Spine

SPINE

a novel

F. E. Mazur

AmErica House
Baltimore

First printing

Excerpt from *Autobiography of a Flea* by Anonymous, published by Carroll & Graf.

Excerpt from "Sad Ann" by Anna Jackson, published in *Ginger Hill*, literary magazine of Slippery Rock University of Pennsylvania, 1966.

Excerpt from *The Poems of Emily Dickinson*, published by Little, Brown & Co.

Excerpt from *The Tin Drum* by Gunter Grass, © 1959 by Pantheon Books.

Excerpt from *The Complete Poetical Works of Byron*, published by The Riverside Press.

Cover design: Nita Kaufman

ISBN: 1-58851-571-0
PUBLISHED BY AMERICA HOUSE BOOK PUBLISHERS
www.publishamerica.com
Baltimore

Printed in the United States of America

For Joan

Author's Note

In the early editions of *Merriam-Webster's Collegiate Dictionary*, nouns for imparting disrespect of a human being included *dumbbell, numbskull, nitwit,* and others with similar connotation. Obscene and repulsive nomenclature, such as *asshole, cocksucker,* and *motherfucker,* were not to be found, their public use insufficient to afford them lexicographic distinction. With the dictionary's ninth edition and online version, this was no longer the case. I mention this to assure the reader that their occasional use here by some of the characters is not gratuitous.

Chapter 1

The distant threat came to him as he broke the water's surface.

"I SWEAR I'LL KILL YOU!"

The squeaky tremor of the excited voice behind the words forced the teacher to smile. Clearly issued by a youngster, it was easy for Grayson Lord to dismiss. The kind of the thing that all children say at one time or another. But soon following the one-line warning were additional sounds more troubling, an out-of-control fusillade of pushed-to-the-limit growls and yelps, and bursts of taunting laughter. Lord, while treading water, pondered a moment. Then, dissolving the smile, he decided to investigate.

He abandoned the shaded swimming hole along a bend on the upper river, a deep spot that was better suited for trout-fishing when one-hundred eighty-five pounds of human flesh weren't disturbing it, and moved northward along the bank. Floor vines grabbed at his wet ankles like wretches from hell while stones and sticks jabbed the underside of his bare feet. The threat from the immature voice repeated, as did the other sounds.

At the bottom of a minor tributary, he hid himself behind a heap of coughed-up brush through which he surveyed the scene. The threats, to his surprise, were coming from his newspaper boy Clipper, a polite, hardworking son of a stonemason, with a maternally inspired red pompadour who would be entering the seventh grade shortly; and he was directing them at an older and much larger teen whom Lord did not recognize, a kid who, in spite of standing a mere foot away from water, appeared dirty all over.

The big teenager, dressed in jeans and a black loose-fitting sweat with the sleeves removed, was holding up Clipper's old beagle by its ears; and the faithful dog named Sy, having given up on growling as a defense, was now whining entreatingly. Every few seconds the kid would swing the animal through a shallow radius, then bounce its rump against the earth before reeling its scared, squirming body once again into the air.

Lord quietly spread the dead brush before him and searched the perimeter. Two other youths were on hand, friends of Clipper, judging by their size. However, they were staying clear.

He started to step out to confront this bushy-haired bully and animal abuser, but hesitated after glancing down at his clay-colored swimming trunks that were actually summer shorts. A single rent on the bottom right, the result of snagging the cotton material on a drawer pull in his apartment's kitchen, served as a staging area for his rubber ducky. That's what colleague Bev Stiles, with her dry humor, had entitled the first performance, and rather than wear briefs to confine the problem, he had simply assigned the shorts to water duty.

Why haven't you just shitcanned these, Grayson? he asked himself hopelessly.

For the moment he stuffed his items out of sight to the left and lowered the trunks with the hole a couple of inches. Then he stepped out.

"All right! What's going on here?"

Clipper turned his way immediately, as did the two spectators off to the side. The head of the kid clenching the frightened dog came roundabout as slowly as a silly duckling he'd once observed attempting to pluck a butterfly out of the air, and there was attitude attached. The boy was as big as himself, maybe bigger, but his soiled flesh seemed to have warped over his adolescent bones, making them too prominent.

"Whattaya say, LBJ, let that canine run away?"

"What the fuck do you want?" the kid mumbled.

"Normally, the first question is, 'Who are you?' 'Identify yourself.' That sort of thing." For sure, this teenager wasn't interested in having the allusion to the thirty-sixth president explained!

"I don't give a fuck who you are, dickhead! So why don't you just hike your tan somewhere else."

"He said he's going to throw Sy in the river, Mr. Lord. Sy can't swim very well. He might drown."

"Take it easy, Clipper. Nobody's about to throw Sy anywhere."

The big kid's eyes dropped away from the intruder's face to his body, yet it wasn't that he was taking measure, as Lord first surmised while he approached. Rather, he could see that the teenager was studying the hole in his swimming trunks.

Crack creep, dammit! And he was already on the right again.

A moment later the kid ceased staring at the rip with its keyhole view of the teacher's penis, but he made no effort to reconnect with Lord's line of vision. Instead, to the cloudless sky overhead he expelled a laugh that was all but silent and filled with derision. Then, spinning in place like some angered track athlete tossing the hammer, he sent the old beagle sailing through the heavy late-summer air.

Fat from age, the dog hit the water like a boulder and instantly went under. Clipper screamed and dashed into the river. The kid advanced upon the other boys who bolted, slipping and sliding out of panic as they did.

"Clipper!" Lord yelled. "He's up!"

The beagle had surfaced, and Lord could see at once that its hind legs were offering minimal help in staying afloat. The terrified dog headed in desperation for the nearer but steeper bank on the opposite side, until Clipper called its name, whereupon it spun around and thrashed in the direction of the boy who was wading out to meet his companion.

But would it make it? Lord wondered.

A drenching rain two nights earlier had raised the river, and there was current stiff enough where the dog was fighting to deny the animal even an inch of progress. Lord entered the water from where he was, dove under, and reappeared in line to intersect with the dog's drift. He fought the current along with a dangerous mass of submerged trunks and branches, trailing long strings of various grasses torn from the banks, until he was able to reach out and snatch the animal. The beagle grabbed at its rescuer's arm as a human being would under similar circumstances.

"Okay, Sy old fellow, enough of this entertainment," he whispered to the dog. "What say we head in and shake off before we both drown?"

Lord took hold of the animal under its front legs, and with strong muscular strokes, single-armed it toward dry land. As he was doing so, he caught sight of the big teen disappearing along the shore to the south, and when the boy swung his head back over his shoulder for the briefest instant, Lord had the alarming feeling that this was a kid who wouldn't be satisfied.

"Thanks, Mr. Lord." Clipper dropped to his knees and hugged the dog.

"You're welcome, Clipper. I don't imagine your buddies will be returning any time soon. You want a lift into town?"

"What about Sy? He's all wet. Me, too."

"That makes three of us. Look, let Sy take a breather, he's earned it; then head upriver. I'm a little fearful that your friend isn't finished with his shenanigans."

Lord took off at a clip, unmindful of his bare feet, and covered the return yardage to his private swimming hole in less than a minute. The kid was waiting, but at a distance. And the car hadn't been touched.

"Check again," he heard the kid say.

"What?"

"Your wheels, asshole."

Lord stepped closer to where he had parked his automobile earlier between a massive oak tree and a large rock, and eventually he realized that, in fact, the gold Toyota had been moved. Not much. Maybe a foot.

"I could have rolled it right into the river."

Funny, thought Lord. It's exactly what had crossed his mind. He brushed the wet hair from his eyes and stuck his head inside the open window to see if the keys remained in the ignition. The kid continued to stand off to the side, crunching idly on a weed. Probably waiting to be asked why he hadn't.

"You ever lay a hand on my car again, tough guy, it'll be you who's the asshole and gets rolled into the river. I'm no decrepit bunny-chaser on its final legs."

And without a punctuating stare, Lord turned away to ignore the teen, reached into the back seat, and retrieved a blanket. He spread it across the front, smoothed out the wrinkles, then got in, started the engine, and waited on Clipper and the beagle. In the rearview mirror he surreptitiously kept a wary eye on the kid who was soon to flick aside the weed and disappear.

"So who is he?" Lord asked Clipper the moment the youngster ran up to the car. The boy bent and cuddled the dog in his arms. "Put him between us."

"I'll kill him, Mr. Lord. I swear I'll kill him!"

"I suppose you could argue that you got cause. Only don't rush into it. For now, just put him on your list. See if he's still there in twenty years."

Twenty years! His Uncle John had once offered him this same advice. Returning home after being backed down by a classmate in the fourth grade and vowing to murder the boy because of the humiliation he felt, Lord had laughed when the man suggested that he keep a mental list of the people with whom he intended to even the score, laughed as he thought he should, because wasn't Uncle John the family's notorious prankster; until the relative, without warning, slapped the boy's face for emphasis, stating plainly that the family didn't need a convicted murderer in its family tree. And what great advice it turned out to be. Here he was nearing thirty and there wasn't an enemy from his early years that he could recall without a lot of bother. They had faded not only from his list; they had evaporated from his memory also. People he mistakenly had thought had significance, in the end had none.

"Thanks again, Mr. Lord, for rescuing Sy. His legs don't work like they used to. I have to carry him up steps."

"So what happened back there, Clipper?"

"Oh, Sy thinks everybody's friendly. I don't think he's ever been hurt. But Asa—that's his name, Mr. Lord, Asa Aftanas—he didn't want him near him, so he picked Sy up by his ears and... well, you know the rest."

"Is this Asa visiting someone? Or has he moved here?"

"He lives here now. Not far from where we live."

He was afraid of that and he was guessing his next question wouldn't be answered satisfactorily either, although it wasn't necessary to ask it.

"He's going to be a senior, Mr. Lord."

"Great." Each year he taught two twelfth-grade English classes. He was willing to give odds that this Aftanas kid would be in one of them.

He punched on the radio, previously tuned to an NPR station, and set the volume more for background than listening. Before backing the car out of the space between the trees, he glanced at the beagle who was staring up at him. He smiled at the dog and gave it the kind of playful noogie that he sometimes gave to his brother's boys when he visited his family downstate.

"Fasten your seatbelt, Clipper," he said once the car was straightened and pointing in the right direction.

"And prepare for takeoff!" finished the seventh-grader, stiffening his arms at their sides.

Playing along, Lord floored the accelerator, causing his human and canine passengers to smile and bark, respectively. He had forgotten the transmission remained in reverse.

It was a road of a thousand ruts through a forest of red oak and pine mixed with sun-shrunken blackberry that wound a half-mile uphill from the river to the state highway, and the kid was again waiting, this time hidden in his rust-bucket of an early model Chevy Camaro. Lord failed to see Asa Aftanas until he swung the gold Toyota onto the shimmering asphalt and, then, there was the reckless teenager, directly behind him, almost kissing his bumper.

13

"*What* is this boy's problem?" he said under his breath. He glanced over at Clipper who was scratching Sy's underbelly, unaware the game was continuing.

The distance to town was a mile, all of it downhill. Lord neither slowed nor increased his car's speed, although he considered pulling the vehicle onto the berm next to the

WELCOME TO
CAREYTOWN, PENNSYLVANIA
WE RECYCLE

sign and stopping. But just as quickly he abandoned the idea because he figured the kid would do the same, that Aftanas was playing some form of cat and mouse game intended to frustrate the adult.

Near the bottom of the hill the road curved to send its traffic across a bridge spanning the river. A few yards before the concrete abutment a pair of mallards suddenly appeared out of tall grass and, with their heads held high, waddled onto the pavement.

Lord reacted, braking hard. The car dipped and faintly swerved to the centerline and back. His eyes alternated nervously from the birds to the mirror. At the same time he threw his left hand out the lowered window with the palm reversed and opened wide.

Aftanas ignored the cautionary signal. As though part of an animated cartoon, the beat-up Camaro fishtailed around the Toyota with its horn blasting, missing the driver's side by inches, and wiped out the lives of both ducks in an instant. And still the teen did not stop, or even slow.

Lord felt stunned. He could hardly believe what he had witnessed. The Toyota now sat idling in the right lane, the sulfurous fumes from its catalytic converter mixing with the hot tar smell of the heated asphalt, but there was no reason for the teacher to open the door and get out. Aftanas had ripped the mallards apart into countless amorphous pieces. A bright indigo feather from the speculum of one of the birds floated earthward and settled on the windshield.

"Your friend again," Lord said, gripping the steering wheel to the point of almost breaking it.

"He's not my friend, Mr. Lord," Clipper sadly corrected him, stretching his neck to peer out the windows at what remained of the ducks.

"No, I'm sure he isn't."

On the boy's softened face Lord read an expression that said, if Clipper hadn't completely believed that Sy could have died at the hands of Asa Aftanas earlier, he believed it now.

"I said I'd take you into town, Clipper, but if you want, I'll drive you and Sy home."

"There's nothing to do at home on a Sunday, Mr. Lord. Dad's away and Mom's with her sister. I'll find my friends again if you just let me off in town."

"All right then.... But Clipper, when your father gets home, you remember to tell him what happened to Sy. I suspect he'll want to have a talk with this Asa's parents."

"I'm not going to do that, Mr. Lord."

"You're not? Why not?"

"Dad doesn't keep lists."

"He doesn't what?... Oh.... You mean, if something needs taking care of..."

"...Dad just goes ahead and does it."

Chapter 2

Was there anything to be done? Not for the ducks there wasn't! Roadkill was everywhere and fresh each morning. Even recounting the incident to someone in town would likely bring about a lecture rather than even a trace of appreciation for his outrage. If there weren't an abundance of wildlife, some would say, if humankind were still hunter-gatherers, Gray, you wouldn't have the daily carnage along the highways. And what was he supposed to do about the kid's barbarian treatment of the aging beagle? Apparently nothing! If Clipper was afraid what his impulsive father might do if the old man ever learned how Asa Aftanas had attempted to drown the family pet, then he ought not to stick his nose further into the matter. Anyway, it was still August. Limit confrontation with teens and their parents to the rest of the year. Why should he put up with the garbage during the summer months if he didn't have to?

Three rooms and a bath above a pharmacy situated on the corner of Careytown's Main and Water streets constituted the living quarters of Grayson Lord. He parked the Toyota in its designated slot in the rear of an alleyway. Although he dismissed himself from further involvement with Asa Aftanas, he doubted that the kid was entertaining a similar thought, forcing him to worry that the car might get vandalized. For if Aftanas dared move it while its owner was near, what might the out-of-control juvenile attempt, say, in the middle of the night?

Yet he had no choice but to leave the car where it was. Park it on Main and it was a foregone conclusion that the police would slide a ticket under the wiper. He clutched the wet blanket to his chest, locked the vehicle, then walked uphill with Clipper and the dog to the front where they parted company. It was four in the afternoon according to the bank clock at the other end of the block, hot with no chance of rain, and only a smattering of people, a few of them licking ice cream cones, was on the sidewalks and shaded lawns. He opened the door to the dark stairs that led up to his apartment. The smell of fried chicken from one of the other apartments invaded his nostrils.

"Hey, Lord!" a voice called out from the upper side of Water. "Hold up there."

He turned around to see Careytown's hometown boy Corey Howser break into a lazy jog. As usual, a step behind the brush cut phys-ed instructor and gridiron coach was a bald, puffy-faced man in a yellow jersey who shadowed his older friend everywhere outside of school.

"What is it, Howser? Shouldn't you be at your pre-season football practice?"

"It's Sunday. We don't practice on Sunday."

"Maybe you should, considering last year's record."

"A regular Jay Leno, aren't you?" Howser responded, reaching out to tap a finger on Lord's bare chest. "And maybe our record would have been a helluva lot better if you hadn't decided to be a hardass and flunk a couple of my linemen."

"Inform your players this year that keeping their grades up is important. So what do you want?"

"I haven't seen you around this summer."

"Well, I've been here."

"We heard talk a couple of months ago that you were quitting. Heading back to the Pittsburgh area."

"Yeah, we thought at first it was your buddy George Nesbitt," said the puffy-face. "You know, every time we hear any rumbles of departure, we all keep hoping."

"But it wasn't that asshole," said Howser, "even though I did hear the same thing about him. Hear it every year, in fact. But this time it was you they were talking about. And I went directly to Orr because I know of someone who would love to fill your position."

"Sorry to disappoint you, Corey."

Actually, the first rumbles had sounded more than two years earlier and if the phys-ed teacher enjoyed a confidence with any of Lord's closest friends, he would have discovered that, the same as he would discover that moving back anywhere near the old homestead was out of the question. But, rumbles were all they were, and it was mathematics teacher Beverly Stiles who had recognized their emptiness:

"You'll be here this year, Gray, and the next because it's so easy to stay."

Yet, mustering his gumption soon after school had let out this past June, he thought he might finally prove his buxom colleague wrong. Sitting down before his computer and optimistically switching on the printer at the outset, he attempted to write a letter to Superintendent Harold Orr and the Careytown School Board notifying them of his decision to leave his job.

However, he discovered that all he could write was a pathetically amusing quibble: "Rather than resign, I've decided to resign."

"So, do you want anything else, or was that it?"

"No, that's it," Howser said, yet the phys-ed teacher made no effort to walk away.

Relieved, Lord eased up on his display of hostility.

"So where you boys off to, anyway?"

"Just heading down to talk to the parents of one of my seniors who busted a collarbone last season. They're afraid to let him play this year.... Say, Lord. That boy who walked up the street with you, who is he?"

"Clipper Ostrander. Delivers my newspaper. He doesn't deliver yours?"

"I don't get the newspaper," Howser boasted. "Never have."

"Still haven't learned to read, is that it?... Sorry."

"Yeah, you are one sorry ass, Lord. There's no argument over that," said the puffy-face, who grinned at his friend and spat a tiny particle of food from his teeth at the sidewalk.

"You're a real piece, Deke," Lord said to the man whose flesh displayed the bloated ugliness of a tumor. "Now if you'll excuse me, I want to get out of these trunks. They're wet."

He opened the door a second time but still did not enter, as he thought he ought to mention Aftanas to the football coach. The kid had size, and if the teen possessed even a shred of athletic prowess, he might help the dismal Careytown Bears to a successful season. And maybe find something in the sport that would make him less of a delinquent and keep him out of jail.

"Any chance there, Corey, you don't know about the new student? He's an intimidating fellow, that much I can tell you."

"Who's that?" Howser asked.

"Must be that family I was talking about a while back," interrupted the puffy-face. "Remember I was telling you old man Eller died and left his place out the Hartwell to a niece of his? She moved in there with a husband two, three weeks ago, and I believe I did hear there's a kid with 'em, and he's a big sucker."

"In that case, I'll look him up," Howser said, nodding. He glanced down at Lord's legs, then winked at his shadow. "Nice swimsuit he got, huh, Deke? Don't you wish you had one just like it?"

Once inside the upstairs apartment minutes later, Lord unfolded the damp blanket across the backs of a couple of kitchen chairs so that it might dry. Then out of sight of the windows he pulled off the ventilated swimming trunks and hurled them into a trash can under the sink.

Naked, he moved into his bedroom where, sniffing the air, he caught the scent of lilac that betrayed the earlier presence of his landlady. Wherever she went, the old lady toted along her aerosol, and in spite of his objections to canned fragrances, she insisted that she freshen the moldy odor of her rental.

From a chest of drawers he removed a pair of cutoff jeans with its end threads so tattered they resembled a mop. Across from the bed the phone on his desk suddenly warbled. He stepped over and picked up, but there was no one on the other end.

No. Couldn't be, he thought, shaking his head. Too soon for the typical follow-up harassment. Not to mention that kids like Aftanas never remembered names the first time they were spoken, right? Probably another goddamn telemarketing outfit automatically dialing more numbers than it had operators.

He hung up the phone without another thought and slipped himself into the cutoffs. Gathering up the mail that his landlady had placed on his desk after he had forgotten to check his slot at the foot of the stairs yesterday, he shuffled into the spacious living room, formerly a waiting room for a doctor's office, reminded that he also had forgotten to leave Clipper the week's money for the newspaper. He stretched out on a wooden bench bulging from the inner circumference of a corner cupola that overlooked the intersection of streets below where students often assembled. Brilliant cardinal tetras schooled endlessly back and forth in a fluorescent-lit aquarium across from him.

As usual with his mail, there was the barrage of credit card enticements, plus a couple of circulars in which he had no interest and the new issue of *The Atlantic Monthly*. But then he came upon a postcard from his nineteen year-old sister who was vacationing with friends on the South Carolina beaches. Since her enrollment in an out-of-state university, they had seldom seen each other. He read eagerly her scribbled words.

Setting aside the postcard, he then tore open a bill for his use of natural gas, noticing at once that the amount due was outstandingly high for summer use. He made a mental note to check the stubs of the previous warm months.

Finally, he ripped open the last piece of mail. Sent from the school, it served as official testimony that another year was about to commence. It contained a schedule for the first day, listing the time and designated rooms for the many ho-hum meetings that he would have to endure. Also, it carried a letter from School Superintendent Harold Orr that he recognized to be much the same as those from previous years: *"We trust you've had a profitable summer and are now ready to re-dedicate yourself to the education of the youth of our community."* He placed the schedule and letter with the circulars and credit card appeals.

Through one of the diaphanously curtained windows on the cupola he saw Clipper strolling his way from a direction that was opposite of where the seventh-grader had begun walking from the intersection earlier. The tired beagle followed at the small boy's heels. Lord rolled off the bench and further raised the window on its track.

"Clipper!" he called down. The red-haired boy recognized the voice and squinted up. "I forgot to leave you your payment yesterday."

"I can't give you a receipt," Clipper said, squinting harder.

"Never mind that. Get it next time."

Drawing back inside, Lord hurried to the bedroom, retrieved several dollar bills from the basket on his desk, then went to the door and swung it open. Shortly, the youth appeared at the top of the stairwell where, with solicitous attention, he lowered the dog from his chest to the floor.

"Here you go," Lord said, extending the bills. "I'm sorry, it slipped my mind."

Clipper took the money and buried it inside a pocket of his jeans, too short in length for his fast-growing body, then excavated another for change.

"Keep it."

"Thanks, Mr. Lord. Since the price went up, I don't get many tips."

Lord motioned toward the dog. "How's Sy doing after his ordeal?"

The boy reached down to stroke the animal between its ears. "He seems all right."

"Did you manage to find your friends? Or are they still running?"

Clipper smiled weakly. "They're okay, Mr. Lord, really. I would have done the same.... What's that gurgling noise?"

Lord cocked an ear. All he could hear was the steady bubbling aeration of the aquarium pump.

"Must be the fishtank. Want a look?"

The boy ordered the dog to stay, and Lord lead the way into the furthest room as Clipper asked if he taught any seventh-grade classes.

"This year just one."

"Do you think I'll be in your class, Mr. Lord?"

"Probably neither of us will discover that until the first day."

Inside the long room Clipper noticed immediately on the far wall the great number of books that filled the shelves framing each side of a fireplace, but a metal item at eye level drew his interest. Lord watched as he picked up the small gold object and examined it. He handled it as a kid respectful of the possessions of others and replaced it on the shelf just as it had been.

"What is that?"

"An embosser. Slide a piece of paper in it, press hard on the handle, and it puts my name in raised letters. Pull out any book and inspect the opening pages. You'll see what it does."

The line of books before the child consisted mostly of paperbacks. The yellow spine of one attracted Clipper's attention.

"Except that one!" Lord exclaimed, suddenly panic-stricken. He glanced into a mirror above the fireplace and mouthed "Idiot!" at himself. "Forget the one next to it, also. Neither one has the mark," he lied. He hurriedly reached around the boy and removed a volume by James Purdy. "Here. Let's look at this one."

That's all he needed, he thought, as he thumbed to the page in *The Nephew* containing his personal circular embossment. Word getting around that he had invited a seventh-grader to explore a sexually explicit underground novel by an anonymous writer of the Victorian Age. No one would care that he had eclectic tastes and read all sorts of things.

The young boy next stared at Lord's small assortment of guns that were displayed on a rack above the aquarium.

"Do you hunt?" he asked.

"Once in a while. Turkey hunting, especially."

"I'd like to hunt turkey. My dad, he always goes. Last year he got him a seventeen-pound gobbler."

Then the boy squinched with his hands on his knees and stared at the rainbows of tropical fish gliding about inside the large glass tank.

"When you tap the glass, some of them swim so fast they look like streaks of oil."

"Supposedly, they accelerate the fastest of all animals," Lord explained. "They just can't keep it up for long. Say, how about splitting a bottle of Pepsi?"

Clipper accepted and Lord returned to the kitchen to pour the beverage under the longing gaze of the beagle who had traded in sitting for the flattest prostration inside the open door. Once in the long room again, Lord listened to Clipper express a wish.

"Someday I want to have an aquarium. With all kinds of fish. And snails, too."

"You do, huh? Then I'll keep an eye out for an old tank," said Lord, nudging the boy at the shoulder with one of the filled tumblers. "I frequently run into people who have one they're hoping to give away or will sell for a few dollars. And if the young of my live-bearers survive after they're born, in that case you'll have your fish. How does that sound?"

Clipper nodded awkwardly at the unexpected generosity and drained much of the glass in a few gulps.

Outside, the traffic light at the corner held red for two vehicles heading up the street. The instant green appeared, the horn of the second vehicle began to blare.

"Mr. Lord! Quick, look out that window. See that truck?"

Lord focused his vision on the dull blue pickup missing its grill.

"What about it?"

"Those people inside, that's Mr. and Mrs. Aftanas. I went over to their house to sign them up for a new customer, but Mr. Aftanas said he had no use for any newspapers and that he didn't want me bothering him anymore. He warned me, too, that he didn't want Sy on his lawn ever again. You should see his lawn."

Lord moved nearer to the window and followed the blue pickup as it passed in front of the pharmacy and continued up Main. There wasn't much to see of the woman sitting on the right except that she had fat legs and was gripping a can of beer. Her coarse-haired husband, the driver, was obviously an enormous man, certified by the elevation of his knees which were pressed against the base of the steering wheel. His face and torso occupied virtually every cubic inch of his half of the cab. And the arm projecting out the

23

vehicle's window showed not only the same patina of dirt that was on the son's flesh, but also revealed an identical skeletal structure, one in which the bones threatened to break the skin so that their owner might grab hold of the biggest, wrench it free from the others, and wield it for a club. The man appeared to Lord to be one cruel mother.

"I should be leaving," Clipper said before swallowing the last of the cola. "Sy's probably getting impatient. Thanks for the Pepsi, Mr. Lord. I really appreciate it."

"You're quite welcome, young man," Lord replied, casting a final and more curious look at the receding truck which had now stopped in the street next to an older couple exiting a revival house. "You're quite welcome. Just knock on the door if you ever want to check out the fish again."

Clipper left the apartment moments later, and Lord watched as the boy literally hopped down the staircase with the beagle at his heels, the short-legged dog flipping its weight carefully from one step to the next, reminding Lord of a slinky.

When the phone in the bedroom sounded, Lord had no doubt that it was the telemarketer again. These people who often hung up after summoning you from two or three rooms away felt no shame about squandering your time and energy. They were certain to call a second time and waste even more of it.

"Lord here," he answered gruffly. "What is it?"

"Mr. Lord, I don't think you should have that young boy up in your apartment all alone."

"What?... Who is this?"

"It's indecent. And you parading around without a shirt on, too!"

"Who the hell is this?"

And then another voice, this one male and threatening, warned, "You should be more careful, Mr. Lord. Remember, this is a small community. Here, people go to bat for their children."

And then both voices on the telephone were gone, but still another one, coming from the street below, was summoning him to the window in the living room.

"Over here, Howser."

"How big is that apartment?" the coach asked as he and his friend sidled under the bedroom window.

"Walk up, see for yourself. I've got a couple of cold ones on hand."

24

"I don't think so," the coach responded with a look that said there wasn't a chance in hell.

"What's the matter? Worried you'll get the plague or something?"

"Or something," said the puffy face, smiling and spitting.

"Didn't your mother ever tell you about flossing?"

"Up yours, Lord."

"Keep wishing, Deke. What do you boys want this trip?"

"Some guy's asking for you," Howser said.

Lord laughed. "Well, he can't be asking too hard, can he? Who is it?"

"I've never seen him before," Howser answered. "Deke here said he looked familiar, but I hear that at least once a day about somebody."

"Did you give him directions?"

"You owe me. He and his wife didn't seem too friendly. Isn't that right, Deke?"

"Said something, Lord, like he wanted to stick your head in your miserable ass and dump you in the river."

"Looks like you might know these people," Howser speculated, observing Lord's expression change.

"I've a hunch I might," Lord said. He raised his eyes and searched the street from one end to the other. "Any chance they were riding in a blue Ford pickup?"

"Matter of fact they were."

Howser then attempted to pry the information out of Lord, but Lord wouldn't budge. Telling stories to Corey Howser and his friend Deke was the last thing he wanted to do. Besides, if the football coach checked out Asa Aftanas as he had said he would, he was likely to find out the story on his own.

Soon after, the long summer Sunday began to disappear. The evening air surrendered its heat to the cool embrace of the northern Alleghenies. The sun raced toward the mountains and through the curtain gap in the cupola it flung a thick knife of gold against the wall supporting the fireplace. Nervous populations of dust tumbled directionless inside the narrow light.

Lord opened the remaining windows on the cupola as an escape route for the heat that would generate from supper's stove. Following the meal, he switched on the television and spun the channel selector to prove that reruns remained in surrogate for fall premieres. Then he pushed it off, electing to read instead. From the hillside portion of the town, where homes and churches lived peacefully together, he could hear the chimes signal the start of evening. Unable to concentrate and knowing the reason why—it had little to do with Asa Aftanas and his family—he soon tired of his book and shut it, more forcibly than he would have expected.

Who the fuck was it? Who the fuck had phoned, looking to stir up trouble?

After a while he turned on the radio, tuning it to the first station whose broadcast came in freely. He set the volume low, then returned to sit on the bench, drawing up his knees and leaning against the wooden frame of the western window, out of the path of the light that swung upward on the wall. He gazed at the quiet streets and particularly the homes above them for a long time through the aperture of the curtains. Only the droning hum from the pharmacy's neon sign beneath him shook the outdoor silence.

The sun raced between the valleys of the distant hills and the street remained quiet. The knife crossed the seam between the wall and ceiling and stretched over his head like a glamorous woman's leg. Neon droned, and the radio voice of a godly man drilled with reluctant susurration at his ear.

"I have a message.... Oh yes, He's told me. HE ... HAS ... TOLD ... ME! He wishes me to give the message to you.... He wants YOU to know what he has told ME."

Try as he did, he couldn't put a face to either voice. And what the fuck did they think was going on up here, anyway?

The sun raced behind its finish line of mountaintops and the sky began to darken. Somewhere on the hillside a wooden screen door slapped against its frame, and a motorcycle exploded into being. The street came alive. Budding-breasted girls rushed in and out of the phone booth on the sidewalk across the way.

"And He's told me more. He's whispered it to ME and He wants ME to tell it to you.... Oh yes, I have a message...from Him."

Girls more fully breasted giggled in and out of the phone booth and he remembered when someone had told him that the morality of a small town might be gauged through the use of its public phones.

"He has related to me much and I shall give His words to you!"

It was ten o'clock, dark; again mostly quiet. He switched off the radio.

SPINE

Nothing to do on a Sunday. And all kinds of people looking for all sorts of trouble. That's likely who had called. Folks who had nothing better to do than look for trouble! Careytown had its share. The whole fucking county had its share.

A few diesel trucks, hauling coils from Cleveland-based steel mills, ran for an early drop in New York and pounded past him, if they got the light. A porch swing creaked at a nearby house, and the stream of television voices leaking through open windows tinkled metallically against his ears. Then from far down the street, the engine of a car growled and tore at the night, releasing him, finally, from the unsettling thoughts generated by his anonymous callers. Its tires screamed forward with smoke from the concrete drag beneath. Gears slammed, rubber chirped, and the engine powered upward to menacing dimensions.

Through the narrow gap in the curtains, Lord watched the familiar machine while it came to a stop as defiantly as a jet on an aircraft carrier. The rusty Camaro rumbled slightly ahead of where he sat above the pharmacy's neon sign that dyed his face a ghostly hue. Other bodies inside the car dangled their arms from the lowered windows.

"I see you've made friends," he muttered to himself.

The car shivered in the street as Asa Aftanas teased the engine with fuel and clutch in preparation for another reckless run. Then with his emotions about to ignite a second time, the kid swept his head over his shoulder and his eyes caught sight above of a narrow slice of a blue Grayson Lord. Aftanas swung his body around, and through the open car window he upraised an arm with the hand extending its middle finger. He spat once, withdrew the arm, then tortured the beat-up automobile up the center of the street.

Chapter 3

"Where the hell is he?"

Randy Aftanas was pissed and getting more so by the minute.

"He said he'll be here, he'll be here," replied his wife Tessie in defense of her stepson.

They were standing next to the blue pickup that Randy Aftanas had parked in front of the weed-riddled walkway to the farmhouse, a two-story box structure that remained square and plumb despite its old age—thanks to the lifelong attention of the woman's uncle—and the centerpiece of a nice chunk of rural property just outside of Careytown. Various weathered, wood-sided storage buildings dotted the landscape. At the backside of the property ran Hartwell Creek, a shallow stretch except during the worst of times and one of several mountain streams that contributed to the headwaters of the Allegheny River.

"He was supposed to be here an hour ago. We'll be starting out at a time I figured to be starting back. It'll be three in the morning before I get to goddamn sleep."

"Renova ain't that far."

"What?"

"It's far enough, but it ain't that far."

What a dumbfuck, thought Randy Aftanas. How the hell did he ever end up marrying this bitch, who didn't have anywhere near the brains of his first wife. And her looks weren't in competition either. The only light was leaking out of the kitchen but it was sufficient to remind him of what he was living with. The matted hair, the stale face. The woman's whole fucking head resembled a big drop of oily water getting sucked by gravity. And all day she'd been wearing the same clothes she'd had on yesterday and the day before. That undersized white banlon jersey without sleeves, so that it was impossible not to see those tubes of flesh hanging at her waist, looking like something ugly inside was incubating. But, the woman could keep a secret, this was something he had to admit, and maybe that was the reason he had married her. That, and he had needed someone to look after Asa back then.

"I'm not returning by the shortest route, Tess. I goddamn told you that already. I'll be driving that car back through county roads, most of them in the gamelands. There's no hunting season underway, so I don't expect to see anyone, let alone a cop."

"Well, don't get yourself lost." She meant this as a joke, as he knew every road there was in the seven-county region, and then some, as he liked to brag. He had lived all over. Paved, gravel, dirt. State, county, lumber. He'd been over them all. He knew the entire region like the back of his hand, which she could see was what he'd be wanting to give to Asa if the boy didn't show up pretty soon.

"You want another beer?" she asked.

He shook his head, topped by hair that resembled discarded barbed wire.

"I'll be right back. I'm getting me another."

"Put a jacket on, too. It's cooling down."

"What about you? All you got on is that rag of a T-shirt."

"I'm all right. Go get your beer."

"You sure?" she asked again, holding up her empty can. It was unlike him not to want another beer.

He ignored her, directing his eyes that were like rivets to the road out front, waiting on his son.

Randy Aftanas recognized a couple of things about himself, in addition to the fact that he rarely grew cold, despite the temperature. One was that he was a monster of a human specimen, so much one that he long ago had learned how intimidating he could be to other men. Merely stepping into a group—and not even its center—would spark a silence, and soon a distancing. And it worked equally well with women, he discovered along the way, with the exception of those who thought if he were that huge overall, surely there had to be a prize of equal proportions below, and then by the time they discovered the truth, it was too late for them. The second was that he was a patient, very circumspect man, although the latter word he would not have used. He thought of himself simply as a man who was deliberate, careful. And after his son had informed him of the incident down at the river and how some stranger had interfered and even threatened the boy, he coupled one quality to the other and drove into town to ask around and show himself off. Just in case the guy was thinking to push on it a little, he wanted word to get back that some big, mean sonovabitch was looking for him. It was a tactic that had worked before, but this time he wasn't so sure.

She came back out of the house.

"Not here yet?"

He watched her drink from the can. She never drank like other women; she was a guzzler.

"You can see he isn't here. If he doesn't show, Tess, you'll drive me down in the pickup. So don't get a fucking buzz on where you can't keep it between the lines."

At that she balked. "I can't drive this truck, you know that. It gives me trouble every time I sit behind the wheel. And you said he's to come back from Renova the regular way, not to follow you through the backroads?"

"That's right."

"Well, I'm not breaking down without you around."

She turned and walked quickly in the direction of one of the smaller sheds, hoping distance would eliminate further discussion on the topic.

"Where you headed now?" he asked, raising his voice.

"You ain't ever going to get around to cutting this grass, I'm going to cut it."

"It's nearing midnight. You start up that mower and..." But he stopped in mid-sentence because suddenly it didn't seem to be such a bad idea. Crazy, yes, but crazy was okay because crazy kept others from coming around and he didn't want others coming around. Especially once he got the car up here and in the garage alongside the other one.

He took another look at the road out front. There was a motorcycle he'd watched racing up it earlier returning in the direction of town. No car, though. Where the fuck was that goddamn son of his?

She was struggling to pull the lawnmower out of a shed. He could hear it catching on other things.

"Is there any gas in this?" she asked.

"Ask your dead uncle! How the hell would I know?" But he left the area of the truck and walked his tall figure over to the shed.

"Choke it a few times and pull the cord," he ordered her.

"What if there's no gas?"

Annoyed, he screwed off the cap and shook the mower, listening for sloshing.

"There's some. Here, I'll give it a tug. Put the cap back and push that rubber button a few times."

The mower refused to start, but his effort was small. All she wanted was that the grass immediately surrounding the house be trimmed back so that she could sit out in it without a swarm of bugs attacking her. Once, she thought she might get the boy to do it, but all he had said was, "Sorry, Tess. I don't do windows." And her own flesh-and-blood Lyle didn't come around all that often.

There were car lights advancing up the road.

"Here he comes," she said.

Randy swung around. He could hear the unmistakable throaty roar of the Camaro, the engine being the only thing that was worth anything on his son's piece of shit. He forgot about his wife and the mower, and hurried back toward the truck.

Asa Aftanas whipped the Camaro into the drive and rolled to an abrupt stop behind the pickup.

"Don't even think about it," he warned his father. The boy's right hand touched the floor between his feet, and his fingers, unabashed, began to walk. "I took Foss home and he offered me a brew."

Randy Aftanas stared at his son, debating if the kid actually had it in him to shoot the ol' man. The first time the threat was made, Tessie and Lyle had been in the vicinity. "Witnesses, boy," the father had said, grinning too, as if he were widening the implications of some joke not thought out all that well. "Not for long," the boy had responded, without even meeting the old man's gaze.

"Foss'll be a senior like me. He lives way the other side of town. He won't be coming around. Anyway, Foss, he don't ever ask a question about anything."

"Think he'd like to mow the grass?" said Tessie, who had walked up behind and was standing on the other side of the truck.

"Shut up about the goddamn grass," Randy warned her.

"You ready to go?" Something about the old man wasn't right to Asa Aftanas. He was looking too intense and his eyes weren't straying, a bad sign.

"You know who he is?" Randy asked.

"Foss. I just told you that. He'll be a senior same as me. And why you acting all weird?"

"He's a teacher," Randy Aftanas said. "And a lot of goddamn teachers have a nasty habit of sticking their nose where it doesn't belong."

"You talking about that motherfucker who jumped into the water after that mutt? He won't be coming 'round here."

"You know that for a fact, do you?"

"Look, if you're that worried for that car, why not leave it where it is?"

"Because we don't own that property, that's why. It's already been sitting there longer than I like."

"Well, another day or two won't change things. Anyway, I'm tired. I don't much feel like driving down there and back at this moment."

Asa Aftanas suddenly opened the door of the car, got out, and took a foolish step toward the house.

The old man seized his son by the arm and swung him around. The other hand encircled the boy's neck and, while the huge body bent the kid over the fender, squeezed the throat as though it were a melon.

"Where the fuck you going?"

"I have to piss."

"Then you piss on your tire and get back in the car. And if that ain't good enough, I'll relieve you of it myself."

In the distance lights appeared. Both father and son directed their attentions to them. They listened, too, as the vehicle changed gears and picked up speed without insistence. Then, about a quarter-mile from the entrance to the property, it slowed and the transmission underwent a steady downshift.

The car turned into the driveway and stopped. The high beams came on.

"You know them?"

"No," said Asa Aftanas, relieved that his father's big hand had let go of his throat.

"You sure it ain't that teacher?"

"That's some kind of minivan. He was driving something else. And why the fuck would he be coming out here at this hour?"

"I can think of reasons."

Randy Aftanas stared into the beams, not blinking.

"You count to ten," he told his son. "If that light ain't out of our face, you pull that gun from under your seat and aim it right at that sonovabitch that's behind the wheel."

The kid looked over at Tessie and grinned before starting to count. "One Mississippi. Two Mississippi...."

"What about you, Tess? That van familiar?"

"I think whoever it is just wants to turn around."

"Then they better do it quick," said Asa Aftanas, who had stopped counting aloud and was now feeling about the floor on the driver's side of his car.

Just as he found the gun, the beams reduced to low and the minivan began backing out and onto the road.

"All right. Empty your bladder and let's go," said Randy Aftanas. "We've wasted enough fucking time."

"You got a plate?"

"I got a hold of one before we pulled up stakes."

Chapter 4

"This is your automated call-back service. The number of your last incoming call was...."

Lord didn't recognize it offhand and grabbed the phone directory from the drawer. The desk clock read three a.m. and the only sound he could hear was the raw wailing power from a truck climbing the rough grade out of Careytown. In the past, when the feature was new and mostly unknown by residential customers, he would punch in star-sixty-nine following a call with no one on the other end and listen for the automated response either to give him the number, or to say "We're sorry...." If the latter, he could be fairly certain the culprit was a telemarketer who had paid the phone company not to divulge such information. But if the other, he would punch in the last seven digits and learn who the harassing current or ex- student was. He'd overlooked using the call-back service to identify yesterday afternoon's meddlesome couple until a few minutes ago when he found himself fully awake with the thought foremost in his mind. No one had rung him since and not wanting to take the chance that someone might want to get a hold of him at sun-up, he had immediately scrambled to the phone.

He checked the number now in the small-town directory against the names of a half-dozen rubbernecks, some of whom lived on the slopes above Main and could view the intersection and its surroundings from their front windows, but to no avail. None of them matched up. And although he gave more than a delicious moment's thought of dialing the number right then in the middle of the night, he decided against it, shut off the lamp, and returned to bed.

But after awaking at eight, he promptly went to it. Receiving no answer each time he pressed the redial button, he nonetheless repeated the instant process every thirty minutes past the noon hour. Still, no one ever picked up and there was no machine. Probably someone like himself who had forgotten about the potential of star-sixty-nine to identify pain-in-the-ass, unknown crank-callers. He chuckled to himself as he thought perhaps the man and woman had remembered the feature in the middle of the night, as he had, and were now fretting over their eventual unveiling.

"Good. Let the nosey bastards sweat awhile."

Now pumped a bit, he figured he'd start some trouble of his own, and he searched for his current utility bill for the use of natural gas, then headed out the door, only to find himself facing his gray-haired landlady, who had her aerosol in hand, ready to blast.

"Mrs. Hampton?"

"Gray, are you all right?" the old woman inquired in a very serious tone.

"Am I all right? Why, of course I'm all right. Why wouldn't I be?"

"Because my neighbor Rose said some man was looking for you yesterday. She said he was going to punch your lights out."

"My lights may already be out," he joked. "Can I help you?"

"That's nothing to make fun of, Gray. I know what those words mean, and Rose said he was a big man and cruel-looking."

"Did he ask Rose where I live?"

"Yes."

"And did she tell him?"

"Well, that I don't know. She didn't say."

"Mrs. Hampton, are there more than a dozen people in town who are not aware that Grayson Lord is the teacher who lives inside the bright orange cupola? Not that they would ever use that particular word. They might opt for 'orange tower' or 'barrel' or something similar."

"Don't make fun, Gray," she admonished him while reaching out to brush a wad of lint from his jersey which fit him snugly.

"Well, you know what I mean. If this man really wanted to find me, he should have had no trouble. He was just blowing smoke. Do you understand that phrase?"

"Yes, I understand those words. But you be careful nonetheless. Rose said his wife looked cruel, too."

"Now you're making fun, Mrs. Hampton. Shame on you." He waited awhile, flapping the utility bill against the outside of his hand. "Is there something else? And I hope you're not here to spray. I can still smell the lilac from yesterday."

"It's the mold you smell," said Mrs. Hampton, lowering the can. With the other hand she daintily smoothed out a wrinkle in her dress which sported all sorts of pink and blue flowers.

"No, it's not the mold. It's the chemical from those cans," Lord said, pointing, "and I don't like it."

"Well, I know better than to argue with a teacher. I won't spray today."

"Thank you." He felt relief at finally winning a battle over the artificial spray. "Your friend Rose, is she one of those who's tuned in to what goes on in Careytown?"

"Yes, Rose knows nearly everything."

"Did she mention anything to you about someone calling me?"

"Who called you?"

"That's what I'd like to know."

"No, Rose didn't say anything. Did someone threaten you on the telephone, Gray? Is that why you're asking?"

"Not exactly. I just like people who ring up my number to identify themselves.... Look, I have to go out for awhile, Mrs. Hampton."

"I said I won't spray, Gray, I won't spray. I'll just empty your garbage, if it's not too much for this old lady to carry."

"All right. I'm holding you at your word about the spray. And remember to lock up, please."

It was none of her business, but she thought she would inquire anyway.

"Where are you going, if I might ask?"

He waved the utility bill in front of her.

"Then you drive down there, Gray," she advised him, earnestly. "Don't go walking."

Lord stared at her with mild astonishment.

"It's barely a five-minute stroll. Do I look that out-of-shape?"

"It's nothing to do with your health and you know it. Rose thinks you teachers should be keeping a low profile, as she likes to say, and I agree."

"Wait a minute! Is this because of the new contract?"

"It's a lot of money, Gray."

"And long overdue!"

"Not everyone agrees with that and there's many who's upset."

"Well, let everyone step inside the classroom and try it for themselves. I'm walking to the local branch office of the Penn North Gas Company, Mrs. Hampton, because it's a beautiful day in Pennsylvania, as a fellow on the radio used to sing out, and if someone wants to run me over because of a few dollars that have been long in coming, then let them."

Mrs. Hampton frowned. After a few seconds, she shook her head.

"Well, don't get into a fight with Donetta Sanders when you're there."

"That woman is never the charmer," said Lord.

"That's true, but she's even less of one, now that she knows more of her money will be going into your pocket."

Mrs. Hampton liked Gray and his friends, who occasionally visited the apartment. Even the one they called Rudy, who had shaved his beautiful wavy hair, only to discover that his head was rife with bumps which everyone laughed at, Mrs. Hampton liked him, too. All of the young men reminded her of the teachers whom she had had when she was a teenager, friendly and outspoken and very sure of themselves. But like her younger friend Rose, Mrs. Hampton didn't think those same qualities in today's public school teachers were much appreciated in her little Careytown. Worse, because of the boys' overriding confidence, she wondered if even one of them would know that a fire was burning under his feet before he felt the heat.

Mrs. Hampton waited until she heard her tenant descend the unlit staircase and exit the building before stepping inside the apartment. She sniffed the air and couldn't resist, although she compromised with herself on the duration. In each room she raised the aerosol can and released but the shortest blast of fragrance. Before leaving, she emptied the contents of three small wastebaskets into a trash bag she had brought along.

"My my," she sighed. "I do hope that Rose is wrong about that boy. I pray that he finds himself a girlfriend. And I pray that it's soon!"

She shook her head, too, as she couldn't believe anyone would throw away a perfectly good pair of shorts that was in need of nothing more than simple mending.

***

Sauntering by the stores on Careytown's Main Street and cutting across the grassy square to the early twentieth-century brick building housing the gas utility office, Lord found himself laughing when he thought of Mrs. Hampton's reminder not to get into a squabble with Donetta Sanders. It was an impossible order and he was certain his landlady had realized it even as she said it.

Cheerless and gaudily jeweled as she always was, the slender middle-aged woman sitting behind the chest-high counter received the bill Lord extended without looking up.

"Teachers and delinquent payment! They certainly go together."

"Nothing's delinquent, Mrs. Sanders. There's a figure at the bottom of that bill that needs explaining."

"Check your oven and burners. Or isn't an entire summer's worth of vacation time enough to keep up with the little things?"

"I'm guessing," Lord said, feigning gravity, "but your father must be president of the company."

"My father worked for the railroad," the woman answered in a tone that suggested he was stupid not to already know this.

"In that case, it must be sex," he said. "That's the only other choice that can logically explain how you keep this position of interacting with the public."

Slowly, the woman raised her head. Her voice lowered and the eyes shrunk to a pair of slits. "How dare you attempt to make fun of me! If I were you, Mr. Lord, I'd start to watch your step around here."

"What's that supposed to mean?" he asked, amazed that the woman was showing an untapped source of nastiness.

"It means what it says."

"Are you threatening me, Mrs. Sanders?"

The door sounded behind him and Lord turned away from the wearisome clerk to observe who was entering. He brightened upon the recognition of his tall colleague he had not seen all summer. A young woman, unknown to him, accompanied her.

"Hel-lo Beverly," he said, issuing the greeting with an emphasis that went beyond mutual acknowledgment.

The striking blonde scarcely nodded.

Lord chuckled. "Glad to be back, are you?"

"As much as you, Gray."

Lord looked at the other woman, who was also beautiful, and guessed that she was replacing a teacher who had left the district over the summer. She was much shorter and her frame bore the delicate structure of a bird, a lively swallow especially, he thought, because her face and everything else revealed the eagerness of approaching a new job. Lord wondered if the district hadn't hired on a dynamo.

He introduced himself, extending a hand that she took after switching a large white bag from one shoulder to the other. She wore the bag on the side opposite from where it hung, as if she had once been mugged.

His colleague pinked with light embarrassment. "I'm sorry, both of you. Gray, this is Janey Renn who's taking Monty's spot."

"One year was all he could endure?"

"It surprised me, too. I hadn't figured him for much in the upstairs department either.... Janey, Gray Lord."

"What do you teach?" the woman asked him.

"Sense, I hope."

"We all teach that. It's a buyers' market in this area."

"I daresay, Bev, you're sounding more caustic than I'm used to."

"I can't imagine why."

"I teach English," he said to Janey Renn.

"THERE IS AN ERROR!"

All three heard the clerk's brusque announcement. The tone did not include a hint of an apology.

Lord's head shook out of combined amusement and disbelief. "Don't you love it? I just informed her of that." He turned back to the counter. "Well, send me a corrected bill, Mrs. Sanders. Then I'll pay it."

After this, as he spoke some departing words to his colleagues, the door opened again and the Reverend Millard Touchstone entered the utility office. The ambitious Pentecostal minister, despite the heat of the day, was in the complete dress of his office—clerical collar, suitable blue-gray jacket with a gold cross pinned to a lapel, black trousers, and his shoes had been seemingly spit-shined, which alone would have distinguished him from other clergy in town. Covering his eyes, as they frequently did, were a pair of aviator sunglasses, which some townsfolk thought could help the minister to pass for a southern sheriff, given a different uniform and place of residence. He paused and loosely combed his wind-whipped air with his fingers. He addressed the women with a "Ladies." To Lord he nodded crisply, vaguely militarily. Then he stepped to the counter and handed his utility statement with the exact payment to the clerk. Mrs. Sanders read aloud the amount before dropping the money into a drawer beneath her waist and rubber-stamping the receipt stub.

"Even God's house doesn't receive its gas for nothing. Isn't that so, Reverend?"

"Indeed not," Touchstone agreed, standing tall. "Like all of us, our Savior has his bills to pay."

"Now if only our teachers would understand that."

Touchstone swung away from the counter and regarded Lord and the two young women. "This year, with their new lucrative contract, they should have no excuses. This year, the bills should be paid, and paid promptly. The rest of us, Mrs. Sanders, will just have to keep an eye on them."

Lord made no effort to conceal his dislike of the successful Reverend whose spirituality, he thought, was less of deep faith, and more of calculation and profiteering. "And if there is a problem, Touchstone, I hope you won't mind if we borrow the money to pay any bills from you and Fifth Third Pentecostal?"

"You ought to be ashamed," said the clerk.

Touchstone was unaffected, but he removed the dark sunglasses. "Make your joke, Mr. Lord. However, someone needs to watch over the faculty of the Careytown schools. Rest assured, I and many others in the community will be doing precisely that."

"And, no doubt, in the name of good ol' God. Isn't he the goat for all your shortcomings?"

"We all have shortcomings, don't we, Mr. Lord?"

"I'm relieved my daughter is through with you," said Donetta Sanders.

"Your daughter was a nice girl," Lord said to the clerk. And, he thought, she has better taste in jewelry. He looked at Beverly Stiles. She was ignoring Touchstone. So also was the new woman who now stepped past the minister to reach the counter.

"I'm new in town," announced Janey Renn, "and I wish to have the gas turned on in my apartment as quickly as possible. I hope that won't be an inconvenience."

Once outside again, Lord paused several seconds to collect his thoughts. It wasn't Touchstone who had called yesterday, he was sure of that, but could the woman's voice have belonged to Donetta Sanders, he wondered. By nightfall, he was certain he would have the answer to this mystery. Then he recrossed the square to Domirock's Hardware where he piddled away much of an hour among the dark, aromatic shelves before finally gathering the few things he purchased. Afterwards, and prompted by the needling threats of Touchstone, he detoured down a side street lined with cape cods and ancient maples to the home of Willis Ruther, president of the Careytown Faculty Association and its chief negotiator. Parties to the new settlement had signed the contract only a couple of weeks before and although he was aware of its significant features, he wanted to fine-tune his understanding of the rest of its contents. Ruther wasn't home despite his black sports car sitting in the driveway, but Lord made a mental note to get hold of a copy of the agreement in the next day or two. Then he started the walk back to his apartment in a breeze that was pulling clouds into the area and as rapidly pushing them out. The sun appeared and disappeared like the light from a flashlight having partially corroded battery terminals.

The time was coming up on two o'clock in the afternoon. On an impulse he decided to have a beer instead of returning to the apartment.

Tilly's was a clean, white-clapboard tavern of two small rooms beside a wind-and-cold protective entrance. It inconspicuously butted the back end of a parking lot along Main Street. The barroom, decorated with a few cheap paintings in place of beer merchandise and mirrors, was about the size of a small insurance office and the bar itself resembled a staple. Any patron could listen to the untamed conversation of others, especially as there was no jukebox and seldom did the owner turn on the television. A pair of narrow windows and their Venetian blinds sliced the periodic incoming sunlight into thin, brilliant strips.

George Nesbitt, another colleague whom Lord had not seen since the last day of school early in June, had parked his long, four-door sedan on the asphalt fronting the building and upon its recognition, Lord entered the tavern with the stealth of a caterpillar, finally easing his head into the barroom to spot Nesbitt's location.

The generally despised history teacher was embracing a draft at the far stool of the square-cornered bar and he saw Lord at once. A broad smile instantly replaced the brazen mask and spread across the prominently reddish features, the latter causing the man to appear more portly than he actually was, like hot coals that quiver and seem larger than they are. He wore a white dress shirt, but without the tie. The collar was open to the third button, the sleeves rolled carelessly to his elbows, and the shirttail covered most of a pair of gray shorts with plenty of outside pockets. On his feet were a couple of worn-out sneaks, no socks.

He swung around noisily on his stool. "Hey hey, how the hell ya doin', Gray? Those fish of yours start biting yet? Jesus H. Christ! How ya doin'? Tilly, give this yoyo a beer."

The two men shook hands and jostled each other's shoulders with mutual exuberance and eventually, Tilly, a small friendly man with terribly thinning hair who rarely left his business for the daylight, joined in their laughter.

"All summer I hear Goige no comin' back, an' in here he walks a few sosoes ago. What you think of that, Gray?"

"I told him," said Nesbitt, "they couldn't do without me in this swell community. Thus, I had no choice but to play Marv Albert and return."

Tilly glanced at the only other customers in the place at the time, a smartly dressed couple in their fifties who only recently had begun to frequent his establishment. He leaned in close to the teachers, his eyes wide with devilishness. "I tell 'im too, someday they goin' to nail his doopa like a turkey. You drink too much, Goige, and teachers no supposa drink."

"Aaah, I don't drink that much," said Nesbitt without attempting to lower his voice while momentarily catching the eyes of the couple. "Besides, I'll tell them what Gray here told 'em if they ever get guts enough to say anything. Some pre-menopause sweetie told him one night down at the Goldenrod that teaching was a full-time job. You know what Gray came back with, Tilly? He told her he didn't know about teaching, but he was sure mothering was a full-time job."

Tilly laughed and wiped a puddle from the bar. "You sure you tole her that, Gray? Mosta you teachers, your stories ar' full o' beetle dung. You all afraid of everybody."

"No, that's what he said to her," Nesbitt repeated. "I was there."

"I had her son that year," Lord explained, elevating his eyes to the ceiling in mock reverie. "Wonderful child," he added facetiously. "Always hungering for the books."

"Mrs. Deisroth's boy," said the woman across from them, both hands cupped around her drink. "Of course, they moved out of the area about last Christmas."

"Now there was a pistol for you!" roared the woman's husband while shaking a finger for emphasis. "That little shit—excuse my language,

Tilly—when he was only twelve, he locked old Dorothea Compton in her supply room. Wouldn't let her out unless she screamed for help, and she wouldn't. The poor woman was missing for a couple of hours. I tell you, I don't envy you fellows having to teach that kind. Your new agreement, though, that ought to make it a little sweeter."

"Oh gawd, yes!" Nesbitt responded farcically. "The more crap there is to eat, the more money we require to ingest it!"

"Now you take it easy," warned Tilly, his pallid skin reddening a shade.

"Go on. I'm fine, Tilly. But Mr. and Mrs. Benson, I'm quite surprised at you. Surprised that you and other parents from the community have failed to see the solution to your school problem and all those big dollar figures it now takes to run the shebang."

"You'll tell us, I hope?" Mrs. Benson said, coolly. "Your friend Mr. Lord, I can see, is also eagerly awaiting your insight."

"Of course I'll share the secret," Nesbitt said, mockingly trustful. "I'm a dedicated professional, I am. The secret solution is this. Are you listening?"

"We're listening, Mr. Nesbitt. Are you listening, Mr. Lord?"

"Okay. Here it is. Listen carefully now. Had you and other parents decided to govern your children in the same manner as parents of old, you might have gotten away with paying the kinds of salaries to us that were paid twenty years ago. As it is, now you're just paying us to eat your crap! Or to be exact, your offspring's crap!"

"Goige!"

"I'm finished, Tilly," Nesbitt said, pulling back from the bar after having made his point. "It's your doing anyway, you know that, don't you? A few minutes ago, you told Gray and me that teachers are afraid of everybody. I think you're right. I think you're goddamn right!"

"And what do you think, Mr. Lord?" asked Mrs. Benson.

Lord lowered his head for the moment and stared into his beer, as he wasn't sure if the woman was attempting to pit him against his friend. Although the Bensons were regulars at the area taverns, as were numerous other couples, Lord saw them as always standing apart, mostly because of their fine apparel and normally controlled speech which, he was sure, the smaller Boyd Benson would later hear about because of his recent indiscretion. But Mrs. Benson owned a history of school involvement that had often gone against teachers, leaving Lord loath to engage in much of a conversation with her. He concluded that she could again be a kind of troublesome troubadour and he was reluctant to become, however inadvertently, the spark or catalyst for some new conflict.

"What I think, is this," he said, trying for some humor. "The Reverend Millard Touchstone is a fink." He adorned the statement with a wet display of his tongue and a eureka-like widening of his eyes, his best Bill Buckley.

He heard Nesbitt beside him laugh at his lame attempt and so also did the woman's husband.

"And why is that?" asked Mrs. Benson.

"Only a short time ago, I exchanged a few words with the good Reverend, not to mention Donetta Sanders."

"About the Careytown teachers?"

Lord nodded.

"Donetta Sanders I can understand," said Mrs. Benson, thoughtfully.

"And why not Touchstone?" asked her husband.

"Because, Boyd, he hasn't appeared at a school board meeting all year, and there wasn't anything heard from him throughout the period of negotiations. Not even a letter to the editor! Now he's talking? Strikes me, at least, as interesting. I wonder what the man might be up to."

"Yes. Well, all the best to the Reverend Touchstone," said Nesbitt, wanting to get off the subject. He grabbed the paper bag Lord had carried in and placed on the bar. "So what did you buy from old man Domirock today, Gray?... Forget it, I'll see for myself."

He opened the bag and inspected the contents.

"Percolator glass."

"Can't make coffee without it."

"Package of screws, faucet washers, caulk.... A box of .243's? Really getting yourself ready for opening day, are you?"

"I look forward to it myself," said Mr. Benson brightly, missing Nesbitt's pun. "Most of yesterday morning I spent in the field next to our house sighting in my .308. Every year I promise myself to get at it early so that my first shot will put the animal down and keep him down, but this is the first year I've done so."

"Redfield on top?" Nesbitt inquired with dramatic mock-interest.

The husband glanced at his wife and lowered his head approvingly. "You hear that, Alva? There's a man who knows his optics."

Chapter 5

Few people in the Careytown School District held the opinion that George Nesbitt was a good teacher. If it weren't for his holding tenure, the argument went, he would have gotten the boot a long time ago. It was the explanation, also, for his offensive, acerbic mouth. But the latter was debatable. Those who had taught and drunk with him in his pre-tenure term testified that he had been straight-up with parents and other members of the local community since day one. Admittedly, there wasn't quite the sulfuric in his repartee then as now, but all those who judged him to be some cowering neophyte when he had begun his job at Careytown were creating an excuse and substituting it as their reason for an inability to deal with him. Some considered Nesbitt actually crazy, wearing but a blanket of sanity. He had a wife and a six-year old son, yet he was gone most summers and, during the school year, spent an exorbitant amount of his time at the county's watering holes. The rumor that he would be absent from the area—and from his family, too—when Labor Day was at an end originated with those locals who had been in earshot of his rambling complaints during the previous winter. From the unusual strength of these voiced dissatisfactions, they had predicted victory, had felt certain he was surrendering up the area and his job, guessed he would leave his wife and kid, too—when had he ever spent time with them! None of them was privy to what Lord and Ruther had heard one bitter wintry night at the Goldenrod where Nesbitt, the history teacher who prompted fractured quotes from students and others—"Those who learn history from the likes of a Mr. Nesbitt are condemned to relive it!"—responded to bullying advice from a colleague he despised.

"If you don't approve of the way things are run around here, Nesbitt, why don't you just pack up your suitcase and leave?"

"A fair question, Howser," Nesbitt replied from a point between sober and drunk. "And here is your answer and an answer for your contemptible beer-drinking suck-up."

"It's a worthwhile recommendation," echoed Howser's shadow, Deke. "You hate it here, dipshit, then go back to where the hell you came from!"

"Yes. Except that I'm not fond of boundaries."

"What the fuck is that supposed to mean?" said Howser.

"It means, I think I'll stick around and change things. And then if you don't like it, you can move your fucking ass the hell out!"

"Whoooee! And Howser didn't go after him," said Blake, a second-year teacher of science, to Lord, the story's narrator.

"He wouldn't!" Nesbitt broke in. He was sitting back in a green Adirondack chair with his feet stretched out on a large stump. "Remove the whistle and muscle shirt and you'll discover a worm. And the other sonovabitch, the inflatable puffball, football has-been, call him what you want, him I ignored."

Ruther stomped out of the cabin holding a ham sandwich and a beer. It was a gorgeously sunny day.

"Tell me again how you found this place. I love it here, George. Ever think of renting it out?"

"What for?" Nesbitt answered. "I don't need the money. This way, I venture out here any time I want. This way, I can do what we're doing now, which is nothing."

The dark log cabin stood at the far end of a deep hollow in an uninhabited section of the county. A steep forested mountain started at its backside, and a shallow creek snaked along its border and under the road several hundred yards out front.

"How'd you find it?" Blake asked. His black colleague's interest in the place stirred his own. He got out of his chair and, while rounding the bill of his logo-free baseball cap, an activity that was more habit than necessity, looked toward each of the four directions of the property. "I got a few dollars saved I might invest in some property."

"Just fortunate," Nesbitt said.

"What did you get it for?"

"Under twenty, Paul. That's in the first year I was here. I say I was fortunate because I haven't any keen eye for this stuff, don't think I do. But somehow I spotted what was starting to happen here with the city hunters, snowmobilers, the trout fishermen and all the rest."

"What do you estimate it's worth at the present?" Ruther asked, looking around. "Fifty or sixty maybe?"

"Hey, just last year I turned down eighty-five, if you can believe that. Three guys from the Philly area offered to buy it."

"Why is it that you've never been here before?" Wallace, puffing on an aromatic pipe, queried Ruther. His hair was starting to grow back, not enough to hide the phrenological moguls, but sufficient to stop the jokes.

"Just haven't been around when George has this picnic. This weekend, however, I'm batchin' it."

"Hey, everyone!" shouted Blake, waving his cap. "We're forgetting something. We haven't toasted Willis."

"Here, here," cheered Lord, and the others all raised their beer cans to their chief negotiator.

Willis Ruther stepped to the center and took a bow.

Wallace said, "I hear Orr is still telling people that he never saw bargaining and persuasive powers the likes of those belonging to Willis Ruther. Tell us the secret, Willis. What did you say to Orr? What did you say to that bozo Rodino and the rest of the school board that was never said in years past?"

Ruther grinned mischievously. "It's not what I said to Orr and the board, Rudy. It's what I convinced the old-timers down at the elementary school to say. Every year contract time came around, Sal Rodino visited the elementary folk, and the older ones, when asked if they would ever strike, responded that they wouldn't. I convinced them to tell Rodino this year that they would at least consider it. Rodino, being the clown that he is, did the rest. He began to lecture them as if they had already walked out on the poor little toddlers, and that was a mistake."

They numbered eight teachers: Nesbitt, Ruther, the hulk McAllister, Jack Schenley, the married ones; Lord and Blake, both unmarried; affectionately-thought-to-be-insane Rudy Wallace, recently divorced; and Diston, an unmarried handsome local who taught at Prosserville some twenty-five miles east of Careytown. They drank their beer leisurely and broached all manner of subjects, limiting time only on the topic of teaching, because each would return to his respective desk the day after tomorrow. Nesbitt and Walt McAllister had brought along revolvers, and for a time in the afternoon, they blew huge holes out of beer cans, laughing good-naturedly at the beanpole Paul Blake who had joined them and, after firing off his first .44 magnum round, stood agape for much of a minute. Diston, an avid bowhunter, had brought along his compound. Lord joined him for a time, flinging arrows at a straw target.

The sun sat on the tall mountain at six o'clock and Nesbitt prepared the grill for doing the steaks. A few feet away McAllister and Lord gathered firewood to be set ablaze as evening drew on. Young Blake started to talk of women, inquiring if anyone had seen Montgomery's replacement.

"I'm sure it's a woman. I overheard some people talking."

"Hallelujah! We need a few more," said McAllister.

"What's the matter, Walt?" teased Nesbitt. "Dot Com doesn't satisfy you anymore?"

"George, I feel sorry for her. The kids make fun of you, you don't give a hoot. You know they're flamers, 'confident fools' as you call some of them. But Compton's from that dominant school of education that says you got to do everything for these kids. You know, that you got to kiss their ass if it'll get 'em to learn something. But, I can tell you from rooming next door that those kids don't give a duck's fuck about her."

"Nevertheless, you all should remember," Wallace interjected, pointing the mouthpiece of the pipe and pretending to be collegial and philosophical, "that while kissing the pupils' ass is supported by the research as a viable incentive for learning, sucking their dicks also has its supporters. As dedicated professionals, if the one doesn't work, I would think we are then ethically bound to consider the other."

"That's an alternative for the boys," Nesbitt played along, laughing. "What about the girls, Rudy?"

"Fuck Dot Com. And fuck you, Wallace! You're a pervert. I want to know about Montgomery's replacement," Blake reiterated.

"Her name's Janey Renn," Lord said, dropping a load of firewood and returning to the pile near the cabin to get another.

"Heyyy...our boy Gray's on it," Wallace said, rolling his eyes.

"Gray's almost thirty," Schenley noted, sitting off to the side. "You should know he doesn't work that quickly, Rudy."

"What's she like, Gray?" Nesbitt asked, still chuckling at Wallace while making another attempt at lighting the fire in the grill. "Did Super Harold do himself and the rest of us a favor?"

"She's beautiful. Not in your overly flashy way though. I didn't see a lot of Maybelline. She's spare, but has big eyes and a smile that warmed my heart. She'll grow on you."

"Ah, the pet-tight look," Wallace said dreamily.

"Not quite, Rudy. Something tells me once she's settled in a place, she doesn't get pushed around."

"Does she carry around this oversized shoulder bag?" Diston asked. "Yeah, it's about as big as she is. Well, I've seen her and if you tire of her, send her over to Prosserville. We'll find something for her."

"Jack, you ain't saying much," Nesbitt said, looking at Schenley, a chemistry teacher, the oldest of them and the only one in his thirties.

Schenley's expressions revealed minor movement. It was a familiar joke that the others were always waving a hand before his face to determine if he were alive or dead. A slight bob of his head told the others he was amused.

"I have Stylish right across the hall," he muttered with last-word finality.

When the top of the grill glowed red, perfect for the Pittsburgh rare they all preferred, Nesbitt forked on the huge, inch-thick porterhouses, instructed Blake to refill the beer tub, told Schenley and Wallace to move a picnic table, informed Diston of the whereabouts of plates and utensils, and finally recommended to Lord and McAllister that they start the fire.

"Where's Willis?"

"He's at his Z getting his harmonica," said Lord.

Night was around them when they finished with their meal. McAllister collected the bones and fat scraps for his dog. Ruther scraped his teeth with a toothpick, then cupped the harmonica in his hands. Countless cottonballs of moonlit clouds floated overhead. Away from the fire there was a starting chill.

"Any requests?"

"Something bluesy," Wallace said, lighting a pipe.

"We got ourselves a fire," Nesbitt said. "Keep that bluesy stuff for another time. What we need is a bit of the 'Red River Valley.'"

Ruther complied, shaking his head at the simple request, and the sad, lonely notes of the old, old western song drifted down the hollow, interrupted only by a weak and sporadic call for help. Lord was the first to hear it and stilled Ruther. All the men waited with their beverage cans away from their lips. Soon the plaintive call came again.

"It's feminine," declared Ruther.

"It's coming from around the drop in the road," Nesbitt decided, setting down his beer. "Let's have a look."

They spread themselves as they went out the gravel lane leading away from the cabin. The call sounded intermittently and always the same.

"What do you make of it?" Lord asked.

The men stopped. Nesbitt cupped his left ear in the direction of the sound and slowly moved it one way, then the other. He looked back at the cabin lit up in the dark.

"A couple of us hang back."

They reached the end of the lane and turned right. Nobody spoke. They searched along the banks of the road, their vision aided by soft, cloud-diminished light from the moon. The cabin stood already two hundred yards behind them and because of the heavy forestation was increasingly difficult to locate quickly. The call now came less frequently.

To Lord the voice in the night sounded too much the same each time and he uneasily questioned their movement in its direction. It lacked the genuine entreaty of one in need of help. It hinted of a Siren.

They walked the road another fifty yards, when suddenly they could hear Blake swearing behind them. Then at the top of his lungs the untenured teacher yelled: "THEY'RE STEALING THE BEER! THE BASTARDS GOT THE TUB!"

Nesbitt instructed the others to fan out along the road and to call out upon seeing anyone. A few seconds later, the galvanized beer tub slammed to the ground, and they could see the culprits racing through the trees as quickly as was safely possible, hear them as they broke off branches in their line of flight. They could see, too, that Blake was not far behind in his pursuit.

Lord, Nesbitt, and the others set out to cut off the two figures hurrying under the darkness of the forest in the direction of the drop in the dirt road, but they all saw they would lose the sprint. Even Blake, the fittest of them, was already falling behind.

The figures leaped a short embankment and hit the road, still running young. From below a car started up and strained in reverse. A door was swinging free on it and the figures jumped in and in a matter of seconds the vehicle, raked by the thudding of stones against its undercarriage, disappeared, leaving a dry drifting dust.

Exhausted and breathing heavily, Nesbitt nonetheless inquired immediately of Blake, who came onto the road and joined them, if anything had been taken.

"Give me a second."

"Anyone tell anything from the car?" Diston asked.

"When the interior light went on, I saw another guy and a girl inside," reported Lord.

"They get anything, Paul?" Nesbitt asked again.

"Not a thing. They dropped the tub."

"You certain they weren't in the house? Those revolvers are sitting right out in the open, on top the fridge."

"I doubt it," Blake said. "They'd jumped the stream when I first saw them. Walt stayed near the cabin too."

"Let's go gather up the beer," Schenley suggested.

"Had to be kids," Nesbitt said, worriedly.

"TEACHERS REPORT ATTEMPTED THEFT OF BEER SUPPLY," Wallace sang out reportorially. "TEENS SUSPECTED!"

"It's not the beer that bothers me so much, Rudy. I don't want them knowing the location of this place. I'm not sure I didn't see that car out here a time or two before."

Rather than go through the forest to discover the tub of beer, which Blake informed them was closer to the cabin than to where they were standing, the men returned along the road that brought them back to the lane. As they were about to make their way onto it, another figure, this time female, appeared from the opposite direction, and to each of them it was evident, despite the limiting light of night, that the girl was exhausted. They went to her.

"Are you okay?" Lord asked. "You're a long way off the track." It was the smallest attempt at humor to determine some level of worry in the girl who looked to be eighteen, nineteen years of age. Even if she were younger, he knew that she wasn't a student at Careytown.

The young woman attempted to collect herself.

"What happened?" Nesbitt asked.

"Did they get your beer?"

"They made an effort.... Who are you? And who dumped you? The way that car sped away, its driver has no intention of returning for you. I hope you realize that."

She lowered her eyes to the ground and kept them there for a time. She was attractive but had a raw, unfinished look, an honest appearance common to many of the girls and women in the region. Like that of a paper doll ripped to shape by fingers instead of scissors.

"Can I get a ride somewhere?"

"Aren't you one of Harley Clouser's daughters?" Diston asked curiously.

A look of worry flashed at their friend told them all she was.

Nesbitt repeated his earlier question concerning the identities of the others.

She shook her head slowly. "I can't. He threatened me, and he wouldn't have kicked me out if he didn't mean it. Besides, I don't really know any of their names, not even the girl's."

Nesbitt glanced at Diston, then at Lord. Each found the response incredible.

"Wonderful. Keep it up," warned Nesbitt. "Keep getting into cars with guys whose names you don't know and someday the police will be dragging your bones up from a swamp. There's a big one not far from where you're standing."

"Can you give her a lift?" Lord asked Diston.

"If one of you will just get me to Careytown, I can call my sister."

"I'll take her," Schenley volunteered. "I've had it anyway." Schenley waved the girl to come along with him, and they started down the lane to where the cars were parked near the cabin. The rest moved at a slower pace behind them.

"She wasn't too elated when Gray offered you to take her home, Dan. What's the old man like?"

Diston waited until Schenley and the girl were yet further ahead of them before he responded to Nesbitt's question. "It's not her father she's fearing," he finally said in a quiet tone. "She was married only a year ago. A few months after... well, you can guess. Same old, same old."

The gathering broke apart before the next hour passed. Lord collected the last of the empty beer cans and bottles from outside and deposited them in their cardboard cases.

"I'm taking off," he announced to Nesbitt from the doorway.

"Stick around, Gray. I've something I've been wanting to tell you. With everyone else around I didn't want to bring it up."

"Sounds serious. What is it?"

"Who's left at this hour?"

"Just Rudy and Paul, I believe. They're finishing with the dishes."

"They'll leave soon enough then. Afterwards, you and I can have another brew and I'll spill it."

Once the others were all gone, Nesbitt did as he had said he would. He popped the tops from two cans of beer and handed one to Lord.

"Let's go back out by the fire. I'll throw another log on."

"Whatever floats your boat," said Lord. He followed Nesbitt outside where the history teacher spent a minute stoking the embers to blazing once again.

"The nights are just beginning to get chilly."

"That heat feels great," said Lord. "Now, sit yourself down and tell me what's on your mind."

Nesbitt threw the stoking stick aside and fell into a chair. He took a slug from the can before speaking.

"Someone's trying to do you wrong, Gray. Was Clipper Ostrander in your apartment recently?"

Slowly, Lord's head shook and he stared into the fire without answering. He could not believe what his friend had asked. Was what he felt apprehension about ever since the phone call coming to pass? Was someone really planning to make something out of nothing?

"Gray, you hear me?"

"He's my newspaper boy."

"That I know. But was he upstairs and inside your pad?"

"I'd forgotten to leave my weekly payment and spotted him on the sidewalk. So I called through the window and up he came with his trusty dog. He heard my fishtank and I offered him to have a look. What's the big deal? You don't invite your paperboy to step inside your home when he comes collecting?"

"I live in a residential area. There's a house with an open front porch identical to mine across the street and on either side. The kid doesn't have to trudge up a long dark stairwell. And, I have a wife."

"What the fuck are you insinuating?" Lord said, although his words didn't imply the tone they would have with someone else.

"Get with the program, good buddy. I'm not insinuating shit. Jack, Walt, Paul, even Willis, they think it's over. We've got a great contract finally and now it's over. But it's just starting and it won't ever be over. Looks like you're the first one they want to fuck, but tomorrow it'll be my turn, then Rudy's, and right on through the line-up. And when there are turnovers, they'll fuck on the replacements too. All because their teachers are now making more money than they ever thought we were worth. You and I are big boys, Gray. They say things about us that's a goddamn lie, I figure we can take care of it ourselves, so long as we know. But these fuckers don't care what happens to the little kid. That's how sucko they actually are."

"Where did you hear this?"

"Down at the Goldenrod. Some locals were talking it up, but they aren't the ones who started it. I know them and they're too goddamn ignorant to get something like this going. But it tickles them. They'll keep it moving. Any idea who might have put it in motion?"

"I got a call as soon as the boy left with his dog. A man and a woman."

"You're not kidding, are you? You sixty-nine them, or were they blocked?"

"They're not blocked, but they wouldn't answer either. I know who it is, though. I read the goddamn phonebook. The number had a double digit at the end, making it a snap. Took all of about ten minutes."

"I'll bet they weren't counting on that," said Nesbitt, laughing in the firelight. "Hell, why the fuck am I worried about you?"

"It was Margo's folks," Lord said.

"Margo of Tom and Margo?"

"And who sop up Tilly's suds and play Liars' Pokers as well as any of us. Only I doubt that her folks would spread it. I've met the old man and he's always on a tear. It's the only way he knows how to talk. But they're good people and I believe this was their crazy way of warning me. Someone else must have seen what they saw. And my guess there would be Touchstone. Or, if he wasn't the one to actually see Clipper leaving my apartment, then he got wind of it and is the one who's spreading it now."

"The good, fat-bellied reverend.... I remember you said you had words with him."

"He hates CFA."

"You think he's enough of a son-of-a-bitch, though, that he'd fuck over little Clipper Ostrander for his own delight?"

"Who knows? If he's intending to display a Hell House this Halloween, he's capable of anything."

"What's a Hell House?"

"Some ministry out west sells a kit to churches that are of the Christian goofball variety. Rudy calls the type Goobers for Christ. I heard Touchstone is planning to set one up. A room for suicides. Another for aborted fetuses. A big one for homosexuals with AIDS. That sort of bullshit. Some parishioner dresses up as Satan and conducts you through the rooms."

"Real fire?"

"Probably paper cutouts come with the kit."

"Sounds like real fire is what's needed." They grinned at one another in mutual understanding. "Well, I just thought you'd want to know, and now you do. So keep your ears up."

Lord hadn't been counting—he never did!—but much experience told him the beer he was now suddenly polishing off with nervous, angry, gulping speed put him in the double figures for the day. And he knew, too, that he wanted yet another. But he didn't outright ask for it.

"You staying out here for the night, or are you heading home?"

"I could easily stay here. I might even allow myself to fall asleep right in this goddamn chair. Listen, Gray. I want to ask you something. Unrelated to what we were just talking about. We've been friends for quite a while and I want to ask you. Do you ever wonder, like a lot of folks, like some of the guys who just left, why I spend so much of my time away from my wife and kid? Why I don't spend more of it at home?"

"I have wondered, but I'm not doing it now."

"You care to know?"

"You mind if I fuck recycling for a moment and throw this can into the fire? It looks hot enough to vaporize the aluminum. Ever see it done? Watch. Check it out...! Goddammit! Look at that! Fuckin' instantaneous. Now where did that aluminum go, huh? I have to remember to ask Jack. You think the aluminum ends up in the soil or the atmosphere?"

"Gray, you wanna know?"

"I get the feeling you're about to tell me whether I want to know or not. But beware I might become bored in the middle of your soul-wrenching explanation and tell you to shut the fuck up."

Nesbitt grinned in the firelight. "Sonofabitch. That's why you're my favorite."

"So talk then."

"What do you think of Stella, Gray?"

"What do you mean, what do I think of her?"

"Would you want to sleep with her?"

"Nooo, I wouldn't want to sleep with her!"

"Because she's my wife."

"Of course."

"Well, hearing that as your excuse will please her. She also thinks you're the best of the bunch."

"Look, whenever I see you two fucking together—"

"Have you been sneaking around our window?"

"I said that wrong. Too much beer. Whenever I see the two of you together, it seems clear you get along extremely well. I've never observed trouble brewing in either of your faces. So if you want to spend time away—"

"—And that's just it. You've touched on the point, my friend. We do get along very well. But it's not because we have a lot in common, which is probably what you and maybe some others think. I drink and enjoy myself. Stella's rarely tasted a drop. I turn the music up, dance and act all stupid. I think I put on a damn good show, better than your exercise videos, in fact. She turns the music down, frowns at my behavior, and tells me I act worse than a silly child. I tell her we ought to get a dog. She talks about fleas and ticks. She loves to fuck. Me, I can take it or leave it. Anymore, I feel a hand on the bird is better than two in the bush."

"You must have something in common! You've been married more than a few years."

"We do. And we talked about it and came upon the answer together. Each of us, Gray, has the seemingly endless capacity to be compatible to the other. That's what the fuck we have in common. A capacity for compatibility."

"So what's wrong with that? Rudy and his ex bicycled, roller-bladed, cross-countried, and shot pool together. They believed all that made them compatible and it obviously didn't. Maybe having the capacity for compatibility is a greater plus than actually having it. Or some bullshit of that sort. This *is* starting to bore me, you know."

"But the problem, Gray, is with how I described it. I didn't say it was endless."

"So I heard. You said it was 'seemingly endless.' What the hell is that?"

"It means if it should come to an end, I'll be out of here for good."

"You could leave your kid, too?"

"You wouldn't think so, would you?"

"No, I wouldn't," Lord said emphatically.

"But, yeah, I'm afraid I could."

Lord stared a moment at his friend and colleague, lit by the fire. "That's bullshit. You aren't going anywhere, George. You'll be here when the cows come home. And now I am totally sick of the subject. So let's drop it and have still another beer."

"Sorry. There isn't any. These two were the last."

"That's a lie and you know it. Remember who you're talking to."

"I'm telling you the truth. There's no more beer in the cabin."

"My ass! You're the one who didn't want any money. Who said you would cover it all."

"It isn't the money."

"Then what? And don't tell me you're out of beer. I know you too fucking well, good buddy. You've been a guy known to run out of patience, gas, and steam. And there's many who'll rejoice when you either run out of time or they run you out of town. But you've never been known to run out of beer. So where is it?"

Nesbitt started to repeat the denial still again.

"Cut the snow job! It's insulting. Keep your ass glued to your seat. Just tell me where it is. I'll get it and get you one, too."

Nesbitt finally surrendered. He wrestled himself out of his chair.

"What the hell! I just told you about Stella and myself. Wait here. I'll be right back."

He turned and went into the cabin, then quickly reappeared with a flashlight. Thicker clouds had moved in, obscuring the moon altogether.

"Follow me."

"Where we going?"

"Just stay close so you can use the light to see where you're stepping."

Lord caught up with him and they padded away from the side of the cabin up a small rise that was absent of trees. A bone-chilling chorus of howls rippled down the mountain on their right.

"Coyotes," Nesbitt explained.

"That's the first time I've heard them. Been here for almost a decade, too. Never heard 'em even once. Never have seen one either."

"I've been out here alone and seen them a time or two. They come bounding down right in front of the cabin. They're cautious once they get here, but not afraid."

"Spooky," Lord said.

"I always thought I should show this to someone, and I always thought it should be you. I just never have."

"Where are we going? Not too far, I hope. I can't see diddly beyond the flashlight."

"Right over here," Nesbitt said. They were at the very top of the rise.

"I don't see anything. And I certainly don't see a brew at hand."

"That's where you're wrong. Here. You hold the light."

Nesbitt reached down to the sod and felt around. Lord watched him pull up on a wooden handle that revealed a trapdoor under the sod.

"Now get a load of this," Nesbitt said, and he lifted the door that was fairly well rotted under the square of sod, setting it aside.

Lord shined the light into the hole.

"Great dust of Hyukatake!"

"Something, isn't it?"

"I'm talking about the hole. I expected the beer."

"I'm talking about the hole, too."

"What's it doing here?"

"The fellow I bought the place from, he poured it."

"What the fuck for?"

"He told me, to keep his tools. Said many of the camps were being broken into over the winter months, and he had thousands of dollars of tools and machines that he didn't want to lose and didn't want to be hauling back and forth from his home. So he built this. We're about two-hundred feet from the camp."

Lord crouched and peered into the concrete hole.

"How deep is this thing?"

"Don't know. Never measured. But there's at least a dozen rungs on that homemade ladder of his."

Lord shined the light up and down the wooden ladder. "There's more than a goddamn dozen."

"So go down and pick out what you want and you can count 'em on the way. Give me back the light."

"Not until I see if there are any surprises down there." Lord moved the light over the floor of the pit, searching for a rat or snake. "It's seems okay."

"It's good you looked. There's been a corpse or two."

"You need to replace the wood in the trapdoor. And probably you ought to keep the sod off."

"I want the sod on. It camouflages things."

"Then when you replace the boards in the door, replace 'em with pressure-treated. That stuff is supposed to work pretty well."

"When did you become a fucking carpenter?"

"All right. Take the goddamn light."

Nesbitt held the light on the ladder as Lord first positioned it, then carefully descended.

"Fourteen," he said, reaching the bottom and peering up. "And don't get any funny ideas about putting that lid back on while I'm down here."

"Wouldn't think of it."

"Yeah? Well, I read a story by a little-known Kentucky writer about a fellow who died in a cistern. His family didn't miss him until months later when the water got to tasting funny."

"Sounds like water you could bottle and sell to the public. 'Fresh to you from the dark, undisturbed cisterns in the rolling hills of Ol' Kentucky...' Can you see well enough to read the labels? Or do you need the light?"

Lord didn't respond. Nesbitt heard him laughing.

"What the fuck's so funny?"

"Two, four, six, eight...sixteen cases of Jacob Best. I never heard of it. I never heard of any of these beers. Five, ten, fifteen, twenty, one, two, three.... You've got seventy-six cases of beer down here, George. Where the fuck did you get all this beer? And why?"

"I don't like to run out."

"Run out? Where'd you get it?"

"If I got to be down around Philly, Pittsburgh, Scranton, any of the bigger cities in the state, I usually stop off at the local distributors. They often buy some of this stuff by the truckload and then have these great sales. I take advantage and load up. I wish they'd do it up here."

"There isn't a one of these brands here that's name."

"So you know me. I'm one of those who thinks it all tastes pretty much the same anyway."

"You're an amazing man, Mr. Nesbitt. How many you want me to bring up?"

"Just make it one. I don't think I got much more in me tonight."

Climbing back up the ladder, Lord handed the case of beer to Nesbitt who placed it on the ground, then helped his friend out of the hole.

"Now you got to promise me, Gray, you don't say a word about this stockpile to anyone. I don't want to take any chance of it getting back to some of the students."

"Not a word," Lord said. "You can cut off my pecker if it turns out otherwise."

"How the fuck did you ever turn out to be an English teacher anyway?"

"Better question. Why aren't you coaching? And why isn't asshole Howser a history teacher?"

Nesbitt understood the implications of the questions and began laughing as he pulled up the ladder from the hole and dragged it several feet away to hide it.

"Those are good questions, Gray. Remind me someday to ask them of Corey."

Chapter 6

"...So the buses will be starting out earlier this year. You should interpret this to mean that our students will be arriving earlier. But I still don't want them in the corridors before 7:55. Those who have the duty? Nothing has changed.

"Study halls. Study halls are larger this year and some of you will have them in the cafeteria. There are new tables in there. Keep an eye out that they're not getting destroyed.

"We're instituting a new pass system this year for the seventh- and eighth-graders. They can go to the library or to one of your rooms only if they have a pre-signed pass from a teacher. But there doesn't have to be a good reason. What we're trying to do is just keep ourselves better informed about where some of the younger kids are going when they're not in one of your rooms and are in the halls instead.

"Some of you still need to learn to direct students to come to my office when you ask them to leave your class. Don't just stand them outside in the hall where they can wander."

"They don't already know that?" Beverly Stiles remarked with a weakened belligerence.

"It's your responsibility to remind them, Ms. Stiles. It's the responsibility of each of you.

"What I don't need to remind you of is how the new contract requires you to be here longer than last year. You're permitted to exit the building at 3:15. You're expected to use this additional time following the last period for professional and educational activity."

"You think P.D. will tire of this bullshit?" Nesbitt remarked to Lord. Some of his colleagues swung around in their seats to look at him.

"You might consider all this to be trivial, Mr. Nesbitt."

"I consider it to be bullshit. You've already ran it off on paper and distributed it to everyone present. Do you think we're illiterate? It's bullshit!"

"I don't believe 'bullshit' is a subject you'll find in academia," the principal said.

"Tell us you're kidding. Ever hear of Harry Frankfort from Yale? Back in the eighties he wrote a paper on it. Sometimes I wonder if you've even heard of Yale."

One hour later, the Careytown faculty, some of its members feeling more verbally bludgeoned than others, departed from the auditorium and went to their classrooms.

At his desk Lord took up the rosters and counted the students in the five classes with which he would meet each of five days for forty weeks. And he counted the number in his study hall. One hundred thirty-two was the total. Although he taught the language, he had a head for numbers, and as he began doing after a parent had questioned his knowing anything about children, because he was unmarried and had none, he multiplied students times hours per week, times weeks in the school year. A single student multiplied in the same manner produced for him an important figure for argument, and with moderate extrapolation came the reasonable conclusion that he spent greater face-to-face time with a child every day than did that child's parents. This wasn't true for all students and parents, but, sadly, it was true for many.

For the rest of the opening day he made out seating charts for his classes, entered each student's name in the grade book (in barely readable pencil as schedules would change), removed from supply lockers the first sets of books for distribution, and filled out numerous forms for the central office.

The next morning the students arrived, shoving and darting through the corridors like rabbits driven from their warren. The terribly grating buzzer sounded and Lord faced the first group, seniors. They sat before him in silence, but he did not fool himself into thinking that the attentiveness would endure beyond a day. The second group filed in and these were seventh graders. They sat quietly too, but in a way that was different from the older students. Here he observed something good, yet his growing cynicism warned him that would change. The distracting buzzer (Why not a chime, he sometimes argued with Waring) sounded routinely throughout the day and throughout every weekday that followed, and Lord wrestled with his classes' minds and with each student's behavior. Each day progressed, digressed, regressed. The weeks connected to each other and the gnawing, eroding familiarity of the job spread across his life like the burnout in a frame of exposed photographic film too long before a hot bulb....

"So why isn't it done?"

"Turn around. Your attention is to be up here."

"Mr. Foss, if you intend to pass this course, you'll have to change some things you're doing."

"Feet off the desk, Bogardus." .

"Eyes on your own paper, Mr. Aftanas."

"Title your composition."

"No, you can't go to the restroom now. You had time between classes and I saw you out in the hall wasting it. And don't refer to it as 'downloading.'"

"No, Jill. Call your mother on your own time."

"It's your education, not mine. Plenty of kids in this country and some will make it and others won't. You decide where you want to be."

"You high, Foss? You look high to me."

"You always look high, Cassie."

"Enough of that language, Asa. Don't encourage him Cassie."

"Of course I don't have to look at it. You can wear your hair anyway you want for all I care. I just thought maybe nobody's told you that you look.... Well, you don't look good."

"You pushed her books onto the floor. You pick them up."

"This is slop. You'll have to do it over."

"You got a problem, Mr. Aftanas?"

"Don't forget. Test tomorrow."

"I've got to get something out of this, too, you know."

"You want to put your name on the paper? I'm not a mind reader."

"Shut up, Mr. Foss, and turn around! And quit marking on the desks."

"Who spit on you?"

"I don't want you stuffing the papers you don't want inside the desks. They're not your personal dumpsters."

"That's three times this period, Mr. Aftanas. Turn around and keep it around or you're out of here. You can talk to Waring.... Yes, we all know you're not afraid of anybody."

"Fuck off, Lord."

"What did you say?"

"I said fuck off. Don't pretend you didn't hear me."

"Gather your things immediately, Mr. Aftanas, and get out of my class."

"I don't take fuckin' orders from a faggot-face."

"Gather your things quietly and go to the office, Asa."

"I ain't goin' nowhere. You want me out of here, you'll have to throw me out. Though maybe you'd rather persuade me by sucking my dick. Or am I too old for you, Lord? I've heard you prefer them younger."

SPINE

For the moment Lord transferred his gaze off the taunting, hateful eyes of Asa Aftanas and onto the rest of his students. Some were anxious, staring silently wide-eyed at their fellow classmate, but most were looking at their teacher standing at the front. And he knew all of them were wondering the identical thing. What was he going to do? At similar times in the past, he had hoped other students would show themselves and speak up in his favor, tell the Asa Aftanases and the Dana Fosses of their classroom to shut up and go away, but it was too much to expect. They were afraid, and they knew what everyone knew but would not admit. The Asa Aftanases and Dana Fosses now ran the schools, a result of the abdication of everyone else by way of some artfully crafted language put to paper in the form of mission statements and related documents that would prove, if ever questioned, school accountability. He knew they thought, too, that their teacher was afraid. There had been students who could have kicked his butt, and Asa Aftanas, he realized, might be another one of them, but he had never feared any of them and he had no fear now. If he feared anything, it was the hassle that might develop afterwards. It was this fear and this fear alone that explained why the kid was still in the classroom and not out in the hall on his ass. It was a game, and sure, he understood it, but the kids understood it better. There were few rules. The first: As a teacher you were to keep your hands off students unless they assaulted you. The second: Teachers must earn the respect of their students. It was a tough game to win if you were the teacher. "Use the power of knowledge to gain their respect," intoned those professing an unfathomable erudition of the matter. It had always seemed so obvious to him, too. Most kids owned little knowledge when contrasted to the amount any individual could accumulate, no matter what the epistemology. You might someday gain their respect through knowledge, but until then, exercising the most obvious power over many of them was the only way, and every student was aware that teachers had been thoroughly stripped of that power. No one ever respected a weakling. No one cared about anything he had to say. Quote the Nobel Prize winners, quote God Himself, and it still wouldn't matter.

Staring at his student, Lord momentarily considered calling Principal Waring on the intercom: "Come and get this joker since you're one of those in favor of always keeping your hands off kids!" And he thought he might summon Schenley and Nesbitt to help him eject Asa Aftanas. However, either way, he would end up the loser in the eyes of the rest of the class. Others would be pulling the same stunt next week. "It's not a contest between the two of you. Remember that." Right. It's a contest between the Dallas Cowboys and the Steelers. They were out of touch, those administrators and educators who pontificated such nonsense. Asa Aftanas wasn't leaving the room except by the physical force of another. Which now brought to the floor the touchy question of exactly how he was going to accomplish such a feat. He wished he were over forty. This event happened less with older teachers. It was normally the younger ones who were in the fight for territory.

He was holding a Merriam-Webster when the incident began and had set it on his desk. He now picked up the dictionary again and thumbed through its pages. It would be acceptable by those to whom he answered to put his hand on Aftanas' shoulder as the first move toward ushering the student into the hall. But the kid would be on the ready, looking to deck him. To avoid the fracas that might result, the kid had to swing first, but he wanted to make sure there was no connection. The colleges and their required methods courses never approached this subject. And the thought had yet to occur to OSHA that the school was a workplace too. You were on your own.

He moved toward the desk seating Asa Aftanas, who had stretched his long legs deliberately across the aisle to block it. Lord shut the dictionary, stared briefly at the legs in the ripped denim that would not be moving, and stepped over them, positioning himself just behind the teen's left shoulder.

"Don't waste your breath asking me to leave again," Aftanas said, tapping the fingers of his right hand on the wooden surface of the desk. A taut smirk extended across his face. Since summer, he had cut his hair shorter. It had undergone some training as well. There was no change in the soiled clothing and flesh. "You want me out? You got to throw me out."

"I want to say something. It isn't for your classmates. It's just for you. Listen to the entire thing, and then decide what you want to do."

"Lay a finger on me, Lord, you'll regret it."

Without focusing on any of them, Lord glanced over the other students in his class as he bent and cupped a hand near the ear of Aftanas, taking care not to touch.

He whispered: "All this talk about sucking dicks, did you want to set up an appointment to have your first experience? Is that what this is about?"

Kids, whatever their age, most could only react. They seemed incapable of engaging in histrionics, as he had just done against his better judgment. In one swift motion Aftanas swung about and uncoiled out of his seat. The right fist roundhoused, but Lord was ready, moving an inch for evasion. He cuffed the student on the side of the head with the weighty dictionary. Aftanas, surprised, lost his balance and misaligned a pair of desks, tried to recover, but Lord immediately shoved him to the floor and stood over him.

"Now get up and get out!"

The kid didn't gather himself at once. And waiting, towering above the boy, Lord thought the incident might not be finished and so prepared himself for his next move. But eventually, Aftanas rose from the floor, the pernicious hatred and malice remaining present, but for the moment dormant. The boy was not going to fight.

As he left the room, he shot Lord an evil eye, of a duration the same the teacher had received from other disciplined students, only this example was futuristically gray and void of redemption. Lord trailed him into the hall where McAllister was passing.

"Walt, will you see that he gets to P.D.?"

The beefy industrial arts teacher nodded a couple of times.

"You know the way, Aftanas."

Twenty minutes remained in the period. Lord realigned the desks, gathered off the floor the crinkled papers that had fallen from their insides, composed himself, and attempted to get his lesson back on track. Foolish of himself, he thought, when the intercom signal came on. It was Principal Waring.

"Mr. Lord, I realize that you have a preparation period following your class, but I need to see you."

There it was again. First, they wasted your time and the time of their classmates. Then more of your time was wasted at the front office when anyone else would have concluded the matter was over and done, at least your part in it. But not in education. Not in the public schools.

"Mr. Lord, we're not going to get anything done today. Can we just talk among ourselves?"

"We can try to accomplish something, Tammy. There's still some time."

"No way, Mr. Lord. Tell us what you said to Asa."

"That was between him and me, Tucker."

"Aw c'mon, tell us. Whatever it was, it really set him off."

"You heard me."

"Then tell us a joke," said Bogardus, a handsome rough-looking boy, sitting way at the back.

"Yeah, tell some jokes. All the other teachers tell jokes, but you never do. Don't you know no good ones?"

He purposefully frowned at them. They all wanted to listen to a joke as a means of wasting class time.

"A joke. You want to hear a joke from me, do you?"

He hemmed and hawed a while longer, running a hand through his hair, before admitting that in his repertory he had one or two that could be told in a classroom situation.

"But I must inform you, these jokes are of a wholly different brand of humor. I suspect most, if not all of you, are not used to it. I've never known but a few people who could understand and appreciate these jokes.

"Try us, Mr. Lord."

"I don't know."

"Aw, pretty please. Widen our horizons."

"Very well, if you insist. And because I'm so fond of all of you. But, for the record, I'm betting that not a single person in this class will understand it and laugh. So here goes nothing.

"For the longest period of time this fellow, whom I'll call Nick, had stacked out behind his house a huge pile of red bricks, building bricks."

"Nick and the brick," Tucker said.

"Yes. Nick and the brick. And one day he decided to do something with the bricks, construct something. But, thinking long and hard as he did, he was unable to come up with a good idea. His neighbor happened by one afternoon, though, when Nick was studying the pile and he told his neighbor of his dilemma, how he couldn't think of anything to build. 'Now see here,' the neighbor said, 'you've been squawking in my ear for longer than a year how you wished you had a garage to park your car in at nights and during the winter. Why not take all these bricks and build one?' Well, our fellow Nick was dumbfounded by his own stupidity—yes, I mean he was absolutely dumbfounded!—and that's what he did. Next morning he selected his spot out behind the house, marked out the four corners employing the Pythagorean Theorem—some of you have heard of that, haven't you, from Mr. Wallace

69

or Ms. Stiles?—transported the bricks alongside and started mixing mortar to lay them all together. Took him the better part of a week it did, and he was very satisfied when he was done, except for one thing. He had a single brick left over, and he couldn't think of what to do with it. This fellow Nick, mind you, could not come up with anything to do with that one remaining red brick. Luckily, his neighbor strolled over to inspect his work on the garage and Nick told his neighbor about the single brick that was left over from the job and how he didn't know what to do with it. 'Why that's easy,' the neighbor advised him. 'Chuck it!' And you know, that's exactly what our boy Nick went and did."

Dead silence.

"That's it?... I don't get it."

"That's not funny. What's so funny about that, Mr. Lord?"

"I warned you. It's a different brand of humor. Most people aren't used to it. Few people ever get that joke."

"So explain it to us."

"There's no sense in that. If you have to explain what a joke means, then it's lost."

"That was a stupid joke."

"Know any others?"

"Come on. One more, Mr. Lord. You said you knew a couple."

"Yes, but I also said it was similar to the other one. You won't get it either."

"Come on. Give us another try."

"Maybe some other time."

"Aw, please."

"Some other time."

When the buzzer sounded, the students uncharacteristically stayed rooted at their desks. He actually dismissed them. On their way out he overheard them continuing to mumble how stupid the joke was. Some said he was stupid, too.

***

Asa Aftanas was sitting beside the faculty mailboxes when Lord entered Waring's outer office where two secretaries and an aid worked. The kid appeared insolent as ever with the legs stretched out and one arm extending above his head and resting against the wall. The monstrous father, streaked in dirt and oil, was already on hand, towering next to his son. He seemed dangerously on edge, as though he were willing to inherit the fight and include the entire school. Waring postured inside his office, issuing instructions to one of the secretaries. Through the window on the outer office he saw Lord approach his door. He held up a hand to say "a minute," and continued talking to the secretary.

Lord turned about to find the old man sizing him up.

"Where do you get off, Lord, saying to my boy what you did? Who the hell do you think you are?"

"I recommend you ask Asa the same question, Mr. Aftanas."

"I don't have to ask Asa shit!"

Nesbitt entered the office to check his mailbox. He glanced at the kid, Randy Aftanas, then Lord. "What's up?"

Lord eyed him closer. "He told me to fuck off, among other things."

Waring emerged from his office, the secretary following. The principal approached the boy and his father with a look not of concern, but professionalism. Always the super-professional, Lord thought mockingly. Whatever that really meant, he wasn't sure it was always for the best.

Nesbitt stepped next to Waring who was talking to the old man.

"...and his behavior, when it becomes disruptive—"

"Ask him what he said."

"What, Mr. Nesbitt?"

"Ask him what he said to Gray."

"I'll handle this, Mr. Nesbitt, if you don't mind."

"Did your son tell you what he said?"

"Mr. Nesbitt! I don't want to have to discipline you too."

"Asa, did you tell Lord to go fuck himself?"

"Mr. Nesbitt!"

Nesbitt inclined his head and raised his voice. "Did you tell my friend to go fuck himself? Answer the damn question!"

"I told him that and plenty more," Asa Aftanas said coolly without removing his arm from the wall. "And you know what else? It goes for you too, sucker. So fuck off!"

"Well, there you have it, dad. The next question's for you."

Waring lost his professional demeanor to anger. He kept repeating Nesbitt's name, but Nesbitt wouldn't have any of it.

"The question, Aftanas, is this. Do you approve of your son expressing his disrespect of a teacher in such a way?"

Randy Aftanas responded slowly and ominously. "You've made a mistake. This wasn't none o' your business." His eyes rigidified and patiently tracked the smallest movement Nesbitt made.

"I guess you do. Okay, Mr. Waring, it's all yours. Because you're not one to ever ask the tough questions, I decided to do it for you."

"I want to see you in my office before you leave today."

"Not a chance!" Nesbitt stared directly into the eyes of both the father and the son, but he was addressing Waring. "You ought to throw his butt out and you ought to keep it out. But you won't. That's why I won't waste another minute of my time."

"This wasn't none of your business in the first place," Randy Aftanas repeated, his eyes continuing to track even the slightest movement of Nesbitt's head. "You made a big mistake thinking it was."

At 3:15, the negotiated end of the school day, Lord and Nesbitt left the building together. The air was cool. There was the suggestion of rain in the clouds.

"Mind a question?"

"Don't bother. I already know it. You're after the reason I butted in. Gray, I've been in P.D.'s office it must be a hundred times when similar bullshit was going on, and that simple sonofabitch never puts the question to the kid right there in front of his mother or father. You know the goddamn kids go home afterward and feed their parents a completely different line about what happened."

"What if my boy would have denied what he said? What would you have done?"

"He say what he did in front of the others?"

"Loud enough for the entire class to hear."

"Then I would have asked one of the secretaries to summon everyone in your class to the office where I would have put the question to Asa Aftanas once again."

"What about P.D.?"

"What about him?"

"You aren't worried?"

"You mean because I'm not meeting with him as he wanted?"

"It might qualify as insubordination, George. Don't give them grounds."

"I didn't think that kind of thing counted under tenure."

They were beside their cars. Nesbitt pulled up short.

"Will you take a look at this!" The right headlight was smashed. Chrome and broken glass littered the asphalt. "Like I care. I'm getting rid of this relic of a roadrunner next week. Trading it in on something new. And if either ignoramus attempts to fuck *it* up, then I will be pissed. What did they do to yours?"

Lord walked all around his car while Nesbitt stood next to the open door of his vehicle waiting on the report.

"Looks the same as it did when I drove in this morning. Nothing touched."

"In other words, you scared them more than I. I must be losing it. Look, I'll stop and see P.D. tomorrow. Let him get off on me awhile just in case you're correct about this insubordination stuff."

"Good idea."

They waved to each other, got into their cars, and seconds later drove out of the parking lot.

The next morning Principal Waring informed the faculty that he had suspended senior Asa Aftanas for a day and assigned him a week of detention.

Beverly Stiles wasn't impressed.

Chapter 7

Two weeks later, the first week of November, Lord discovered a note in his faculty mailbox from Careytown Schools Superintendent Harold Orr. "See me soon," it read. Freed up from class because of school pictures being snapped on stage in the auditorium, he strode down to the Superintendent's Office at once.

An ex-basketballer at a state college before it began to boast itself a university, Harold Orr stood very tall, his posture exquisitely erect, his movements correspondingly clean and precise. His eyes and lips were drawn tight like the closure line on a baggie, yet his teeth, when displaying, revealed the brilliant white of a successful crooner's. His voice was controlled and deep, producing the tone of a hollow drum. He was a stark contrast to the much shorter Principal Waring who reminded the faculty of the Pillsbury Doughboy and into whose bellybutton Rudy Wallace vowed he would someday poke his finger to test if the man would giggle.

Like many of his colleagues of the day, Harold Orr did not super-intend to do anything. Rather, he managed. And while he endeavored to control the school and even the community, it was his career that he managed most. He was so deft at the activity that he deluded town residents into believing that he was, in fact, turning education in the district on its ear. He forever was completing small surveys, several varieties of statistical analyses, and last year, with Montgomery's talented help, he had produced a passel of beautiful charts and graphs, all labeled with new acronyms. They were showed off at school board and other meetings, and in the local press, and generous amounts of his explicative and complimentary verbiage accompanied them. Watching and listening long enough, a taxpayer couldn't help but think the entire student body must certainly be destined for Harvard and Princeton, or Penn State, at worst. Eventually, his goal became clear. Pointing to his surrounding brethren north, south, east, and west, he informed the local citizens that he would have to stay on an economic par with the other superintendents, or be forced to leave. It worked every time but for the occasional snag. And he would deliver then some statement or perform some act that had the faculty in its belittling focus. The school board and taxpaying residents were reassured. He was on their side and on the sides of the children. He would keep those greedy, arrogant, lazy teachers in line. We need him. We shouldn't go losing him because of a few dollars. At the same time, there was a minority of others who believed his stay at rural Careytown, with its elementary building and a combined junior-senior high school, was only a résumé builder. Orr was in his third year. These people gave him one more.

"Thank you for responding so quickly, Mr. Lord. Take a seat."

Lord dropped into a cushioned chair next to an oak bookshelf filled with educational volumes of which he performed a rapid scan. Not a novel in sight but one—*Lord of the Flies*. How appropriate, he thought.

Orr shut the door to his office before stepping back behind his desk where he continued to stand.

"Months sometimes pass before I hear what a certain teacher is doing. Then, suddenly, I hear something different about that person every day for a week. That's what I find has been happening with you."

"You must be referring to Asa Aftanas for starters."

"His stepmother Tessie called me at home and delivered me an earful about both you and Mr. Nesbitt. Randy must have filled her in, as he would never telephone. He prides himself on taking care of business himself. Or so I've heard. I'm glad Bill Waring apprised me of the situation. Tessie Aftanas claims you said something obscene to her boy, and she repeated it over the phone. But I must tell you, Mr. Lord, that I have always found you to be never anything less than fully professional, which I cannot say for your colleague Mr. Nesbitt. Bill Waring briefed me on his outburst as well. In any case, while I have no illusions that you said something befitting the occasion to young Asa Aftanas, I told Tessie I was quite sure Asa's, or Randy's version of it—it's likely he added some curry—was out of proportion to the reality of what you said. And I stick by that now."

Lord was unsure what to say, or even if he should respond at all. He hoped whatever expression was forming on his face was a grateful one.

Orr smiled at him, the lips opening to display the beautiful teeth.

"I've also been informed that you've started telling jokes in your classes. Rather 'stupid' jokes, as I've heard them described."

Lord began to explain.

"There's no reason to apologize. Understand, I don't mind an occasional joke being told in the classroom by the teacher. Our students, I believe, need to develop an improved sense of humor. They need to see there's more than their kind of simple, often out-of-the-gutter humor. I suspect what they are calling 'stupid' is really more abstruse, esoteric. More conundrum than joke. However, that's not an invitation to hear one, no offense intended."

Lord kept the amusement he was experiencing under the surface.

Orr moved to the front of his desk.

"I didn't summon you to my office because of your latent desire to be a Mike Tyson or Jerry Seinfeld. As you know, the second Thursday of the month is the school board meeting, and I want you to attend next week's. I asked your department chair, June Ferris, to be there as well. Millard Touchstone is heading up a group that's having trouble with some of the things we're assigning our students to read."

"Like what?"

"Well, he didn't care to elaborate. He asked to be placed on next week's agenda, which I've agreed to. He said he would elaborate then and there. Still, your name was mentioned."

"Count on it then. I'll be there."

"Offhand, can you think of any examples of books and stories you are doing, have done, or will be doing in your classes that he might object to?"

"Dr. Orr, I can imagine the Reverend Millard Touchstone objecting to just about anything."

He wondered then if the Superintendent had heard the same things Nesbitt had heard and informed him of out at the camp just before the start of school. The bullshit involving little Clipper Ostrander.

"I really don't understand what this is all about," Orr said convincingly, "but it may be about me as much as you."

"How's that, if you don't mind my asking?"

"It's not a problem. Touchstone had been after my wife and me to join his church until I could no longer put up with his badgering. He didn't much appreciate it when I told him to his face that I wanted to hear no more about it. That my family was quite satisfied with the church we've been attending. That we weren't interested in helping him build his own little empire in the county, which I do fervently believe is what he is doing. So far, he's managed to attract our chief of police, supervisors Witter and Sproull, Bob Earle down at the bank, and I recently was informed that Judge Zonarich has joined the congregation, too. Touchstone's already enlarged his church, built a recreation hall, and I'm certain he has plans to erect a school."

"Perhaps he thought you would have an interest in running it."

"Hmmm. I see why your students might have difficulty with your humor, Mr. Lord. No, I think whatever is being generated by Reverend Touchstone relates to the fact that no one from the administration, faculty, and staff has taken up membership in his church. He has no connection here, and that probably isn't sitting well."

"Careful," Lord said. "Next year's Hell House might include a room for the noncompliant school administrator."

Orr appreciated the humor. "He would be better advised to construct a room for himself, Mr. Lord."

***

That afternoon, Lord stayed after the final buzzer to grade a set of compositions. Normally, he had read enough by the end of the day, his eyes and mind fatigued. But tomorrow was TGIF, a day every teacher could get through, regardless of how bad it might turn out, and he refused to haul correction work home for the weekend.

After shutting the door to the classroom, he occupied a seat in a student's desk at the rear, out of view from the window on the door. At 4:30, the task finished, he closed his briefcase, locked up and left. There were still people loitering in the halls, students in sweats and some adults from town whose business there was often questionable. He ambled down the corridor and saw that Janey Renn was standing outside her classroom door with her coat on.

"I haven't seen you remain this late," she remarked when he caught up.

"I don't make it a habit, that's for sure."

They accompanied each other through the corridor toward the school entrance, the first time each was in the other's presence without another colleague close at hand.

"So how's it going?" he asked after a while.

"How do you think it's going, Gray?" she asked back, the intonation serious but playful.

He didn't confess that he had worried about her. First-year teachers with tiny frames, men and women equally, often were earmarked for trouble from the outset.

"You know, I've passed by your room and heard you raise your voice on occasion," he said.

"And you don't approve."

"Not at all. I believe there's value to be gained from a good, infrequent tongue-lashing. Being nice and understanding doesn't always cut it with some of these kids."

"So you're not afraid of humiliating them?"

"Excuse me, but I think I know the difference between humiliation and humility." He could see that she was having fun with him, and he liked it.

At the entrance he opened the door for her. There was a cool drizzle in the air that immediately refreshed their faces, moistened the lines where chalk and other dust had settled. The sky was already darkening.

"So where to now?" he asked as they stepped onto the parking lot. "Home?"

"Well, I suppose. I haven't heard you make a better offer."

The reply took him by surprise, as his question had really been meaningless, and he stood silent for a moment, biting his lip, a really old habit resurfacing. The look on her own face seemed to say, "Why the hell are you taking so long, Buster?"

"In that case, care to join me for a drink? I was thinking of running over the hill to Prosserville."

"How imaginative," she said, tossing her head. "I'd love to."

He followed her to her home, a rented apartment out behind the bottle factory, where she parked her automobile, hurried inside to check the feed and water bowls of her cat before returning to get into his.

They drove over the hill, actually a small series of shouldering mountains, passing an occasional camouflaged bowhunter leaving the woods, to Prosserville and the Revolution's Inn. It was a large white colonial building on the distant end of the town's main street. There were thick columns at the front, a stone porch, and a central door made of stout oak, framing numerous pieces of beveled glass. Thick shrubbery encircled much of the first floor. Most people patronized the place for its dinners and desserts, but it had a small interesting bar, dark around the edges, and it was never crowded. The bartender was a white-haired, egg-headed man, always vested, who regarded his job as a profession. He once told Lord he had been mixing drinks for thirty-eight years and that he no longer could list off the names of the countless towns and places where he had plied his trade.

Lord pointed to a table in a corner. "Go ahead and sit. I'll be right back with the drinks."

"I see why you favor this place," she commented when he returned. "It's on the main drag, but it certainly has that out-of-the-way flavor to it."

"It's always struck me as a place where famous writers would meet. If only there were some around."

"I can see that," she said, again surveying the room.

"So your classes are coming along okay for the most part and you can stomach Careytown."

"I think so. I'm not sure about Mr. Waring. He observed me recently, and his write-up was less than encouraging."

"Nothing to worry about, Janey. P.D. does that with everyone who's new. He wants them to believe that they're being molded into great teachers and that he's the architect or potter."

"His observation didn't include much in the way of suggestions."

"If you catch him when he's being principal, he can be worth listening to. Too often he's running scared of the parents."

She took a long sip of her drink. He liked how her dimples became accentuated and her already slender nose sharpened. He was quickly realizing there was a lot about art teacher Janey Renn that he liked.

"Gray? A question."

"Anything."

"Don't be too sure. The bartender. Why does he keep looking at you? He seems to be staring straight at you. Now why is he doing that?"

"I'd rather not say. The owner recently hired a new fellow and I was hoping he'd be here instead of the one you see."

"Tell me why he's staring? I have the feeling there's a story here."

"Oh, there's a story all right. Your presence is upsetting him. You see, he's always hoped I was gay. Like the fogey would have a shot."

"No fooling," she said, stiffening her posture while stifling a light guffaw. "What makes him think you might be so, dare I ask?"

"Probably because I'm in my late twenties and single. And come to think of it, I've never brought a date in here. You're the first."

Her eyebrows went up. "So this is a date?"

"Maybe we'll have a typical one some other time."

She didn't respond at once, as it wasn't clear whether she was suddenly being taken for granted. But he looked away. Almost sheepishly, she thought. "Okay, Gray.... I can't believe it. He can't take his eyes off you."

"You want to hear more? You probably do. He reads behind the bar when he isn't mixing drinks. He has a paper open most of the time. You can't see it unless you step behind the bar."

"What paper?"

"Well, that's just it. The first time he learned that I was an English teacher and unmarried, he asked if I ever read *Screw* magazine."

"That's the paper...? I never heard of it."

"It's the size of a tabloid and it has a lead story, complete with pictures. You sure you want to hear this?"

"Are there reasons I shouldn't?"

"I can think of a few."

She deliberately squinched her nose to her eyes. "Let's throw caution to the wind. What was the lead story about?"

"'My First Blow Job.' That was the title of the feature piece."

"Omigod!" She laughed, nearly spitting on herself. "How was it?"

"How the hell was what?"

She couldn't stop herself from laughing. She looked away for a few seconds. Then she surprised him further by dipping a finger in her drink and flicking the liquid in his face.

"The article. I meant the article."

"Oh, you meant the article." He rallied quickly. "Poorly written I thought. And no balancing view besides."

Her laughter was infectious. He started laughing too.

Neither of them had much to say afterward, which was no surprise to Lord. There was no sign on the outside that his head was shaking, but inside was another story as he parodied to himself what had just occurred: *Since this is our first date, Miss Renn, I suggest that we could get to know each other best if we talked about meaningful things. How do you feel about blowjobs?"* Several minutes passed. Occasionally, she allowed a snicker to escape and would secretly point a finger in the direction of the bar every time the bartender glanced their way. Lord half-expected her to stick the finger in

81

her mouth as Blake did in his when he told Wallace to "Go wah-wah the Big One."

"Are you hungry?" he asked her. "We could take our drinks and shuffle into the dining room. My treat."

She struggled to contain herself, seeing that he was serious with the offer, not just trying to get away from the bartender. "Thanks, but no. I don't want to stay long. I also left some items out to thaw. Maybe on that future date. For now, let's just have this drink, and maybe another."

When they drained their glasses, he rose to walk to the bar to order the second round of drinks. Several steps away from their table, he hesitated and glanced back. Yes, she was grinning again. But she still wasn't imitating Blake, thank god.

As he received and paid for the drinks, his friend Dan Diston and two men entered the barroom.

"Gray, my man."

"Hey, Dan."

"What are you doing over this way?"

"Just wanted to flee town for a quiet drink. I brought Janey Renn along. Care to join us?"

"I'll be right over," answered Diston. "I've never met her and I'd like to. Let me get something first."

"I'll wait."

Diston ordered a beer, what the vested bartender called a designer beer, excused himself from his friends, and followed Lord back to the table where he was introduced.

"Did you invite yourself, Dan, or did Gray do it?" Janey asked.

"Look, I don't mean to intrude."

"You aren't intruding," said Lord. "She's just having some fun at my expense." He saw her tongue half-ballooning out one of her cheeks. He secretly wagged a finger at her from tabletop level.

"So what's happening here?" Diston asked curiously, observing that some friendly jousting was being exchanged between the pair.

"It's nothing," Lord said.

"Okay, if you say so." Diston couldn't refrain from smiling. He gave a once-over of Renn while she was regarding Lord and raised his eyebrows at his friend in approval.

"Sit down," Lord said.

"I don't think I should, Gray. Those fellas I came in with begged me to join them for a couple of drinks.... By the way, remember that incident out at Nesbitt's camp near the end of the summer?"

"The beer thieves and the girl abandoned on the road? I remember. She's from Prosserville. I seem to recall you informing us of that."

"She is. She'd been married not too long before we saw her there."

"What about her?"

"Well, not about her so much. But do you remember, too, that besides the kids that were running with the beer, there was a fellow and a girl inside the car? The fellow it turns out is Lyle Kaster."

"Never heard of him."

"Didn't expect you would. But it was a young stepbrother of his with him who attends Careytown. Name's Aftanas."

"Asa Aftanas."

"That's it! You must have him."

"Unfortunately, I do. A senior. Nothing but trouble."

"I'm told that's what the family's all about. They're trash you bury, forget the recycle. They've been all around the region and Harley Clouser said it would be a helluva contest to find anyone who has a good word for even one of them."

Lord recognized the name of the girl's father. "You told him?"

"How I see it, I did her a favor. Maybe it'll keep her clear of that swamp George mentioned. And the old man, he's okay. It won't bother him to keep his son-in-law in the dark. Look, I'll leave you two alone now to enjoy your drinks and each other. Janey, it was nice to meet you."

"And you, too," said Janey.

A short time later, after his friend had excused himself and they had finished their drinks, Lord and Janey drove back to Careytown under a rising full moon. As the gold Toyota crested the final hill, Lord gazed across a valley at several deer lingering at the edge of a field and underwent a familiar, intoxicatingly real sensation. Easing the vehicle gradually off the top of the hill, he first observed the tiny town snuggled securely against the upper Allegheny River, whose narrow waters quivered in a plaited pattern of soft, consoling light. From the twin stacks of the glass factory oozed smoke lighter than cotton, while a pegboard of lamps identified the clusters of homes, streetlights, small businesses, and plant departments operating through the night. Then he viewed the roads leading out of the town. One wound upward, only to drop again shortly. The other two gazelled through long, fingerlike valleys.

Following his survey came the transformation. He accelerated smoothly, steadily, with his hands gripping tightly on the wheel, with his hands sweating, and the car flashed to a sleek phantom jet whose mission was to destroy a quiet night and resting town—confident, serene, complacent—with his eagle hurtling low for hitandbegone out a fingerlike valley. All there it was and yet all futile because he tried to pull up when he realized he was too low and his hands and body pulled hard on the plastic wheel to bring it up, to bring it up, but the car hurtled down and the lack of response caused him to come back, to ease off the accelerator and glide into town, to home, his apartment.

"...What? Is there something wrong?"

She had her back pressed against the car door, her head in a state of alertness. She was staring wide-eyed at him.

"What is it?" he said.

"Gray, you have to take me home." She was unsure of what had just taken place. "Whatever were you doing just now?"

"I wasn't doing anything."

He'd played the flyboy before, but never when someone was with him. What the hell had he been thinking?

"You were. You looked like you were on a bombing mission."

"You mean like Tom Cruise and *Top Gun*?"

"Exactly." Pretending more gravity than she really felt, she peered well over her shoulder toward the rear of the car, as though she were inspecting and attempting to identify the type of vehicle in which she was riding. "Tell me, does this automobile convert to an airplane or something?"

This question he naturally left unanswered. But after a long moment of silence, he ventured, "So you think I look like Tom Cruise, do you?"

The traffic light at Main and Water was malfunctioning when he stopped at the crosswalk minutes after dropping her off. Above, his apartment was mostly dark, illuminated faintly by the blue neon light just under the cupola and the fluorescent bulb above the aquarium. The pharmacy on the first floor remained open and it was brightly lit, although there didn't appear to be more than a customer or two inside. Next door was a coffee shop, and six people crossing the street were heading toward it. He became fed up waiting for the light to change from red to green and turned onto Water.

He parked his car in the reserved spot behind the pharmacy and walked uphill from the rear of the building around to the front. A boy and a girl were now hanging out on the corner, chatting.

"Hi, Mr. Lord."

"Good evening, Tammy. Good evening, Bogardus."

He passed them and entered his apartment's stairwell that was unlit, retrieving his mail and newspaper at the bottom. A woman from one of the other apartments was on her way down as he started up. They exchanged hi's.

He inserted his key into the lock, turned it less than ninety degrees, when to his surprise the door opened. He hadn't to engage the tumblers on the primary lock.

"Goddammit," he swore softly to himself.

He snapped on the lights in all the rooms and inspected each. Everything appeared to be okay. He pried off the plastic lid from a coffee can atop the mantel of the fireplace. The three twenties he had stashed inside the can after cashing his most recent paycheck were still there.

"Goddammit, I told her...." Agitated, he trailed off again and went immediately to the phone. He dialed his landlady's number.

Just the machine. He left a message.

He moved through the apartment once more, this time slowly, inspecting carefully. Still, everything appeared just as he had left it that morning. Nothing seemed disturbed. Not even the guns.

Chapter 8

"All right, there's about five minutes remaining in this period. You can use it to start the weekend's reading assignment."

"Hey, Mr. Lord?"

"What is it, Tucker? Did you lose your book again?"

"Aw no, Mr. Lord. I got it right here. See?"

"Which reminds me. If you're reading the books and you dog-ear the pages and make a few marks inside, that's one thing. But if you're not reading them and have no intention to, then I don't want you doodling in them. Understand me?"

"Sure, Mr. Lord."

"Okay then, what is it you want?"

"Remember that joke you told us about the brick?"

"What about it?"

"I told it to my parents and they thought it was stupid."

"So?"

"Yeah, they said it was really stupid. But my grandparents from Florida showed up just yesterday to stay with us for a while and I told it to them. Guess what they said about it?"

"They liked it. Thought it was the funniest joke they'd heard in all their years."

"You got to be kidding, Mr. Lord. No, they said it was stupid, too."

"So what is it you want, Tucker? You could be reading."

"Well, my grandparents said something else about it too."

"I can hardly wait."

"No, this is good. They said the joke was stupid and all, but they also said at least it was a clean joke you was telling, and that it didn't make fun of no one."

"So they really thought Nick was a bozo, huh? All right, enough. There's still some time. Everybody just open your book and get to reading Monday's assignment."

"What now, Tucker?"

"Tell us another joke."

"Open your book."

87

"Nobody wants to read now, Mr. Lord. It's Friday. Come on, tell us another one of your jokes. Maybe we'll understand this one and laugh."

"I've warned you, you wouldn't get my kind of humor, and yet you want me to present you with a second chance to call my jokes stupid."

"I'll bet we get this one and howl. Look around, there ain't no one reading. We're all listening to you. We love listening to you, Mr. Lord."

"Right. The same as you love learning to speak proper English."

Lord checked the clock. They were set up again, and if he timed it correctly, he could end the joke at the buzzer and send them off with their heads spinning.

"Very well, Tucker. I'll give you and the rest of this class one more opportunity to comprehend the kind of humor that I'm accustomed to. But if you don't get this joke, don't bother to ask again. I promise you I won't take the time."

"Hey, that's cool."

"Then listen carefully, all of you. There's a bus, a commercial bus, not one of those uncivilized yellow vehicles which most of you ride and cause mayhem on and which none of your parents seems to realize could be the death of you all, thanks to your underriding concern for the bus driver's sanity."

"You're editorializing, Mr. Lord."

"I am, Tucker. And next time, I'll remember to feel ashamed when I accuse you of having learned nothing in my class. This bus makes a stop whereupon a man steps aboard, a rather fat man. The bus is crowded, not a seat for the obese man to sit in but one, and he naturally takes it. It's an aisle seat, of course, and next to him is a little old woman who's clutching to her heart a dog, a rather tiny dog. What Fido fanciers call a 'Pomeranian.' You all know what kind of a dog that is, a Pomeranian? They're fairly small."

"And they yap a lot!"

"That's right, Mr. Jesse Bogardus, they yap a lot. And what do you think this Pomeranian was doing?"

The class in unison: "Yapping a lot!"

"Correct. Maybe you all will get this joke after all. Maybe I've been misjudging you people."

"Hurry up, Mr. Lord. The buzzer's gonna sound."

"There's still a minute. Anyway, the bus is filled to capacity, and also it's summertime, so all the windows are down so that fresh air can come in. Well, this fat man, what does he do but ignore the posted signs about No Smoking. He pulls out a big cigar, almost as fat as he is, and shoves that Havana stogie into his mouth—"

"You can't buy Cuban cigars in this country, Mr. Lord."

"Thank you, Tucker. Shoves that imitation Havana stogie into his mouth whereupon he lights it and starts puffing on it like there's no tomorrow. Pretty soon, the little old woman can't stand it anymore and she politely asks him to toss the cigar out the window. He answers by saying, 'Lady, you may not approve of my cigar, but I can't take much more of this yapping mutt of yours. I'll tell you what. I'll throw my cigar out the window if you do the same to that mutt.' Well, she's almost mortally offended, is this little old lady, but she recovers nicely. She grabs the cigar from between the fat man's lips and chucks it out the open window onto the sidewalk. The fat man can't believe his eyes. He lurches at the woman, wrestles the Pomeranian from her clutches, and tosses it out the window. The poor little woman was then beside herself, screaming 'Stop the bus! Stop the bus! Please stop the bus.' She pushed her way in front of the fat man, who didn't make it easy for her, and raced up the aisle to the driver. By now, you see, the bus was already two, three blocks from where the fat man had tossed the dog. But a scheduled stop was just a hundred feet away and the driver pulled to the curb. Lo and behold, when he opened the door, there was the dog waiting to board the bus. And can you guess what that little critter was grasping in its mouth?"

The class, again in unison, and louder: "A CIGAR!"

"No, I'm sorry, that's incorrect. In the little dog's mouth was a brick."

Dead silence. Then long grating buzzer. Perfect.

"You're all dismissed," he said. "See you on Monday. And have a good weekend, boys and girls."

Once they were gone, many having exited the room like zombies and either mumbling to themselves or throwing him a sidelong stare, he gathered some papers, locked the door to the room as it would not be used the next hour, and maneuvered down the noisy corridor filled with students to the faculty room that was empty. He went directly to the coffee pot and poured himself its last cup. Bev Stiles entered seconds later with Wallace and Blake close behind. Wallace prepared a pipe, but did not light it.

"You look ridiculous," Stiles said to him.

"You're right," said Wallace. "So why don't you all just ignore the rules and let me smoke."

"Forget that.... Gray, before one of us gets away, I was just at the office and your landlady called. She was told you had a class and apparently it was nothing that couldn't wait. There's a message in your box. Are you thinking of moving?"

He shook his head. "I want to check on something. When I got home last evening, the door wasn't double-locked."

"Someone broke in?" said Blake.

"I don't think so. Nothing seems to be missing or out of place."

"Then what are you worried about? You must have forgotten to double-lock when you left in the morning."

"I don't forget that. And she hasn't either since I emphasized to her that I wanted it done whenever she's leaving the place."

"Why do you let her go in whenever she pleases anyway?" asked Stiles. "She doesn't have that right as a landlord."

"I know that, Bev. It's just that she's a nice old lady. I told her that I'd prefer she wouldn't do that, but it didn't take, and I haven't pushed it."

Blake asked, "When she's there, what does she do? I've been to your place. You're not a slob."

"Once in a while she removes the bagged-up garbage and recyclables. But mostly she sprays a fragrance all over the place."

"Gee, Gray," said Stiles, sniffing, "I never realized you stink."

He grinned back, thought about flipping her the bird just for the fun of it, but instead asked: "How long ago she call?"

"Ten minutes, if that."

"Nobody pilfer my coffee. I'll be right back."

He left the faculty room for the main office where there was a phone teachers could use. A log book for recording long-distance calls had been placed next to it. He dialed his landlady's number. She picked up without his waiting much.

"Hello, Mrs. Hampton? This is Gray. Thanks for calling back."

"Is there something wrong, Gray?"

"Were you in my apartment at any time yesterday, Mrs. Hampton?"

"Yes, I went over and sprayed."

"I didn't smell anything."

"I went early. Maybe I should spray twice a day."

"No, that's quite all right. Did you remember to double-lock the door?"

"I always double-lock the door to your apartment. That's what you told me you wanted. 'Always use the key and double-lock,' you said."

"You're sure?"

"Is something wrong, Gray?"

"No, no. Everything's okay. Thanks, Mrs. Hampton."

He hung up and returned to the faculty room.

"What did she say?" Blake asked.

"She said she double-locked."

"So there you have it."

"But it wasn't when I got home. That's the point."

"Seems to me you're making a mountain out of a molehill, to quote my father," said Wallace. "You said the place was the same as you left it. Maybe she failed to completely punch the button to double-lock and when she shut the door behind her, the button popped out. It doesn't seem like much of a mystery to me."

Lord stared for a moment at Wallace whose hair was regaining its waves and curls. "You got it wrong. It's the button that was locked. She would have had to forget to insert her key to secure the second, more important lock. She's saying she didn't."

"Why is it bothering you so much, Gray?" asked Stiles who was dismantling the coffee pot for cleaning.

"I don't know, Bev. It just does."

Wallace hesitated several moments to see if the matter had run its course. It apparently had.

"All right, changing the subject," he said. "What time do we meet in the morning?"

"Seven's what I understand," Lord said.

"Schenley's?"

"Yep."

"What about George? He joining us this time?"

"As of yesterday he was."

"Will he be able to keep up?"

"He can find his way around okay. We won't lose him."

91

SPINE

Beverly Stiles stood looking off through a window, listening and rolling her eyes. She had heard this kind of conversation in previous years and wondered which of them would be the first this year to use the phrase.

"Bev, dear" Wallace said. "Why don't you tramp along with us tomorrow morning? I got a gun I could lend you. You might just be the lucky one to nail the ol' wily bird."

"Congratulations, Rudy," she said, turning away from the window. "You're this year's winner."

Chapter 9

When they hunted turkey, they walked. And they walked rapidly, a brisk stride in every one of them, including Nesbitt for a time. Up a mountain, down one, across a stream, across a flat, their postures straight with shotguns out front. No stalking stealthily, no waiting patiently, no calling with a box. Just walking in a spread-out line, fast and furious. If they hunted all of a Saturday, they later bragged they'd covered ten miles at least—*at least!*—and the next morning usually confirmed their estimate.

The turkey, or "turkles" as Rudy Wallace often referred to the large birds, never expected any human being to be moving so swiftly in the forest, and so they were always victims of surprise. They were so again this Saturday minutes before noon, twenty-four of them, all hens except for three, so the briefing afterward determined. Willis Ruther, flanking far left, spotted the large flock on the ground amidst fairly mature trees, each bird pecking away to its stomach's content.

"TURKEY!" he yelled at the top of his lungs, and the rush forward was on. The dark birds, clumsy on the ground but smooth when airborne, scattered in all directions except the one behind them. Some found air rather easily, and Lord and Schenley stopped, planted their boots, lifted their guns, took their cracks. The heavier ones, unable to lift off a short runway, found Wallace and the others racing behind them, firing away. Smarter birds, the wiliest, maneuvered to turn the tables. They ran at each other across the front of the line in the hope that one of the hunters would lead them too much and maybe, just maybe, the lead shot intended for them would end up in the hide of a fellow gunner.

The blasting-away of the shotguns endured for thirty seconds, though it seemed much longer. When it ceased, there wasn't a single turkey crippled or killed, and the crew holding the shotguns was laughing at one another. What the hell, it was fun. Who gave a hoot whether a turkey was nailed anyway? It was a good attitude, for they nailed very few, although turkey that had been taken in seasons past were never wasted, were quickly cooked and consumed.

"Time for lunch," Schenley announced, setting aside his gun. "This spot pass muster?"

"Looks good to me," Wallace said cheerfully. He slipped a pint of brandy from a coat pocket. "Anybody for a swig? Paul? George?"

"No thanks. I don't often drink that stuff."

"How 'bout you, Gray?"

"Thanks. I brought my own, XO Rare."

"Ooh, good stuff. Willis, Jack? What about you, big boy?"

"No thanks," said McAllister who had selected a log to sit on and was wasting no time unwrapping a sandwich. The others followed his example. Nesbitt popped a tab on a beer.

"How you doing, George?" Wallace asked. "Think you can keep up with us in the afternoon?"

"Where you planning to hunt?"

"That's to be decided. Does it matter?"

"I'm not running up and down any more mountains today. If you plan on staying on the flats, fine. If not, I'll head out. Maybe see you all for a drink afterward."

"Perfect," Wallace said. "'Cause I'm anxious to go down into Slumber Hollow and climb the other side if everyone is up for it. I've never been over that way."

In his always soft, uninflected voice Schenley said, "By the way, George, I've been meaning to ask you. How's that new machine of yours running?"

"It's alright, Jack. No complaints, except for the price."

"It's becoming tougher to get a deal of any kind," McAllister said. "More automotive dealers are doing this thing where it's the same price for everyone. You know the price isn't in your favor."

"Not that. The deal was good enough. I managed to get eleven hundred out of them for that gas-guzzler I traded in. But any new car you buy today.... Christ! You likely need to take out a mortgage. It's a fucking crime is what it is."

McAllister said, "What the hell, George! A few months back you told me you were seriously considering buying yourself a four-by-four. Something more in tune with the terrain around here. What made you change your mind and buy a big old luxury car again?"

Nesbitt shrugged at the question. "I don't know. Guess I'm just hopeless, Walt."

"It's a wise move," said Blake, who they all realized was a car buff. "The big luxury vehicles are holding their value longer. Used to be, that was true of the four-by-fours. But now everybody and their brother owns one, and every car manufacturer builds one."

For a half-hour, they relaxed in the woodland and ate their sandwiches and chips, munched their apples and pears, and sipped their drinks. Wallace lit a brief pipe. The sun broke through for a time and warmed them. The conversation got around to the upcoming school board meeting.

"What's it about?" McAllister wanted to know.

"Hell, I would think you know the answer to that question," Wallace said.

"And why would you think that, Rudy?" McAllister countered with comic suspicion.

"Well, you don't live that far from the Touchstone Kingdom. And there is such a thing as 'religion runoff.' In fact, I've occasionally listened to you spit out the word 'Hallelujah'."

"You're something else," McAllister said, shaking his head.

"Ask Gray," Nesbitt said. "He's the one Harold called in."

"Hell, I got most of your kids," Wallace said. "And I see their English texts when they come in. What's Touchstone's problem?"

"You got me," Lord said.

"What do you have this year, Gray?"

"Two senior classes, one seventh, and two freshman groups, Jack. The 9-3s and 9-4s. But I don't see where we've done anything that would be offensive to even a nun."

"So what are you doing?" Nesbitt asked.

"With the seniors, American Lit, watered down for the one. They're still reading Franklin at the moment. I'm already a month behind. The ninth-graders have a text with short, easily readable stories. There's nothing to them, believe me."

"And the seventh-graders?"

"We're jumping around the anthology. And again, there's nothing anywhere in that book that I can think would piss off anyone."

"Well, something is chewing at Touchstone's ass," Schenley said. "You can be sure of that."

"Speaking of ass," Wallace said, "what's the word on you and Renn, Gray? I ran into Dan. He said he saw the two of you out for a drink and you were having a little fun with one another."

"What do you mean, 'Speaking of ass'?"

Wallace let out an abrupt laugh and began to dance in front of Lord.

"I was testing you, buddy, and you failed! You've got the hots for her, don't you? You got the motherfucking hots for Renn!" He pointed a finger at his colleague's crotch, then transferred the mockery to his own. He pretended his cock had swollen to gargantuan size and that it was completely controlling his movement. He put one hand into the air about three feet above the other and tried to wrestle the thing into obedience, but now it was growing in diameter. He stumbled all over the clearing, bolting from one man to the next, his hands being shaken violently by the monstrous erection, yet they held on trying to tame the beast.

"No wonder your wife divorced you," Schenley said, laughing.

"Maybe that's what he promised her, Jack," McAllister said, "and when he didn't produce the goods, she up and split."

Nesbitt and Lord glanced at each other, and they too were laughing at their colleague.

Wallace ignored the remarks from his audience. Instead, he began speaking to the invisible giant phallus.

"Whoa, boy. Easy. Come on, I'm not going to hurt you. Whoa now."

"It's not listening," said Schenley.

The right hand then delicately traveled up and down the side of the thing as a man would play a trumpet, pushing valves.

"Rudy," Nesbitt called. "Knock it off. We've got company."

Wallace, straight-faced, dared to remove the left hand from the other side of the thing and he placed it near the top where a single finger began to tickle the glans.

Nesbitt caught Lord's attention and nodded in the direction of the visitors who were some thirty paces from entering their chosen lunch area.

"Oh shit," said Lord.

He rose from the log he was sitting on and went quickly to their nutty colleague in an effort to bring the masquerade to a speedy end. But Wallace was doing that himself. The tickling finger had accomplished its goal, and once again the invisible penis was catapulting its owner all about, even worse than before, and spewing invisible come over everyone, though Schenley was seeming to protect an unwrapped candy bar from getting splashed. Wallace's last act endured longer than needed. Finally, the shaking stopped, his hands were lowered to show the beast was now flaccid, and he grinned thankfully toward the sky.

Still laughing and shaking his head, Schenley said, "I always knew you were an asshole, Rudy. I just didn't know how big o' one."

Wallace was about to say something regarding the candy bar, but Lord showed him the visitors.

"Oops," said Wallace.

"Hello, Tucker!" Lord called out, louder than would have been normal.

"Hey, what's happening, Mr. Lord, Mr. McAllister? What were you doing, Mr. Wallace? Some new dance?"

"Think fast," said Schenley.

"Turkey trot," Wallace said, looking away.

"We haven't seen a bird all morning," Tucker said.

"Who you got with you?" Lord asked. He didn't think it was the father. "That your dad?"

"This my cousin. We hunted around here last year and he knocked a hen out of the air."

"She didn't weigh in as no trophy," the cousin added, "but she was mighty good eatin'."

"And I think we best get ourselves in gear if we intend to get anything," Wallace said, anxious to get away. "Let's go. Let's get our butts in gear."

The men, their faces still flushed from the recent bout of inane comedy displayed by their friend, crushed the bits of paper garbage they had made and stuffed the matter into their coat pockets. Under Tucker's eye, Nesbitt retrieved two empty beer cans and replaced them in his belt pack.

"All set?"

"Lead on, Rudy," said McAllister.

"I'll see you all at Tilly's later this evening," Nesbitt said.

"Don't forget to look for the birds on your way out," Lord advised. "Some may have taken a wide swing and doubled back."

Nesbitt gave an all-inclusive wave of farewell and departed from the group.

"Hey, Mr. Lord. I got a joke for you."

"We're out of here, Tucker," said Wallace.

"This won't take long, promise. There's this kid, Mr. Lord—"

"What's his name?"

"Huh?"

"He must have a name, this kid in your joke."

"I can't tell you his name."

"Then this isn't a joke, is it?" said Wallace.

"Yeah, it's a joke. Mr. Lord'll laugh. This kid, he wants to bring something into school that isn't allowed."

"Like what?" Wallace said.

"It's not one thing. It's a bunch of things," Tucker said. "See, he doesn't know which one himself."

"This kid whose name you can't give us."

"You won't understand this joke, Mr. Wallace."

"I don't think your cousin is much impressed either."

The cousin was digging into his nose.

Tucker altered his body's direction just slightly, but it was clear to Wallace that he was now to be ignored.

"This kid has all these things he could take to school which are against the rules, Mr. Lord, but he can't make up his mind which one he should choose. So what do you think he does?"

"I don't know, Tucker. Tell me, and be quick about it."

"He asks a friend. Yeah, a friend comes by as he's looking at all this stuff, and he asks the friend what he should do. Well, the friend—I can't tell you his name either—he looks over everything and after a while he suggests—"

Lord cut him off. The idea struck him that this was to be a truly stupid story. That Tucker was trying maybe to see how long he would listen before catching on that his time was being wasted.

"You need to hone your storytelling skills, Tucker. The joke's already boring the daylights out of me. Work on it and give it to me some other time. Besides, we're all anxious to get started again. Good luck to you and your cousin. Keep your eyes open, too, because there's a lot of turkey around."

Wallace turned himself to Lord's ear. Clandestinely, he said, "Now can we get the fuck out of here, Grayson dear?"

Chapter 10

It hadn't slipped his mind that he wanted to share a bed with her, but he wasn't dwelling on the thought. Instead, since their evening at the Revolution's Inn in neighboring Prosserville, Lord discovered that he was thinking of art teacher Janey Renn in positive, self-reflecting ways. Each morning and throughout the parade of hours he realized that he was feeling upbeat, that he wasn't spilling out the usual gloom and doom to himself about his job and his life. And the reason, he was certain, was this beautiful energetic female with the pixie haircut who was more upbeat than anyone he had previously met. He didn't think there was any problem or stroke of misfortune that could get her down. And if there was, it certainly would not defeat her or even keep her in the pits for very long. For the first time in his life he believed that he had met a woman with the much touted, proverbial moxy. He re-examined this thought for several seconds, as Bev Stiles popped into his mind. True, Bev had moxy too, he admitted, but hers was of the withdrawal type. Bev Stiles, if she were talking face-to-face with anyone of importance, couldn't be ruled out from pivoting an about-face and walking away without a word of explanation. But Janey, he believed, would never walk away. She could interact with anyone.

He had been wrong to worry that her classes might take advantage of her diminutive stature. She was no Miss Compton, a thirty-year veteran grateful to student Jesse Bogardus for replacing the long familiar, debasing "ol' lady Compton" with the jazzy "Dot Com." On those occasions while passing by her room and overhearing the raising of her voice, he had concluded wrongly that Janey was losing control. The truth was, she exhibited greater command of her classes than he did of his. He permitted his own classes to loosen up far more often than did most other teachers because it was the only way he knew how to teach. Even as a child, learning had been fun and he wanted it to be the same for his students. The problem arose from those who wanted fun only and weren't inclined to learn much of anything. These teens were impossible to bring back into a serious fold with a simple snap of the fingers or a mild reprimand. No, students like that you had to bust your lungs and shout at and pretend that you were about to lose it. Only then did they tighten themselves and return some attention to you and what you were attempting to teach.

It was a few days before the weekend, but he decided not to wait. Classes were changing. He could see her posting outside her door with arms crossed. She was issuing short, friendly comments to favorite students passing by. He strode down the corridor to where she stood.

"Got a proposition. What are you doing tonight?"

"Wednesday night? Nothing as far as I know."

"Good. How about having dinner with me? I'm cooking. You can get a firsthand inspection of my cupola. You're not a veggie, are you?"

"No, but I sometimes think I could be.... Wait a minute, Gray." She called to a junior girl who was rifling through a locker. "Mandy, this week are we having the yearbook meeting after school tonight or tomorrow night? I forget which we agreed upon. It's tomorrow, isn't it?"

"It's tonight, Miss Renn."

She turned back to Lord. "Failing memory and I'm young. Not a good sign. Can we eat late? These yearbook meetings last to about 7:30."

"Anytime you say will be fine."

"Then expect me between 8 and 8:30. You know, this invitation should be the other way around."

"How's that?"

"I apologize for not asking you in for a chicken breast the other night. It didn't take me long to throw a meal together. You wouldn't have had to go home hungry."

"I made something for myself when I got back. But thanks just the same. Maybe another day. By the way, I still don't want you to regard this as the official date we spoke of."

"Why not? Eating in restaurants turns old quickly. Inviting me to your place and you do the cooking.... Now that I find appealing!"

She showed up at his apartment door, which he purposely left open because there was heat in the stairwell, a few minutes before nine. A wind outside was knocking about like a testy inebriate and every fifteen seconds its brief eruptions resonated from the street to the second floor.

"I'm sorry I'm later than promised," she apologized as she shook out her hair to restore its set. "But I wanted to give you this, and I had to cut the mat. Are you aware of how nasty it's becoming outside?"

She slid a framed black-and-white photograph from a large brown envelope and handed it to him.

"I thought you might like this."

"Jeezus, Janey, it's beautiful," he said with genuine appreciation. "Did you take it...? Oh, yes, I can see you signed and dated it." He stretched the print to arm's length and held it there for several seconds. "It's really very beautiful. Thank you. As you can see by this room alone, I don't have much of anything decorating my walls. The tiny plaque above the stove is it."

"'Vee get too soon oldt und too late schmart,'" she read.

"A leftover from the previous tenant. Can I get you a drink? A seven and seven? Some wine?"

"I'd love a little wine."

"Make yourself comfortable, okay? The living room is at the other end. Can you take the picture with you?"

"Vee can, yah."

She removed her coat and draped it over a chair next to the door, and knowing that she had made him smile with her Swedish imitation, disappeared into the room with the cupola. She set the framed photograph on the mantel above the fireplace while he remained in the kitchen to pour drinks. The covers of two paperbacks beside the embosser attracted her attention.

"What are your intentions for these romance novels, Gray?" she asked sportively when he came in with the drinks. "Are you planning to emulate the appearance of the men on the covers?"

"Damn! I thought I already did," he said, feigning disappointment. "Actually, I'm reading them because they're a genre I've never read. And because they're quite popular, I thought I ought to learn firsthand something about them, being an English teacher. Have you read any?"

"Two or three, no more. My oldest sister, that's all she reads."

He took a sip of his drink at the same time she took one of hers.

"Is that a horse that you owned?" he then asked, now taking the time to inspect the photograph closely. "Or one you stumbled upon in your travels?"

"That was my father's horse. An Arabian named Dutiful Sun."

"He's absolutely beautiful. Except for his eyes, there's not a speck of color on him."

"He was as white as they get, at least on this side," she said. "The land surrounding him is part of my father's farm. It's beautiful, too. Do you do anything with photography, Gray?"

"I own a Pentax, and I even have a wide-angle lens. But that's about it."

"Want a lesson? It's free."

"Sounds like a bargain I'd be foolish to refuse."

She moved over to the picture and employed a hand in her explanation.

"If you have only one major item to focus on in your picture as is the case with Dutiful Sun, you might consider positioning it as I did. It's called the rule of thirds. You divide the frame up into thirds both vertically and horizontally, and then you place the subject at one of the points where the lines intersect. It's often more pleasing than the center. Of course, it's not recommended for portraits."

"The rule of thirds. Place the subject at an intersection. I'll remember that."

They ate before they finished their drinks, a winter stew that he was fond of making, and he had purchased a pie from a local bakery for dessert. Afterwards, they returned to the room with the cupola.

"This bench alone makes this apartment worth it," she remarked as she sat on the inside shelf, once upon a time used to display a physician's magazines for his patients. She stretched one leg over the other. "Do you sit here on nights when you don't feel like venturing out?"

"I do, Janey. And quite often."

She saw that he was contemplating something.

"What is it?"

"I was thinking about how the students often congregate on the corner below. It's something to listen to them talk when they don't know you're only a few feet above them."

"What do they talk about?"

"Nothing of much substance, it seems to me. They're all bored, and none of them catches on that each is boring the other. It's rare any of them makes a suggestion to actually do something."

"Like snap some photographs?"

"There you go," he said, shooting a finger at her. "They all enjoy seeing pictures of themselves, but it doesn't occur to one of them to borrow their old man's camera and record some of their young lives."

"You should suggest the idea to them, Gray. Tell me what they talk about."

"Usually it's a mixed group, so you don't hear too much about sex as you might if it were just the boys. Or girls, I suppose. Beer. They talk a lot about beer."

"Drugs, too?"

"Not so much drugs, thank god. They talk about the stuff, but not as often as a lot of people might expect."

She stared down at the corner below.

"Anyone stake out a position?" he asked. "Or has the wind thwarted them tonight?"

"There's a few."

He went over and joined her on the former display shelf.

"The girl trying to light up is Tammy Riznick," he said.

"I don't have her, although I've seen her with one of the girls in my 11-1 glass."

"I hate to say it, but she'll probably end up the same as her sister who got pregnant in her senior year. I remember the following summer I was playing tennis on the school courts, George Nesbitt and myself. He doesn't care to do it much anymore. She came running over from the parking lot, singing out, 'Mr. Lord! Mr. Lord! I have a baby! I have a baby!'"

He shook his head. To this day, the boast struck a nerve.

"I had friends like that when I was in school. You must know what the unspoken conclusion is, Gray. What she didn't say? 'See! I can do something, Mr. Lord. I can have sex and make babies! All of you teachers were wrong about me.'"

The statement sounded callous, but it made sense.

"They all appear to be seniors which I don't have any of," she said. "Who's the good-looking boy in the dark jacket? I notice he's the only one of them who seems to enjoy facing into the wind."

"Jesse Bogardus. He's in that class of mine you've heard about. Could be a nice kid if he tried. And next to him working hard to be cool is Aaron Little. He's also in the class. The girl in the white jacket must not be from around here."

"Who's the girl with the stance?"

"Kathy Raye. She's confident all right. She'll probably be this year's valedictorian."

"I'm seeing something else."

"She's all of that, too. Gets it from her parents."

"That's the class with the Aftanas boy, isn't it? How has he been behaving?"

"He's alright as long as I'm facing him. Who knows what he's up to when I turn my back to scratch something on the board?"

"Bev can't stand him. She said there's not a redeeming quality in that boy."

"And she's probably right. He laughed in Howser's face when football was brought up."

For the next half-hour they relaxed on the inside shelf, facing each other, sipping their drinks, and talking. Several times she raised her right hand to massage her left shoulder. Finally, he couldn't help himself.

"That shoulder appears to be troublesome. If you'll turn around, I'll be glad to rub it." He fluttered his fingers in the air. "It always feels better when someone else does it."

She pursed her lips to show that she was about to disappoint him.

He spread his palm as a gesture of honesty. "I promise I won't try anything."

"Gray, this is the second occasion I agreed to be with you on little more than a moment's notice. If you haven't yet realized, I love spending time with you. My not wanting to have you massage my shoulder hasn't anything to do with you."

"You're not about to tell me you're hiding a husband, I hope."

"No, I'm not. I'm telling you that I have a boyfriend."

"Well, bully for me." This he remarked in the tone of a born loser, and he glanced at the street below. All the kids who were there earlier had departed. Two young boys he did not recognize had taken their place, which meant they were younger than seventh graders. Both were smoking cigarettes. One was practicing flicking off the ash at knee level.

"I have a boyfriend and I'm trying to end the relationship, only it hasn't gone well. Do you want to hear this? I hope you do."

He nodded stiffly.

"I met him in college and we graduated the same class. He accepted a teaching offer in a wealthy Pittsburgh suburb. Fox Chapel. You may have heard of it."

"Quite wealthy."

"I came here. He's driven up, must be a half-dozen times already, and I've let him know each time."

It didn't agree with his moxy assessment.

"Why haven't you just refused to see him? Tell him to take a hike."

She dropped her head, an entreating sign to encourage his understanding. "I'm afraid of him. It's the reason I want to be free of him. When we dated, he did something which convinced me that in the years ahead, if I were to marry him, he would ultimately use his fist on my face."

"What did he do?"

"For the first year we were together, I don't recall his doing it. But later, I seemed to become his possession. When we walked or stood together among his fraternity brothers, he would curl his hand around the back of my neck. As if I were a puppet and he was controlling me."

"He was informing you that he could break your neck if you didn't do what he wanted! There's a number in the halls who do the very same. I wish the girls would wise up. It's the first sign they should dump the guy."

"I've always been honest with him, Gray. And I know it's the only thing that will make him go away and stay away. He's already accused me many times of sleeping with someone else, but I haven't and I've told him I haven't. I've told him no other man has even touched me. If that weren't true, he would know. Somehow, he would know. That's the reason you can't touch my shoulder, or anything else. I want him to realize it's nobody else. I want him to finally understand that it's him. When he does, I'll never see him again."

The time was approaching eleven. In the aquarium the beautiful cardinal tetras with the blue and red neon bands schooled from one end to the other. The angelfish were doing what they did all day, every day. They were on their backs, so to speak, searching for an opening in the tight overhead crystalwort that might afford them a quick gulping attack on the tiny young of the swordtails and the guppies. It wasn't long after that she made to leave. He asked if she wanted to watch the news, but she declined.

"I'll get your coat then."

"So the photograph of my father's horse, do you—"

"—I love it, Janey. It'll be hanging on my wall for many years to come."

They were at the door. The wind continued to whistle through the spaces around the exit to the street.

"I wonder if we might not get some snow before the morning," he said.

"Oh, I hope not. I'm not ready for it.... Gray, before I leave, I want to wish you good luck tomorrow night at the school board meeting."

He shook his head in puzzlement. "I've still no idea what reading materials Touchstone might want to complain about," he said.

She thanked him for the dinner and left. He returned to the windows in the biggest room and watched her get into her car that she had parked opposite the pharmacy. As she eased out from the space, she glanced up at his window and waved.

Afterwards, he switched on the TV to watch the tail end of the eleven o'clock news and Leno's monologue. Something continued to bother him about his apartment. It had not been bothering him for the past few days, but while he and Janey had sat on the inside shelf of the cupola, the disquieting feeling started again and stayed with him. It was with him now. For a brief time during the evening he had considered that it might be the framed picture of the Arabian horse, reduced in size and set in a lower intersection of imaginary lines according to the rule of thirds. The magnificent animal was gazing into the picture, almost all of which was a great expanse of dark, threatening sky. It wasn't the horse, the new thing in his living space. This that he felt contained the quality of violation. And what he was now sure of was that the violation was most contained in this area around the cupola and fireplace where tonight he and Janey had spent much time. Someone—perhaps a stranger, maybe a friend—someone had entered his home uninvited. And there continued to be some detail—altered, added to, removed, he didn't know which—that was different.

Chapter 11

Adjacent to the Superintendent's Office located at the front of the Careytown Junior-Senior High School stretched a windowless room approximately three-quarters the size of a standard classroom. It had a long dark table positioned down its center, the sides modernly converging at the ends like a surfboard so that the people sitting at its edge could see each other without straining their necks either left or right. Along two of the walls rose white-enameled metal bookshelves that ran the length and width of the room, the capacity of each wholly filled, but in a jumbled manner. What filled them, however, weren't mostly books, and the reason that what filled them was in disarray was not the result of constant use. Tomes of printed paper, bound in every imaginable way except a professionally published one, occupied the greater space of these shelves. Many of their authors were state committees, special commissions, and governor-appointed task forces; and such authors may have been the only persons to have read such boring volumes in their entirety. This room displayed a plastic sign on its door to prove it was the meeting room for the Careytown District School Board that numbered seven members, and these materials were purportedly to be of benefit to it, as well as to the school administration. Yet no one other than Dr. Harold Orr ever consulted this ton of printed matter. And most of the others, who lifted the tomes merely to judge their weight, were not frequenters of libraries, so that these board members replaced the materials on the shelves in the same manner they might have put back a can of sauce in a supermarket which they changed their minds about purchasing: they set them wherever. A dozen wooden folding chairs, reserved for visitors attending the meetings, rested against one of the walls absent of shelving. The chairs were as old as the room, yet their urethane remained glossy and unscratched.

The seven-member school board also was ancient, as voters had re-elected five of its cast three and four times. Only the two remaining members were relatively new, and although they alone garnered the respect from the men and women on the Careytown faculty, they wielded little influence in spite of their thoughtfulness. They, too, rarely consulted the printed advice by state agencies, but this was because they did not desire to plow through the gobbledygook of newly invented, high sounding words that were more obfuscatory than enlightening. Their elected counterparts did not read the governmental and professional tomes of advice because they were people who never cracked open a popular novel, let alone a reference book.

Of the thoughtful pair, one was a housewife with a degree in nutrition from the University of Pittsburgh. Her daughter, a seventh-grader, had told Serena Cantor that Mr. Lord was a funny teacher who made all her classmates laugh. Lord had met the woman and her husband earlier in the year during Open House and he hadn't minded answering her questions, as they clearly had revealed a daily interest in her child's education. The other half of the pair was the owner of an electrical shop whose sons and daughters had graduated from the district several years prior.

There wasn't much to say about the other five members of the school board, except to question their presence on it. None expressed a true appreciation of education and how a good one could serve a young boy and girl in the development of their lives. Instead, each seemed to cling to a personal agenda to somehow stifle the efforts of the very educators the board itself had hired. This observation appeared ironical to Lord, for having another agenda other than the one to instruct children was an accusation often launched at teachers by these same board members. Rarely did it cross Lord's mind that a particular colleague was out to fail or deliberately punish a student. All seemed to want the adolescents in their classes to learn and prosper, even when a few like himself were at the same time bitching about this student or that. Sometimes, the bitching simply was needed, if only to shake out the anger or disappointment. But that's all it ever was, a few moments of therapeutic complaining.

By far the most destructive of the five remaining school board members was the chair, Salvatore Rodino. In his early sixties, Rodino was the oldest and he saw himself as some kind of powerbroker, though if he were, it would have been difficult to prove. He was an ignoramus without equal, or so did the Careytown faculty regard the ineffectual man with a kingfisher's hair. They regarded him also as they figured he must regard himself, as the big fish in the little pond. Often Rodino visited the school during hours and hung out in the faculty room where he tried to hobnob with the teachers. But he seldom spoke of education in any meaningful way. More often he talked about the "dog problem" that most faculty members who lived inside the town limits judged to be no problem at all. Thirty years earlier there reportedly was something of an overpopulation of free-running dogs, and volunteering for the low-paying job because he had been without work for more than a year and his wife was threatening to leave him, Salvatore Rodino took to his new duties with almost unheard-of vigor. For his efforts he received a great deal of praise and consequently appointed himself to be the patron devil of canines for the rest of his time on the earth.

"You better hope when you die, Sal, they conceal your grave," Nesbitt once dared to tease him during one of the man's faculty room excursions. "You don't, and every pooch within a five-mile radius will be defecating on your head. You know the definition of that word, Sal?"

Salvatore Rodino was wanting to fire Nesbitt, but he was unable to, because the history teacher had gained tenure before the board chair discovered what he was really like.

Still, despite their low opinion of Sal Rodino, faculty members forced each other to admit that the man possessed *something* to account for his longevity both as board member and chair. But as educators, a typically hopeful and resilient group, they inflated it with more mystery than needed and, for a brief time, allotted Rodino more stature than he deserved. Nesbitt, who seldom suffered the common afflictions of his colleagues, soon corrected them. Salvatore Rodino, he said—and not without occasional comic imitation—had maintained his heightened stature because of three behavioral characteristics: a turbulent sinking of his voice when he took exception to something said; the swift, back-and-forth darting action of his face in the direction of the faces of others; and a look of hard, sincere intensity that endured throughout all meetings. The last encouraged one to believe that the man was listening and permanently recording every word spoken, whether directly to him or to the board as whole. In truth, he captured only one version, and it was always the first.

"The man's head is a rock, a genuine boulder," Nesbitt preached to his colleagues. "Scratch on it whatever you wish, but what you scratch on it first will be what's remembered. If, when he was a child, he was told to spell cat k-a-t, he'd be spelling it the same today."

Likewise, Superintendent Harold Orr realized this about Rodino, and yes, the board chair was a simple man to manipulate because of it, but Orr sometimes wished that weren't the case.

"Sal, what are you doing?"

Rodino and the board secretary, who doubled as Orr's administrative secretary, were busily setting the agenda and other papers at each member's place of seating along the table with the sloping sides. The monthly meeting would start in forty-five minutes.

The chairperson seemed baffled by the Superintendent's question, the evening's intense look of readiness already present.

"Millard Touchstone's on the agenda, remember? And I'm sure there will be a substantial number of his congregation with him. I instructed Mr. Vittitow and his custodial staff to set up tables and chairs in the auditorium." He dropped his head and raised his brow as he briefly diverted his attention to the secretary, a nattily dressed woman in her forties. "Apparently I forgot to mention this change to you, Leah. But I did mention it to you, Sal."

"Then our meeting won't be in this room, but in the auditorium," said Rodino.

"That's correct," Orr said. "The meeting will take place in the auditorium. And Sal? Remember what else I advised. Touchstone is the fifth item on our agenda, but you need to inquire at the outset whether his business with the board will be short. He might well be expecting considerable discussion of his matter. And if that's the case, then he goes to the end of the list and we conduct all our business first. Is that clear?"

The Rodino head with its seriously constricted eyes darted sharply from the papers he was recollecting to Orr, to the board secretary, and back to the Superintendent. It exhibited the sharp movement of some birds as they searched the grass for insects to eat.

"I've made a mental note of that," he said with a sternness to convince Orr and the secretary that he was fully on top of the matter. "I'll ask the Reverend first thing, if you think that's wise. That way, we won't have to interrupt the meeting later on."

Most of the discussion to which Lord was a party regarding Touchstone's intention to speak at the November meeting had transpired inside the school walls. Outside, he had overheard only the barest mention of it at the bakery, at the convenience store and gas station, even at Tilly's on those occasions when he had stopped by the cramped bar to down a few beers. After a while he concluded that Touchstone on the agenda would not be any big deal. This attitude changed the instant he swung the car into the school parking lot, as vehicles jam-packed the asphalt and he had a hard time finding a slot for the gold Toyota.

Walking unhurriedly, he nonetheless walked a little apprehensively, from the deepest end of the lot into the brick and glass-block building that offered classes on two floors and in a pair of converted, concrete-walled storage rooms in the basement. The auditorium was off to the right just inside the entrance and bright lights illuminated its stage and seating sections front to back. Many town residents were standing but an equal number had selected a seat. It was a sizable auditorium for a small school. Those present wouldn't overfill its fire capacity, but they would come close. Lord chose a seat in a side section, nearer to the exits than stage, just as Rodino banged the gavel and brought the meeting to order.

As the chair had said he would do, he pointed immediately at Touchstone seated in the first row and inquired how much time the minister would require to address the board.

"Why does that matter?" Touchstone asked, at once suspicious.

Without dropping the facial intensity, Rodino mixed in a smile. He explained to the minister his reason for asking the question, but then he added, "All of those sitting out there with you, Reverend Touchstone, may not want to hear what you have to say. They might rather get in their car to go back home and watch television."

The minister outright laughed in the chairman's face. "Who are you kidding, Mr. Rodino? So few residents attend your meetings that it's something of a joke around town. These people are here—virtually all of them—because I am here and I do have a matter to take up with the board that is of interest to them and which they support."

Orr leaped in.

"I suspect that you will have much to say, Reverend Touchstone—"

"And so might the members of my congregation, Dr. Orr. Nor would I think for a moment that the board and yourself will not want to discuss the matter, at least to some degree, here and now."

"Fine," Orr said, throwing open his hands. "Then we'll save you for the end. We'll carry on with our customary business, and once completed, you may have the floor before we adjourn." He shifted his eyes off Touchstone and onto the audience. And he allowed himself to light up pleasantly. "Of course, that means that all of you will have to endure the rest of our agenda.

But I must say, I'm quite happy about that. It's true, as Reverend Touchstone has pointed out, that few citizens of the community come to these monthly meetings. However, I wish more would. And so I encourage all of you to take a greater interest in what is happening with your school board."

This was a lie, Lord believed. Orr, he thought, would have preferred that no one ever show up at a meeting, just as he would have endorsed the elimination of local school boards altogether. To run the district the Superintendent felt that he could easily do without the taxpayer's lollygagging, which only slowed him in his own pursuits, as it forced him to finesse the contributor of any input into another, more conducive way of thinking.

In fact, Lord now noticed that the lectern wasn't miked and normally it was. When Vittitow and his crew unstacked and lined up tables for a special meeting, they also wired a microphone before the speaker's station, but tonight Orr must have told the custodial chief to forget it. Touchstone, of course, was gifted in oratory and would do fine without the electronic amplification, but those in the audience, if they wanted to put in their two cents, would have to do it clearly, articulately, loud enough so that everyone in the auditorium could hear, and probably from where they were standing at their seats. Orr understood there was likely no chance of that. Not offering others the opportunity to use a mike to express themselves this evening was an advantage the Super intended to keep. It was his meeting and it would remain his meeting.

Rodino banged the gavel a second time, and the board absorbed into itself like a poked amoeba as it proceeded through the agenda items.

Waiting with the others in attendance, Lord now did what many of them were doing. Most were darting their heads about and glancing over their shoulders to learn who all were present. And soon a thought occurred to him that he did not especially like because its possibility of being true brought to mind other possible truths. Just by the way the people in attendance were sitting, rigid and in groups, he felt certain that nearly all of them must be members of Touchstone's church. This should not have been troubling except that it reminded him again of how he had heard so little on the street about the matter, and this suggested a conspiracy within the growing Pentecostal church to keep the minister's petition to the school board to speak publicly and for the record among themselves as best they could until its release this night. Certainly there were town residents who were not members of the church who had heard that Touchstone was having some problem with the school. But until it received billing as a bona fide issue, they would stay away from any public meetings, no matter whose side they would support. Such a strategy by Touchstone—and the more he pondered it sitting in the auditorium, the more Lord felt it must be true—would permit the minister to make the initial attack with only the slightest opposition.

And so the more serious question came to mind: Exactly what was the minister intending to attack and lay waste to?

If it was only a religious objection to specific reading materials, an attempt at censorship, as Orr had implied during their meeting in his office—although with frank reservation, as the Superintendent had admitted also of the possibility that he himself might be Touchstone's stimulus to action—it did not seem to Lord to be a matter requiring church secrecy, because, after all, no one could possibly think that the board would resolve it in a single session. And he still found it difficult to believe that the department's curricular materials would be objectionable to anyone at all, while at the same time admitting that the disbelief was quite likely to be a product of himself. He was an English teacher. He read all sorts of materials, as he had always believed he should. But others who didn't might object to the new multicultural texts. And perhaps in the books he was using in this year's classes there was something too complimentary to gays, or too trumpeting of evolution. It could be these and a dozen other viewpoints to which the Reverend would soon be detailing his objections.

But if secrecy and a deliberate conspiracy of silence among the congregation, his mind rolled on like a train on schedule, was not something to go hand in hand with its church leader's public denunciation of certain books, then why was it done? The community was normally so apathetic that it would relish a disturbance arising from a religious objection to school reading materials.

The answer scared him.

The object of the attack demanded a conspiracy of silence when the object was not an object at all, but was a person; for the attack hit hard and with surprise and permitted a defense by the accused that was only minimal and unprepared, without tactics and soberly assessed strategy. Of perhaps greater importance, those who might side with and defend the accused would not be present. And afterwards, reading the regional newspaper that covered the local school board meetings of small towns only by telephone, some of these same defenders might begin to have doubts, for the overbooked reporter telephoned only those who were in attendance of the meetings. A balancing view of a personal attack could well be lacking.

Lord all of a sudden felt that he should have been giving more serious attention to what Orr had apprised him of. And he wished too that he had asked Nesbitt to come along this evening. George would be quick to defend him.

He sensed that minutes from now the Reverend Millard Touchstone would be attacking someone and he was certain it would be himself, Grayson Lord.

He suspended his thoughts and focused attention on the stage to determine where the board was in its agenda. How much longer before Touchstone would gain the floor and begin addressing everyone?

One of the members was arguing for the expenditure of discretionary funds to cover some unexpected debts incurred by the school's largest club, the Rifle Club. The man wasn't having much success as the others were choosing to ignore him, Serena Cantor being the exception. The item was clearly under "New Business." That meant that Touchstone would be out of his seat very soon.

Lord forgot about the board and went back into himself. He noticed how some of those around him were occasionally staring in his direction. If what he thought would happen was going to happen—and at the moment he believed without any doubt that it would—he needed to come up quickly with the plot that had brought Touchstone and himself to this point in time.

And it was a plot, and he thereby benefited by this fact because of the plots of many novels he had had to explain to his students who often became confused in their reading, or in some cases, his reading to them. In his mind he did what he sometimes asked his pupils to do after completing a novel and what they complained to no end about, claiming it was an impossible assignment. He compressed the whole of the story into one or two sentences: *The leader of a local church seeks to gain influence in the public schools, and he attempts to do so by open denunciation of one teacher which he believes will diminish the stature of all while elevating his own.*

Not bad, he thought. It coupled to what Orr had related to him concerning the minister's ambitions and further underscored Nesbitt's early admonitions that someone was out to get him.

Lord did not believe that Millard Touchstone was so foolhardy that he would introduce the name of Clipper Ostrander because involving the boy in any *actual* way would be sure to backfire. No wrong had threatened the seventh-grader, and Clipper Ostrander was a child who always told the truth. Touchstone or, more probably, a congregational member whom the Reverend could easily encourage very likely had circulated the filthy rumor of which Nesbitt later informed Lord at the close of the summer out at the history teacher's camp. The motive behind the rumor, it seemed obvious, was to stir up and bring to the surface some foul, untrue sediment of Lord that had been in existence now for more than a few years, the opinion that he was a pervert and was therefore a threat to the children of the community. Yet this would be a significant upgrade in the community's view of perversity, he realized. Usually, the sentiment was that he was gay, or rather, queer. To this day he occasionally discovered his name and phone number scribbled on a wall of a local restroom—doubtlessly done by former students of his who, in spite of being now old enough to drink and frequent bars, continued to nurse a grudge—and while at one time it must have crossed his mind if men ever punched such numbers, it did no longer. Over the years he had disappointed more than a few late-night callers.

This step up in perversity meant to inflict severe damage. It suggested that he might be a child molester, and everyone understood this was a practice that would not be coming out of any closet. Pedophiles you had to drag into the open, and even then they would deny their revolting proclivity. Lord realized he was the ideal target for Touchstone to go after. Excluding Wallace the divorcee, Blake and another department colleague of Schenley's were the only other unmarried male teachers, but both were fairly new to the district and neither had tenure. It would be nothing to get rid of them. What statement, if any, would their dismissals make? No, for a statement Touchstone needed to get rid of a Grayson Lord who held tenure and was still single. He didn't see why people would take the leap, yet he didn't doubt they might if their leader presented the story effectively.

"But an effective presentation is likely to be a problem for the self-righteous bastard," he mumbled under his breath as the idea of a counterattack upon the minister became attractive. The plot was exceedingly thin and it was filled with slander. Maybe enough for a successful lawsuit, as there wasn't a thing concrete. Damn! Was he all of a sudden becoming paranoid?

The restrained exchange of voices on the stage in the distance came to a stop, and Rodino raised his as he invited Touchstone to speak. Lord watched the minister, who was holding a thin black briefcase, proceed from the seating section, and the belief that he was just suffering some atypical paranoia gained in strength, to his relief. Touchstone appeared extremely affable, without any sign of pent-up agitation, and he acknowledged many of the people seated in the first and second rows. Mounting the stage, he uttered several words indistinguishable to the audience. All the board members either grinned or laughed, and Rodino darted his head at each. Lord wondered if any members of the school board also belonged to the minister's church. Orr had made no mention of that.

Off to one side, but well on stage, loomed the lectern and the minister might have begun speaking from its usual placement. Instead, he slid it closer to the tables of the board, and on the end of the table nearest, behind which sat Serena Cantor, he opened the black briefcase. Cantor, it seemed to Lord, considered the move an intrusion, if not an outright rudeness. Touchstone again said something to the board that he couldn't make out, and the board, minus Cantor, laughed again, this time louder; and they all, minus Cantor, darted their heads. Wasn't the Reverend a funny, personable man?

Lord supposed he must be. What else would explain the impressive growth of his church?

Tonight the board had conducted its business in an hour and fifteen minutes, but Touchstone seemed not to be in any hurry and Lord lapsed further into the palliative belief that he was acting paranoid.

Let's hope it doesn't develop into a habit, he chided himself. He found himself sitting back and relaxing in his seat, as though he were a dedicated moviegoer. He even crossed his legs.

Millard Touchstone was a tall, imposing man, though not so tall as Harold Orr whose own height had towered above everyone in Careytown until the arrival of the Aftanases, and he could strike a stance. It was a bias of all those who disapproved of Touchstone to describe him as fat and overstuffed, but the minister carried only the extra weight of approaching middle age, and it was still much less than many men who had reached their forties. He grew a rebellious head of hair and often reached up top with his fingers to rake and settle it. His eyes were a strong feature. They were dark and probing. But often equally dark sunglasses through which the eyes would still penetrate covered them to give to the minister, what appeared to many outside his church, a sinister visage.

Touchstone got to the business at hand. From the briefcase he had set down in front of board member Cantor he retrieved some papers and two books. He shut the lid on the case and placed the papers and books on top.

Lord uncrossed his legs and stretched forward slowly, unable to believe what he was seeing. The sanctimonious sonovabitch *was* out to get him after all!

Throughout his life Lord had enjoyed the capability of recognizing small familiar items, even when they were at a distance and distorted. Driving down a highway at a speedy clip, he knew immediately the brand names of the soda and beer cans strewn in ditches. Often they lay crushed or caked in mud, their colors faded from having lain so long, but neither factor ever fooled him. And he could do the same with books, as he had recently. He had only one passionate collection, the World War II novel. Two Sundays earlier, the sun had been shining and a family dared to have an off-season yard sale. Passing by, he spotted a table supporting several books and recognized instantly the spines of John Hersey's *The War Lover* and Gwyn Griffin's *An Operational Necessity*.

He had no difficulty recognizing either of the books on the briefcase. Both were paperbacks. One had a yellow spine, the other a red. They were two underground Victorian novels, their pages drenched in sex. What's more, he recognized these copies to be his very own. He was absolutely sure they were.

It did not strike him until many seconds later that the strange unease he had been feeling in his apartment stemmed from the removal of these volumes from his bookcase. Touchstone, or more likely a devoted member of the congregation, must have entered his apartment during the day while he was at school and removed them from the shelf. Whoever it was probably had followed Mrs. Hampton up the enclosed stairway, and while the old woman was in the farthest room from the door activating her aerosol can, the intruder had slipped in and hid himself, or herself—there were a lot of women in the minister's flock—in one of Lord's closets. Then, after his landlady had left, the person withdrew from the second-floor apartment, capable of opening both locks from the inside, but incapable of relocking both from the hall as the double lock required a key.

Thinking of all this, Lord could only reluctantly listen to Touchstone who was reading from the sheets of paper he had pulled from his briefcase. The minister's voice was becoming more insistent as he addressed the board on particular stories and poems that he and his flock found offensive. Lord surveyed the board members to see how each was reacting. Rodino, of course, displayed his typical look of great attention. Cementing the look to his face would not have improved it. Some of the others appeared to be listening with rapt attention as they thought the matter was serious and might force them to react.

One board member who was not listening was Serena Cantor. The confident look on her attractive face told Lord that she considered Touchstone to be a man who was too full of himself. He noticed, too, that one of her fingers was dancing on the cover of the first book, the one with the red spine entitled *Autobiography of a Flea*. The conceit of the tiny tell-all pest had it residing in the pubic hairs of a beautiful young maiden visited often by several men of the cloth. Finally, her hand turned the paperback book so that the title was right end up and the finger dug between two random pages. He watched the expression of Serena Cantor as she read silently from the story. The eyebrows went up, and rather quickly. The head pulled back and the chin shrank. Next, the long painted finger shifted randomly, seemingly reluctantly because of what it might find, to another section of the book. Moments later, the woman's head turned slowly to one side while the eyes, narrowing, remained on the printed words.

Lord realized he was openly grinning, but he couldn't help himself. It didn't matter which page she turned to, Serena Cantor would find vivid sexual action underway. This was the criteria that Rudy Wallace and he had established for great literary pornography. Get such a book and open it to any page. Perform the test at least a half-dozen times. If the action wasn't there, sorry, the book didn't qualify for pornographic distinction.

Being an English teacher and holding a Master's Degree in Comparative Literature, he had known about the underground Victorian novels whose anonymous authors, according to scholars, were at the time mocking the

118

superficial primness of their island country, but he had not ever even looked at one, let alone read an example. This changed at the end of last year, just before the holidays, around a jovial table at the Goldenrod. Wallace, a math teacher, had read several and was hyping them to Lord, Blake, and Dan Diston. Lord asked to borrow the books, but Wallace went one better as he had picked Lord's name out of the box for the faculty gift exchange. He purchased his colleague copies to keep. They were the same ones setting on Touchstone's briefcase.

But what is the man planning on doing with them? Is he intending to read a passage or two before Orr and the entire school board?

Gawd, didn't he hope the minister would! If it happened, he would be unable to control himself. He was sure he would burst out laughing. And not because Touchstone was reading, but because of the material itself. It's what it did best, at least to him and to Wallace, too. There was no denying it could raise an erection, but only a hormones-in-flux teenager could maintain a flagpole for the length of the work. Mostly, it made Wallace and himself laugh. Sometimes they fucking howled at the authors' unwavering, almost dutiful effort to see that hot sex was *always* underway! How could anyone not appreciate such devotion? Or the attention the authors had given to the creation of their metaphors? If he lived a hundred years, "rampant steed" would remain stuck in his memory. Or the dialogue, written deliberately prim and proper:

> *"Father Ambrose?"*
> *"Yes, Father Clement?"*
> *"Let us fuck."*
> *"Amen, Father Clement."*

And there was Rudy's favorite. More than a couple times in May when the weather was hot, his colleague had raced into the faculty room, unmindful of all who were there, shouting, "Quick, Fanny! Sponge me off!" Lord alone knew the crazy math teacher wasn't speaking gibberish.

The inquiring finger of the board member now pushed the top book aside and began to perform the same random exploration of the paperback advertised by the yellow spine that contained Rudy Wallace's favorite quotation. Already Serena Cantor appeared inured to the findings. Her face appeared at ease.

Lord continued to watch as she went purposefully to the pages at the front of the book. She stopped on one, having found what she was searching for. She spun the book in a circle to better read the raised embossing mark. Then she lifted her eyes to look out over all those in attendance. She found him in his seat.

Lord interpreted her stare at him to be one of more amazement than alarm. And her next move seemed to confirm his judgment. She interrupted the minister, who was now under full power.

"Excuse me, Reverend Touchstone. Mrs. Ferris on the right apparently has something she wants to ask of you. And Mr. Rodino, either he hasn't seen her, or he is choosing to ignore the Chair of our English Department."

Rodino flustered and took exception, but Cantor, without a show of personal fanfare, cut him off as she nodded at Mrs. Ferris to speak.

June Ferris was a heavy-set, much older woman who would retire the year after next. Lord got along fine with her. He had a single complaint—she was a comma freak. Students he taught who had had her for their teacher in previous years passed in compositions inundated by commas that he was unable to get them to remove, for the simple reason that she wielded more influence with these students than did he. And the reason explaining this was simple, too. Mrs. Ferris was extremely strict with her classes. She told no jokes, brooked no rude interruptions, and absolutely insisted that things be done her way. She was not a compromising woman.

She rose awkwardly out of her seat and stood. "Thank you, Serena. Reverend Touchstone, you are wasting the time of everyone in this auditorium."

"I beg your pardon," Touchstone said, instantly provoked. "This is a matter of great importance to myself and countless members of my congregation, Mrs. Ferris, many of whom have sons and daughters under your and others' tutelage. For you to assume it is a waste of time mocks their concerns."

Mrs. Ferris' head shook with impatient annoyance.

"Before you compiled your list, you might have inquired as to whether a policy already exists concerning reading materials that you and others like yourself deem morally objectionable. You see, Reverend Touchstone, there is. It has been in place for longer than a decade, and I take credit for putting it there. Parents who object on some moral ground to a reading assignment given to their child can request that another work be substituted. They may offer their own recommendation even. The latter, of course, must meet with our approval because, as educators, we might find that we have an objection to some of your favorites. But there is much in the middle. You need only to make your concern known on a personal basis. What you are attempting to do here, frankly, I find suspect."

Mrs. Ferris collected her things, intending to leave. She had said her piece.

"You should stay," Serena Cantor warned her. "I think the Reverend has some additional business on his mind. Isn't that correct, Reverend Touchstone?"

Rodino, as the table's centerpiece, appeared lost. His head tossed about in all directions, like a weathervane on a blustery day. The look on his face had intensified so greatly it seemed the flesh might crack and disintegrate into pieces.

"Are we hearing correctly, Dr. Orr? Is there a policy in place?"

The Superintendent made a slight movement with his right hand, signaling Rodino to be still.

"There is, Mrs. Cantor," Touchstone said with forced solemnity to finally answer her question, "as you've well discovered for yourself these past several minutes."

Touchstone then took hold of the paperbacks and placed them on the lectern before himself.

"But this other matter is not so easy to put before the board as the first because it involves people, and it pains myself and my congregation deeply. There was great discussion among the members of my church as to how this should be approached and how we should proceed. There were those who encouraged the matter to be taken up privately, secretly. But others reminded us that, all too often, matters handled in such a manner permitted the perpetrators of morally distasteful and objectionable behavior simply to leave and to repeat their sins elsewhere without shame or punishment. We can feel sorry and we shall wish that it had never happened, but in our own community we will not allow it to be swept under the carpet. Dr. Orr, Chairman Rodino, Mrs. Cantor, all of you, I hold a petition signed by virtually every member of my congregation who resides within the Careytown School District, demanding the immediate dismissal of teachers Grayson Lord and George Nesbitt!"

There was no applause, which Lord had half-expected. Touchstone's followers remained fixed and silent, their eyes glued to the lectern and the man behind it. Only those men and women in attendance who were not of his church turned in their seats to stare at Lord or search for Nesbitt.

The minister left the lectern and stepped to the front of the board where he handed the petition to Sal Rodino who became visibly inflated.

"Millard, you could have mentioned this earlier. What are your grounds?"

"They will be laid out fully, Dr. Orr, trust me."

Returning to the lectern, Touchstone paused first to peer out across the auditorium like a too proud leader, scanning those in attendance as though they were more a mathematical matrix than an audience of human beings.

"Let our concerns first go to Mr. Nesbitt," he finally began. "Is there a single one among us this evening who is not aware of how ineffective a teacher this man is and has always been? Yet despite that collective knowledge, George Nesbitt has been allowed to continue his employment in our school district and draw a substantial salary from the taxpayers of this community. And the reason for that? He has tenure. Tenure protects him, as it does most teachers, against termination because of poor performance in the classroom. But recently Mr. Nesbitt made a serious mistake that we can neither overlook, nor should we protect. Recently, in the office of the school principal Mr. Waring, before women and children, Mr. Nesbitt repeatedly made use of the foulest language. And even when his superior warned him and threatened him with a reprimand, George Nesbitt ignored Mr. Waring, choosing instead to pursue his tirade rife with obscenity. Such behavior can have no place in this school district. We will not tolerate it from any teacher, even those tenured. And we certainly will not forgive it from an ineffective teacher like George Nesbitt."

He paused a few seconds, long seconds. Lord expected the man to look his way, to seek him out, however briefly, and so make certain that everyone knew where he was seated, but Touchstone did not.

"Now as for Mr. Lord," he said, plunging his voice an octave. "With Mr. Lord I'm afraid the matter is worse, our objections even stronger."

Lord listened then as Touchstone developed the case against him. The minister hinted carefully, avoiding a declaration, that he was both a homosexual and a child molester. The first charge stirred barely a reaction in the board members. It was ancient innuendo. But the suggestion that they had long ago given their approval to the hiring of a disgusting pedophile made several cringe. Lord felt sure Rodino himself was ready to terminate Nesbitt's and his own contract on the spot.

Orr glanced at his watch and interrupted.

"Millard, these are serious charges that you're making against Mr. Lord. Is there any substance to them? Or is this just an attempt at slander?"

"You don't wish to adjourn this meeting yet, Mr. Rodino. There's abundant substance. I'm surprised that Dr. Orr is feigning ignorance. Arising out of the same incident regarding Mr. Nesbitt, Mr. Lord attempted to establish a sexual relationship with a male student. That student will testify to that fact before this board if necessary." He paused, but only for a moment. "And then there are these!" He elevated the paperback books in his right hand, as though they were an offering.

"What have you there, Reverend? I can see they are books, but is there something special about them?"

"Mr. Rodino. All of you. These books contain the worst filth imaginable. None of us could possibly imagine what is inside them."

"And these books, are you saying they belong to Mr. Lord?"

"They do, sir. It is not conjecture either. Mr. Lord thinks so much of these horrible books that he has proudly embossed his personal ownership of them in their pages."

Touchstone flipped to the pages containing the embossing mark and held them in the air in spite of the raised white mark's invisibility from a mere ten feet away.

"We'll want to look at those," Rodino said.

"Of course. I'll leave them with you. You'll be shocked, Mr. Rodino. All good people would be shocked."

"I have a question, Sal. I'd like to learn how the Reverend came into possession of the books."

"They were presented to me by a member of my congregation, Mrs. Cantor."

"And the name?"

"That I will not divulge, I'm sorry. This good man came to me in turmoil after being lent the books by Mr. Lord. You see, he was not expecting what he received. He was totally and horribly shocked. He could not believe, *he did not want to believe*, that a teacher of children would ever be in possession of such smut. I will tell you also that he was not in favor of making this matter public because he did not desire to visit trouble on Mr. Lord. Others and myself had to persuade him of that. We had to convince him that it would be in the best interests for the children of the district. But even now this man broods that he might be wrecking another man's career."

Lord had heard enough. He shot up from his seat near the rear of the auditorium, threw out an arm and pointed a finger at the minister.

"They were stolen!" he shouted. "They were stolen from my apartment, plain and simple! And the Reverend knows that."

"You'll have your opportunity to respond to all of this, I'm quite sure, Mr. Lord. Including your solicitation of a juvenile. But for now, I have the floor."

"Yes," Rodino added, "we'll want to hear from you, Mr. Lord. These accusations are quite serious. And I'm sure you'll want us to listen to your side of it."

However, once the minister finished and Rodino recognized him, Lord discovered he had little to say in his defense. He did not step to the stage but stood where he sat, feeling sapped of much of his strength, the eyes of everyone inside the auditorium pinned on him, and he only repeated that the paperback books had been taken from his apartment without his approval or knowledge. He hadn't given them to anyone, he said. Was the minister lying then? Damn straight! The minister was blatantly lying.

Chapter 12

June Ferris was part of a small group of teachers who did not frequent the faculty room. She visited the oasis during her lunch period only, toting along a brown paper bag that lasted all week and that concealed one or two plastic containers holding leftovers from a home meal. Unlike the others, she went every day. She never had the cafeteria duty, and Principal Waring was not about to argue with her refusal to accept it. She contended, however, that Waring knew only that she did refuse the duty. He did not remember her reason in spite of her having explained it to his face. June Ferris refused cafeteria duty because she understood she would not be permitted to force food-fighters to clean up their mess, and she would be damned if she would order old Mr. Vittitow and the other custodians to do it for them. "The occasional smashed crinkle fry on the floor is a part of their job description," she had lectured Principal Waring. "Three thousand of the things are not!"

On Friday, bag in hand, Mrs. Ferris waddled down the hall to the faculty room. Inside, next to an opened card table, she took a seat that her younger colleagues always left for her to occupy, and pried off the lids from her containers. Because last evening's school board meeting wasn't the usual yawn, news of it had disseminated rapidly. By noon every teacher, student, counselor, aid, and member of the secretarial and custodial staffs was aware that Touchstone was seeking to relieve Lord and Nesbitt of their jobs, and everyone knew also of the audacious evidence the minister had presented to support his petition.

In a corner opposite Mrs. Ferris, under a bulletin board advertising various computer software seminars and outdated applications for Fulbright Scholarships, sat Paul Blake and Jack Schenley. The vocal Blake was grasping a small can of V-8 in one hand and in the other a copy of the list of literary works that Touchstone and his congregation was striving to have banned. Several other teachers were spread out along the walls, eating their lunch.

"Some of these books have been around for ages," Blake remarked incredulously to no one in particular. "And he's just now getting around to—"

"—He obviously has nothing better to keep him busy," Mrs. Ferris interrupted. She had not dispelled her annoyance with the minister from the night before. "His objection to some of those works is ridiculous."

The door to the room opened and Lord walked in with Rudy Wallace talking into his ear. Wallace was laughing, Lord shaking his head.

"Mr. Wallace! Did you think you were fooling us last evening?"

The question from the Chair of the English Department stunned the comical math teacher. He stopped short and stood suspiciously erect.

"Really, did you think there wouldn't be anybody who would recognize you? What sort of get-up was that? Mr. Wallace attended last night's meeting in a disguise. And he looked absurd. You looked incredibly absurd, Mr. Wallace, I hope you know that."

"Then you're the only one who recognized me, Mrs. Ferris. Gray didn't. I was just now telling him about it. He can't believe it."

"I couldn't believe it either," said Mrs. Ferris. "Wherever did you get hold of that greasy mustache?"

"Is that what gave me away?"

"It didn't help once you called attention to yourself by sitting alone. Except for Gray and yourself, everyone else sat in small groups. And if you employ a cane ever again when you travel incognito, be sure you learn how to walk with it."

Mrs. Ferris concluded her criticism of her much younger colleague with a wink to show that she was only having fun with him. Then she switched her attention to Lord.

"Now, Gray, as for you. What are you intending to do in the wake of Reverend Touchstone's accusations? Will you see a lawyer to protect yourself? It might be wise."

"I haven't the money for a lawyer," he replied. He had already toyed with the idea, but he had to be realistic. There just wasn't that kind of cash sitting in his bank account.

"Then at least place a call to our union rep," said Schenley.

"Gray," Mrs. Ferris began, "don't take this the wrong way. I personally don't care what you or anyone reads, just as long as it isn't the only thing he reads, and I know all too well that is not the case with you. But I want to ask you a question, face-to-face and in front of your colleagues here, because last night you were ambushed by the Reverend. Perhaps the meager response you offered wasn't well thought out. Maybe you felt you had to say something to defend yourself."

"Ask anything," Lord said, noting that the eyes of every teacher in the room were focused on him.

"Were the paperbacks stolen as you claimed? Or did you make up that allegation, thinking that it might cast a shadow over Millard Touchstone?"

"I didn't make up anything. I didn't have to. For some time now I've had an uneasy feeling that someone broke into my apartment. When I returned home last night, I went immediately to the bookshelves. I know where those books should be located. They weren't there."

Corey Howser, a smirk breaking across his face, started to speak, but Lord stayed him to make a point that he wanted the others to be aware of and understand. It wasn't only that two books belonging to him had been taken.

"Other books were there in their place," he stressed to his colleagues. "Titles I didn't recognize. Consider that for a moment."

The implication of a setup underwent digestion by the others in the room. Some heads nodded.

Having waited patiently, Howser finally broke in. The smirk hadn't gone away.

"Am I mistaken, or are those books of yours the same your buddy Wallace there surprised you with at the last Christmas party?"

Rudy Wallace manifested the glummest of looks. "Gol-lee, Mr. Dillon, ya caught me."

"Yeahhh, I caught you. You better hope the Reverend doesn't learn of that minor detail, else you'll be leaving on the next stage with Nesbitt and Gray."

Wallace sobered in a blink.

"It's not a fact that anyone's leaving yet, Corey my boy."

One of the other teachers, sitting next to the soda machine, asked how Nesbitt was taking the matter.

"He's out today," Wallace said. "Called in sick."

"I'll bet," said Howser, grinning.

"Does he know?" Mrs. Ferris asked.

Lord nodded. "I located him last night and filled him in on everything that went down."

Howser wasn't finished.

"Hey, Moody Rudy, explain to everyone here why you went to the meeting disguised. Halloween is over."

"Just a gag."

"You're not going to tell us?"

"No, Corey, I'm not going to tell you. So you can change whatever that look is on your face to something pleasant."

In this instance, Wallace was not sticking it to Howser, as the football coach assumed. Before entering the faculty room, Wallace had explained to Lord his motivation behind attending the previous night's school board meeting in a disguise that he had borrowed from a friend of his ex-wife. In the auditorium he had sat by himself but in the vicinity of many of Touchstone's followers in the hope he would overhear some interchanges that he wouldn't hear if they realized he were a teacher. But it turned out to be a disappointing experiment. Nothing worth noting was revealed. And now he was not inclined to explain the whole matter once again.

Blake, shifting his attention from Wallace and Howser back to the list of objectionable literary works, blurted out in disbelief: "What is Touchstone's problem with this selection?"

"Which one is it?" Lord asked.

"'The Creation' by James Weldon Johnson. You'd think his ministerial buns would be tickled pink that you're using a piece such as that."

"You'd think so. You know it, Paul?"

"No, but I'm guessing it isn't a promotion for evolution."

Schenley asked, "Gray, is that the poem you were telling Willis about this morning outside homeroom?"

"Willis said he plans to get up in the Reverend's face and ask exactly what the man's objection to it is. Last night, Touchstone skipped over this one, as he did with a few others," Lord explained. "It's a wonderful poem, poignant and moving. Are you familiar with it?" he asked Mrs. Ferris.

"I don't believe I am, Gray."

"It's a poem which doesn't so much describe the creation of the universe as it does the mental and emotional state of God while He did it. He's very lonely in the poem, until He creates Man. Maybe Touchstone regards loneliness as a weakness that God wouldn't have."

"But you don't think that's what it is, do you?" Wallace asked.

"That's what Willis intends to find out. During His act of creating Man, Johnson compares God and His solicitude metaphorically to that of an old black mammy. I wonder how Touchstone feels about that."

***

Throughout Friday the mind of Grayson Lord lacked its normal control. Despite his best efforts, it acted less like a man who had once enjoyed the writings of Hamsun, Gide, Hesse, Grass, and Lagerkvist and more like a simple dislocated moth in a large lighted room, flitting in all directions, bouncing off everything. At the end of each class period he felt he had squandered the time of both his students and himself. By the end of the day he questioned if he had earned his pay.

When the week ended at three-fifteen, he felt greater relief than was typical when weekends arrived. He exited the building alone and returned to his apartment above the pharmacy with the intention to spend most of Saturday and Sunday there, just reading and maybe writing a few letters to friends residing elsewhere. He put aside all thoughts on visiting the local bars for the next day or two, with the exception of Tilly's. The taunts were sure to be there and they would be too much for him to handle at this early point. Some former student bearing a grudge would show up likely and might even attempt a swing at him, now feeling he could attack a teacher on the outside with impunity too.

Around eight a dozen teens, none from any of his classes and some no longer students, crowded the sidewalk on the corner of the intersection below the apartment. Tonight, he tried not to listen to their conversation, but he found it impossible as some were elevating their voices for his benefit. He attempted to use the television to drown out their derision, but those below who recognized his effort pitched their voices still higher and louder. Finally, he waited for something to distract them, to move them elsewhere, and when it did, he hurriedly left the apartment for his car.

He drove—ironically, he realized—to the school that was dark except for the bright illumination in the gym, attached like a stereo component to the rest of the building. Inside, he felt himself begin to relax, which happened when he entered the vacant school at night. The building itself seemed to be taking a deep breath, relieved that its young destroyers had abandoned it for a time.

His walk echoed in the long hallways, undefiled once again after the broom and buffer of the custodians. The tough linoleum floor glimmered in the occasional spot where there was an exit door with windows, and an outside light shot a quiver of dim rays into the building. Way in the distance, when an interior door to the gym opened, he could hear the ping of a dribbled basketball. The school radiated a refreshed aroma, and most of the billions of germs had left the brick building with their carriers.

He unlocked the door to his classroom and switched on one of the two rows of overhead fluorescents. Like the halls, the classroom was again orderly and clean, except that if he bent himself over a few inches, he could see the assorted pieces of student garbage jammed inside the desks. Because the custodians did not usually empty them, he periodically asked his classes to perform the task while a student or himself circulated the waste can up and down the aisles. But too often he forgot. There was fresh heat rising from the register under the windows and it was pleasant to inhale.

From a book closet at the rear he selected a volume with an owl on its cover, then went to his desk upon which he rested his legs. After a while, he was moved to look left and saw that Janey had appeared in the entrance to the room.

"Hi," he said, dropping his feet to the floor. "How long have you been standing there?"

"Long enough. Are you okay, Gray?" She attempted to read his mood.

He nodded, inserting a crick at the end. He was and he wasn't.

She went over to him and glanced at the cover of the book.

"That's a novel. Coming down the hall, I'm sure a poetry recital was underway."

He looked up at her with the childlike quality she had seen before.

"It's a strategy I first employed during my appointments with the dentist," he explained. "You know, when they want some chemical compound to set up and it'll take a few minutes. You want to gag, but you have to stifle it because if you don't, the whole process has to be done over. I used to sit in the chair and recite every poem I ever memorized. Now I do the same thing when I can't clear my head.

"'Care-charmer sleep, son of the sable night / Relieve my languish and restore the light.' Samuel Daniel, sixteenth century, with a line intentionally missing so I get the rhyme at once. 'Much Madness is divinest Sense— / To a discerning Eye— / Much Sense the starkest Madness—.' Emily Dickinson."

"What was that I heard about a 'two-faced man'?"

"That would be a poem by Philip Booth. A fellow pretends he's someone else and in the end gets the two faces mixed up."

"Brings to mind people I know."

"And 'Sad Ann, she could not feel for her man whom she should love / Because he's so godawfulniceandpleasant' are lines from the pen of one of my college co-eds. Then, I usually dine with 'Cliff Klingenhagen,' enjoy Gunter Grass's reversals in 'Where's the witch, black as pitch? / Here's the black wicked witch,' and often finish with Byron and a little Greek: 'Maid of Athens, ere we part, / Give, oh, give, me back my heart. / Or, since that has left the breast, / Keep it now and take the rest. / Hear my vow before I go, / *Zoa moo, sasaga po.*' Some I can recite in their entirety, others just a stanza or two. But I can while away an hour with barely a break."

"That's truly wonderful," she said. "You make me regret that I never took the time to memorize my favorite lines."

She moved behind him and began to massage his shoulders. He looked back at her questioningly.

"I never said I couldn't touch you."

"What are you doing here on a Friday night?" he asked.

"Yearbook. Matter of fact, they began pasting up the faculty section this evening. The photo they've selected of you makes Grayson Lord appear genuinely philanthropic. Know the one I mean?"

"Where I'm sitting on the window sill?"

"That's the one."

"And I look philanthropic on a window sill."

"Hard to believe, I'm sure.... Gray? Let's get out of here. Let's go have a drink somewhere."

"Where do you want to go? Over the hill to the Revolution?"

"I was thinking we might stop at a few of the ones in town. Tilly's is always fun. Let's begin there. Then maybe the Lark Hotel and the 3-Mile. Or even Resch's. I suppose I could stand it for a drink."

"You forgot Domirock's Bar and Grille, not to mention the Goldenrod."

"Sorry. I draw my line at those two."

"The clientele at those will have to continue to think I'm a fag and molester?"

He stared at her several seconds, and she returned his emotionless look.

"Do you really think it will help?" he finally asked.

"It can't hurt, Gray."

"Well, not me, perhaps." He shook his head after a time. "Let's just forget it for now. I think it's best if I drink alone until this is over. And knowing I'm not helping to ruin your career, I'll sleep better."

Chapter 13

The game played at Tilly's wasn't shuffleboard, Bowl-O-Matic, 8-ball, or darts. Those traditional games and a new video assortment enjoyed popularity throughout the week at the other taverns. The game at Tilly's was Liar's Poker, and not the boring kind, examining and comparing the serial numbers of dollar bills; but Liar's Poker played with a full deck. The staple of a bar was perfect for the game as everyone could see everyone else, and the game wasn't about winning or losing for those who took part routinely. The fun was in making the lie heartfelt, sincere. The fun was in the acting. The fun was also in the surprise of the occasional truth.

"Who's in?"

"We're all in, Tilly."

"Goige, why you think you can—"

"All right, who isn't in?"

"Skip me. The wife gives me hell when I gamble."

"This is hardly gambling," Lord said.

"Well, I know that and you know that, but Alva doesn't."

"Pour Gray and me another beer, Tilly, before you deal."

"I'll just watch," said Boyd Benson.

"You'll have to do more than that if you continue to sit where you are," Nesbitt said.

"I can pass the hand. Alva wouldn't object to my doing that."

Tilly set the beers before Lord and Nesbitt, turned off the barely audible sound of the television where a football game was underway, then gathered up the deck and did a short shuffle.

"Twos and t'rees wild," he said and dealt five cards to a balding, thin, friendly-faced man sitting on a stool at the far left, Warren Hoverton, a regular and the citizen most responsible for organizing the community's springtime canoe races down the Allegheny River.

Hoverton, the only person smoking, collected the cards, ordered them quickly, then folded them together and reached out and dropped them on the bar before the man sitting two stools to his left.

"Four sixes."

Nesbitt laughed out loud from the other side. "You be wary of him, Tut. I played with him long enough I know he likes to lie right out of the gate."

Hoverton made a face, pretending to be offended.

The hefty farmer Tut picked up the cards and studied them through dirt-smeared spectacles.. **3♠ 7♠ 9♦ 10♣ K♥.**

"He lie about those sixes?"

"Naw, they're here. He don't dare lie to me, George. He does, he knows I'll take him outside to the parking lot and tan his hide."

Tut discarded two cards and Tilly gave him two.

"Pass these over to Margo, Boyd. Four tens, Margo."

The woman named Margo Worth didn't hesitate to scoop up the hand. She kept the pair of wild cards, got rid of the rest with barely a glance at the farmer.

"Three, Tilly. I don't think I'll even look at these before presenting them to my hubby," she announced. "Here, Sweetie. Four jacks."

Everyone laughed.

"You're not about to buy that, are you, Tom?"

"Now hold on, Gray. Hold on, all of you. She's been awfully lucky as of late, almost psychic. I told her she ought to open up her own psychic hot line and bring in some extra money. Her mom and daddy told her the same."

"Where is Alva, Boyd? Why you travelin' alone tonight?" Hoverton asked.

"I don't think it would be appropriate to say," answered Boyd Benson.

"Four jacks and a five to you, Gray. And they *are* there."

"All of a sudden you want to spare Gray's and my feelings?" Nesbitt said. "Tell him. It's a small town. She's with a number of other women strategizing on how to aid Touchstone and Rodino in getting rid of Gray and myself."

"Well, that's not exactly true," Benson said. "I'm sorry to disappoint you, George."

The four jacks were there in the form of a single one-eyed jack, a pair of treys, one deuce, and the five was also there. Lord threw away the jack and the five, and Tilly dealt out two cards from the top of the deck.

Lord checked the altered hand. "Four aces," he said crisply and flicked the cards to a bearded young man sitting next to Nesbitt on the staple's other side.

"You wouldn't be lying to me now, would you, Mr. Lord?"

"You don't know who this is, do you, Gray?" Nesbitt said.

134

Lord inspected the young bushy face while it drank from a mug of beer.

"You do look familiar, I can't say you don't."

"DeWitt Wainwright," Nesbitt said.

"Well hey, so it is Dewitt. You aren't so recognizable behind all that hair. You didn't have that when I had you." Lord reached over, extended a hand, and Wainwright, surprised, awkwardly did the same. "What are you doing here?"

"I've been working across the line, but I got laid off. Thought I'd see if the glass plant was hiring. What'd you pass me?"

"Aces. Four of them."

"You wouldn't be lying to me, would you, Mr. Lord?"

"I'm a teacher. Teachers don't lie. Didn't George and I teach you anything?"

Wainwright grinned and gathered up the hand, but he didn't open it.

"Now how's this go? If I turn these over—"

"If you turn them up and they're there, then you get the dooley," Hoverton said from the other side. "If they're not, Gray gets it."

"And then I'd have to buy a round for everyone?"

"Not until you get three dooleys," Nesbitt explained. "And dooleys are what Tilly calls poker chips."

"Don't turn them over," Lord warned. "Besides, George looks like he's in a buying mood. Sell 'em to him."

The young man grinned again and spread the cards in his hand.3♠3♠2♣ A♣ 4♦.

"I'll take one, Tilly.... Mr. Nesbitt, four jacks and a—"

"You got to beat aces."

"I'm sorry. That's what I meant to say. Four aces and seven. Are you buying?" Wainwright held the hand to his heart like a schoolgirl would hold a note from her lover.

"You're more deceitful than you look. I'll buy. Give 'em here."

Nesbitt took the cards and fanned them for himself.

"I think there's a helluva lot of lying underway in this here joint of yours tonight, Tilly. I should probably throw away the whole lot and start over. Two."

Tilly dealt out two cards and Nesbitt put them with those in his hand.

"Here you go, Tilly. Five big—B-I-G—nines to you."

"Sumtin mus' be there, huh?" said Tilly. He accepted the hand, looked at it briefly, seriously, dealt himself one.

"Fi' queens, Warren."

"Now how the hell did this get back to me!" Hoverton picked up the hand, shaking his head with exaggeration from one side to the other. "I can't believe this.... Alright, make it one, Tilly, and make it good.... Tut, you ready for this? You'll be between a rock and a hard place but I've left you some room. Five kings." And then pretending to whisper so the others couldn't hear, he added, "And only one of them with a face. Get me?"

"Turn 'em up," said Tut.

"Not so fast now. I'm telling you you're making a mistake. Sure, I lied last time, but not this time. This time, I'm swearing to you. Look!" He raised his right hand in the manner of a boy scout. "All you gotta do is draw an ace or another wild card, and that deck in Tilly's hand, if you haven't been watching, is thinning. Not to mention somebody over there was fibbing about aces. Now here. I'm pushing them over to you slowwww-like. Think about it. Don't act rash."

Hoverton eased his hand off the cards as if they might explode were he to jostle them in the least.

The big farmer immediately turned them face-up.

"Damn!" Hoverton said.

"Hey, someone threw away some wild cards," Wainwright exclaimed in amazement.

"Goige," said Tilly.

"Give me a chip," Hoverton said, "and the deck."

"What do you mean when you say, it's not exactly true? What isn't exact about it?"

Boyd Benson pretended not to hear Nesbitt. He even appeared embarrassed for himself. Nesbitt repeated his question, then said it again when Benson still did not respond.

Hoverton came to Boyd Benson's rescue as he shuffled the cards and dealt five to the farmer Tut, then returned the deck to Tilly.

"They're strategizing on Touchstone's caper of last Thursday to get rid of you, yes, but with one modification."

"I thought you were the one who asked about Alva."

"I knew about the meeting same as you. Just didn't know the time."

136

"What's the modification?"

"They're omitting Gray. It's only you they're going after, George."

"Anything wild?"

"Make it one-eyed jacks. We'll keep this round simple."

"Pair o' tens. Pass it to Margo."

Margo Worth picked up the hand from Tut and opened it, but she was also picking up on the talk by Hoverton, as was her husband.

"I can see by the way both of you are looking this moment," Hoverton said, "didn't neither one of you hear about this."

"No, we didn't," Lord said. "At least I didn't."

"I didn't either, Gray, or I would have passed it along. So what's behind it? And what makes your wife, Boyd, and the other women think Touchstone will stand for it."

"Don't ask me. I think this is pretty dirty business trying to lose a man his job."

"You do?"

Benson nodded awkwardly.

Margo Worth passed two pair to her husband, tens and deuces.

"Give Boyd a drink on me, Tilly," Nesbitt said. "I mean it. Give him one."

"You don't want to hear what's behind this?" Hoverton said.

"If you know, I do," Nesbitt said.

"What I know, George, is what's getting around. Whether it's true is another question and one I can't answer. But what's going around makes sense."

"Then let's hear it."

"Well, first off, Touchstone made a poor calculation concerning Gray. Seems your students are quite fond of you, Gray, in spite of your pissing off a few of them—excuse my language, Tilly, Margo. Not too many folk outside the Reverend's congregation consider you to be gay, as they once did, and no one believes you're a molester of children."

"What!" shrieked DeWitt Wainwright, spilling some beer on himself. "They really used to think that? Why didn't anyone ask those of us who had him for a class?" Wainwright started laughing and couldn't stop.

"Serena Cantor's the batter on that one," Hoverton continued, "and she can hit hard when she wants."

"Here, Gray. Three tens."

Lord accepted the hand, certain Tom Worth was lying. He threw away all five cards after looking at them and Tilly dealt an equal number of new ones.

"And nobody can really believe you said to the Aftanas boy what he claims you said." Hoverton paused, coolly lit another cigarette. The man often surprised others with his frankness, and Lord suspected Hoverton was readying to surprise him now. "So, Gray, did you?"

"Tell me what you heard."

"Well, I can't say it verbatim. I guess you asked him to have oral sex with you."

"No, no, no."

"I'm sorry, Tilly. I don't know how else to say it."

"Seriously?" Lord said.

"No say at all," said Tilly. "Or you get out."

"I'm sorry."

"Three kings, DeWitt. Remember, one-eyed jacks are wild."

"What about those books I heard about?" Tom Worth asked. "I heard they were pure porno."

"I think it's 'impure' that you mean," said Tut, grinning.

"Weren't you distributing them? I heard you were passing those books about."

"They were taken from my apartment while I wasn't there, Tom. I'm still eager to put a face on that."

Lord could see Margo Worth smiling to herself. He had never mentioned to her the phone call from her parents and he wondered if they had told her.

"What's so funny, Margo?" he up and asked. "Are you the burglar?"

"Honest, I'm not laughing at you, Gray. It's something else."

"And that is...?"

"You've been seen out a few times with that new art teacher. She's lovely and everybody I've ever talked to likes her. That won't help Millard Touchstone."

Lord thought Margo Worth remained quite beautiful herself in spite of her middle age, and he wondered momentarily how she had ever hooked up with Tom, a nice fellow but rather simple in his thinking.

Nesbitt was staring, but at no one in particular. The former student Wainwright passed him four kings.

"I don't think so this time," Nesbitt said, abruptly turning up the cards. The fourth king was missing, and DeWitt Wainwright frowned when Tilly skidded a poker chip in front of him.

"Warren!" Nesbitt didn't have to ask the next question because he already knew the answer, but he was curious as to whether Hoverton, who also was aware of the answer, would voice it.

"I dealt the last. It's Tut's turn."

"Not that. Since you seem to be informed on the matter, do you know the reason I'm not being granted the same amount of consideration as Gray?"

"Come on, George. We all know the answer to that. Not too many local folk fancy you and they sure as hell won't miss you when you're gone. I will, of course. I've always found you to be quite refreshing."

"Are you saying George is a hoot?" said Margo, coyly.

"I guess so. I guess I am saying that George Nesbitt is a hoot and that he can count me among his small legion of fans."

"Was that 'legion' or 'lesion'?" Lord asked jokingly.

"I wouldn't take it too personally though, George. They're really wanting to get rid of you for the same reason some would prefer to get rid of Gray."

"What reason is that?"

"Someday they'll try to give the ax, too, to that Wallace fellow and maybe to Stiles as well. I don't agree with it, but it's something that's been going on for quite awhile and not just here either."

"What the fuck are you talking about?"

"Goige, I no like that language. You get out now!"

"I'm sorry, Tilly. It slipped out. It really did."

"I think it did too, Tilly," Margo said with an appeasing whisper.

"They want to homogenize all you teachers. And they're succeeding," Hoverton said. "I think it's a mistake."

"I don't follow," said Boyd Benson.

"They want to make all of them the same. I hate to say it, but Alva strikes me that way when she gets to talking about the schools."

"No, I got to defend her on this one," Benson said. "She's just looking to have the teachers be consistent."

"Exactly. And I think that's a crock. It isn't that way in the real world, Boyd. No reason it oughta be in the schools. You're doing the kids a disservice. Nowadays, that classroom belongs to the kids and the parents.

Used to be, it belonged to the teacher and that's still who should run it. Forget about consistency. Join the military if that's what you're after. Long as each teacher runs his or her classroom within reason, everyone else should stay the hell out of it. It was like that when I was in school, and I believe I got a good education and am a better man because of it."

"You should run for the board," Lord said.

"I've considered it."

"Are you saying there shouldn't be standards, Warren?"

"No, that is not what I'm saying. What I'm telling you, Boyd, is this. What appears today as a concerned attitude for children and their education is nothing but a look-good mentality. Waring's probably busy tonight putting together another newsletter that will tell us all how wonderful it is up there at the high school. I mean, a newsletter! What the hell do we need with a few sheets of word-processed paper that's basically a P.R. tool? Or what about that thing out front? The lawn marquee, or whatever you want to call it, that lights up the school slogan?"

"It's a motto, Warren."

"'Where Caring and Success Are One'? It's an advertising slogan! You know what was chiseled in stone at the school my wife attended? *'To Strive, to Seek, to Find, and Not to Yield.'*"

"Tennyson," said DeWitt Wainwright.

"That's right, DeWitt. Tennyson. Hey, you taught him well, Gray. And at my old school the words above the entrance read, *To Thine Ownself Be True.'*"

"Shakespeare," Dewitt said. "Two for two."

"*I am master of my fate, captain of my soul* at school my son gone to," said Tilly. "They write it in floor so you see when you walk in."

"But then they tore the building down," Hoverton said, "constructed a new school, and now they have a marquee and a slogan too. You know, there's still some life in the Careytown faculty."

"So where did you go?"

"I graduated from Prosserville, but today they're more homogenized than milk. That friend of yours, Gray—Dan Diston—he's about the only one who isn't."

The farmer shuffled, sprayed a few cards onto the floor, retrieved them, shuffled again, and laid down five new cards in front of Boyd Benson who slid them over to the woman Margo Worth who, in turn and again without looking at them, passed them to her husband.

"Pair of eights," she said.

"Aces and deuces are wild," Tut said.

"In that case, make it three eights."

"Well, if my wife can do it, so can I," said Tom Worth. Leaving the hand face-down on the bar, he pulled off the top two cards and asked Tilly for the same number of replacements. These he didn't look at either, but placed them with the rest, then slid the cards to Lord.

"Three aces," he said.

Lord kept up the cards' momentum and pushed them to Wainwright.

"You're not even going to take a card?"

"Don't need to," Lord said. "I can read the cards from the back and Tom made a mistake. Four aces."

Hoverton and Tut were shaking with gentle laughter, as was Tilly. Dewitt Wainwright appeared totally perplexed.

"You better look at them, DeWitt," Nesbitt said. "I'm not as easy as the rest."

The young man picked up the cards, opened them, and scratched his head.

"Not there, huh?" Hoverton said.

The young man then began trying out various facial expressions, and he took two cards from Tilly. The expressions worsened.

"I think DeWitt is finally getting a taste of how this game is played," Hoverton said.

"Too late," Nesbitt said.

Wainwright opened his mouth to start the sale, but Nesbitt turned the cards over and the young man received his second dooley. They played three rounds after this and DeWitt Wainwright bought everyone a drink, including Boyd Benson. Tut, too, treated the bar to a round, and the farmer hadn't received a single dooley.

Lord and Nesbitt walked out of Tilly's together, as the second half of the football game on the television was getting underway. The town was quiet and the streets were glistening wet. The temperature was falling sharply.

Nesbitt shivered in the middle of the parking lot. "This is weather I hate. I've always hated it."

"Assuming Hoverton's correct, why do you think I was included in the first place?" Lord asked, leaning on the roof of his car. "Touchstone isn't an idiot. He had to have some idea."

"It's no different from asking for a raise, Gray. He doubled what he'd settle for. If he got us both, so much the better. If not, he'll still have his influence."

"That's what Orr said he's after."

"Sure. When Orr leaves for bigger and greener pastures, Touchstone'll want to be heard on who his replacement is."

"What are you planning to do, George?"

"I won't be attending this month's meeting, I can tell you that much. Wouldn't be any sense it in. I already talked with the regional rep, but he's aware of what Hoverton was saying. There's no support for me from the community. So he'll do nothing and hope he can capitalize on some other issue later just because he's not being a pain in their ass now. I'm going home to Stella. It's becoming too cold out here for me."

Chapter 14

She was there to block him.

"I'm sorry, you can't come in here, Reverend!"

"Then apparently you haven't heard of the Sunshine Law, Mrs. Cantor."

"This matter has gone to committee. The Sunshine Law does not apply. If I have to call someone to remove you, Reverend Touchstone, let me assure you I will."

Serena Cantor felt certain the tall imposing minister was intending to walk over her to gain entrance to the meeting room. But at last, without even a nod or further word, he turned and walked away.

Displaying no sign of her small victory, as it was not in her character, she then called the meeting of the Personnel Committee to order.

Alva Benson and her concerned group of women had already contacted each member of the committee to make known their position on the two teachers that Touchstone was seeking to have dismissed, and before the strictly ceremonial rapping of the gavel, the members had talked independently among themselves. It was a foregone conclusion by the Personnel Committee that it would not recommend the dismissal of Grayson Lord to the full board. Although Warren Hoverton had been correct when he stated that support existed for Lord, it was not what motivated Benson to action. She, too, saw that Touchstone was after influence in the Careytown public schools and she was determined to keep it minimal, especially after she had witnessed his awful and insensitive display open to the public during Halloween. She would have preferred that the power-hungry minister have no sway whatsoever, but George Nesbitt had opened the door that she realized accurately she could not shut altogether. She was angry at Nesbitt because of this. She would have fought for him, too—much to his surprise, she was sure—but he had left her no room. So, it was the smart thing to call for his expulsion from the payroll. That way, she and her group appeared to be fair and judicious, whereas Touchstone then looked only vindictive.

The number of women she had summoned to action amounted to fifteen, and each was aware her vote counted more than the votes by the women in the Pentecostal congregation. The reason for this was simple. In building his church, the outspoken charismatic minister had first appealed to the people in the outlying townships, and most whom he had wooed were women who had experienced no involvement in civic affairs. Thus, they rallied nicely to the consoling and therapeutic leadership of Touchstone, but each was lacking in what to do alone. Benson and her cohorts, on the other hand, recognized the times they should come together, and when they did assemble, it was only to determine what they should be doing independently. This independence marked their strongest suit and exponentialized the power of their vote. More than anything, they knew how to work the phones.

If Alva Benson had not marshaled the important women of the community on her own initiative, Harold Orr was prepared to telephone her and request that she do, and for the same reason: to diminish Touchstone's attempt at grabbing some power in the local schools. But, unlike the women, the Superintendent had given no thought to keeping around history teacher George Nesbitt. He would welcome the man's dismissal. Nesbitt never was one to play along and there were always reports that he drank too much. He liked Grayson Lord, on the other hand, and was ready to defend the young man, although he realized the precarious possibility that his support could backfire. And it wasn't because of the teen either that a backfire could happen. Asa Aftanas, as was true of the entire family, possessed little, if any, credibility with the general population. He had no doubt that Lord had responded with a carefully thought-out remark that brought the kid exploding out of his seat. But exactly what that remark was he didn't know and he didn't want to know, and it's why he had not asked Lord directly, even after receiving the phone call from Tessie Aftanas. No, what made the matter touchy and made him feel that he could be going out on a limb were the books. There would have been no question if the books were contemporary porn purchased at some brown windowless building sitting along a highway in the middle of rural nowhere. Lord would be on his own and the Superintendent could just about guarantee that he soon would be interviewing for a new English teacher. But the fact the books were almost two hundred years old and written in Merry Old England somehow put a different light on the subject, especially since the man did teach the language. It helped, too, that the books had been removed from his apartment without his knowledge, and just about everyone now believed this to be the case because Lord continued to say on one occasion after another that he wished he could learn the identity of the person who had entered his apartment without his invitation. He voiced this hope enough that people actually began thinking about it, and when they did, they began thinking also that something might be fishy about the dear Reverend Touchstone.

The many machinations under steam by those concerned with the matter were already known to Serena Cantor, for she was not only intelligent, but also she was thoughtful, in the truest sense of the word. For instance, she recognized there would be a push to get rid of Nesbitt with the utmost immediacy, but she would not allow that to happen, not so long as she was heading up the committee! The investigation would be thorough, despite the ending everyone knew it would produce. If at all possible, she planned on talking to each individual involved.

Not long after Touchstone went away, Salvatore Rodino then entered the meeting room, his intention to muscle a recommendation from the committee, one that was stated and not just understood, as he, too, realized that Lord was staying and Nesbitt wasn't.

"The taxpayers want a resolution on this matter and they want it without the dilly-dallying, Serena."

"They'll have to wait a while longer, Sal."

"We have to give them Nesbitt now. Otherwise, it'll look like we're defending his behavior." Rodino switched his attention to the two other members of the committee, assuming if he could move them, Cantor, too, would fold. "You all know that's true. We'll look like fools if we let this drag on." The serious bird-head darted at the committee's other woman.

"Have you talked with Orr?" asked the man, Cantor's usual ally.

"About what? He confides with me on all sorts of matters."

"You just like to think so," Serena Cantor said.

"Well, he won't favor dismissing Nesbitt before Christmas," the man said. "If he didn't tell you that, it's only because the thought has yet to cross his mind. But it will, Sal. Harold won't be wanting to fire anybody with the holidays so close."

"You should have thought of that yourself, Sal," Serena Cantor scolded him. "And even though you didn't, you might want to mention the idea to him anyway. You know. Score some points."

Rodino grunted. Everyone realized the chairman was terrible at taking jokes. "Okay, if we're intending to let Nesbitt stew for a time, then we do the same for Lord. We issue no statement at the next meeting that says the district intends to keep him on."

"And why do that?" Cantor challenged him. "Why play games, Sal? Touchstone realizes his claim against Lord isn't gathering support outside his church. And he'll concentrate to make sure the same doesn't happen to Mr. Nesbitt."

"I don't care. There's enough question marks around Lord I don't want him getting off this easy. And I don't want any of you sneaking behind my back to do otherwise!" He threw his head at the others. "Your word?"

Both nodded.

Serena Cantor was glad Rodino did not ask for her word. She had yet to speak face-to-face with Grayson Lord and it was her intention to definitely do so.

Lord received her call shortly after arriving home from school the following day. At his invitation she agreed to come over to his apartment the same evening.

When she pulled next to the curb outside the pharmacy, he was sprinkling flake food to his fish, but saw her through the windows of the cupola. He went to the door and opened it, even stepping outside the apartment to watch her mount the stairs without her aware he was standing above. She didn't just ascend them one after the other, but inspected the stairs themselves, the wooden newel post, the poor lighting overhead, and the walls on either side. She even paused once to turn around and stare at the entrance door below. Finally, she saw that she was being watched from the top of the stairwell.

She knew better than to bring up the Ostrander boy, but he figured that ugly rumor was the reason behind all her examination.

They exchanged greetings and a light handshake, and he showed her to his apartment.

"Should I leave the door open?" he asked, suddenly feeling awkward. She was an attractive woman, not much older than himself.

"Not unless you're expecting others," she answered.

"Then can I get you something? To drink?"

"Nothing at the moment. Where can we talk, Mr. Lord?"

He led the way into the farthest room and invited her to sit wherever she pleased. She chose the sofa next to the aquarium. He settled on the shelf inside the cupola.

"Are these where the books were taken from?" she inquired, indicating the bookcases flanking the fireplace.

"Third shelf down. The blue volume in the center and the one to its right were substituted."

Then she asked what he thought was a curious question.

"Have you attempted to read either of them?"

"You think there might be a message for me in one of their chapters?"

"Well, I don't know. But when morality is at the heart of the matter, it seems there's quite often some extra game that is going on."

"Not in this case. I did, in fact, give each a fair shake, but there's nothing exciting in either volume. Whoever they belong to must have felt the same. They were copyrighted ten years ago, but the pages hardly crack open. They've been collecting dust on someone's shelf. Now they'll collect it on mine. I can't stand to throw out books, no matter how terrible they are."

"Still no idea on who your intruder might have been?"

"Not a one, sorry to say. But I haven't given up."

Continuing to stare at the shelves, she bunched her lips as though to say it was a mystery that she, too, wanted very much to learn the answer to.

"I think you realize that I didn't come here this evening to discuss my daughter, Mr. Lord."

"It would be a waste of time," he replied, smiling. "Julie's a wonderful student. She owns a great perspective. You should be proud of her and I'm sure you are."

"Well, thank you. I appreciate that. Her father will, too. I came here to ask some questions which don't seem to be getting asked."

"Careful now. That's what started this whole thing. Well, not my part, but it's what started it with George. P.D., he said, never poses the tough questions, so George burdened himself with the task. But before either of us proceeds any further, I need to hear something out of you. I don't know that I'd lie to you, Mrs. Cantor, because I believe you're an ally. But I don't know that I wouldn't either. Some people have told me that George alone has something to worry about. If that's true, I'd prefer to hear it from a person with some authority."

"You understand, don't you, that Sal Rodino wouldn't approve of this," she said, leaning forward with her hands clasped together. "Offered the chance, he would use this against me whenever possible. So keep that in mind, please. Between the two of us, Mr. Lord, it appears matters with you will not be advancing any further, unless, of course, you were to again immerse yourself in hot water. But, officially, you won't hear of this for at least a month. Fair enough?"

He nodded, without expression.

"First question then...."

She began with the things she considered of lesser importance and worked her way upward to the most awkward of the questions. She started by asking his opinion on the many literary selections to which Touchstone was objecting and specifically if he thought the minister's reactions to "The Creation" were racist, as charged by Willis Ruther. Lord answered that it wouldn't surprise him if that were the case. His Catholic upbringing was telling him it was impossible, yet today there were no surprises. He felt sure there was a substantial number of ministers and church higher-ups from all over who accepted willingly the donations from people of other color and sexual orientation, while at the same time holding fast to their contemptible prejudices. Next, she asked about the two books that had been removed from his apartment. Was she correct thinking that he had received the books from another teacher as part of a Christmas gift exchange, and was that teacher Rudy Wallace? Lord answered truthfully in each instant.

"What do you honestly think of those books, Mr. Lord? Do you approve of them?"

What kind of a question was that, did he approve of them? Did he approve of movies he watched in which a dozen people were sensationally slaughtered?

"Well, do you?"

"No, I don't approve of them," he finally said, careful not to lose the controlled tone of his voice. "Look, before you got here, I didn't rush about stuffing dirty magazines under my mattress. That's not to say I don't look at a *Playboy* on occasion. I'm a few miles from over the hill. And believe it or not, I do read the interviews. But there's something more that was going on with those works when they were written, you have to remember that. Quite often, the young girls getting violated aren't much older than your daughter. So how could I approve of that? More than anything when I pick up those books, I find myself laughing. Laughing from the almost deferential nature of the writer pounding out 'We're gonna have sex, sex, sex, and more sex.' I mean the stuff that's out there today, the porn without the pictures, I've looked at some of it. It doesn't compare. There's something else, too. Search the shelves, Mrs. Cantor. You won't find any others."

"All that tells me is that you didn't join the book club." She waved a hand in the air immediately after uttering this to let him know it was only a joke. Just in case he was becoming uptight talking about the subject, and it seemed he was.

"June Ferris told me you're a very avid reader of almost any genre. Is there any writing that you can't stand to look at?"

"Student essays," he said, not entirely facetiously. "Not all of them, but certainly too many of them. Not much cogitation going on inside those adolescent heads, I'm afraid. Even less about the benefits of learning how to communicate your thoughts and feelings effectively.... You know what I'm saying, don't you? Despite the fact it's an important part of the job, sometime you need to take a time-out, go to the cabinet—that's under the kitchen sink in this place—and pour yourself a healthy belt or two."

He had made her laugh. Somehow she was identifying. Maybe she herself had taught school for a period. Or had substituted. He asked her again if she wanted anything to drink—coffee, tea, juice, he could mix her something, too—and to his relief, this time she accepted a cup of coffee. When he returned from the kitchen with it, he could see that, although still sitting, she was studying the framed photograph presented him by Janey.

"How old are you, Gray, if you don't mind my asking?"

"I'll be thirty shortly," he answered, aware that she had addressed him more familiarly.

"Any plans for you and Miss Renn to marry?"

"We've never talked about it. It hasn't been that long."

"But sometimes you just know that you've met the right one."

"Excuse me if I sound impertinent," he said. "But most of the students dating feel the same way—especially the girls—and you must know it isn't going to work out for most of them if they go through with it."

"I was fortunate. It has worked out for Don and me."

"Thank your lucky stars then."

"Oh, I often do.... Those students, do you do anything to discourage them?"

"Sure, I have my speech. I doubt it does any good. They're all well-intentioned, which is the sweet thing about it. They all expect to be married to the same person for their entire life, so that's where I start."

"What do you tell them?" she asked, stretching forward, but not seeming too eager to hear.

"I tell them that since they've all lived some sixteen, seventeen, eighteen years, they each know how long it took to get here, and that if they intend to stay married, they will have to put in that same amount of time again. And then again, all the while refraining from shaking their bawling baby to death so that they can stay out of prison. And God willing, yet again. And maybe even once more because the genetics were right from the beginning and some drunken idiot never crossed into their lane and they never ran up against any of the million losers who would put a bullet in their brain for the hell of it."

"And you doubt that has any effect on them?"

"Would it have worked on you?"

"It might have. Because I probably would have had a crush on you the same as my daughter.... Does it get to you? You sound as though it might. Touchstone warned me that you've been considering tendering your resignation anyway and by firing you, we'd be extending you a favor."

"When I leave, it'll be on my terms. Not on those of some self-appointed moralist."

"Well, I hope that won't be for a while, Gray. But if not, I want you to tell me now. What the Reverend was suggesting, he uttered after a rather sinister laugh."

Lord didn't immediately understand.

"If we formally recommend that you be retained and then you up and leave.... It's the proverbial egg on the face. I don't want it on mine."

"Long as I can get enough out of it, that won't happen. School is more than just about the kids. Too many people believe mistakenly that teachers get into teaching because they love working with children. I suppose that's generally true of the elementary faculty, but it isn't always the case with the secondary. Some of us became teachers because we love our subject and think it's extremely important that students gain an adequate understanding and appreciation. Some of us are just arrogant enough to think we're perfect for the job."

"Did you really say to that boy what he's claiming you said?"

If she thought she would be surprising him with the question, he disappointed her. Besides Nesbitt, Warren Hoverton had been the only one to ask, and Tilly had kept him from answering.

"I said it. He wasn't leaving when I asked, and there weren't.... Yes, I said it."

"All because he told you to—"

"—He prefaced it with a lot more. He as much said I was luring every little boy I could up to this apartment to do you know what. What's more, he said this in front of the entire class. At least what I said I whispered to him and him alone."

"But why do it at all? You had to understand it was completely out of line for any teacher to say that sort of thing and that it could lead to what it has."

He opened up his arms as if to plead. "Do you really think I have options, Mrs. Cantor? That any of us do beyond the magic that might exist in some of our personalities? The options, anything that could possibly work and maintain the line between an adolescent like Aftanas and an adult, they're long gone, sealed. And woe to anyone who suggests revisiting them! P.D. likes to furrow his brow and tell everyone on the outside that there are consequences and that the students know they will face those consequences if they break the rules. The kids laugh at this. When P.D. assigns a student to detention, he must also assign a teacher to be in the room with him so that the physical room itself is protected. I guess what I did, I did because I wanted Asa Aftanas to know that with me the line was still in existence and that I wasn't going to let him get away with showing me that kind of awful disrespect. And I can tell you that George Nesbitt holds identical feelings. But why are you asking now if nothing's to happen? Or was this right along a set-up which I've foolishly bought into?"

"It would have been a slick one, wouldn't it?" She smiled to erase his smallest doubt. "First, Gray, I was merely curious, nothing more. Second, because I chair the committee on personnel, I want to understand the issues which come before us better than anyone. It's the way I work. Simple as that."

She was being candid and at ease with him. He appreciated that. He got up and refilled her cup with coffee, although it wasn't in need, and they talked a while longer.

"Those options you mentioned," she said. "Are they the same ones that are deemed abusive in today's legalistic climate? Is that what you're getting at?"

"In their frenzy to safeguard children, they lumped them all together, put a circle around the entire package and a diagonal line through the center. No more paddling, no more standing a kid up against the wall, out with the ruler on the knuckles—"

"Lose the sarcasm, please."

"But look what else they threw in. I have Waring telling me to lower my voice when I'm attempting to discipline a student. Last month he pulled Walt McAllister off to the side and warned him not to get into the face of Dana Foss after the delinquent ripped off the doors in the boys' room. Jack Schenley was warned about becoming angry in front of the class. Bev Stiles tapped a kid on his head with the eraser on her pencil. Just a light, friendly tap-tap. The kid told his mother and she called Orr and he ordered Waring to talk with Bev. I just wonder if we aren't abusing them now in a silent fashion, one that makes a lot of the adults feel good. There's nothing been changed in Asa Aftanas. All of it is just being kept under wraps for the time being. And I think school should be about altering behavior in children that is dangerous and unacceptable. If Aftanas doesn't come at myself or at George, he'll eventually unleash it on someone else. It's all the result of doing away with *in loco parentis*, Mrs. Cantor. Remember that phrase? Teaching is now little more than high-grade baby-sitting and paper shuffling. Why, just this year, soon after the start, Orr insisted that I be on a committee, a paper committee is all it is, about discipline, and I told him my time would be better spent reading the two hundred-forty new books Mrs. DeRose ordered for the junior-high wing of the library, many of them Caldecotts and Newbery winners, some of them so beautifully bound that they're inviting to a kid just holding them in their hands. Wouldn't it be great, I said, if I could both recommend these books and discuss them with my students? 'I'd like you on the committee,' he said, and I could tell that he was thinking I wasn't serious about reading all those books. I mean, he really didn't think I was serious! We're supposed to get kids excited about reading. What better...."

"Mrs. Cantor, you take a book from these shelves and hand it to a kid, he'll at least look at it, thumb its pages, read the blurb on the back cover, maybe even start the first chapter. But before you present it to him, if you bend it back too far and break its spine and its pages are already threatening to fall out, that kid would rather toss the book in the wastebasket. That's what's happened to the teachers and what's happening to the kids."

That was it, he shut himself up. He'd most likely said too much already and he wasn't even sure if was making any sense. He looked back at her and she was staring at him, studying him, he thought, wondering probably if she was making the right decision in sticking up for him. Maybe he was jaded, burnt-out, and Touchstone was correct. Perhaps the district should do the man a favor and send him on to other pursuits. She broke her gaze, turned her head toward the windows where she noticed the darkness and, without a signal, rose at once.

"I promised Don I wouldn't be long."

She carried her cup into the kitchen and set it next to the sink. At the door she became suddenly buoyant again. "I suppose you're looking forward to your Christmas vacation?"

"It'll be welcomed, the time off."

"And does your family get together like mine? We'll have a house full. All ages."

"Sounds like the Cantors know how to enjoy the holidays."

She offered her hand. "Well, you try and do the same. Merry Christmas to you, Mr. Lord," she said, switching back to the professional address, "because I probably won't see you again before then."

"Merry Christmas to you and your family, Mrs. Cantor."

"Try not to ever say anything again like you said to the Aftanas boy, please."

***

Lord had been saving what he thought was a great in-class assignment for his seniors.

"Mr. Lord, can we have a party tomorrow?"

"No party, Tucker. You'll no doubt be having them in some of your other classes. Besides, we don't meet tomorrow because of the early dismissal."

"Then let's party today."

"I got something better I want you all to do."

Some of them openly groaned.

"Now pay attention. This is a fun assignment. One hundred years ago, a little girl in New York by the name of Virginia O'Hanlon wrote a letter to a newspaper called the *Sun*. In her letter, she asked if there was a Santa Claus. She said her father had told her that people could trust what they read in the *Sun* and that's why she was asking them. I'll show you the newspaper editor's response once you're finished with what I want you each to do. So listen up. I want you to think of a little boy or girl who trusts you. Perhaps it's one of your younger brothers or sisters, or maybe it's just a neighbor. It doesn't matter who, just so you feel they trust you. Now I want you to pretend they've asked you the same question Virginia O'Hanlon asked of the *Sun*, and I want you to answer. This isn't take-home. I want you to do it in class. Any questions?"

Some of them began laughing at the assignment and making light of it.

"You understand what I want, Tammy? Tucker, you clear? Bogardus, any questions? Kathy, Asa, Aaron, anything?"

"Mr. Lord, I don't know what to say. What's the point of this?"

"Ah, Tucker, say what's in your heart."

"He don't got one, Mr. Lord."

"But what's the point, Mr. Lord?"

"Yeah, what's the point?" echoed a few others.

Lord stared at them. He could sense his head shaking ever so slightly. No one was writing. They all were staring back, many with their mouths open.

"The point is this," he said, exasperated. "I'll learn which of you people will grow up to be the Nation's psychopaths of tomorrow. Now, please, get to work."

"I'm writing to my brother," spoke out Aaron Little. "You stupid kid, I'm gonna tell him, when did you ever see a person who could fit down a chimney. How 'bout you, Mr. Lord? You got a bro?"

Chapter 15

Yes, he had a bro.

Brother Bradford, the first of favorite names by Eileen Lord who had convinced herself that proper nomenclature for her three children would assure them success in life, was the eldest, some five years older than Grayson. He was married with a pair of sons and worked for a small company as a glazier, an almost predestined occupation as glass had fascinated him since he was a small boy. None of his co-workers called him Bradford. To them he was "Fordy Lordy," uttered sometimes with respect, other times out of fear. Bradford Lord was a strong, muscular river-rat (the much wider section of the Allegheny just before its confluence in Pittsburgh with two other major rivers) fond of the summer tan and disdainful of the perennial melanoma warnings, a weightlifter in his school days and military days, and he knew how to fight and was not afraid of becoming bruised and dirty. More than one of his fellow high school students had made the mistake of threatening Bradford with the directive, "Let's take it outside." Bradford then had no fear of consequences. Before teachers and others, he hit his enemies before the end punctuation.

And he was intelligent, too, though it wasn't clear that he realized this about himself because the subject of intelligence too frequently dominated his discourse, dominated by soon overtaking whatever topic had given rise to conversation. Bradford Lord would fall back in his chair and pontificate, turning from the issue to the quality of thought behind the opinions on the issue, and without fail he declared the opinions of most others to be "stooopid," spitting the word out as if it were coffee grounds, while implying peremptorily that his own analysis was thought-out and the correct position for all Americans.

His younger brother wasn't ashamed to say often that it was indeed a fresh approach and attempted to further the discussion, making it fuller, more inclusive, more detailed. But the honest gesture turned out always to be pointless. Grayson Lord long ago had learned that a comment from himself to Bradford, whether contrary or complimentary, was but an invitation for the older brother to set up his sibling and show that, despite being a college boy, he wasn't so smart.

SPINE

Although the Christmas recess for the Careytown district began at the close of school on the twenty-third, Lord did not depart immediately for his mother's home, a three-and-a-half hour drive, as he sometimes had. Nor did he leave on Christmas Eve as he usually had. Instead, he and Janey agreed to spend these hours together. Her college boyfriend had come through for them, and although she, like Gray, was driving to her family's house for the holidays, the full complement of her brothers and sisters would not be showing up until later on Christmas Day.

"So let's decorate your apartment," she had said with a big grin flooding her face.

Right off, Lord suggested buying a tree but she discouraged him, taking the position that it would be sinful to kill a tree for just one night. Instead, she purchased a couple of yards of quilted holiday material, from which she cut out and hemmed the outline of a pine tree. Together, they stretched it on the wall opposite the cupola. Beneath it they set their gifts, a single wrapped package for each they had bought earlier in the day after agreeing to separate for an hour at the nearest mall just over the New York-Pennsylvania border. Also, Lord set under the tree this year's faculty exchange gift. The one book had a red spine, the other a yellow.

Janey laughed as he neatly tucked the wrapping and ribbon around the books.

"You never did tell me who bought you those. Who drew your name? Was it Rudy again?"

"Take a guess. Someone you wouldn't expect."

"Corey Howser."

"Well, he fits the bill, I'll admit, but it wasn't him."

"Who then? Dorothea?"

"My chair."

"June Ferris? You're kidding."

"You know what else? I think she read them first. Pick one up. The pages aren't as flat as they should be for a new book. I think she read them, being careful not to crease or break the spine."

"So what if she read them?"

"So nothing. It's one more reason I appreciate June Ferris, is all."

He stood up and reached for her hand.

"Let's go pop the cork and have our toast," he said.

156

He led her from the big room, through the bedroom and into the kitchen, and removed a bottle of wine from the refrigerator. Without letting go of his hand, she fumbled her free one through a drawer containing the puller.

"You must be looking forward to seeing your sister again," she said as he worked the cork. "Will you invite her to visit on her spring break? I'd like to meet her."

"I would," he said, "but she won't come."

"Why's that?"

"Would you give up Florida and warm Gulf water for this? I do miss her because we were close growing up. But a Christmas visit, remember, also means a dose of my brother Brad. You want to meet him, instead?"

Dose. That's what it had come down to, the relationship he now had with his older brother.

"You don't get along?"

"He continues to think I was the one who called him stupid growing up. 'Dumb as a wet fly,' to be exact. Our father the great fisherman called him that and it was my mother who was always comparing him to me. I had nothing to do with it." He looked directly at her and his eyes narrowed. "Are you familiar with the 'Fucking Idiot' game? Brad plays it with me every time we get together."

She could see that he was suddenly agitated and more serious than a moment ago, and so she just shook her head.

"Here's an example," he said, placing the bottle on the counter so that he could free up his left hand. "How many coins do I have in my pocket?"

"I don't know, Gray."

"Come on, take a guess."

"All right then. Three."

"Zero, you fucking idiot!" he screamed, and he laughed right in her face. "Some game, huh? He plays it all the time with me. I'm sick of it and sick of him."

"Perhaps he won't be there."

"He'll be there," he assured her while retrieving the bottle of wine again. "He and Rita and their two children. Them I don't mind."

On Christmas morning, after he and Janey parted, he still felt no great hurry to journey to his mother's house. He had slid into his car, then reversed himself and went back inside the apartment where he brewed a pot of coffee that he poured into a thermos.

The roads were mostly empty, a steady snow was falling and sticking. He drove slowly, more slowly than normal for him, thinking frequently of Janey and their intimacies of the past night and sipping at the coffee from the thermos cup. The snow was falling evidently throughout the state, and at some of the higher elevations where it was collecting faster and where there was a view, he pulled over and got out for a time, wondering if she was doing the same. He continued to be amazed by how quiet and empty the highways were.

It was after two when he rolled to a stop in front of his mother's house whose exterior continued undecorated, unlike the distant past when he and Brad had helped their father to tack up the outside lights each year, running the wires and dozens of Rudolph bulbs along the gutters and down the spouts and around the porch railings. But without those lights, his mother thought the interior lighted wreaths she once placed in the windows appeared hopeless, and so they had been collecting dust in the attic year after year. She still kept a tree, although now it was a plastic one all silver and glitter and no bigger than a birdcage, and she stationed the dozens of holiday cards she received across one or two rooms. Some Lord could see through the windows. The hours she spent in the kitchen of course numbered fewer than when he and Brad and their younger sister were at home, and accordingly, so did the resulting fresh buns, cookies, and loaves of nutbread. Still, Lord appreciated that his mother every year continued to make some attempt to celebrate Christmas, though anymore she lived so alone.

Besides his brother's big sport utility, there was also a red station wagon and a rusted-out Chrysler, belonging to his mother's sisters and their husbands, that were crammed into the narrow driveway. He was glad he had dawdled on the trip down. He wouldn't have to endure Brad by himself, and his uncles were fun-loving pranksters.

He grabbed a couple of presents from the backseat, slid out of the car, scuttled up the edge of the driveway where the others had walked and packed the snow, and went up to the door. His brother's youngest boy, a brightly lit towhead, opened it.

"Hi, Uncle Gray! Merry Christmas."

"Merry Christmas, ace. Man, you look a whole lot different than you did last year. How much you grow?"

Others were entering the room and coming toward him.

"Here he is! Where the hell you been?" He recognized the deep, booming voice of his balding Uncle John.

"Here, take your present. Give this one to your brother. And do me a favor and retrieve the others in the car."

The uncle extended a hand. His wife came up behind him and Lord kissed her at the same time.

"Here's our teacher, Eileen! Now you can start to make merry."

Eileen Lord entered the room with the other sister and uncle behind. Bradford and his wife drifted into a corner. His own sister stood at the back, making a silly face in his direction.

"I thought you would have been home yesterday," Eileen Lord said to her younger son while glancing at his feet to determine if his shoes were clean. He kissed her on the lips while waving a hand behind his mother's back at the other aunt and uncle. "Why weren't you here yesterday? I had to go to church this morning with Brad and Rita. I like to go to Midnight Mass."

He wasn't sure he wanted to make it any of their business just yet, so he answered generically: "A friend and I wanted to spend Christmas Eve together."

Too generic, he realized at once. The old looks were immediate, stimulated responses expressing the terrible worry. His brother's was the worst, a combination of sucked cheek, faint nod, and shrunken eye. He'd always known his younger brother was a fag and now he was just about admitting the fact to the family. Bradford Lord glanced at his wife whose own look agreed with her husband's. Only his sister and mother had faith.

Eileen Lord said, "Does she have a name? And is she pretty?"

"Her name's Janey," he said, only to his mother, although the rest could hear. "I work with her, and she's very pretty."

The looks on the faces of the aunts and uncles flashed relief. Only Bradford's countenance remained suspicious.

Eileen Lord started pulling her son toward the kitchen and dining room.

"Dear daughter, welcome your brother and wish him a Merry Christmas."

"I'm just waiting for you all to finish, Mom."

Bradford and Rita ventured over next. Bradford offered a hand.

"Merry Christmas, brother. And thanks for the gifts you gave the boys. They weren't expecting anything from you, I know that."

Rita kissed her brother-in-law on the cheek. "Merry Christmas, Gray. I'm happy you made it. Your mother was looking forward to it."

Once they turned away, his sister moved in.

"You said the name was what?"

"Janey. Janey Renn."

Her face was mocked up to appear serious and her lips buttoned tight against each other.

"Remember the movie *Marathon Man*?"

"Remember it? It makes my teeth ache just to think of it."

"There was a character named Janey."

"That's right. She was—"

"She was a man!"-

"Sumbitch. Don't tell that to Brad or Rita, for godsakes."

"Not to worry," she said, and they hugged.

Queers, that was the worst topic to bring up for discussion with Brad and Rita. They hated queers, never allowing the group the descriptor of "gay." And it was never himself who introduced the subject, and quite a while before he had realized the reason why it was often brought up in the first place. From his responses, Brother Brad was hoping to determine, once and for all, if his little brother was one of that kind. The worst occasion had happened more than a year before when he had driven down for his mother's birthday and gone out to his brother's house the following evening. Bradford had developed more focus for the discussion. Queers in the school. Queers who were teachers. Or, as Lord had observed, queers *that* were teachers. Don't allow them any human identity.

"I ever catch one of those sick sonofabitches trying to do something to one of our boys, I'll kill the sonofabitch. He won't be luring any other youngsters to join him in his perversions, I can guarantee that."

Killing, too. Bradford often talked of killing something. He'd killed cats. The reason? To bring the rabbits back that used to inhabit his two acres. And he'd placed a bullet in each of his dogs after he judged them to be infirm and of no use to themselves. Lord sometimes thought that killing another human being was something his older brother felt missing from his life, and that he wouldn't be satisfied with himself until he accomplished the goal.

"Any queers teaching in your school? Or don't you know?"

There had been talk at the time that Rudy Wallace was maybe gay and the opinion still surfaced even now, mostly because of the recent divorce. But the consensus forming on the math teacher was that he was just a super jackoff, and Lord didn't think even that was close to accurate.

"I don't think so. But how can you tell anyway?"

"Well, you can't tell them all, but you can tell some. Especially those that sashay. The swisher sweets."

He wasn't fond of the sashayers either, he had to admit. Otherwise, he had no quarrel with gays. Usually, he opted out of the discussion and let his brother run out of self-prompted things to say. But on this occasion a neighbor was present with his wife, neither of whom he liked very much, and they held the same opinions as Brad and Rita, so that the subject wasn't going to be put to rest as easily as in the past. He listened politely for as long as he could. When he realized his head was shaking in an arc that grew wider and wider with every stupid comment from this man and Brad, he exploded.

"What is it with you people? Do you think that all gay men want to do with their lives is clamp onto a goddamn upright dick? That they pass each day searching industriously behind doors and in lockers, hoping to find a thousand erections so they might suck their way into oblivion or the goddamn here-fucking-after?" Tmesis. Always the proof to himself that he was really pissed. And when he was aware he had used it, for some unexplained reason he laughed inwardly. It was a kind of governor on his anger. It kept the lid on. His classes always laughed outwardly when he did it in front of them.

Rita looked away, offended by his language.

"Yeah, that's what I think," said the neighbor, inflating from the belief that his friend's educated brother had just unwittingly proved his point. "That's exactly what I think."

Lord considered informing the man that he was an asshole. He glanced over at Brad.

"Hey, don't look to me to stick up for you on this one."

"I got it," the man said, grinning now. He was probably ten, even fifteen years older than Brad and a lot of gray had already slipped among his hair and whiskers. "You think with these guys and gals that like their own, it's because of this genetics stuff. That it's natural. To be expected and accepted. Well, it ain't and we don't. That's nothing but a convenient excuse these queers are trying to get some mileage out of, now it that's all over the goddamn news everyday."

Actually, he personally thought it was more gravitation than anything, if it wasn't already in the genes. It wasn't hard to imagine a son to this man turning his head and marching the other direction. What better way to get back at the old macho bastard than to like your fellow boys—and mean it! And it was even easier to imagine a scenario for the women. Date a few or, god forbid, marry one like this jerkoff neighbor to his brother and you could easily start to feel it isn't worth it, no matter what the religion, no matter what the common thinking.

"You don't think it's a choice, do you?" the man said. He was continuing to grin at Lord, certain of his perspective.

"Apparently, you do."

"That's right, little Lord, I do. And so does your brother."

"In other words, these 'queers' as you like to call them, could have done the same as you. They could have chosen to take a woman?"

"That's right, they could have. But they didn't."

Lord chuckled to himself, two swift vibrating clucks that seemed to originate somewhere behind his nose, but some of the mockery escaped and both the neighbor and Brad took notice.

"What the hell," he said mostly to himself. He met the man's gaze. "So what you're telling me and the rest of us, including your wife, is that, being the contemplative person you obviously are, you thought long and hard yourself about becoming a queer, and it's probably only some heterosexual perk that put you over the top and convinced you to become what you are today. Is that it?"

The fucker, he could see, knew right away that he had been scored on, smashed in the face with nothing but words, unsure exactly how it had happened. Lord continued to meet the eyes of the man who was repeating some of the verbal uppercut silently to himself. Which was just as well, he thought. He wasn't looking to duke it out with anyone. He switched his attention back to his brother and Rita. "You'd all be better advised to worry more about the girls in school. Worry because their older male teachers might be trying to nail them. Take it from me, that happens more often than the other. But I got a feeling a young girl getting laid by her teacher wouldn't bother you."

"I don't know about that," Bradford said.

"But you wouldn't want to kill the sonovabitch, would you? You'd be more understanding about the matter."

It was no use. Like so many others, his brother could not recognize his own insecurity in his hatred of gays. But just mentioning the young girls as he had, brought to mind how enticing and threatening they could be. They certainly had been that for him, in the first few years especially. Then, just out of college, he was but four or five years older than many of the students he taught, and he suffered many erections in the late-night hours when he thought of the more beautiful girls. And he always knew, too, that he could have fallen in love with a special one, had she only given him a sign in return. To this day he still found her occasionally slipping into his thoughts.

There was no sit-down dinner because his mother had covered the table with food. Everyone filled a plate and went elsewhere in the house, though most went into the living room where the small tree was lit.

"Gray, you ever think about coming back around here to teach?"

"Uncle Phil is talking to you," said Eileen Lord.

"I'm sorry, what is it you wanted, Uncle Phil?"

"You ought to think about coming back here to teach. All the districts around here are expecting to have a ton of openings next year, according to the paper, and they pay teachers well. More than what you get up there in the boondocks, I'll lay wager. And your mother could use having you around. Brad's got his own family to take care of and he can't be running over here all the time. You should think about moving back."

"I already thought about it, Uncle Phil. Long time ago. It's too crowded around here anymore. Takes a half-hour it seems just to pull your car onto the main highway. Besides, I like it where I am. I like living in the mountains. And when I quit my present job, believe me it won't be because I'm looking to do the same thing somewhere else."

"What about your mother?"

"She's doing okay. I told her she ought to get herself a small job. Something maybe at Penney's or Sears."

"I worked enough in my life," Eileen Lord said. "I don't want to work no more."

"It's nothing to do with work, Mom. It'll keep you out among people. You're too cooped up here."

"I worked enough raising you and your brothers. You don't *know* how hard I worked."

Uncle John boomed out, "He'll be back down here looking for a job one of these days, once they fire his ass up there."

For a moment Lord feared that his uncle, by some incredible circumstance, had come to learn something about Touchstone's attempts to have him dismissed, but the familiarly devilish look soon formed on the bald man, so Lord played along.

"Why would they fire me, Uncle John?"

"Why would they fire you? They won't let you pinch those little girl titties forever and ever. You're going to have to get your own tittie to pinch."

"You're terrible," the man's wife said, punching him. "He's terrible."

Uncle John continued to laugh.

"They won't fire him, John," Bradford said. "They can't. He's one of those that got tenure. And when they get that, you can't get 'em out with a crowbar and dynamite."

"Gray's pinching titties," Uncle Phil said, "they'll fire him, no matter how much of that tenure he got."

"Now he's got you talking filthy," said the other aunt. "Thank you, John. Thank you very much. And it being Christmas!"

Uncle John did not respond. The old man's mind was stuck on titties.

Later, from under a kitchen cabinet, Bradford removed a bottle of whiskey that his mother had asked him to purchase for the occasion. He made highballs for the men.

Uncle Phil asked, "So what is it you teach anyway, Gray? Science?"

"He teaches English," Bradford answered, handing a highball to his brother.

"English? You mean those children in the mountains don't speak the same language as you and me?"

"Why the hell you teaching that stuff for anyway?" huffed Uncle John. "These kids today, they don't read. All they do is watch television. You ought to teach science, or something doing with computers."

"You need a major or minor in it to teach it."

"So get one!" Uncle John ordered him. "You're pissing away your time, not to mention taxpayer dollars, teaching what you are."

"It's not that easy," he said, holding back a grin.

Bradford said, "That science today, it's not all it's hyped up to be either."

Lord recognized instantly the tone in his brother's voice. "So what? You got something against science teachers?"

"Not just teachers," Bradford said. "The professors, too."

"What do you got against them?" Uncle Phil asked. "Christ, they took us to the moon."

"I'm glad you mentioned that, Uncle Phil. There's a good example of what I'm talking about."

"They did go to the moon, big brother. You're not about to tell us you think the same as Uncle Ted did, I hope. Uncle Ted was Dad's brother from St. Louis and he was convinced the moonwalk and the rest was done in a government studio."

"He wasn't the only American who thought that, you know."

"So what do you got against the goddamn scientists?" Uncle Phil repeated with greater earnestness.

"Let me tell you. For one, it was the engineers who took us to the moon."

"Wait a minute," Lord said. "The scientists—"

"I'm not saying the scientists didn't do a thing, only that the engineers did plenty and they don't get much credit."

"They're all one. It's a team."

The uncles were switching their eyes from one brother to the other. Bradford took a swallow of the whiskey highball.

"But here's where they screwed up and nobody seems to hold them accountable. How many times we land on the moon? Must have been five or six. They still don't know for a fact whether the moon will support life."

Lord laughed out loud, he couldn't help it. Bradford took notice and the cool, smug response told him his older brother had come up with something by which he was once again going to demonstrate how goddamn smart he was and how fucking stupid some other part of the world was. It was the scientists this time who were about to get the poker up the ass. Lord thought hard as to what his brother might be about to say, but came up empty.

He said what was expected.

"What do you mean, they don't know whether the moon will support life. They know, and it won't."

"They don't know that for a fact."

Uncle John said, "I thought they knew all that before they ever went to the moon. Christ, did I miss something?"

"They did," Lord said.

"Not for a fact."

"Well then, I don't know what the hell you mean by a 'fact.'"

"They didn't plant a tree or shrub while they were there," Bradford said. "I never heard of them doing that."

"It would die."

"Neither you nor they know that for a fact. They could have planted a seedling of some kind and threw some water on it. Maybe even some fertilizer."

"You think it might have evolved just like that?"

"If I were a scientist, I'd want to know for sure," Bradford said. "I don't have a goddamn degree or anything, but I'd sure enough have the common sense that if I set foot on the moon I'd plant a tree and learn firsthand whether it would support life."

Lord rattled the ice in his drink. Bradford, as always, became a blight on his spirits. He looked at his Uncle John, and it seemed to him that the old man didn't want to hear anymore about it either. It seemed to him the old man was once again dreaming of titties.

And so Lord, too, began dreaming of Janey's.

Chapter 16

"It stinks, Mr. Lord."

"Oh, you'll have to clean it up."

"I didn't mean that. It's just that you can still smell the fish, and it don't smell so good. Pee-yoo." Clipper pinched his nose.

The aquarium lay in the open trunk of the gold Toyota, and Clipper was running his other hand over its chrome-plated, hinged top.

"Mr. Lord?"

"Do you like it?"

"You bet. But Mr. Lord? How much do I have to ask my father for? I probably don't make enough with the paper."

"Are you sure your parents are okay with you having this? I never thought to ask."

"There's no problem with Dad. He likes fish. Mom, too. But if it's too much..."

"You and your father don't have to give me anything, Clipper. While at my mother's over the holidays, one of her friends stopped by, and to make it short, she has a son who's now in his first year of college. He left the tank behind. He told her just to get rid of it. I tried to give her something for it, but when I informed her that I wanted it for a student, she wouldn't take anything. You can't ask for a better deal than that. And everything works, even though it's old. The pump, the heater, the fluorescent bulb. But you will have to spend some time cleaning it, especially washing out the gravel. It's what smells."

"Wait'll Sy sees it after it's all set up and there's fish in it. I know he'll sit and stare."

"Sounds as though old Sy might have some feline in him."

"Huh?"

"Look, will your father or mother be home around six? I have to go back inside for a while. But once I'm finished, I'll deliver this to your house later this evening."

"They'll both be there."

"Then you better run along, else you'll miss your bus. I know where you live, Clipper."

SPINE

***

Snow was common to the region and most years it began in earnest during January. On the second Thursday of the month eleven inches covered the ground. In spite of that, the buses were running.

There was commotion exploding from inside Nesbitt's first period history class. Lord and Blake, standing nearby, stepped into the room, whose door was open wide.

"What's going on here?" Lord demanded. "What's all the ruckus?"

"Mr. Nesbitt's left!" a student shouted at him.

"What are you talking about?"

"He's gone, Lord. Gone for good."

"How do you know that?"

"He's not here, is he?" said another student.

"You all pipe down a little now and stop moving your desks around. Other classes are underway. Mr. Nesbitt's probably late because of all the snow."

"We're waiting on three buses," Blake explained to the rowdy group.

"Well, I say he's gone and I'll put up money."

"How much, Bogardus?" challenged Nesbitt. He squeezed between Lord and Blake and sailed his briefcase onto the desk before turning back to them. A few unmelted snowflakes remained in his hair.

"The drift against my garage must have been eight-feet high. That's where I've been. Haven't even had a cup of coffee this morning. Lucky I didn't suffer a heart attack shoveling that stuff." He then addressed his class, which had become muted. "Sorry to disappoint so many of you. How much were you willing to put up, Jesse?"

"I might have put up ten."

"Last of the big spenders is what you are."

Lord and Blake floated back out into the hall and Nesbitt followed.

"Well, tonight's the night. After tonight, they won't have George Nesbitt to kick around anymore."

"Oh hell, George, they still aren't ready to fire you. Correction, they're ready, but it won't happen tonight."

"Why's that? Christmas is over, Paul."

"Think about it. Semester exams are coming up. They get rid of you now, who can they hire that will test your classes with any degree of accuracy? It'll turn into a mess and the parents of your kids will be bitching their rear ends off to Orr and P.D. and all the rest."

"He's right," Lord said.

"You're giving Rodino and that crew a lot of credit, Paul."

"Sal Rodino's a hard-on. I learned that as a first-year teacher. I'm referring to Orr. He's not about to set himself up for a headache. It's next month's meeting they'll fire you, once you've corrected and recorded all the test grades of your students. That way, they can safely bring in somebody new."

"Oh Christ!" Nesbitt remarked. "Check who's coming."

Waring was striding down the hall in their direction.

"You know what he had the gall to do yesterday?" Lord said. "As he was passing by my room while I had the door open, he overheard me tell Aaron Little that his answer to a question I asked was wrong. He called me out and said. 'Never tell a child that he's wrong. Tell him he's not quite right, or that his answer is possible but not what you're looking for.'"

"That self-esteem stuff. Doesn't matter if they get out of here having learned anything! Just so long as they're confident and possess great self-esteem."

"Classes began several minutes ago, gentlemen. Mr. Blake, I believe your class is at the other end of the hall."

"Only two people have showed up."

"They still require teaching. So get up there. Your colleague's problems don't concern you."

It turned out Paul Blake was right about the school board. They did not vote to invalidate the contract of George Nesbitt and thereby terminate his employment with the Careytown School District during their January meeting. Touchstone attended as expected, and he pushed on it, but Rodino and the board made excuses, which they thought everyone believed, that would keep the history teacher around for first semester exams. But the following week, Paul Blake found himself laughing all the same. Lord might have found it funny as well, except that he realized he was now missing an important friend.

169

It was Waring who had walked into the faculty room during the second period to break the news.

"It's been snowing all night. How do you know he isn't just late again?" Lord asked.

"I wish that were the case too. But his wife called. She said he won't be back."

"He won't be back? What does that mean?" questioned Schenley.

"He's left, Jack. She said he packed his things last night and that was it. She has no idea where he'll go. I've already arranged for a substitute, but it won't be easy for her. His departure leaves his classes in chaos."

"I'm surprised you don't have that covered," remarked Beverly Stiles with the thinnest of grins.

Once the school day was finished, Lord drove over to the Nesbitt house, some four blocks away.

Stella opened the door to the front porch. She was a shapely woman with a bland but inviting face, and her flesh had stayed young and smooth. The back of her hair was worn in a twist which she had flung over a shoulder, giving her somewhat of an old-fashioned look, but one that Lord and others who knew her appreciated.

"Come in, Gray."

"Maybe this isn't a good time."

"I'm fine. Please. Come in."

He had been inside the house on several occasions and each time he couldn't help but notice a few special details, or their lack. For one, there were no photographs displayed anywhere of her husband, and there was none of her parents and in-laws. In fact, he counted only three pictures on the first floor. Two were of the boy who appeared to have inherited all the genes of his mother and none of his father, but neither color print was very large or appropriately framed. The last was a small photo of herself hugging her son, attached magnetically to the refrigerator door that was in plain view from the hallway. The photo had been there a long time, evidenced by specks of dry food and liquid on its surface. The other details had to do with the unfinished look of the interior windows. Though she and George had lived in the house for many years, the majority of them lacked any blind or curtain.

"Let's go into the kitchen, Gray. I was fixing myself something to eat. Would you care for anything?"

170

"No thanks. Where's—"

"He has a cub scout meeting. He doesn't know that his father has left us."

"Are you certain of that, Stella?"

"Am I certain?" She said it with mild surprise. "Why aren't you, Gray? Is there anybody in town who didn't think he would do this eventually? This thing with this Aftanas boy, George was setting himself up to do what he's wanted for a long time. He just needed an excuse and the threat of being fired was it. He took all his clothes, Gray, and a lot of other things, including the new car. He left me with the van. He even took his gun, the handgun with the big bullets, which was probably the first thing he packed. I can see that surprises you too."

"What surprises me is that you're taking this so in stride."

"Why? I've known George for a long time. His leaving isn't any surprise, and I doubt it's a surprise to you. He must have talked with you, Gray. I know he considered you his closest friend."

"Yes, he once told me he could leave the two of you, but I didn't believe him."

"Well, you should have."

"Do you think he'll be back after a while?"

She sweetened at him. It was the kind of sweet that said she accepted his innocent ignorance.

"He won't be back, Gray. Someday, someone will find him dead. He will have used that gun to kill himself. You know the gun I'm talking about, don't you? He generally had it with him wherever he went. He didn't advertise it, but he never made much of an effort to conceal it either, except when he carried it to school. Were you aware he took it to school with him?"

"He didn't have it at school every day, Stella. I don't believe that."

"No, it wasn't like his briefcase. But he did carry it there more than once."

"When he had his club and they had their fund-raiser with the pizzas, he had it with him, that I know. But he had a reason. He was the one collecting the money for deposit, and at the time there were some students who had dropped out who were making threats at him every time they saw him in town."

"There's nothing in the house to drink, except for beer. He left a few, and now that I think of it, he probably left them for you, expecting you would come by. Maybe he thought your girlfriend would be with you too. Would you like one? Or can I make you a coffee? It would have to be instant and black. I'm out of milk."

"I'll pass on both, thanks."

"How involved are you, Gray, with Janey Renn?"

"We're not engaged if that's what you mean. But neither of us are seeing anyone else."

"Well, good luck. I hope it works out for you. You've been single too long and you'll make a good husband for whoever is lucky enough to get you. George wasn't a bad husband. It's just that he's always had this dark side to him and he wouldn't see anyone about it. He covered it all the time when he was among you, Jack Schenley, and those others, so maybe you never saw it. But he didn't always cover it at home, and I couldn't expect him too. Something like that has to have a stage that it can act on occasionally."

"He once told me that the two of you were compatible. That compatibility was your saving grace."

"Yes. That was an important revelation for us. God knows, we didn't seem to have much in common. And we both questioned how we ever came to be a married couple. It may have been what allowed him to leave finally. And it may be the same thing which is allowing me to take his departure 'in stride,' as you say."

"I'm sorry."

"Don't be. You're right. I'll miss him, don't think I won't. It's only that I expected this."

"Well, I don't mean to stay. I just wanted to hear it from you directly instead of P.D. And I wanted to check if you were all right."

"That's sweet of you."

"If I can help in any way, Stella."

"Thank you."

"And if you're wrong and he does call..."

"Believe me, I'll be sure to let you know. And don't stay away either, Gray. I've always thought we were friends, too."

***

The following morning, before he was out of bed, the phone warbled. It was

Clipper Ostrander's father.

"I hope I didn't wake you, Mr. Lord."

"No, I was just getting up to get ready for school. Is something wrong?"

"There is, and it's the reason I'm calling. Sy is missing and Clipper is pretty upset."

"Oh man, I can imagine. What happened?"

"I don't really know. He just wandered off."

"How old is Sy?"

"He's two years older than Clipper. He was my dog originally. I believe I know what you're thinking and I'm inclined to think the same thing. And even if he didn't go off to die, his vision is poor and his ol' beagle sniffer ain't nothing close to what it used to be. I doubt he could find his way back home if he's gotten himself lost. Especially with this snow on the ground."

"Have you had an opportunity to search for him?"

"We went out last night while there was light, and I've already been looking this morning. But no luck."

"So what can I do?"

"I don't think there's much that can be done, Mr. Lord. I called because I'm sending Clipper to school today. He doesn't want to go, but I promised him I'll keep looking for Sy. Maybe you can talk to him, though, and help him see the reality here. He thinks a great deal of you."

"I'll do what I can, Mr. Ostrander."

He first saw Clipper in the halls from a distance and the boy clearly was worried. When Clipper got to his class, he wasn't showing any sign of improvement and Lord wasn't expecting him to. It would have been better for him to have stayed at home. The boy was worried sick for his old dog and attending school and going through the motions was not about to change that. Besides, Clipper differed from the rest. When he missed work, he made it up and he did so in double-time. An endangered species.

The buzzer sounded.

"Stay a minute, Clipper. What do you have next?"

"Study hall in the cafeteria with Mr. Wallace."

"I'll write you a late pass. I want to talk with you."

There was a study hall in his own room that was filling with upperclassmen.

He really didn't know what to say to the boy, so he said what he believed to be the truth.

"I spoke with your dad this morning, Clipper. He told me about Sy being missing."

"Dad thinks he might be dead."

"Your father might be right. Sy is a very old dog and he might have gone off to find his place to die. You have to accept that possibility."

"That ain't right what you're telling him, Mr. Lord."

"Tucker, if you're in this study hall, just find your seat and open a book."

"But it ain't right what you're saying."

"Tucker, quit hassling Mr. Lord and this young man. Take your seat."

"Just a sec, Ms. Stiles. It ain't right, Mr. Lord."

"Do you even know what this is about, Tucker?" Lord asked through a tone of mounting exasperation.

"Sure. He lost his dog, right? Sy's hobbled over to my place a thousand times to see our beagle Tippy and take a dump. Clipper don't live but maybe a half mile from us. And you're telling him he oughta give up on 'im because the animal's probably dead, and that's wrong of you to say that. How can you give up on something when you don't know what happened?"

"What?"

"How can you give up on something when you don't what happened? He don't even know for sure what direction that dog went."

"Take a seat, Tucker.... All I'm saying, Clipper, is that you have to be prepared for the possibility that you might never see Sy again."

He was disappointed with his performance, and when he entered the faculty room a short time later, he was inclined to blame his inadequacy on Tucker.

"What's wrong?" Blake inquired, observing that his colleague was upset.

"Aw, that damn Tucker can never keep his nose out of other people's business. I was trying to talk with one of my seventh-graders who lost his dog yesterday. The dog's really old and chances are it keeled over in the woods. I was just trying to get him to realize that he might not see the animal again, but damn Tucker kept butting in, saying 'You shouldn't give up on something if you're never sure what happened.'"

"Do you know much about Tucker?" June Ferris asked.

"You mean besides the fact that he can sometimes be a royal pain in the tush?"

"Gray, when he was only eight year's old, Rodney Tucker's mother disappeared. At that time the family was still living in Prosserville. The police never found her. They never found her car. And there's never been evidence to suggest anything of any kind, and there isn't to this day. No one knows whether she's alive or dead."

"Wouldn't she have called at some point if she were alive?"

"One likes to think so. Except she rued the day she ever married and she never took any interest in her son. So where do you go with that? I don't know. But it might help you to understand where Rodney Tucker is coming from."

It did help. He wasn't sure how, but it did help because Rodney Tucker was one of those students who were in the middle. He wasn't a Dana Foss or Asa Aftanas, and he wasn't on the other end, one of the small studious band of kids that you needn't worry much about because you knew they were all but certain to make out in this world. Rodney Tucker, more often than not, appeared to be out of it. But for the fact he was a likable jackoff, Lord could have written him off, a sorry action no teacher would admit openly to, but it happened all the same. Except there were times when Tucker caused him to shake his head, as was the case one day when the teenager had skipped into his room and started telling him how Mr. Nesbitt had said some idiot people were going around claiming the "holy ghost" never happened and that all those millions of Jews and others being killed was a lie. It wasn't close to "holocaust" and Lord couldn't believe that any senior could be that stupid, and so he was shaking his head, until he remembered the one reason he kept trying to teach his subject to the boy. Tucker, like himself, enjoyed playing with words. He once told Lord that he liked using "self-defecating" humor. Seldom did he read the novels and the essays that his teacher assigned, but if there was a poem with a rhyme scheme, that was different. The boy would raise his hand. He would attempt even to answer questions.

Chapter 17

The thirty-five year-old woman who signed on as a full-time substitute and agreed to teach world civilization and U.S. history for the remainder of the school year was hoping for such a chance ever since moving to the region three years earlier with her husband, who had accepted a supervisory position at the bottle factory. She learned immediately that Nesbitt had left her without first-semester exams and was also advised by Waring to administer essay tests in place to the students. It would require more work on her part to grade, but it seemed the sensible thing to do. However, during her first day of substitution, she discovered the exams and answer keys in a locked locker at the back of the classroom. None of the long tests were stapled or even collated, but Nesbitt had marked each clearly with a header, indicating the class for which it was intended.

No one heard from George Nesbitt in the weeks and months that followed. More than once Lord telephoned Stella, not trusting that she would reciprocate and do the same if George renewed contact with his family. And in March on a Sunday, with Janey alongside, he had stopped by the house. The boy, the elementary teachers were saying in a worried voice, continued to bring to school a picture of his father and was showing it to classmates again and again. He showed it to Lord and Janey, too. It was a rather old photo of George. In it, the male history teacher appeared much thinner. The face, too, was very different. It seemed friendlier.

Lord missed his friend a great deal and much more than expected. He still could not believe that the father had just up and left his family. His son, particularly. Janey offered the only explanation that seemed plausible.

"I have married friends older than myself who decided against having children for that very reason. Women and men both."

"You mean they all were teachers."

"Some still are. But it's taken their toll. They no longer feel that need to have a child of their own. Perhaps George began to see his boy more as a student and less as a son."

At other times Lord found himself wondering if George Nesbitt was really a brick or two short of a load, which was what Stella had been suggesting. This, too, he could not accept. George had been different, certainly unconventional, and to some intractable. But he'd not once struck

177

Lord as being off-center, and they had drunk many a beer together. It was hard to accept that he might never again see his friend. And impossible for him to believe that the outspoken man could ever commit suicide.

Sy, too, continued missing, but almost everyone who knew of the fat waddling dog felt certain it had wandered off and died. Clipper, in the end, handled his loss with a maturity that was greater than his years. One day a week, Lord directed all his classes to write about whatever they wished. These were not papers that he ever graded meticulously because he encouraged his students relentlessly to play with the language. Have some fun with writing, he told them. Don't think it always has to be a chore. He graded the papers only on the effort they reflected. If there was little or none, the student received an F. But if there was honest effort, then the grade was always an A, regardless of the composition's quality. F or A, there was nothing in between. For many weeks after Sy's disappearance, the boy wrote about his dog. After a time, Lord realized that Clipper was committing his memories of the beagle to paper to insure they were recorded with proper details and to help keep them forever in his mind. Lord learned important facts from the canine's history. For one, he learned Sy was not a he, even though Clipper and his father both had used the pronoun. From a litter of six, the father had meant to take home the only male, but had carried away mistakenly a female with very similar markings. Because he had named the pup immediately, he stayed with it. Clipper noted in his paper that Sy seemed "never to care that everyone thought he was a boy when he was really a girl." Lord learned, too, the reason for the dog's peculiar walk. Overweight even at birth, Sy started to waddle only after the rear legs had been ensnared by barbed wire. From then on the short legs remained at a funny angle, and Sy didn't amble a foot forward without also displacing a few inches of air on either side. But the condition hadn't weakened the animal's devotion to those who cared and provided love. Sy went everywhere Clipper went, until just a year ago. Then, Clipper started to carry his pal up steps. Lord recalled the steps leading to the Ostrander front door. Fifty, if there was one. Their steepness reminiscent of pictures of early Andean civilizations. But Clipper wrote that Sy had scrambled up and down them every time he himself had done the same. Clipper was an active, growing boy, and he had heart. Sy must have had plenty of heart, too, Lord realized. And more than himself, he confessed, reminded of a certain momentary misgiving out of the past—what a relief when the old man had descended the steps to retrieve the heavy aquarium from the trunk of the Toyota.

As the sun increased its appearances and the weather warmed, the value of much school activity became questionable. Too many, students and teachers alike, waited anxiously for the end of the term, a fact that seemed not to enter the minds of those who favored increasing its length. People like Sal Rodino who, as Nesbitt had pointed out, still believed he was unable to read a book because they all had too many pages and he didn't have the time. People who would have been astounded to learn that one might read two and three books in a single day. Lengthening the school year meant only that what the kids weren't doing now in 180 days, they wouldn't do in 200. It was a joke to many, including Lord.

The seniors proved to be the worst for doing nothing during this time. They realized they weren't just being released for summer; they were getting out once and for all. And most felt ready for it. Lord took their inactivity in stride, as did most of his colleagues who had been in the classroom for more than a few years—although it had been easier to do so in the past. In the past, when the temperatures had risen, he would escort them out to the Leathers amphitheater next to the tennis courts to act out dramatic scenes on its moderately sized stage. The sun, the fresh air, and the flowery fragrances wafting out of nearby fields complemented a welcomed break. But then P.D. issued his "white paper." Among other things, it said classes could no longer be conducted out-of-doors, except where certain subjects dictated otherwise, such as physical education. "I think we all know and agree," Waring wrote, "that if any learning is to take place, it will occur inside these walls, not outside them."

Paul Blake found the seniors' slowdown impossible to simply swallow. In just two years he had established a reputation for himself as a teacher who never let up on his students. Walt McAllister, everyone agreed, had said it best after listening to some of his industrial arts students complain with unintended gratitude toward the science teacher. The difference between Paul and the rest of them, he said, was the difference between most people who merely pounded nails and others who drove them.

"It's probably because I was schooled in New York, the reason I keep pushing them," said Blake.

They had crowded into Lord's homeroom—Janey, Blake, and Rudy Wallace—waiting for time to tick off the clock.

"Why is that a reason?" Janey Renn asked.

"This room of yours is a dump, Gray," said Rudy Wallace, idling about the back of the classroom like a bored puppy. "Orr's liable to make you install a plastic liner before too long. Man-o-chevitz, look at the insides of these desks!" He reached a hand into one near the back. "They require state regency exams, Janey. Paul and his buddies had to work to— Jesus Christ!" His hand withdrew gingerly from the desk and held up a crumpled and badly soiled item of underclothing.

"What is it?"

"Forget it, Paul. They're too big for you."

Blake stuck a finger in his mouth.

"Tell me that isn't what I think it is," Lord remarked, sitting behind his desk with his legs stretched out.

"BVDs. Size thirty-four." Wallace wrinkled his nose and stuffed the underwear back inside the desk.

"Thanks a lot," Lord said.

"Hell, I didn't put it there."

"That's what the kids always say."

"Let's get back to those regency exams," Janey said, straightening the photos of famous authors tacked onto a display board. Merely one year and already nothing seemed to faze her. Not even dirty underwear stuffed in a desk!

"They're not as great as Rudy thinks," Blake said. "Yes, we worked right up to the end, and that's why I do it now. It's habit, that's all. But my teachers taught only for the tests. The last few weeks of every year we even did the regents from the past. I can't say I blame them. Under the circumstances I would have done the same. But in my opinion, it sucked, being taught to an exam. We rarely discussed anything. Sometimes, when I pass by your classes, Gray, I can't help but stop and eavesdrop. You get those kids involved in some interesting discussions."

"So why don't you do the same?"

"Well, I might if I didn't have Kathy Raye to contend with. Our personalities clash."

Wallace was continuing to mosey about at the back of the room, now opening and closing his colleague's unlocked storage lockers. He laughed at Blake's excuse. "Too smart for you, is she, Paul?"

"Too much a pain in the ass," Blake responded, glancing and wincing at the room's open door. "Is she really going to be this year's valedictorian? I like to think those who study hard and read constantly are somewhat appreciative of us. That they understand what we're all trying to do. Not Kathy Raye. She thinks we're the enemy!"

"There isn't anyone who can catch her at this late hour. You know what she once asked me? She asked if my name was really 'Rude' rather than Rudy."

"What made her ask that, I wonder?"

"Sorry, Janey. I don't always qualify as the jerk some think I am. On this one, I didn't say a thing to invite such a question. That's, really, why I agree with Paul. The young lady's a pain. Who's working with her on her speech, Gray? You or Ferris?"

Lord shrugged.

"It wouldn't surprise me if she avoids working with either of you."

"Any of you been blessed with meeting her parents?" Blake asked.

"Interesting thing about them," Lord said, "is that they're not a great deal older than she is. I doubt either one is beyond the mid-thirties."

"Well, then you know that she's no different, other than being a lot smarter."

"Enough of Kathy Raye," Wallace said. "Enough of this discussion, too! Let's get our tired carcasses the zip out of here and go have a beer somewhere. I could use one." He immediately started moving to the front of the room as encouragement to the others.

"We can't leave yet," Blake said, checking the clock.

"The hell with P.D. It's only a couple of minutes. Isn't this supposed to be a profession?"

"I'm up for it," Lord said, rising from his chair.

"What about you, Janey?"

"I can't, Rudy. Too many end-of-year projects coming in."

"In that case, we'll think of you if Gray'll let us. Come on. Let's go. And anywhere but Tilly's."

"What's wrong with Tilly's?"

"Nothing, except I'm running short this month. I can't afford to buy the entire bar a drink, and I invariably lose when he pulls out the cards."

They settled on the Goldenrod located five miles out of town along a curved section of the main highway reaching toward the New York border. A bar that illustrated a contradiction, it offered fights every night of the week and dancing on the weekend to reputable bands. The building stretched across several lots and was spacious inside as well. The bar itself could seat thirty patrons, always a mix of education, incomes, and political views. The food continued to be its biggest draw as it was home cooking at its best, and a newcomer might have expected the same of the drinks. But this wasn't the case, especially with the draft beer. The Goldenrod remained the only bar in the region that had not subscribed to the equipment cleaning services of a local man, and the rubber tubing connecting the compressed air tanks and the kegs continued to taint the beer, although some customers weren't sure it was the tubing alone. A three-pound coffee can sat on the drain grate underneath the tap to collect the afterdroppings. When it was full, the bartender would retrieve the can, disappear momentarily through a pair of swinging doors, then reappear with the can once again empty. This action might not have aroused suspicions except for the fact there were sink-drains out front.

Lord and Wallace, in separate cars, coasted into the gravel parking lot together.

"Why in the fuck did we come here?" Wallace said when they stepped out of their vehicles and stared at the building's ugly plywood facade. "What a dump! And I'm not even hungry!"

Lord was thinking the identical thing as they entered. The inside of the building was depressing in a worrisome way. He pointed to an area of the room that was mostly empty of customers and they took their seats at the bar.

Paul Blake joined them a half-hour later, and the barroom filled over the next two hours as people got off work. The three teachers continued to drink and alternate in their now frequent urination. At seven, they decided they had had enough and rose to leave. But Corey Howser and his friend came through the doors and stopped them.

"No you don't. You're not leaving yet. I want to talk with you boys."

"What about?" Lord asked.

"Sit down." Howser signaled to the bartender for a round and put a hand against Wallace's chest, pushing him back onto his stool. "I said I want to talk, Rudy."

"Why is it I always think you're an asshole, Corey my boy."

"Maybe it's you who's the asshole," answered Deke.

"Who the fuck are you, *anyway*?" Wallace said. "I've often wondered that."

"Somebody who'll kick your ass if you're not careful."

"So what is it, Howser?" Lord said.

"Heard from Nesbitt?"

"No."

"Aw, come on now. You must have."

"He said he didn't hear," Wallace said.

"You gotta big mouth, teacher!"

Wallace turned to look over his shoulder to find the new speaker, a man in his late twenties with dark swirling hair and tight facial flesh. "Now who the fuck is that? Who the fuck are you?"

"Somebody else who'll kick you're fucking teacher's ass."

"All right, Lyle. Leave. You're finished."

"You really cuttin' me off?"

"You're done," the bartender said. "I warned you when you came in."

"You ain't fuckin' cuttin' me off. 'Cause I ain't fuckin' drunk."

"You're getting no more here. You get out now, else I'll call the police."

"You're gonna call the goddamn police on me?"

"I'll call the police."

"Why's it matter to you if I heard from Nesbitt?"

"I might be interested in his place. I mean, seeing that he was talking through his ass when he said he was planning on sticking around and changing things to his liking."

The phys-ed teacher couldn't resist flashing a grin of self-satisfaction.

Lord refused to recognize it. "His wife's continuing to live there and I don't think she has any immediate plans for moving."

"I'm talking about the place in the woods, numbnuts. His camp. It's pretty goddamn nice from what I've seen from the road. She won't be using it."

"Well I haven't heard from him."

"You're sure."

"Fuck you."

"Isn't he a little old for you?" Deke said, smirking.

"He obviously isn't for you," Wallace said without looking at the man.

A patron came rushing into the bar. "Roddy, you got trouble in your parking lot. Some guy's out there with a hammer and he's already smashed the headlights on your Ford."

"That no-good sonovabitch!" cursed the bartender.

He dropped his rag, swung from behind the bar, and immediately ran out of the building.

"He would have done better to call the cops," said Paul Blake.

"He won't never call the cops," Howser said. "The man's a criminal himself. He doesn't want to get mixed up with the police."

Within seconds, the bartender re-entered the bar, teetering toward them. He was drenched with blood.

"Jesus Christ!" Wallace said, big-eyed.

He and Lord rushed from their stools to the injured man, who was already shaking uncontrollably, and pushed him into a booth.

"He hit me with a hammer."

"Someone call an ambulance!" Wallace shouted. "Call the police too!"

"No," the bartender objected, stammering. "No police. I'll be all right."

"Call 'em!" Wallace repeated his orders.

"No police."

Lord left to get a towel from behind the bar and returned quickly. He dabbed some of the blood from the bartender's face who continued to shake.

"He may already be going into shock," he said.

"Will one of you assholes please call the goddamn police and ambulance?"

Howser and his friend had drifted over. They were still clutching their beers.

"Anything we can do?"

"Make the calls," Lord said.

"He said he don't want 'em."

"Get out of my way," Wallace said. "I'll make the calls myself."

"Why you gonna do that when he don't want it? He must got his reasons."

"You think I'm doing it for him, Corey? I'm doing it for myself. I'm doing it because, unlike you, I value my life. I mean I *really* value it. And I don't aim to walk out in that parking lot and have that sonovabitch stick that claw hammer in my skull. Now get the fuck out of my way if you're not going to make the call!"

Chapter 18

They arrived in Careytown right at three. They had planned to allot him a few minutes to change his duds and do whatever else he did after returning from school. However, he hadn't appeared. They waited in the car parked along the curb beneath the orange whatever-the-hell you call that thing until four-thirty, but still he hadn't shown. Where the fuck was he? the driver wondered, irritated. *What do you mean, where is he? You know all too well where he is!* The aunt was the first to grow hungry and his wife suggested a place that she had noticed sitting back and away that looked rather quaint, so he started the car and they drove the short distance to Tilly's Bar. But now they were back, waiting again, and the gun was finally loaded. Although he had been the only one to hear, because it was he who left the room and went up to the tiny bar for drinks, he had managed to whisper the news to his wife.

"Maybe he leaves his apartment unlocked," Rita said. "We might be waiting out here for nothing. Did you try the knob, honey?"

"Why didn't you call?" Eileen Lord asked. "I thought sure you or Rita would have called him first. What if he's not in town? What if he went somewhere for the weekend with his girl?"

"I doubt that," Brad said, glancing at his wife.

"Well, what are we planning to do, nephew?" the aunt asked. "My veins are strangling me."

"He'll be along. Don't worry."

"Walk up and see if his door is unlocked, Brad. You never know in these small towns. Take the beer with you and set it by his door."

Bradford Lord surrendered to his wife and got out of the car. He stood on the sidewalk a moment, gazing up at the bright orange cupola, before he unlocked the trunk and removed a case of beer. The others in the car were watching him, and so no one saw Lord as he turned at the light. A minute or two later, he shuffled up from his parking space behind the building and heard someone say, "There he is."

He spun about to look in the direction he had heard the voice and there was his mother's older sister smiling and waving furiously at him through a car window. He saw his mother and she was waving too. The three women got out of the car as quickly as possible, as each felt cramped from sitting all day.

"What are you doing here?" he said.

"Brad just went up to your apartment to see if it was open," Rita said.

Lord elevated his head to peer into the car.

"We left the boys with Aunt Carrie."

"So what are you all doing here? Are you on your way to somewhere?"

"We came to see you, my son. Aren't you surprised?"

Eileen Lord put her arms around him and kissed him. His aunt did the same.

Lord smiled awkwardly, wondering what this was all about.

"Okay, we might as well go upstairs as stand here on the corner."

He opened the door leading to the second-floor apartments. Brad was about to start down the staircase when he saw the others ascending.

"So he finally showed. Where the hell you been?"

"What are you doing here?" Lord again asked, pausing on the stairs with the others bunching behind.

"We came to visit you, little brother."

"Hell, I've been in Careytown since I got out of college," he said curtly, and resumed the climb.

Brad curled an arm around his brother's shoulders when Lord made the landing.

"This looks like it might be a neat little pad."

"What's this?"

"I brought you a case of beer."

Lord unlocked the door and entered. Brad grabbed up the case and followed with the women behind him. He set it on the kitchen counter, tore open a side, and began removing cans to the refrigerator.

Lord took hold of one of the cans.

"You haven't given up on the suds, have you? It's good beer. Pabst makes it. The big breweries are feeling threatened by the micros, so some of them are putting out new labels to give the impression that you're buying a micro. You remember Dugby's Distributors, don't you? They moved to a bigger location, ordered a truckload, and put it all on sale. I picked up six. Rita said to bring one up for you."

"You should have called before coming."

"Well, I figured I would. But when I didn't, suddenly it was too late. We only decided on coming yesterday, Gray. Mom said she never saw this apartment and.... How long you been here?"

"Three years."

"—And she wants to meet this Janey you talked about at Christmas."

Eileen Lord revealed a trace of hope in her face to say this was true, but not enough to convince Lord that it was her idea.

"So call her up. Invite her over."

"Yes," Rita said. "We all want to meet her. You spoke so well of her last Christmas."

"You know she's in her twenties."

"Of course. She wouldn't be allowed to teach if she wasn't," Brad said, chuckling.

"And so I did tell you she had a job."

"What are you getting at?"

"Are you hungry?" He directed the question to his aunt and mother. "I can put something together. Or we can go out."

"We ate," the aunt said. "Though it was nothing to speak of."

"Where'd you go?"

"A tiny place called Tilly's."

Lord chuckled. "Tilly doesn't serve much food. A hamburger and that's about it."

"That's what we had," said his aunt. "At least it was something."

"Well, make yourself comfortable. But let me ask you a couple of other questions. How long are you planning to stay? And where? You're welcome to bed down here, but I only got my bed and the couch."

"You sleep where you always sleep," Eileen Lord said. "You need your rest. We'll get a motel. There must be something around here."

"There's a few, either direction. What about my first question? This isn't to be a fish-and-visitors thing, I hope."

Rita shrunk her brow, befuddled by the fish and visitors connection.

"We thought we'd stay overnight and leave tomorrow afternoon. Maybe you could show us around during the day. Maybe you and Janey both."

"Brad, don't you get it? You're not the only one that works."

"Hell, can't you just take the day off?"

"But I'm not sick."

"Hey, don't pull that bullshit on me, little brother. You teachers are privileged with what are called Personal Days, which you still get paid for. And you can take them any time you want."

"Not without prior approval, and after a written request. Look, do whatever. I'm going to change. There's munchies under the counter. There's soda and juice in the fridge. There's even a couple of cold Rolling Rocks on the door."

He turned his back to them and headed for the bedroom.

"Gray, what's that on the back of your sleeve? It looks like blood."

"Syl's right," Rita said. "Are you bleeding?"

He stopped and tugged the sleeve to the front where he could see three stains, two of them smeared.

"I was out with some friends for a few beers, and—"

"Did someone attack you?" his mother asked, shocked.

"Not me, Mom. The bartender. Some unruly hit him in the head with a hammer out in the parking lot."

"Why? Was he gay, too?"

Lord swung about and stared at his brother in the silence that followed.

"'Too'? What do you mean 'too'?" Brad had already lowered his gaze to the floor and was compressing his lips against each other. "Look at you. You're not even claiming that isn't what you intended."

"It isn't what I meant to say."

"Somehow, as hard as it is for me to believe, that's why you're up here, isn't it? You've had a bug up your ass forever about this. And when I mentioned Janey over the holidays, you thought I was playing some stupid game with you and you wondered if she really does exist."

"Does she?" Rita asked.

"Piss on you, sister-in-law."

"Now you watch your mouth, little brother."

"What are you two getting into an argument about?" Eileen Lord said. "We don't have to stay here, Brad. There's motels."

"You overheard something, too, didn't you? When you were at Tilly's."

"Sometimes, where's there smoke, there's fire. I think I will have a Rock."

Bradford moved to the refrigerator and opened its door. Lord reached out and slammed it shut.

"You made the smoke. You always made the smoke. Why the hell am I being so nice about this, goddammit! Get out of here. Get out of my home, now. I want you out."

Brad laughed. "You're kidding. You're actually throwing me out of your apartment?"

"You and Rita. Out! Mom and Aunt Syl can stay. You can pick them up tomorrow. This is where I live and I'll be damned if I'll feel like shit in my own apartment because of you."

Once they left—Rita in a huff, Brad smiling and shaking his head in a save-face fashion—Lord made a decision to inform Waring that he would be taking the morning off. P.D. normally asked no questions, and he was one to understand how any person on the spur of the moment might require the morning or afternoon off. So long as it didn't become a habit.

"See, there was no reason for the two of you to be fighting. He went to get a room for him and Rita after all."

"It wasn't about a room, Mom. Do you know what the fight was about, Aunt Syl?"

"I try not to listen when anyone in the family starts shouting."

"Look, don't either one of you worry about it. You both can share my bed for tonight. I'll sleep on the couch. I've made arrangements to take the morning off. So tomorrow, we'll get up early, I'll show you around the region, some of the sights like the Austin Dam, and we can have either a late breakfast or early lunch. It's been a while since you were up this way, Mom. And Aunt Syl, I don't think—"

"—I've never been here, Gray. I've tried to convince John that we should visit you. Get Carrie and Phil to come along too. But he always said, wait till you were married."

"Are we going to meet this Janey or not, Gray? We want to meet her."

"And you will in time, Mom, if it works out."

"You mean it's not working out?"

"Our relationship is just fine. Someday, we'll drive down and surprise you, and I'll introduce her to everyone."

"Well, you better," his aunt said.

"Yes, you better," Eileen Lord said.

SPINE

When morning dawned, he did as planned. And when his mother and Aunt Syl asked why Brad and Rita weren't with them, he lied. He told them that Brad had wanted to drive around and look at hunting camps for sale.

Chapter 19

Both the fib and the tour gave him an idea once the weekend arrived.

"Hello?"

"It's me."

"Gray, what time is it?"

"It's early. I thought you might be heading somewhere this morning. I didn't want to take a chance."

"I was intending to clean the place, that's all. But apparently you have something else in mind."

"What a keen intellect, and at such an early hour. Remember what I said about the day I spent with my aunt and mother?"

"You said you had a fun time showing them around."

"That's right. But I'll have an even better time showing you around. You haven't been over too many of the county's roads, have you?"

"Very few."

"So let's pack a lunch and spend the day cruising them."

"All right if I have a cup of coffee first?"

"Brew enough for us both. I'll bring my thermos. And don't worry about the lunch. I went shopping and the cupboards and fridge are full."

They drove to some of the same places he had shown his mother and aunt, including his personal favorite, the Austin Dam. The great slabs of broken concrete remained where they had been pushed by the megatons of water that continued rushing down to destroy the town, a community that had rebuilt and now claimed itself to be "the town that wouldn't die." It was easy to see the history, for the valley was narrow and the town wasn't too far below the dam. There had been minutes only and all the men and women heroes had acted without much forethought because they had to. Those who died had probably acted the same.

By noon, the thermos was empty and they had eaten most of their lunch. Lord reached into the back seat and retrieved a topographical map detailing their part of the county.

"Can you read these?" he asked. She didn't answer for a couple of seconds and he glanced over. "Well, some women can't."

"Some men can't either. What do you want me to find?"

"Look for Crossfork Road. And then decide what's the easiest route to get there."

"What's the name of the road we're on?"

"This is Hribar Hollow we're on now. It's somewhere there in the bottom right of the quadrangle."

She leaned over and methodically studied the map, her eyes scanning the various text left to right, top to bottom.

"Here it is, Crossfork Road. And we should be able to get there without much trouble." She raised the map so he might better see where she was tracing her finger. He slowed to avoid driving onto the low shoulder.

"Good. I just hope none of the roads are too badly rutted or washed out after some of those rains last week."

"What's on Crossfork Road?" she asked.

"George Nesbitt's camp is a few miles off it."

"And you have a key. Ahhh, I should have suspected." She grinned from under a bowed head.

He returned the look. "Too bad I don't, huh...? Sorry, I just have an urge to see it again. I got to thinking about it when I told my mother that my brother was checking out hunting camps. And the day before, Howser was pumping me about its status. He said he's interested in buying it. It's a wonderful place. It was a good time a number of us had there every year when George put on his picnic."

"Turn here," she directed him. "Then make another left, which should be a ways."

They finally came onto the road that led to Nesbitt's hideaway camp almost an hour later. The distance hadn't been far, but the dirt and gravel roads wound severely in every direction and the recent rains had left their imprint. The county crew had blocked the entrance to one of Janey's selected roads, but Lord dared to drive around the wooden barrier.

"I've never approached it from this end, so keep an eye out." He described the camp so she would know what to look for, and she spotted it immediately as they descended off the mountain.

He swung his car into the lane leading to the cabin and braked at once. Deep gullies sliced the length of the entrance, exposing several huge rocks.

He went easy with the car, not wanting to lose a muffler. The rain had washed much of the gravel to the bottom.

They got out, and he took her hand in his at the front of the car.

"Doesn't look like anyone's been around for a while," he said, surveying the camp and its surroundings.

"Were you thinking that George might have been living out here for a time?"

"The thought had crossed my mind. But the place isn't really set up for a winter-long residence."

They proceeded across the grass and stepped onto the porch to peer through the cabin's windows. Janey tried the door. She heard him laughing to himself.

"What is it?"

He pointed to the inside. "I see an empty beer can on the counter. It brings to mind something from our get-together last September. After the others had left, George showed me this big hole in the ground where he stashed his beer. I can't remember how many cases were down there, but, jeez, Janey, there were plenty. And all of them were these off-brands that I never heard of. I wonder if, before he left, he stopped to retrieve them. Of course, he might have been coming out here right-along throughout the fall so that there wasn't anything to retrieve. George liked his liquid grain, you know."

"You want to take a look?"

He pivoted around and gazed out, away from the building. "Other than the general direction, I'm not sure where I'd begin. It was dark when he showed it to me and we had only a flashlight. The grass was trimmed up, too. I think he said it was about two hundred yards or so from the cabin. Forget it. It's not important."

"The ground is rather wet, too. We should have worn boots."

"But isn't this a beautiful place?"

"Oh, it's delightful. I could live here."

They remained at the hideaway for another twenty minutes, stepping around to the back of the cabin, and then drifting down to the stream where springtime vegetation was punching through the earth. He showed her where they released their arrows and shot off their guns, emphasizing the echoing, booming resonance that shook the air between the mountain out front and the one behind. He even mentioned hearing the coyotes.

"So what becomes of it now?" she asked him as they headed up the lane, back toward the car.

"I confess I don't know anything at all about how this kind of thing is handled. I suppose he might start a divorce from wherever he is. Or maybe she can do the same. All I really know is that Stella is predicting he'll someday shoot himself. Of course, if that happens, then this is hers to do with as she wishes."

"Do you think he'll shoot himself, Gray?"

"She told me he had a side no one ever saw. But I still don't believe George would do himself in. I'm not persuaded that she knew him any better than I did."

On their return to Careytown, they encountered another barrier and one that was impossible to drive around, as part of the road had collapsed. They followed the detour. About a mile into the road he sounded the horn at a boy pedaling a bike. The boy waved.

"Who's that?"

"My paperboy, Clipper Ostrander."

"He lives out here?"

"I'll point out his house when we pass it. He's really a remarkable kid. Delivers to about a hundred and fifty customers. Most of them are in town, but he has a dozen or so on these backroads. I suppose his father must help him at times because the route must cover four, five miles. Now this house we're coming up on to our right is the home of Rodney Tucker. Also a remarkable kid, but in an entirely different way. I'm sure you've heard me mention Tucker."

She nodded, staring at the house as they passed it.

Then, a quarter-mile further:

"And there's this gem of a family." He slowed the car considerably as they approached a gray house set back a distance from the road. Six weathered-gray outbuildings of various sizes surrounded it.

"Who lives there?"

"The notorious Aftanas clan." She glanced over, smiling, as he had uttered the words in a deadly voice. "I'll be relieved when the boy graduates and is out of my hair."

"And that must be Clipper's house I can see in the distance. I remember you telling me about the steps."

"They're something, aren't they?" he said as they drove past the house.

196

SPINE

"They're something, all right," said Janey, awestruck. "How does anyone in that family do that day-in and day-out?"

Chapter 20

"Hey, Mr. Lord. I saw you drive by my house on Saturday. You and Miss Renn. I waved but you didn't see me."

"No, I didn't see you, Tucker. If I had, I would have returned the wave."

"I was in our garage trying to fix a tire on an old motorcycle my uncle gave me."

"Can I ask you a question?"

"Will I know the answer?"

"I sincerely hope so. Tomorrow are your finals and except for a few hours on Wednesday, your last day of twelve years of school."

"I didn't hear a question, Mr. Lord."

"Why are you doodling, Tucker? Why aren't you putting this study hall to good use and studying for those finals?"

"Am I flunking English?"

"You don't even know?"

"Ah, I'm passing everything. And Ms. Stiles, she don't care if we fool around in this last study hall. Where is Ms. Stiles, anyway? She's better looking than you."

Truthfully, he didn't care either. He'd likely done the same when he was a senior, anxious to exit for good. He smiled at Rodney Tucker, even squeezed the boy's shoulder, and peered over it to take a closer look at the doodle.

"If I'm not mistaken, you were sketching the very same thing when I had you during junior high, Tucker."

"I like drawing cars."

"But why not sketch something newer? That's a fairly old machine you got there."

"It's the only car he ever draws," remarked a student two seats to their left. "That's what his mother drove, Mr. Lord, when she ran away."

"How do you know she ran away?" Tucker confronted the student, an extremely overweight sophomore with scraggly locks dripping down his forehead, who reminded Lord of a Nero played by some actor named Charles Laughton, one of those minor details that had settled in his mind for life. "You don't know anything," Tucker said to the fat boy. "So shut up about my mother!"

Bev Stiles came striding in and Lord was relieved.

"Thanks, Gray. This isn't a study hall you can leave unsupervised for a minute, and I had to get these tests run off."

"No problem."

"By the way, June is looking for you. The last time I saw her she was in her room."

The Chair of the Careytown English Department was correcting papers. Lord found the quiet of her empty classroom at the end of the hall inviting.

"Searching for me?"

"Yes, I was, Gray. Would you work with Kathy Raye on her valedictory address? She wouldn't come out and say it, but I got the strongest of feelings that any help from me would be rejected."

"What makes you think she'll accept mine?"

"You had her in class this year. She's likely to feel more at ease working on it with you. I told her to stop by your room."

He waited the rest of the day for the Raye girl to come see him, but she never showed. The following morning he sought her out in Schenley's homeroom and took her aside.

"She didn't *order* me to see you!"

"Be that as it may, Kathy, one of us needs to have a look at the speech you intend to deliver."

"Why? It's my speech. I should be allowed to say what I want."

"I won't be telling you what to say. I'll act much as an editor acts."

"I don't need an editor. You said yourself I'm a very good writer and I have the grades to prove it. I also won an essay contest, remember?"

"You're a good writer, all right. But don't confuse that with being a mature writer. You won't want to stand in front of your classmates and an auditorium full of people two weeks from now, and say something inadvertently that will embarrass you, do you? That's how I'll help. I'll try to make sure that doesn't happen. And when it's over and everyone says what an absolutely dynamic speech it was, you'll get all the credit. And that's the way it should be."

She stared at him with hardened eyes. The young woman was a thinker and he could almost hear the wheels up top turning slowly and deliberately. *What makes you think you're some kind of spectacular writer? You're a goddamn English teacher. Most of your students could have cared less about what they wrote for you.*

"I won't be able to meet with you before the end of the day," she said.

"You can't possibly have an exam every period, Kathy. What about meeting during a study hall?"

"I plan on using them to prepare."

"Right up to the last minute?... Then you're the exception. Very well. I'll wait for you in my room at the end of the day."

To his surprise she had the valedictory address fully composed when she arrived, although it wasn't representative of her best work. It appeared she had made little effort to correct and edit things herself. He worked on it with her for forty-five minutes, advising her to change a word here, a phrase there; encouraging her to re-order a couple of items. The speech contained the basics of most valedictories. The mention of hallowed halls. The reminder that commencement meant beginning, not end. The phony, self-congratulating group pat on the back, a presumption that every student had been sweating his and her butt off for the past four years. The talk of grit and determination to pursue the individual dreams in the years ahead. The other reminder not to forget in the future who they were and what they had become. If he hadn't heard it before, he might have found it inspiring. He supposed some of the more sentimental students would. And the parents would be hearing what they wanted.

He sent her off with an itemized list of additional considerations and recommendations but told her to come back with any incorporated changes before the underclassmen were let out one week later. But when she hadn't shown by the following Tuesday, he realized she would not be returning for his approval. She was a tough one, determined to have it all her way. Too believing in the contemporary promotions that you could! Well, maybe she was one of those who would. Who was he to say that her stinking attitude would come around to bite her head off? Nowadays, that no longer was a feel-good rule-of-thumb for the victims of such attitudes. She'd likely make the perfect speech on commencement day. So what the fuck did she need him for?

It was the first week of June, and the following Thursday Lord sat alone in his classroom with his door open, finalizing grades and talking to himself. The entire school sang with quiet.

"There. That's it. They can go down later. Now what's next?"

At the back of the room, on the floor, stretched a skyline of books. He withdrew a form from the center drawer of his desk, and from his seat, tried to inventory the columns of various workbooks, novels, and anthologies. He lost count too easily, got up, and went to the back where he immersed himself in the skyline and its numbers.

"Hey, Mr. Lord. Whattaya doin'? Puttin' books away?"

He recognized the voice without turning, though he did.

"Now what are you people doing here? You couldn't wait to get out, and already you're back."

Tucker grinned and shrugged.

Bogardus said, "We still haven't graduated. Not 'til Saturday."

And Tammy Riznick informed him, "I told Ms. Stiles I'd help her put away her books and papers."

"You people are just a wee bit pitiful, I hope you know."

"Mind if I come in, Mr. Lord?"

"No. Come on in."

"I'm going to find Ms. Stiles."

"What about you, Jesse? You coming in?"

"I don't think so, Mr. Lord. You're probably setting us up for one of your stupid jokes. Besides, I came here for a good reason. Coach Howser has a jersey of mine that I want."

"Mr. Lord?"

"Who is it now?... Ah, Mr. Vittitow. Yes, what can I do for you?"

The chief of the custodial staff widened his eyes to their fullest and pointed at the desks in the room.

Lord shamefully understood at once. "Ah, shit. Shit, shit, shit."

"Mr. Lord. Remember, I haven't graduated yet."

"That's right. Damn. Damn, damn, damn."

Mr. Vittitow stood at the door, laughing. "You don't have to put the stuff in the can. Just dump it onto the floor and we'll get it all with the broom. Maybe that feller with you will lend you a hand. He looks like a pretty good guy."

Lord had risen to his feet when Tucker appeared. But now he bent over and peered into the twenty-eight student desks that filled his room. Each was stuffed full with garbage.

202

"When do you people do this?" he asked. "Get the can."

"He said—"

"—I heard what he said. We'll do what I was supposed to do. Get the can."

Tucker hurried to the front of the room and grabbed the waste can next to Lord's desk.

"I'll flip you," Lord said, holding a quarter in the air.

"What are we flipping for?"

"To see which of us sticks his hand in and pulls out whatever's inside, be it dead or alive."

Tucker smiled as Lord tossed the coin in the air.

"Heads."

"This must be your lucky day, boy. You move and hold the can. I'll do the wading."

They started at the back of the row nearest the door and worked to the front, then emptied the second row front to back. At each desk Lord plunged his arm into the dark shelf beneath the scarred wooden surface and shoveled the olio of debris into the wastebasket that Tucker was guiding. Some papers and other items missed the can and Tucker bent over to retrieve them. The desks seemed to contain a little of everything, but unlike a general store, all of it was worthless. Gum wrappers. Severely chewed pens and pencils stuck with chewing gum and hair. Crumpled dittoed worksheets. Postage-size crib sheets. Personal notes. Uneaten chunks of candy bars growing frizzy white mold. Ice cream wrappers and crushed milk cartons. Lost paperbacks. A golf ball. Pizza and corn and beans and french fries. A Bic lighter and empty packs of Camels and Luckies and Marlboros. Skoal cans. Stiff, wadded Kleenex. Q-tips and bobby pins and combs and brushes. Cheap barrettes and bandage strips dotted with dried blood and lint.

They started up the third row, arrived at its middle desk.

"I wonder what diamonds we'll find in his," Lord said, sarcastically.

Tucker was already laughing.

Lord reached his arm deep into the desk, bowed it, and swept everything out before it. Two of the cans dropped into the green wastebasket. Two others bounced off its rim, clinked to the floor, and went rolling.

Tucker's friendly laughter was now audible.

"Remember that joke I was telling you that day in the woods during turkey season, Mr. Lord, when my cousin was with me? Remember it was about..."

Lord stood up and stared at the cans rolling down the aisle.

"You ever hear of that beer, Mr. Lord? I never have."

He reached down slowly into the wastebasket and pulled out one of the empty cans of Jacob Best.

"I myself only saw him drink one of them."

"I'll take care of the rest, Tucker. You can go."

"Oh, I don't mind helping."

"No. Go. I got some things I have to take care of. I'll see you at graduation. Don't forget to wash behind your ears."

"Behind my ears...." Tucker laughed again, not understanding if there was really meaning to his teacher's comment. But Lord would not look his way anymore—in fact, the teacher appeared worried—and slowly he left the room, not sure of what had just happened.

Lord then completed the quickest end-of-year book inventory ever, delivered his grades, gradebook, and keys to the front office, then went to find Janey.

"How close are you?"

"I'm there. Is something wrong?"

"I want to run out to George's camp again."

"Why are you driving out to Nesbitt's camp?" Wallace asked from the doorway, his briefcase in hand.

"You come along too, Rudy."

"Something happening?"

"Ever hear of the beer brand Jacob Best?"

"Don't think so."

"I'll explain on the way."

***

The camp appeared the same as when he and Janey had left it. Wallace mounted the porch, cupped his hands, and peered through a window.

"There's one of those cans on the counter," he said.

"You didn't think this hole in the ground would be easy to locate," said Janey.

"We have to find it. Listen. There was a long wooden ladder for climbing in and out. He dragged it into the brush where it couldn't be seen. The two of you search for it. I'll look for the hole."

"Just what are you hoping to discover, Gray?"

"What I'm hoping to find, Rudy, is George's stash of beer. It's what I'm not hoping to find that I'm afraid of."

They uncovered the ladder first, but it had been broken in two. Lord ordered them to drag it over anyway as he kept on searching. He was on his knees now, certain that the deep concrete hole in the earth was nearby.

Suddenly, the soil under him gave way with more spongy flexibility than the ground he had previously crawled over. He scrambled to the side and felt beneath the sod for the door.

"This is it!" he shouted. "I've found it."

Wallace and Janey hurried over to join him as he pulled up on the rotted door and removed it.

Filtered sunlight flooded the dark hole. Fresh air mixed with the incarcerated smell of death. The body rested at the bottom against the side in an almost upright position. It had been dead a long time.

"Can either of you tell what it is?"

"Well, it isn't George, thank god," Wallace said. "How much beer did he have stored in this box?"

"It was a lot, that's all I remember. But maybe he drank and pissed it away before he left. Or maybe he took what was remaining with him. It would be just like him. Or maybe Asa Aftanas did steal the entire supply. In any case, he didn't put George down here, which was my biggest fear."

"What do you want to do?"

"See what that is. Give me the longest piece of the ladder. I might still be able to climb in and out of here with some help from you."

He lay down and extended the broken piece of ladder as far as he could toward the bottom of the hole before dropping it. Then, he swung around and extended his legs. Wallace gripped him tightly at the wrists.

"Okay, my shoes are touching a rung."

Wallace released him and he descended the ladder the rest of the way into the hole.

"My God!" they heard him say a few seconds later. "It's Sy. Clipper's beagle."

"What! Are you sure?" asked Janey.

"He's well decomposed, but some of his fur remains. I'm certain it's Sy."

He looked up. Janey and Wallace met his gaze.

"How do you—"

"Asa, Rudy. Last summer, he pitched the dog into the river just for the hell of it."

Janey switched her attention to the other half of the ladder lying on the ground. Her smooth unblemished face grew taut and thoughtful.

"What is it?" Lord asked.

"Why destroy the ladder, Gray?"

"I don't get you."

"Why destroy it? Why bust it up? To show a dead animal that you mean business?"

Lord let it sink in, her hypothesis that the ladder may have been broken right before the eyes of someone cast into the hole. After a while, he began a close inspection of the concrete walls, using both his eyes and fingertips.

"It was just a thought," Janey said.

Wallace hadn't understood. "What are you looking for, buddy?"

"I'm trying to determine if there's any possible way for someone to climb out of here without a ladder."

"Man, I don't see how!"

"I don't either. But there's a few scratches that could have been made by a human hand."

"They could be Asa's," Janey said. "That, or perhaps the dog scraped his nails as he was falling." She was now eager to discount the other possibility, which she had made more possible through reason alone.

Lord wanted to discount it, too.

"Give me a hand," he said. "I'm coming up."

"What about Sy, Gray? Clipper will appreciate it if you take him out of the hole and bury him. If you'll wait, I'll find something to slide his remains on."

"All right. And a shovel, too."

While they waited on Janey, Lord ran his hands again over the scratches on the wall.

"Gray, goddamn Michael Jordan couldn't leap out of this pit," Wallace remarked.

They buried the beagle behind the cabin next to a spreading patch of Dame's Rocket. Worried what Clipper's father might do to Asa Aftanas if he found out about Sy, Lord advised Janey and Rudy not to say anything to Mr. Ostrander and his son until more was learned.

Chapter 21

The widest of the weathered outbuildings rested the deepest on the lot and doubled as a garage and workshed. Weeds grew tall at the sides and corners, a few in white and yellow bloom. A haze of dirt replaced the transparency of its tiny windows. Heat vapor, distorting the air, could be seen rising like a curtain of clarity from the metal roof. A pole some fifty feet away supported an electric wire running to the building from the house.

"Come nightfall, you pull one of them outside. I'm fed up that I can't move around. Wasn't made for three cars, and I gotta be able to work."

"We sure as hell can't move the new one out."

"But we can either of the others."

"How do you figure? We pull this one out and he sees it, he'll know it. We pull out the other one, I guarantee he'll be interested and will come snoopin' around. Won't matter that I told him to stay the fuck out of my space. I told you, he came over here twice when you and Tessie weren't home. Thought we might become friends 'cause we're neighbors. He almost went snoopin' in the garage. I still think we ought to hang a lock on it."

"Fine! You put a lock on it. And every time I want to get in, you make sure you're there to open it. And when I want to leave, you make sure you're on hand to lock up too."

"Well, I ain't ever been makin' this up about him. He's fucking crazed! Drew that picture of the car every chance he got."

The old man pointed to the almost junk of a car on the right, the same year and model as the one to its left that, despite its age, was in excellent shape. "Has to be this one then. If you really think he sees this he'll come asking questions, take a sledge to it. Got all I need off it. Why not get Lyle to help ya?"

The old man's humor. No one had seen or heard from Lyle since he tried to install a hammer into the skull of the bartender at the Goldenrod. The police were continuing to search for him.

"Take a sledge to it. Then drift it around back in the thick weeds. Throw some shit on it. Maybe put an old tarp on top, but not those blue ones that attract. There's a couple of black ones from Tess's uncle in one of the sheds out front. Couple of weeks, it'll look like it's been there forever." He moved away, the matter of no further concern to him even though he was an extremely careful man, and stepped closer to the new car on the left. He ran a hand over its paint, tracing a contour. "This a fine vehicle you got hold of, you know. We'd never be able to afford something like this."

"Thirty Gs. That's what they start at."

"Fuckin' teachers. You gonna be able to wait like your old man before you drive it?"

"I'll wait."

"You sure you got my patience? I'm talking eight, nine, even ten years, you don't want to get collared and end up in prison. Time goes on, you remember to check the ads and junkyards for one just like it."

"You sound like you're still considering driving her car. I told you, you better take it somewhere and sell it."

"Won't get nothing for it no matter how good it looks. No matter how low its mileage. It's an old car."

"Well, don't drive it around here, I'm warning you. Soon as he sees it, he'll know it belonged to his mother."

"Dint you say he's a senior?"

"Yeah, but he ain't going off to college or no army. He'll be around."

What they had in common. Neither liked being told anything.

"Okay, you warned me. Now let me tell you something. Don't go taking that revolver off this property."

"Why you worrying about that?"

"We don't know he had that gun registered or not. But if he did and you fuck up and some cop wants to see it, then we're all in big trouble. You play with it here, nowhere else. You want to carry one, you carry the one you always carried."

The old man started to walk off and he watched him go.

"You coming to graduation?" he called after.

"What's that?"

"Graduation. You comin'?"

"When is it?"

"Saturday."

"You want me there?"

"Hell, I don't want to be there myself."

"Well, Tessie appreciates you stuck it out. She could never get Lyle to go back. She'll be there. But if you don't care whether I show or not, then I won't."

The sky was free of all cloud and the day was heating up rapidly. After his father disappeared into the house, Asa Aftanas stepped over to his car, the Camaro, a flat brown rust-bucket with loose linkages and a hundred thousand miles on it. He opened it and reached under the seat for the revolver. It was a helluva gun. Weighty. And the walnut grips were nicely shaped.

He had driven the car home under the cover of darkness and squeezed it in the garage beside the other two. In the morning he went back out, cleared away the snow that had accumulated at the shed's side door, and began rummaging through the suitcases in the trunk. The gun had lain under a layer of socks and underwear, along with two boxes of ammunition.

Since doing the deed, more than once he had felt the strange urge to travel back out to the remote camp and peek under the cover. He couldn't help wondering which of them died first. The old hound, probably, as it seemed ready to die anyway. He wondered, too, if either, in the end, had licked the concrete walls in an effort to get water. And had they given a go at each other once they realized their fates were sealed? Throwing the dog in, that was just some crazy idea that hit him after he had spotted the animal on his return. An idea tied to a book that put a dog and a weasel inside a darkened barrel. What was the name of that book Lord had said they might want to read for extra credit? It had something to do with killing stinking pigs. He hid the luxury vehicle, jumped into his own clunker that Lyle had driven, and drove back up the road alone to find the beagle.

The fucker still thought, being a teacher, he was something special.

"You're doing the right thing, Asa. You came back. You're conscience is working. That's a sign of a man's humanity."

"Shut the fuck up, Nesbitt."

"Then why did you return? What are you planning to do?"

"What! Now you think I'm figuring to shoot you? I brought you some company, that's all."

He stepped back from the car and brought the revolver quickly to the level of his eye, sighting it on a baby rabbit munching on the distant grass. He turned it on its side as they sometimes did in the movies. Suddenly, the gun swung down between his legs, and he began laughing loudly.

The dumb fuck must have figured we evened the score when we busted his headlight.

He stood up straight and, while holding the gun, cupped both hands around his mouth. "He said 'big' mistake, fucker!" he shouted into the air. He held the revolver to the side, away from him, and looked at it. Then, he placed it back under the seat, still laughing.

As evening approached, bearing the old man's morning decree in mind, he prepared to move the parts vehicle that had provided a new identification to the Tucker car. He grabbed a couple of cold beers from the kitchen fridge and tramped out to the garage. The old man had located the sledge hammer and thrown it atop the hood of the car where his son couldn't miss seeing it.

The windows were first. Despite the restraining space, he sailed the sledge freely into the laminated windshield, producing a hole no bigger than the hammer's head. Most of the glass, although now broken into hundreds of diamond-like pieces, remained connected yet within the frame. Finishing with the windows, he smashed the heavy sledge into the hood, then into the trunk. He climbed onto the car and, looking like some crazy monkey, wreaked havoc on the roof. The side panels were impossible—no room to swing. Maybe a few hits outside, it wouldn't take much. There were already a thousand dings in the body, anyway—the reason why the old man had got the car for nothing in the first place. "Tow it out of here, mister, the title's yours. You'll be raising property values."

The side door to the workshed opened and the woman stepped in.

"I could hear you working hard out here. I brung you a beer."

"You drink it, Tess. I brought my own."

He reached for one of the cans he earlier had set on a workbench and popped the tab. She did the same with no reluctance.

"Somethin's bothering me, Asa."

"You let things bother you."

The old man had said to tell her. "Only no details for her neither." It was some kind of rule of his. The authorities couldn't get out of you what you didn't know. So he had told it to each of them, in one or two sentences, omitting Lyle's involvement. He knew they both assumed that Nesbitt was dead, but neither could imagine that he had left the mouthy teacher to die of thirst and starvation in his own beer pit. *Shit! Should have given him back a six-pack just for the fun of it.*

He put his head out the door to see if the sky had darkened sufficiently.
"So what's bothering you, Tess?"

"You sure you're graduating? I talked to your friend Dana's mother. She said sometimes they get all dressed up in that gown and silly cap, go on stage and get handed their diplomas, but when they open them up, it's nothing but a blank piece of paper. She said they do that so as not to embarrass some of you that aren't graduating."

"You've seen my grades. I'm graduating." He used his arm to wipe sweat from his forehead and took a gulp of beer from the can. "But you're thinkin' something else, I sense."

"That smart-ass English teacher Lord. He don't like none of us. And then there's Touchstone who tried to use you for his own purpose. Now I know that's supposed to be over, but maybe it ain't for Lord. He can't do much to Touchstone, but he still might have it in for you."

"Then we'll just have to wait and see. Don't let it worry you, Tess."

"He's not like the others. You should know that. No teacher would say to you what he said. And what you told us, you told us the truth, Asa, didn't you?"

"I told you true, Tess. The sonovabitch asked me to suck his dick."

He stared at the woman with the fat rolls hanging from her arms and clinging at her belly. He wondered if the old man ordered Tess to suck his dick. She was no looker—not even by the longest stretch! And his mother was, one of the reasons he had got to wondering at all. The old photographs confirmed the memory of his mother's good looks. There were questions all around needing answers, but he had never known how to ask them of the old man. For one, he noticed that Tess would always avoid looking at the Tucker woman's car. She was avoiding it now, and she was standing right behind it. And he had once seen a picture of Rodney Tucker's mother. Fucking-ass dynamite, that woman!

What he understood wasn't much. Somehow, his father had come to know the Tucker woman and learn of her misery, as well as her threats to up and leave her husband and boy. The woman was dead and buried somewhere in the mountains of the county, that much he did know. The words straight from the old man's mouth. But then the rule had been invoked. Still, he was sure his father had murdered the woman. What eluded him was the reason. Had the old man merely taken advantage of circumstances to get himself a new car, the same as he himself had done last January, evening a score at the same time? Or had he fucked her and then killed her to keep her from talking? Their bullshit sessions usually implied the first. But he'd never felt convinced.

Nor to this day was the matter with his mother herself very clear. Why the divorce when he was five? First, divorce, followed by her accidental death in her auto. Two years later came Tessie, and a year after that Tucker's mother.

"Randy said he won't be going to your graduation. You okay with that?"

"Drink your beer, Tess. You'll be there. That's all I need."

He weaved his way to the front of the garage and opened its doors.

"You going to help me push this car outside? I thought he'd be along."

"These cars were driven up from Renova and into this building under the cover of dark. Why can't you drive this one *out*?"

"How come you don't like these cars, Tessie?"

"Who said I don't like them?"

"I said. You don't touch 'em. You don't look at 'em. And I bet when the time comes, you won't be riding in this nice one."

"I'll wait and ride in yours."

"How come?"

"I'm going back inside. There's bugs coming in and I'm already being bit to hell."

She turned around and left, without again looking at the boy, catching a sandal and stumbling a step through the side door, guzzling the beer left in the bottom of the can.

I *should* drive this wreck out, he thought, studying the car. Only now there were sharp pieces of glass covering the seats, and he couldn't roll any window down to crawl inside. No way a door could be opened either.

He pushed the front of the car to test if it were in gear or had its emergency brake engaged. Neither.

"All right, let's roll this piece of shit the hell out of here," he ordered himself, "and be done with it!"

Setting his beer on a flat spot of the hood, he hunched his body and spread wide his arms, shoving with all his strength. The vehicle started to ease out the garage. He let off, allowing inertia to take over. His hands came together and ran over the spot where on the other vehicle there was a blemish, still discernible despite the old man's touch-up. It's what had got him the story. That the car was stolen, he'd realized since the first of three moves in the region—the old man always moved the car late-night. But that it was more sinister he never suspected until meeting Tucker the past year. The mark, a tiny smiley face but with a head shaped like Tweety Bird's, decorated every one of his classmate's drawings. Tucker told him he had scratched it on his mother's car when he was still a tyke. The old man shucked and jived, doing his best with the lies, but the son wasn't buying any of it.

"Okay. Then I'll mention it to the moron that it's on one of our cars as well," he threatened the old man.

That was all the blackmail required. Randy Aftanas surrendered and pointed slowly up into the hills.

"She's buried out there. But you don't need to know where. I don't know that I could find the spot anymore myself."

Outside, he moved behind the car and rolled it into the high weeds in back of the garage, forgetting that he wanted to crumple the sides with the sledge hammer. He ought to roll it all the way down into the Hartwell, he thought, although he wasn't serious—the creek was too shallow in most stretches. Retrieving the tarp he located earlier, he stretched it over the destroyed vehicle, then stepped back to regard the finished scene.

"Fuck. It'll work."

He bent over anyway, raked up a double handful of sticks and branches, and pitched them on as well. But what he was really thinking about now was the money and where he'd hidden it. It was a shitload of dough and the old man wasn't about to get a penny if he could help it. The funny thing was, he hadn't asked. Not a single question about what kind of cash Nesbitt had been carrying. Yeah, the ol' man had fucked her. He was pretty goddamn sure that had been the intent. The car was a freebie, part of a two-fer. Like a second pizza on the house, after having paid for the first.

Chapter 22

George Nesbitt's plan had been to travel to the Southwest. He had taken along plenty of cash and his own credit cards, ensuring that he need not make contact for quite some time, if ever. He was still not absolutely certain that he could just up and walk away from his half of the house and camp, but he had always been sure that such uncertainty would not deter him when the time was right to leave his wife and son. The year-round warm weather, however, the trading in of one compatibility for another would have to wait a while longer. He had Asa Aftanas to thank for that.

On that January night it happened, he had observed the lights behind him, keeping a distance. Although he thought them worthy of watching, he did not consider their presence alarming. But the car pulled in soon after his. When the driver got out, he could see the bristling hair in the partial moonlight, and there was another figure inside.

"Stay where you are."

"It's Asa Aftanas."

"That's hardly an invitation."

"Hey man, I didn't follow you out here to make trouble."

"What did you follow me for?"

"You didn't see me when you stopped for gas. I was in the other aisle filling up."

"And?"

"While you were inside paying, I couldn't help but notice your car was all packed up. People around here, I've heard, have always said that one day you'd just take off and leave, with no good-byes to anyone. Is that what you're doing?"

"What I'm doing is none of your business. Who's that in the car? Your father?"

"I'm not after trouble. But I thought, if you're leaving, then maybe I ought to apologize for that shit I started last year."

"Grayson Lord. He's the one to whom you owe an apology."

It was a quality common to all teachers. Give the students the benefit of your doubt. Aftanas dared to move toward him and he allowed it.

The kid peered through a window of the teacher's car at the shirts and suits hanging from a crossbar and at the boxes on the seats.

"This is it, ain't it? You're leaving like everyone said you would. What's your plan? Stay here maybe a couple of days, then move on? Maybe until after the storm that's on its way? This is a dynamite camp."

"Don't act like you've never seen it."

He thought the kid was smiling as his gaze dropped to the earth.

"You're not fucking planning to stay here at all. This is just a stop to pick-up some of your goddamn beer."

And then his left hand went calmly behind him. When it reappeared, he was holding a gun.

"Worthless stop, asshole. Lyle and I have been cleaning you out all along, and two nights ago we finished the job. Now, if you don't want a bullet in you here and now, turn your ass around and march over to that pit of yours. But first, the money out of your wallet. You can keep the rest."

"Asshole" was fucking right! Why hadn't he believed what he knew? And yet it happened again—the benefit of his doubt. When the kid returned, he was sure it was to help him out of the hole. He'd just wanted to strike fear in him for a while. Show the teacher that he, Asa Aftanas, wasn't someone to fuck around with.

But then the dog was lifted overhead and cast heartlessly to the bottom of the concrete pit, where its neck was broken. When the rotted cover followed, there in total darkness he realized, giving no more benefits of his doubt, that the kid was leaving him to die. To die a terrible death from thirst and starvation. If he didn't freeze first.

The dog was the hero. It hadn't died at once. He could hear it on the other side, still breathing. Once in a while some internal part of its body moved and the poor thing moaned. In the blackness he felt his way next to it and rested a hand on its side. It allowed him, and they remained that way for more than an hour. And then he listened to its breathing become altered and less involuntary. Finally, the beagle died with his hand still gently stroking it.

He liked to think the dog had realized that it must die if there were to be any justice for this crime against them. He had continued to sit next to it, waiting for its dead muscles to stiffen, testing one now and then. When that condition began to set in, he stretched the animal out. At the height of the stiffness, he placed the body against the wall in a sitting-up position, as though the dog were begging for a treat. Maintaining a locating hand at the

218

side of its skull, he then placed his left foot between its ears and sprung quickly upward off the rock-solid corpse, reaching for the ledge at the top.

Catching it, he struggled to secure the other hand in the same place and pulled himself up against the rotted wood, shoving the cover aside with his head. It was well after midnight and the snow assaulted him. He replaced the cover over the hole and rushed to the cabin to warm himself.

He had right along maintained the cabin with adequate provisions—a variety of soups, frozen milk and bread, coffee, a steak or two, several pounds of quality beef jerky dried and sent up by an old friend from downstate. And there was clothing, including a winter coat and an old pair of high-top boots. There were even a couple of beers left in the refrigerator.

Why empty only the pit? he asked himself. Why not break in, too? Do the usual scenario and vandalize the joint. The senseless shit too many of them loved to do.

On the morning of the second day, a black Jeep pushed through the snow-covered road, and later a pair of four-wheel drive pickups. Each time he rushed to the window to see if the vehicle was turning in. The thought had occurred to him that the sicko kid might come back just to see how his killing was progressing, what stage it was in. On the fourth day, still unsure of his next move, he attempted to bury the dog. Beside the creek where the earth wasn't frozen. But the discovery of the broken ladder thwarted him and he returned to the warmth of the cabin.

Decide, that's what really needed doing. He must decide what he was going to do. The more recent indoctrinations of teacher professionalism surfaced first. Inform the office. In other words, tell the police, let them handle it. But the inculcations of real teaching, the stuff he'd learned from everyday battle, wouldn't allow it. Truth was, he wasn't sure the kid was even eighteen. And if he wasn't, the whole thing might end up in juvenile court. What did he have to offer anyway, either way? He was convinced the car was already trashed. The kid would have rummaged through the bags and found the revolver and the rest of the money, some five thousand dollars, then taken the customary reckless joyride before dumping it in the water somewhere. It wouldn't surprise him if his new car was now submerged in the nearby swamp. And the revolver would be useless as proof that a crime had occurred. It was never registered. Then there was the crime itself. Who the fuck would believe it? Who the fuck wouldn't think that he was making up such a preposterous tale? The Aftanas family had no credibility, but there was no sense fooling himself. Neither did he.

He stayed at the camp a total of six days, until the firewood stacked at the back ran out. On the morning of the seventh, he walked out, still uncertain what he himself would do to avenge the wrong against him, but by no means uncertain that he would not be contacting the police. There were only two persons who might look into the hole, three if he counted Lyle. But despite the earlier thought, he seriously doubted Asa would return to the pit so soon. Like a lot of them, the kid was ignorant, not stupid. In his mind he had pulled off a perfect crime. Nobody would miss George Nesbitt; everyone would think he was alive. The kid and his friend might come back for a glimpse under the cover, but not until the flesh had separated from his bones. The only other person who might be curious was Gray. And all he would find was the skeleton of a small animal.

He tramped along the road for several miles in the direction opposite from Careytown, grateful for the tracks carved out by vehicles, fearful that another would appear with passengers who would recognize him. This fear became great enough that he considered leaving the road, trudging over the mountains instead. But that, he couldn't lie to himself, would be too dangerous. The many times he had visited the camp, he had run into only a handful of people who were from Careytown.

He made Crossfork Road after a couple of hours and a storm of snowmobilers rushed at him from a hole in the woods.

"Need a lift?" their leader asked.

It was difficult to see their faces under the helmets, but no one appeared to be acting as though he were familiar.

"What happened to you?" the driver asked him as he swung onto the seat.

He hadn't thought about it. "My machine gave it up," he improvised.

The driver swung his head around to stare at him. "I don't mean to preach, but it's not a good area to be exploring alone. You ought to consider getting yourself a suit, too. How far's the spot? Where your sled stopped?"

"Thanks, but forget it. I've a couple of brothers on the other side of this mountain," he said, extending the lie. "We'll get it later."

"Whatever you say. Only that fellow on the Ski-Doo is one super mechanic in the field. And I can tell you you won't be imposing."

"Thanks again, but you got your own day planned. Just drop me in Crossfork. I'll appreciate it."

He slept the night in a room atop a bar in the extremely tiny village, aware of how a plan of revenge was formulating without yet defining itself. It made for a strange, though not uncomfortable, feeling. He had amazed himself by how easy the lies had floated off his tongue.

The following day he crossed into New York after going down to the bar in the morning and inquiring if any locals made regular trips across the border. There were two fellas, the owner told him, who went up two, three times a week.

"And don't ask why, I line up a ride for you. You understand?"

He understood. He posed no questions to the driver, although he wondered if the journey were for pickup or delivery, and the driver reciprocated.

At a town named Antilis, three times the size of Careytown, he stepped out of the van. The region wasn't completely unknown to him as he'd driven through it in years past. It lacked what he wanted it to lack—malls and the popular outlet stores. There would be little, if any, reason for a resident of Careytown to motor to its downtown district. His first item of business was to secure some money, and so he went to the bank where he withdrew a substantial sum on his credit cards. Next, he found a diner and, while eating, scoured the local classifieds for a place to stay and a car. He got lucky on both. An old man with a pugilist's features watched him from the counter. The man rose finally and approached.

"What are you looking to buy there, stranger? I got a big-ass barn not too far from where you're sittin', and there's a little something of everything stored inside. What's more, it's all for sale."

"I'll bet it is," Nesbitt responded good-naturedly.

"So what is it you need? Tell me what you're after." The old man sat down without invitation.

"I need to rent a couple of rooms for several months. And I need some wheels."

"That's what you're looking for?"

"Not what you have to offer, is it?"

"Oh, I got a coupla cars for sale, but they're nothin' you'd want. Don't neither of them runs, you see. You know, they're for restorin'."

"No, don't need anything like that. I just want something that's dependable. Something to fill in until I settle a matter."

"Well, I can still help you. Fellow named Howard Whitley. He's got an old Gremlin he wants to sell. It's in great shape for its age, same as me, and he's been looking to get rid of it. It might be what you're after."

"You have a number?"

"He's in the phone book. Hell, if you're genuinely interested, I bet he'll come pick you up."

"If it's such a great car, why hasn't he already sold it?"

"If you knew, you wouldn't be askin'. He's a guy that does all kinds of work, and he works hard and does it well. But he's one of those that when it comes to taking care of the little things—like gettin' hold of a for-sale sign, or putting an ad in this here paper—well, the man just can't seem to get his ass in gear to do it."

"I can sympathize."

"Yeah? You don't look the type, you know. I called you 'stranger' earlier, but maybe I'm mistakin'. Maybe you're someone from around here I just never met."

Nesbitt shook his head.

"But neither are you just passing through, I gather."

"Just not this moment."

"So what is your business?"

The lie was already at the tip, but he had to be careful. If the lies became too involved, you were bound to lose track. The danger arose when someone else didn't.

"You don't want to say."

"I don't want to be rude, Mister."

"Just tell me it's legitimate. I don't want to get myself mixed up in something that isn't."

"It's on the up and up, no problem there. But I don't want to talk about it with you or anyone."

The man stared hard at him for several seconds. "You left your wife, my guess."

"Can you help or not? I need a place to stay for a time."

The man continued to stare at him before folding to his own reasoning.

"Sure. I can help on that, too."

Nesbitt noticed the immediate change in tone. The man was now less of a salesman, more of a Samaritan.

"Correct me if I'm wrong. It seems to me you wouldn't mind spending this time by yourself."

"That would be fine."

"Then I've got just the place. A friend of mine owns a cabin a short distance out of town, and he rents it out each year about this time. Only this year, he hasn't had any takers. Interested?"

Nesbitt nodded.

"There might be a problem, though, with how long you're staying. He don't rent it out much past September. The first of the hunting seasons starts soon after, and he hunts 'em all."

"I doubt I'll be there that long. What about trout season? When April comes, will he expect me to move out for a time?"

"He don't fish."

Before the day was over, he had purchased the Gremlin from the man named Whitley and signed on to stay at the cabin. The owner pressed him to commit through August, but he refused, saying he was sure he couldn't stay beyond June. He had no real idea where this information came from, where it had been stored. And he had no idea how it had been decided, even whether he had had a hand in it. Formulation without definition, that's what it was. It moved him along as though he were a stick in water, and he allowed it.

On the clear blue morning of June twenty-third, a Saturday and Graduation Day for the seniors of Careytown Junior-Senior High School, George Nesbitt abandoned the cabin outside of Antilis, New York, and returned to his own in Pennsylvania. The distance was less than sixty miles. The time required to drive it one hour and thirty minutes.

Chapter 23

Principal "P.D." Waring had excluded commencement exercises from his "white paper" for several reasons: the lack of air conditioning in the building; in recent years more parents, siblings, and visitors attending than the auditorium could accommodate; too many video cameras and too many people moving about for a selection of shots. Wiser to seat the graduates in the folding chairs, most everyone else in the stands, and hope that it wouldn't rain.

The afternoon before and throughout the morning, Mr. Vittitow and his custodial staff prepared the football field for the commencement ceremony. They mowed the grass, wiped off the bleachers, transferred tables and two hundred folding chairs from a storage room off the cafeteria, assembled a large raised platform, pushed out a piano in the manner of Egyptian slaves, and miked a lectern. The forecast held.

No contract between the district and faculty association had ever included the stipulation that teachers attend the end-of-year ceremony. And in early years few of the teachers did. George Nesbitt was one of them. Somber-faced and standing consciously erect in a side aisle of the auditorium, each June he had applauded the town's newest graduates. Over time others joined him. Waring had instructed Mr. Vittitow to set aside twenty-five of the folding chairs for the faculty.

Lord, one of the instructional staff who would be attending, roamed the first floor and its various rooms, in which the graduates were donning their caps and gowns, in search of Kathy Raye.

"There you are."

"What do you want?"

"You know what I want, Kathy."

"Ooooh," swooned another girl. "Mr. Lord, you know she's not eligible until Mr. Orr hands her the diploma. You're liable to end up in another mess if you're not careful."

Lord felt certain more blush was showing in his own face than in the valedictorian's. Raye started to walk away.

"No you don't, Kathy. I want to see the speech you're planning to deliver."

"You saw it, remember? You recommended changes. Well, I made changes. But they're not exactly the ones you think they'll be."

"Yes, I'm quite positive of that. The draft you showed me, that was done simply to get me off your back. I should have realized it then and there because it wasn't of the quality I've come to expect of you. But I gave you the benefit of the doubt, thinking that you were overly busy with countless end-of-the-year things. Where is it?"

Several other students were now listening to their exchange. He could see they were puzzled. Whatever the young woman was intending, she had planned it as a surprise to everyone.

She stood away from him but stared angrily back, and he met her gaze. He could see there would be no thanks. In the years upcoming, she would complain about him to her friends and family.

She walked over to a bookshelf beside a window and grabbed a file folder lying on top. She thrust it out at him.

He stepped forward, took the paper from the folder and read it quickly. The sort of thing he feared wasn't far from the top.

"Let's go somewhere else."

He led her into the hall and into another room that was empty.

"Don't do this," he said.

"But it's true. It's what inspired me. I want to make sure I'm never like Mr. Nesbitt."

"You don't know George Nesbitt, Kathy."

"I know enough."

"You believe all your classmates are in synch with your feelings? They're not. Many of them liked Mr. Nesbitt and were sorry to see him go."

"You sure about that? I never heard any of them say a good word."

"They went with the flow. It was easy. It produced laughs for some of them. Go ahead and ask a few. Get them alone and ask them what they really thought of their history teacher."

She was strong, and if she straightened, someday she would be a terrible adversary.

"I won't let you do this to yourself. And I won't allow you to do it to my friend. Especially when he's not here to defend himself."

"How can you stop me? I've memorized that paper you're holding. I can recite it by heart."

"I'll stand and interrupt you, Kathy, if I have to. I'll rise from my seat and in front of everybody—your classmates, their families and your family—I'll voice my objection."

"Then you'll look like the fool."

"That's right," he said, nodding intently. "I'll look like the fool. But I would do that for you."

What more could he say. It was really up to her. He turned and walked quickly away, then toured the hall to find Janey who was helping some of the girls to adjust their gowns.

"Hey, Mr. Lord. Are you and Miss Renn going to the parties afterward?"

"Are you holding one, Tucker?"

"No. But there's a bunch of them to go to. Why don't you stop by?"

"We'll think about it. In the meantime, you be careful."

"I don't drink, Mr. Lord."

"You don't? Well then, good for you."

"Oh, I have, but I don't really like it. My mother, she didn't drink anything but juice."

"Looks like you're starting to line up, Tucker. And Miss Renn and I should get out there and take our places."

"Okay, Mr. Lord."

"Wait. I might as well say this to you now as later. Congratulations. You were a wonderful addition to my class and I enjoyed having you. I mean that, Tucker. I wish you the very best."

"Thanks, Mr. Lord."

He found Janey and they left the building for the football field through a rear door on the gymnasium. Wallace, already sitting, spotted them and patted a hand on the empty seats to his right.

The car passed slowly on the road outside the gate. It was a small car, a compact—he couldn't remember the brand—and the driver, who was alone, appeared to be severely crammed behind the steering wheel, much like a pheasant in a can. Later, when the graduates marched to their chairs, Lord observed the car again. This time it stopped for a few minutes and the driver, still sitting awkwardly with his shoulders pressed into his neck, flipped down his visor, even though the sun was behind him.

Chapter 24

Nesbitt returned again to the camp that he had found to be much as he had left it during the winter. Only the remains of the dog were missing. The good heart of his friend Gray must have put it to final rest.

He had risked driving into town and near the school, where others might recognize him, for one reason only. He wanted to learn beforehand if Asa Aftanas were still around. Waiting at the camp and not knowing for sure was not an option. If Aftanas failed to march onto the football field with his classmates, it would mean that the kid had checked under the cover on the pit, understood the truth, and fled the region for good. But luck had been with him. He had no difficulty identifying the boy dressed in the gown of his school colors.

The start of the definition came at five. A perforated green pickup truck bounced into the washed-out lane. Nesbitt watched from inside the cabin. He had parked the Gremlin next to the rear of the structure where it wasn't visible.

The driver of the truck climbed down and removed three cases of beer from the bed to the dropped gate.

Goddammit, they planned to use his camp to party, the sonsabitches! Though why not? They could whoop it up to a frenzy, and who would know? Or even care. In the years that he owned the camp, he had never once witnessed a state trooper or deputy sheriff cruising the road out front. But this guy, he thought, appeared a little old to be mixing it up with seventeen- and eighteen-year-olds. Nor did it appear that the man had come prepared with ice.

The driver squared all three cases in the stack and heaved them off the gate. Nesbitt expected he would carry them somewhere near the large galvanized tub hanging from a hook at the side of the cabin. Instead, the man lugged the cases onto the rise and set them next to the cover of the pit. Then, he sauntered off into the neighboring brush and found the two broken sections of the ladder.

"Sonovabitch!" Nesbitt heard him yell. "Why the fuck did he do that? Goddamn that boy's ass!"

Spinning on his heels, the man stomped back to the truck and extracted a hammer and some nails from a container in the bed. He smashed the hammer against the side metal panel, producing yet another remarkable dent in the vehicle.

Nesbitt left the cabin through a rear door, and waiting until the man hauled the pieces of ladder next to the pit, approached silently from the back.

A twig snapped underfoot. The man whirled and Nesbitt stopped in his tracks. The person before him, it was obvious, was no believer in apparitions.

"You must be Lyle."

"See. I didn't think you were a twin."

The hammer struck. He stepped to one side, feeling it graze him on that shoulder, inflicting a numbing pain.

"The boy's going to have more of a surprise to show his friends tonight than he thinks. He ain't counting on you looking so fresh, Nesbitt."

The man lunged again and the hammer came at him again, but he was expecting it, stepping aside in plenty of time so that now it missed him completely. He drew the knife from his pocket. About to run at him a third time, Lyle Kaster hesitated as he eyed the blade, some four inches long.

"I didn't think you'd be much for talking," Nesbitt said.

"When's the last time you used it? Tip's all rusty It's been lying in that cold cabin, hasn't it?"

They eyed each other without words for a brief while.

"I get that knife away from you, I'm going to gut and skin you like a fuckin' buck. I ain't spending time in no slammer."

He was no clever fighter himself, yet he thought his opponent would come at him yet again in the manner he already had. And he was right. Lyle Kaster, while glancing off into the trees, made what he thought was another unanticipated lunge. But Nesbitt danced aside like a talented bullfighter and plunged the knife into Kaster's ear.

The man collapsed like a cake. Blood gushed from his ear. The mouth quivered and his body began to shake. Reaching out a weak hand, he tried to speak.

"I don't intend to go to prison either," Nesbitt said, sickened by the sight before him. No portion of the blade could be seen. Only the handle was visible, sticking out of the ear like a long stalk on shucked corn. "You know I can't trust you'll tell the truth if I get you to a hospital. That means you'll have to wait until I nail your buddy."

Even so, he thought he should do something. Help the man in some way. He bent down and tried to lift Lyle up, to move him closer to the cabin. The man's arms flailed at his effort. One hand continued to grip the claw hammer. He pried the tool from Lyle's fist and it dropped to the ground. The man was no longer trying to kill him. The pain was simply too intense.

Nesbitt left the man beside the pit and hastened back to the cabin for a bandage. He wasn't sure he could extract the knife from the ear, or even if the man would let him. But by the time he returned to the rise, the doubts required no additional thought. Lyle Kaster had died. There was a final definitive shudder to the body even as he realized this.

Out of the silence that then developed he soon became aware that some vehicle was approaching his direction. Acting quickly, he removed the rotted cover from the pit and dragged the body closer. Similar to what he had done to the beagle, he planted the sole of his shoe on the head of Lyle Kaster, then reached down and yanked the knife free, but at an angle so that the tip broke off and remained in the skull. The release of steel from bone issued a wet, squeaky note. The engine of the vehicle grew louder. He gazed out at all the rich foliage between him and the road. There were three or four small openings that might allow a glimpse of the spot where he was standing. He rolled the body of Lyle Kaster into the pit and replaced the cover. One of the boards loosened from the nails and with the hammer he beat it back in place.

Replace it with pressure-treated.

The memory of his friend's advice brought forth a smile, though it was cancelled instantly by the vehicle that passed on the road without slowing.

He dragged the broken ladder into the brush, then picked up the hammer and carried it, along with the three cases of beer, to the cabin. There he waited for night and Asa Aftanas.

Chapter 25

Waring had beat his gums too long at the podium was the consensus, but the commencement ceremony was finally over, and now it was time to celebrate. Wallace suggested they all get a Tillyburger. He was starving.

Lord and Janey were the last of the group to swing into the parking lot of their favorite bar. They ran into DeWitt Wainwright who was leaving.

"What's happening, DeWitt?"

"Mr. Lord! You know, you're brother's inside looking for you."

"My brother?"

"That's what he says he is."

Lord searched around the crowded parking lot and identified Bradford's big sport utility.

"Is there a woman with him?"

"No, he's by hisself. But he has an audience. He's been telling stories about your dad and the two of you."

"You ready for this?" he said to Janey.

"Are you? That's the better question."

"Kathy Raye restored my faith today. Maybe the same will happen with my brother."

A horde of customers occupied all the stools in the front room of Tilly's, as well as the space between and behind them, many of the patrons having come from the graduation ceremony. They discovered Bradford holding court near an angle of the bar. He had captured the interest of Tom and Margo Worth. Warren Hoverton was listening, too.

"Here he is!" Margo Worth announced. "Gray, squeeze in here. Your brother's been telling us all about you."

"Heyyyy, brother," Bradford greeted him with a healthy grin. "I can see you're already wondering what brings me up here again."

"It was crossing my mind."

They only shook hands, although Lord, too, displayed a genuine smile, a facial conclusion that required some time to reach, like the delayed opening and closing of a damp camera shutter. It was his lone brother. What the fuck was he supposed to do?

"Who's this with you?"

"This is Janey Renn. My brother Brad."

233

"Nice to finally meet you," said Bradford, who revealed difficulty with expressing the smallest formality.

"It's nice to meet you."

"So what's your answer?" Lord asked.

"My answer?"

"To my question. What brings you here a second time?"

"Rita's idea. I drove up to apologize. She says we're all getting too old to let these arguments linger. It was a bad one, she said, and neither of us ever seems to call the other. She insisted that I clean up my end of it and that I do it in person." Bradford looked at the Worths. "Can you believe this fellow threw his big brother and sister-in-law out of his apartment?"

"Gray, you want beer?" Tilly asked, looking frazzled.

"Tilly, give my brother and Janey whatever they're drinking. And you had some others come in ahead of you."

"They're in the back room, Tilly," Lord said. "You better check with them first. And I'll just have a ginger ale."

"I'll have the same," said Janey, who noticed Bradford glance at her.

"Not drinking tonight?"

"Maybe later, Brad," Lord said. "Today was graduation."

"Ah, so you have parties to attend."

"Nothing like that. We crash some of them. The ones that are likely to get out of hand and result in an accident. Tradition for prevention. It started about five years ago."

Tilly delivered the ginger ales. The noise from conversation in the matchbox of a bar rose to another level.

"We'd like to order a couple of burgers, Tilly. I believe everyone out back does too."

"Okay, but it take time."

"Why'd you kick your brother out of your house, Gray?" Margo Worth asked coyly. She looked at Janey afterwards, as though they shared some secret.

"He thought I was gay. What else?"

Tom Worth glanced at Bradford who had been listening without much eye contact. Bradford now appeared surprised that his young brother had so readily brought up the subject of homosexuality in public and before Janey.

"Well now, there was that thing with the Aftanas child," Hoverton said, feigning reverie while elevating his head. "We shouldn't forget about that."

"Oh, go paddle your canoe, Warren," Lord replied dismissively. For his own self-amusement, Hoverton enjoyed extending family tiffs that developed at the bar. It was meant to be an innocent pastime, Lord knew. But the man didn't know his brother Brad.

"Where the hell were you guys, anyway?" Hoverton said accusingly. "The community always anticipates whipping you teachers in the canoe races. This year, none of you showed. Not even Howser."

Lord saw that Bradford still hadn't picked up on Hoverton's original intentions. The older brother stared at the man almost stone-faced while the Worths were at the same time chuckling and nodding.

"He's putting you on, Brad."

"How's that?"

"Tell him, Warren."

"Tell him what?" Hoverton said, lighting a cigarette and unwilling to end his fun.

"Admit that you're gay," Margo Worth said, coming to the rescue. "Come out of the closet once and for all, Warren dear."

Lord, Tom, Margo, and an eavesdropper laughed immediately. Hoverton choked on the first draw of smoke from his cigarette and started laughing, too.

"I owe her one, Tom."

"I think you do," said Tom Worth.

"Say, Gray. You ever hear from our boy George?"

"You know, I thought I saw him today. Except the person was driving a compact car. One of those old AMC uglies."

"For sure that wouldn't be George," Hoverton said. "He was partial to those big boats. Land cruisers and roadwagons he called them."

Lord and Janey soon excused themselves and joined the teachers in the other room. Invited to accompany them, Bradford left his stool and tagged along. Lord again made the introductions. Much later, after everyone had eaten, they planned their evening. Rudy Wallace said he had the poop on all the parties, who was serving beer and liquor, and who wasn't. They would skip the dry celebrations.

Lord could tell that his brother disapproved. Kids were entitled to a few drinks the night of high school graduation. Teachers ought to stay the hell away.

Soon after, the chairs slid out from the table as everyone got up to leave.

"You're not planning on driving back tonight, are you?" he asked Bradford.

"I don't want to intrude. You and Janey probably have plans."

"Forget me," said Janey. "I'm headed home."

"Bring him along, Gray," Wallace said. "You never know when we might have to kick some butt."

Blake inserted a finger into his mouth.

"Go wah-wah yourself," Wallace said to his younger colleague.

"C'mon, Brad, you might as well," Lord said. "This really won't take all night. The kids'll probably think you're a state cop or some kind of narc. It'll help to keep them honest."

"Yeah, you'll be our mystery man," Wallace said to Bradford.

"You really think you'll keep these kids from drinking tonight?"

"It might help," Schenley said, a trace of dislike attached to the words.

"But the real deal, Brother Lord, is this," Wallace explained to Bradford as he put one hand onto the big man's shoulder. "Some parents will know that we know. So maybe they'll pull the plug on the booze. You get what I mean?"

Chapter 26

According to teacher-sleuth Rudy Wallace, eleven graduation parties would soon be getting underway inside the school district. Of these, four would be serving beer, wine, and maybe hard liquor. And one of these they discounted because they knew the hosting parents who might allow the graduates to toast themselves and each other on their milestone accomplishment. But if the young people were figuring on holding high their glasses all through the evening, they could just forget it at the Bogardus household. Of the remaining three parties, two were occurring in town. Jack Schenley, Walt McAllister, and Paul Blake volunteered to visit these. Rudy Wallace and the Lord Brothers were headed for the other, some ten miles south of Careytown.

Lord drove the gold Toyota, with his brother up front. Wallace slumped in the backseat.

"Why didn't your girlfriend Janey come along?" Bradford asked about a mile out of town. "She didn't decide against it on my account, I hope."

"It's her first year and she's too close in age. Some of the boys, now that they're out.... Well, you know. There's always one or two who start feeling bigger than their britches. She didn't want to chance an ugly scene."

"But not to worry, Brad," Wallace said, straightening and gazing out a window. "We might appear a trio of gay amigos when we sidle in, but they all know different. Not that either Gray or myself has anything against gays. But that's not the case with a lot of folk around her, their offspring included. Maybe you heard what some of them tried to do to your brother? Some of the more religious ones?"

Lord could sense that his comical friend was winding up, and in an area that was best left untouched.

"Well, your brother isn't gay, but you already know that because of Janey. But he isn't bisexual either. Trisexual. That's what Gray is, Brad. This sonovabitch of a brother of yours will try anything sexual. No, just kidding. He's not gay, and neither am I for that matter. And I only bring myself into the equation because there are some who think I am because of the way I act sometimes. Sometimes, I act like the biggest jag-off you could ever imagine. Isn't that right, Gray?"

"Sometimes. Not always."

"That's right. Not always. But some of these forever uptight assholes, unless they see some seriously dopey mask on your mug every minute of the day, which the fuckers regard as the ultimate outward sign of maturity—"

"—and professionalism," Lord added.

"—and professionalism, fuckin' A, they figure you're some kind of wimpy fag. You probably never realized this, Brad, but did you know there are no gay mathematicians? That's right. No gay or lesbian mathematicians out of the past, and still none in our day and age. A fact you can take to the bar and amuse your friends with. And the reason for that is that none of them has ever proven it by the numbers. Mathematically, that is. So until they do.... I'll shut up. I think you get my point."

There was only one point his brother was likely to get, Lord thought while stealing a glance to his right. The guy in the backseat was a fucking queer! Couldn't be anything but!

Wallace sobered in mood as he always did after delivering a salvo of deliberately asinine behavior. He sat up even straighter and crossed his arms over the front seat.

"Know where the Foss house is, Gray?"

"It's out here on the right somewhere. A big square house in need of paint."

"It's just this side of the Tutweiler farm. You can't miss it."

Although Lord had taught Dana Foss in a couple of classes, including senior English, the teen had not made much of an impression. Mostly, the kid was a back-stabber, petty thief, spray-painting graffiti man, and mumbler. He had done just enough to pass the course and graduate. Neither Lord nor Wallace had ever met the parents.

The first quarter-keg was visible to them from the road even though the sun was well over the horizon and the sky was darkening. They saw the second quarter-keg as Lord swung the car into the driveway.

"They got stuff in the woods, too," Wallace said, briefly pointing through the windshield. The Tutweiler farm bordered the house on the left, but to the right and behind it stretched nothing but wooded state game land. Several kids were going and coming through its foliage.

Every room of the tall house was lit and many of the windows were without curtains. There were bodies floating by each. After leaving the car, the three men walked in the direction of the second keg where more activity was occurring.

"See anyone remotely resembling a parent?" Wallace asked sarcastically.

Lord spotted Bonnie Riznick. The young woman was without her child, holding a styrofoam cup filled with beer. He didn't think she qualified as an answer to his colleague's question. As he gazed around, he saw several others who were past graduates, young men and women now in their twenties. The party had an ugly feel to it. Plenty of drinking taking place, but nothing much to speak of in the way of upbeat celebration.

"Mr. Lord, Mr. Wallace."

"You enjoying yourself, Tucker?"

"Yeah, it's all right."

"So what's in the cup? You told me earlier you didn't drink?"

"I don't. This is probably all I'll have tonight. I just got it to get in the mood with everyone else."

"What mood is that?" said Wallace, who eyed the gathering with distaste.

"Well, I hope you're telling the truth," Lord said. "I don't want to see you ending up in a box. What are you eating there anyway?"

"Go get yourselves some. Dana won't care. It's all snack stuff." He held up a Dorito. "Hey, Mr. Lord. Do you know why they call nacho cheese 'nacho cheese'?"

"I can't wait."

"Because it's notch yo reg'lar cheez."

Tucker laughed at his own joke and slapped a leg. Lord grinned an appreciation, while Wallace rolled his eyes. Again, the brother gave no sign that anything of a humorous nature had just taken place.

"Even Mr. Ruther chuckled at that one, Mr. Wallace. You know, Mr. Lord wished me the best. You got anything you want to say to me?"

"Like what do you want to hear? Some advice, maybe?"

"Advice would be good."

"All right then, Tucker. Don't let your ding-dong drabble in the dirt. Rap it up in cellophane and stick it in your shirt."

Tucker slowly shook his head. "I don't know about you, Mr. Wallace. You're one truly loony dude."

"What's that line you like, Gray?"

"Long live the romantics, screw the deconstructionists?"

"No, the other. The one from Hemingway, I think it is."

"'Isn't it pretty to think so?'"

"Yes, isn't it pretty to think so, Tucker."

Bradford was staring intently at the side of Wallace's head, and Lord was certain he knew the thought that was passing inside his brother's own. No wonder the schools were fast going to hell in a handbasket!

They left Tucker and went moving about the lawn, eventually stepping inside the house. Several grads came up to them, some encouraging them to pour themselves a beer. Aaron Little thought if he poured it for them they would accept.

"Forget it, Aaron. We're just here to make sure none of you get on too much of a buzz."

"You're not going to call the fuzz on us, are you?"

No, they weren't planning on doing that, but it was always an option. And if they had found them already soused, then perhaps the cops would be en route this minute. Perhaps. Lord didn't know for sure. The drinking was a cultural thing. And though the complaints were always about the drinking, really the objection was one of drinking too much. That's what it really was. Getting bombed and losing control. It was un-American. If you got bombed, you were supposed to maintain control in spite of it, always. Besides, the cops weren't stupid. Probably, they were aware of the location of every party around. So why hassle the kids and make them run off to somewhere they didn't already know about.

Tammy and Bonnie Riznick approached them when they returned to the outside where someone had ignited a fire for warmth. The older sister lasered her eyes on the muscular Bradford, and Lord introduced his brother to her and several others that included a few of the boys. Most had observed the confident swagger of the strong man, who looked out of place. Lord and Wallace continued to rephrase their alcoholic warnings to those with whom they talked.

They saw Asa Aftanas before he noticed them. The kid emerged from the state woodland behind the house and asked another kid the whereabouts of a certain girl. When he turned in the direction that was pointed, he stopped and a twisted smile spread across his face like an oil slick. He walked over to where they were standing near the fire. Wallace had accepted a Coke and was tapping the top of the can to make sure it didn't spray once it was opened. The kid positioned himself squarely in front of Bradford.

"You a new teacher or somethin'?"

"This is my brother, Asa."

"Your brother.... Well now. He don't look to be much like the faggot that you do."

"Let's put that tedious item to rest, Asa. It's a brand new game now. No more teacher and student stuff."

The kid's eyes switched back onto Bradford. Nothing was going to be put to rest.

"You don't know it, but we got something in common. Your brother once said I was a tough guy. Well, he don't know how fucking tough I am. I think you think you're a fucking tough guy. Are you, O faggot's brother? Are you a fucking tough guy, too?"

Bradford maintained a silence that Wallace concluded to be a strange behavior. Certainly this muscle man was going to say something, something cool, wasn't he? Lord saw his colleague throw him a questioning look. But the silence wasn't strange to the younger brother. He had watched Brad in similar face-to-face confrontations when they were kids. Opponents who mistook it for fear or something similar often suffered in the end. What it was was concentration. Watching for the first sign of the sucker punch. If Asa attempted that, he was sausage!

The kid ran his tongue along the inside of his upper lip to bring an end to his smirk, pivoted on his heels, and headed back toward the woodland. At its entrance, he turned back for a few moments.

"You know, Lord, I'm thinking I ought to invite you..." He let himself trail off. "No. Wouldn't be smart. Be fun, but wouldn't be smart.... Aaron! Find Cassie. Tell her I want to see her. And tell her she can keep her clothes on. Another thing. Don't go running your mouth to anyone."

"What about Rodney?"

"Him most of all."

Aaron Little lowered his voice. "But he's been watching us. He knows something's up."

"So if he asks, make up something," Aftanas whispered. "But I don't want him in on this, you understand?"

Tucker was off to the side of the fire, standing in darkness. He wouldn't miss any of them down the road. And he especially wouldn't miss Asa, neighbor though he was. He'd never done anything to him and yet... Mr. Lord was who he'd miss.

In the darkness the boy recollected his first encounter with his favorite teacher. Then it was junior high and he had sat always in the back row if possible. There was a reason for it, too. Hard-ons. He'd been thinking of nothing, trying to listen to the reading out loud of the story "Mateo Falcone," when suddenly out of nowhere, there it was, and he couldn't help but slide his hand onto it.

"What are you doing, Roy?" came the voice from the front. Not even his given name.

And what had he said in reply? How did he answer the teacher's question? With the exact same words, even the exact same tone: "What are you doing, Roy?" What an idiot he was then.

Lord, he remembered, had looked toward a window and smothered a smile. He had known immediately, and yet he did not attempt to have his fun at a student's expense like Mr. McAllister sometimes did. Mr. McAllister would have made him stand up and answer some stupid question. Stand up so that everyone could see the bulge in his pants and have a good laugh.

"Well, Mr. Roy Tucker, I suggest you pay all your attention up here. That goes for the rest of you, too. Turn around. Roy's business isn't yours."

Tucker watched his fellow graduates Aaron and Cassie enter the woods, and he followed, keeping a distance so that he wouldn't be seen.

There was no fire beside the keg under the trees, and all those surrounding it were becoming loud, interrupting and one-upping each other at every opportunity, the boys shoving each other's chest, punching each other's shoulders. He couldn't funnel every word coming out of the mouth of Asa Aftanas as the disturbed youth spoke to Cassie. But he was able to pick up enough, and the rest he could get later. A group of them were driving out to a camp that belonged to Mr. Nesbitt. The history teacher had hidden *mucho* cases of beer out there, Asa told them, and he knew where to find it.

Chapter 27

The house remained dark. He could hear her snoring, hog-like grunts and guffaws exploding through the screen of the upstairs window and drifting into the shed. He deliberately did not click on its lights either.

There were a number of things to say that it hadn't been Nesbitt. And now, standing next to the automobile that he had protected and hidden for most of a decade, preparing to move it to another location, he thought perhaps he was putting himself on edge. The details didn't fit, at least not together. The whole thing was eluding his understanding. Where had Nesbitt been all these months? Had the boy only wounded him and put him in the hospital, so severely that it took this long to recover? Earlier he had hoped his son might return home after receiving his diploma before heading out to the numerous parties so that he could learn exactly how the deed had been done. But that hadn't happened, and not knowing the answer to his questions bothered him. The cops should have already arrested Asa, he thought. If Nesbitt wasn't dead, they should have picked up Asa a long time ago.

He had rode in with them on their way to the ceremony, Tessie warning him not to get too drunked up on Asa's day. It was a half-hour or so after they had dropped him in front of Domirock's Bar and Grille, just after the owner asked him to slide off the stool and stick an empty pop case against the door to let in some fresh air, that the small car floated by, like in a dream. He might not have given it a second glance, except the lone person inside was all scrunched up, much as he himself would be, only worse, if his own tall frame were sardined behind the steering wheel of a compact car. The driver hadn't looked his way, and so he confessed it was only a side view that he had. Still, he was sure it was Nesbitt.

What he hadn't been sure of at first was what he should do. At first, he had thought of leaving his beer on the bar and rushing over to the ceremony to inform his son, but the affair most likely was underway and an interruption, it was his belief, wouldn't fly too well. It was also a belief of his, a cunning one that rigidified his eyes into cold stones, that he best be careful where he talked with his son. Showing up at the ceremony, but not really attending, might be enough for the cops to tie him to Asa's crime if it got that far. The boy had fucked up apparently, probably getting too cute instead of just snuffing the wise-ass sonovabitch and being done with it.

He returned to his beer, but in the next several minutes as he turned everything over from the perspective of reason and self-preservation, the car came to mind. The Tucker woman's car. His own crime. The last thing he wanted were cops sniffing around the property. And if they arrested Asa, then for sure they would be.

He shook his head in violent frustration. Perhaps the man in the clownish car had not been George Nesbitt at all. Perhaps that was the reason nothing was fitting together.

It wouldn't wash. That day in that chickenshit principal's office he had memorized Nesbitt's facial features so he wouldn't forget them. Don't be a fool and take a chance at this late date, he admonished himself. They might get your boy, but there's no reason they got to stumble onto you. *If you have any sense, Randall Aftanas, you'll move Vera Tucker's car the fuck out of this shed and to a spot where the cops won't think of looking, and thereby save yourself a visit with the needleman.*

Where to deliver the car, however, continued to be a problem. He had people elsewhere in the region and even south in Renova, and there were Kasters dotting the landscape as well. Trouble was, though everyone got along with everyone, none of them were *that* close. They were all too tight-assed to do him any good. They'd ask too many fucking questions about why he suddenly wanted the automobile off his own property and he wouldn't have the answers to satisfy them. Even if the husbands were willing to do him the favor, the old ladies would be complaining 'cause most of them never did trust him. Best to keep them all the hell out of it as he always had.

He then considered the metal storage sheds that were popping up everywhere. There was a long string of them just the other side of Prosserville. What the fuck did people keep in those things anyway? Dope, he imagined. And the conjecture made him again think of his son, but for a different reason. Lately, the boy was spending money that the old man didn't think he had. Dope was dirty business and it was too easy to get your ass shot up by some fucking mean sonovabitch who didn't like the competition. Anyway, the self-storage sheds. Fuck it. You had to rent the damn things and he just didn't have the extra money.

Okay, so what the fuck was he going to do? Drive around in the goddamn thing like it's one of those always on-the-move Russian missiles he once saw in a newscast? Then he recollected a discussion from last year's hunting season and the answer to where he would hide the car was immediate. He could store it away at a distant camp. Last winter he'd listened to some of the men at the bar talk of a few places back in that hadn't been used in years. Places owned by absentee sportsmen from downstate who were too rickety to hunt and fish any longer, but who also didn't need the bucks they'd receive by putting the structures on the market. Evidently, the old fuckers were keeping the camps to will to their families following their deaths. Because the buildings had gone unused for such long periods, each now presented a worthless exterior of terribly weathered boards, moss-covered eaves and roofs, and a cracked windowpane or two. Vandals left them be. Firebugs, too! The goddamn joints appeared dry but were actually damp as sponges because of the vegetation that also had gone unattended. One camp talked about, he recalled, boasted a large outside barbecue pit and a two-car garage. He felt certain he could find it, though it might take him the better part of the night.

It was time to move. Should he wake Tessie, he wondered, have her follow in the blue pickup? He mulled the idea and decided against it. The less she knew, the better it was for each. He could sleep over in the car, it was a warm night, walk a ways in the morning and eventually hitch a ride. He felt his way in the dark to the front of the shed, stretched his hand through the space between the large doors whose boards had shrunk over time, and flicked off the outside latch. As he pushed open the door, on the opposite side of the space separating the shed from the house, a figure moved.

"Who the fuck's there?" he called into the night.

"Mr. Aftanas, is that you?"

"Who's there?"

"It's me, your neighbor. Rodney Tucker."

The boy spun away from the house and hurried in the direction of the garage. Aftanas had not stepped outside, which, if he had, would have made his next action acceptable to Tucker. Instead, he started to close the door from the inside at its hinges, which cheated him of any mechanical advantage.

"Hey, what are you shutting it for, Mr. Aftanas? You just opened it."

Tucker was too swift at arriving and he put out a hand, stopping the door before it was perpendicular to the rest of the building.

"What do you want?" Aftanas asked, at the same time checking behind himself to determine how visible the car might be under the starlight and the weak residual rays streaming from distant streetlights. But Tucker, he saw when he turned back, was focusing on the second car, Nesbitt's new boat.

"You going to tell me what the hell you're doing here at this late hour when everything's dark and Tessie's sleeping?"

Tucker moved his eyes slowly off the new car and onto the older car which sparkled even in the diminished light. He cocked his head a measure to see around Aftanas whose body was blocking much of the vehicle.

The hard edge wasn't working. Aftanas lightened his tone.

"Didn't you graduate today with Asa? Why aren't you partying with the rest, son? What the fuck you doing here?"

Tucker briefly met his eyes. His tone of voice now changed and became synthesized.

"I was. And we're about to do some more. We're meeting here at midnight and traveling out to some camp way out of town in just a couple of cars. I parked mine at home and hoofed it over."

"Who was it told you to meet here? Wasn't Asa."

"Aaron Little," Tucker said, tonelessly.

"Shit, he was lying to you, son. Pulling your leg. Ain't nobody meeting here tonight, I can tell you that. You a big drinker? Might be the reason this Little fellow didn't want you along."

Tucker loosened his tight expression.

Aftanas took advantage of the moment to reach out and attempt to shut the door. Tucker refused to remove his hand, and in fact, fortified it with greater strength. Aftanas finally released his grip, and after swinging the door all the way open, the kid blindly felt behind its frame with his other hand for a switchbox.

"How do I turn the lights on?"

"Now what do you want lights for?"

"I want to see this car behind you, Mr. Aftanas."

The whole thing was moving too fast.

Tucker moved a couple of inches to improve his view of the car. Aftanas moved to block him. He had to think. First, stall.

"Go on home, Rodney."

Tucker didn't answer, but kept stretching his head.

"Look, if you don't drink—"

"—Who said I don't drink?"

246

"Come on, boy. If you don't drink, why you want to go out to this camp?"

"It's my graduation. I want to be involved. They never involved me before in anything. Where's your lights?"

"I was running a buffer earlier and it tripped the breaker," Aftanas lied. "But I ain't going back in the house to reset it for you, graduation day or no graduation day."

He thought the kid might laugh at this, but Tucker's eyes remained attached to the car.

"I want to see the front of the car, Mr. Aftanas."

Sonofamotherfuckingbitch! The sick little bastard already knew and was just toying with him. Now he wanted to confirm what he knew by finding the smiley face. He should have sanded it off a long time ago instead of just touching it up with paint, but the scratched-in image was so small and that's why he hadn't. He had to think hard now. Come up with something, and fast!

"Your old man still working the overnight at the bottle factory?"

"Ten to six. Same as always."

Tucker moved to walk around the man to his mother's car. Aftanas stopped him by putting a hand on the boy's chest.

"You let him know?"

"What?"

"Did you let your old man know where you are so he don't worry?"

"Of course," Tucker said, with a strand of annoyance evident. "My car's there, I didn't want him to wonder I wasn't. I left him a note in case he gets back before I do. I want to look at the front of this car, Mr. Aftanas!"

"Easy now, son. You want to see the front of this car, that's no big deal." He reached into a pocket and withdrew the keys. "But there's some junk in the trunk that might interest you more."

"Junk in the trunk."

"Junk in the trunk, yes. I'm a fucking poet. You didn't know that, didja? What are you looking so alarmed for? Here. Open it yourself. Inspect things all you want. You'll be surprised."

"There's no light."

"There's a light inside comes on."

Tucker inserted the key in the lock and the trunk lid popped open. He stepped back quickly, nervously, watching Aftanas.

"Why the fuck you all of a sudden acting like a scared rabbit? Go ahead. Have a look."

Tucker raised the lid cautiously to its full extension.

"Back in the corner," Aftanas said, indicating with his head.

As Tucker stretched, Aftanas acted. He grabbed a thick wad of the boy's hair and, gripping it to the scalp, wrenched Tucker backward. With indifferent brutality and overwhelming force, he slammed the head downward into the steel staple of the lock.

A searing crack erupted at the front of the skull. Through incredible pain Tucker could taste the blood that seemed to come from everywhere. In seconds his body went water and the upper half collapsed into the open trunk.

Aftanas gaped at the interior of the carpeted storage area. Blood had spattered throughout. Small dark globs even glistened on the exterior of the car. His shirt was wet and he felt the liquid on his pants, too.

"You little sonovabitch! You and that fuck of an old man of yours should have stayed in Prosserville." He swung a booted foot and kicked the limp body in the leg.

He inspected his shirt again, quickly removed it and tossed it into a box with burnables. From a nail, he pulled another shirt, this one thick with oil and grime.

Leaning over, Aftanas grabbed the boy's legs and flipped the rest of Tucker into the trunk as though his neighbor were a marionette, then slammed the trunklid shut. No way he'd let Tessie help now! Removing the keys from the lock, he scurried around to the driver's door, got in, started the engine, and pulled away.

Seconds later, the car swung into the driveway of Tucker's home. Aftanas could hear a dog confined in the basement.

The back door was unlocked. Inside on a table he found the note Tucker had left for his father and stuffed it into a pocket. Before leaving, he located a dishtowel and used it to open the refrigerator.

The car returned to the road out front. For the first quarter-mile or so, its speed did not exceed thirty miles per hour. Attempting to calculate how he would dispose of the boy in the trunk, he was incapable of matching his thinking to a higher velocity. Two cars rushed up behind him and passed him without increasing their own speed. He popped the top off one of the beers he had swiped from the refrigerator and grabbed a wad of chipped ham from the bag of lunchmeat that he also had taken.

Suddenly, the accelerator was pushed to the floorboard and the engine surged like a rushing ocean wave. He figured he could make the swamp in just over an hour.

Chapter 28

"Sharp. Eighty-one Crown Victoria.... It's a car."

"We know it's a car."

Staring at the edges of the road, alert for deer about to spring from the darkness, finding it hard to believe that they were en route to another place, Bradford thought, Here's another one! His brother's friends were wearing on him. First the clown asleep in the backseat looking like he might throw up on the inside of the window. Now this skinny shit who was trying to impress him that he knew about automobiles. He should have gone back home to Rita. He and Gray were just too different to be spending time like this together.

"Some people have never heard of it," Paul Blake said.

"What I don't understand is how you can tell the model and year when it's pitch black out there.

"We also flew past it like it was standing still," Lord added in support of his brother. Paul Blake sometimes amazed him too.

"First of all, it isn't pitch black. That bright thing out your window, Brad, that's Jupiter. There's plenty of stars out tonight as well. It's just the moon that's missing. Plus there were lights on that car and on ours. You're forgetting, too, you got a few years on me. I was growing up in those years and I could recognize all the makes and models.... Hey, Rudy! Wake up! You'll make us all fall asleep before we get to George's.... I'll tell you something else about that automobile we just passed. I'd be surprised if its odometer isn't under 10K."

"Give me a break," Bradford complained in the sorriest of tones.

"I'm not bullshitting," Blake said. "There was something about it. The tires. The paint. I don't know exactly what, but that car's been sitting in some old lady's garage, it's my guess."

They were so immersed in their talk, the long Crown Victoria roared by them before they noticed and disappeared quickly around a bend in the road.

"It isn't healthy for a car to sit all the time either. I mean, if it was, why not buy a pair of new cars at the same time for the same price. You know, as a hedge against future inflation.... Hey, Rudy! Wake up!" He smacked his colleague in the back of the head.

Wallace jolted to life. "Stop the car, Gray! Put this motherfucker outside before I beat his head into hamburger. Let him go back to riding with Jack and Walt. Why the fuck did you switch anyway is what I'd like to know?"

"What do you think? Walt's been releasing church-creepers ever since we started out. My olfactory system couldn't take it anymore."

Lord chuckled in the mirror. The reference to farting was amusing his brother as well. It was the first time he'd seen Bradford lighten up since they'd gotten into the car and traveled out to the Foss party.

Blake turned and looked out the back window at the station wagon that was tailing them. The driver momentarily high-beamed them.

"Gray, you got a cell phone, don't you?"

"In the console. Who you calling?"

"Schenley. He's got one with him and I remember the number. Let's get the latest flatulence report, what do you say?"

Wallace laughed. It was more of an involuntary regurgitation. "You want a report? McAllister's likely to put the phone directly under his ass and present you with it firsthand."

Blake laughed in response and appeared to abandon the subject. "Man, am I glad this school year's over," he said. "Did you ever think of becoming a teacher, Brad, when you were in high school? What is it you do anyway?"

"I work with glass," Bradford replied dryly without turning around.

"So then you know the reason behind the wavy glass in old houses and barns."

"He knows," Lord said. "He probably knew that glass was a liquid before I was born."

"And no, I never wanted to be what you are," Bradford said to Blake, still without turning around.

"Good thing," Blake said. "I mean it's a good thing you're a glassmaker and not a teacher. The kids would eat you alive."

"You're talking inside."

"Yeah. Inside the classroom."

"This kid isn't going to be too thrilled when we show up again," Bradford remarked to his brother.

"Tough. He shouldn't be out there in the first place. But wait'll you see this camp, Brad. I guarantee you'll fall in love."

"How much do you think I'll see at this hour?"

"Get out the cell phone. Call Jack," Wallace ordered Blake.

Lord fished the phone out of the console for his colleague and extended it backward over the seat. Blake took it, rolled down his window, and waved it outside over the roof of the car.

"What the fuck are you doing?"

"He has to see it to turn his on."

The lights again flashed up, then down. Blake punched in the number and held the phone out so everyone could hear.

"Yes, Paul?"

"What's it like back there, Jack?"

"What's what like?"

"The fellow riding shotgun still poisoning the air?"

"No, Paul. Matter of fact, the air cleaned up soon as you left. But put Gray on. There's something Walt and I want to know."

Chuckling, Blake handed the phone forward.

"What's up, Jack?"

"Walt and I have been wondering why Cassie Bateson sought you out to snitch on your boy Asa. That sort of thing doesn't happen often. What's your read why she done it?"

Wallace shouted from the backseat. "I think Aftanas and a few others, like maybe Foss, gang-banged her! And I don't think she liked it!"

"We copied that. You think the same as Rudy, Gray?"

"It's a possibility. At the beginning of the year she thought it was cute, how he was staring at her and throwing comments her way. But I judged them to be more than just hitting on her. The kid's fucked up, that's the bottom line. For all we know, he might have raped her during the year."

"And she isn't the type to go public, is she?"

"Cassie? No, she isn't. But she's also not the type to remain afraid."

"What'd I tell you?" said Paul Blake, pointing through the windshield.

"Is that it, Jack?" Lord asked. "Because you know, the roaming charges. Won't matter that we're only a hundred feet apart."

Lord and Schenley cut their connection as Wallace lifted himself and stared through the front windshield too.

They were now on a long straight stretch of road and they could see that the taillights of the Crown Victoria far ahead of them were randomly flashing off and on. Finally, the red lights extinguished completely and the big car bumped onto the berm.

"It's no good when a car sits. Sometimes it's the motor. Sometimes the seals. Sometimes it's plain old electrical."

"And I suppose you want to stop and see if Grandma could use a hand," Lord said.

"It was a man driving that car," Bradford corrected them emphatically.

Blake rolled his eyes at Wallace sitting across from him and mouthed the words, "No shit."

"You wanna stop?"

"Pull in behind him, Gray," Wallace said. "If Asa's intending to torch the cabin, he won't do it till they finish their beer."

"There isn't any beer, Rudy"

"I meant what he has with him. He and his buddies aren't heading out there empty-handed, you can bet your ass on that."

Lord slowed the car. The driver of the Crown Victoria, who, he could see, was very tall and wearing a shirt far too grimy for the black metallic beauty surrounding him, had gotten out and was stepping toward the back.

Schenley pulled alongside in the left lane of the deserted road and McAllister lowered his window. Lord and Blake did the same.

"Man, I can smell it already!"

McAllister smiled at the younger man, then nodded a "What's up?" at Lord.

"He might need a hand," Lord answered through the night air.

"I'll pull in front," Schenley shouted, leaning across, and the station wagon increased its speed.

"Just pull up alongside him," Bradford said, who now lowered his own window. "And click your beams on."

Lord did as his brother requested and now recognized the other driver as Randy Aftanas. He glanced over his shoulder at Wallace who had also taken notice.

Bradford did the talking.

"Do you need some help?"

"Nah, everything's okay," Aftanas responded while his eyes attempted to read the numbers in the car. "You can move along."

"You sure?"

"What'd I say?"

"Just trying to be helpful, that's all. The headlights fizzle out like your rears and you're liable to meet a tree, or worse."

"I said everything's okay, didn't I?"

"We can probably give you a lift. Or if that doesn't suit you, we got a cell phone—"

"What'll suit me is you all get the fuck out of here."

Lord watched as Aftanas turned to check the disposition of Schenley's station wagon.

"Fuck him. He's fine," Blake said, who did not recognize Aftanas.

Bradford raised his window, as though in confirmation.

Lord said, "For your information, big brother, the man you just talked to? That's the father of the kid who got up in your face at the party."

Bradford peered back immediately through the window at the tall dirty man who hadn't moved, but continued to stand next to the trunk, watching them.

"That's Randy Aftanas," Lord said.

"Pull off on the shoulder then," Bradford said soberly. "We need to get out."

"What the hell for?" Wallace objected. "He said he doesn't need our help."

Bradford turned around to glance at Wallace and where he was sitting in the car. "You kept your window up. You didn't hear it either."

"Hear what?" Lord asked.

"There's something alive and kicking in that trunk of his. I was going to let it pass. Not now. Pull over!"

"Wait a second! We could be asking for trouble," Wallace warned. "That crazy fucker might have a gun."

"He doesn't."

"How the fuck can you be so sure?"

"He would have went for it the moment he saw us slowing."

Lord pumped the car some gas and drifted in behind Schenley and McAllister.

Blake was staring back at the Crown Victoria.

"No wonder the lights went out. Whatever's back there is ripping at the wiring. I'll bet the rotten bastard has locked up a dog."

Schenley and the big teacher McAllister were already outside the station wagon and striding toward the others.

Wallace looked back, too. "Well, if we're planning to confront him, we ought to do it fast. He's heading back to the wheel."

They got out quickly now, without further word, Blake waiting on his older colleagues from the other car so that he could apprise them of the situation. Wallace and Lord scuttled in the direction of the Crown Victoria's right side while Bradford, several yards ahead of them, stayed a few feet inside the road. As he neared the car, he moderated his pace and at the same time raised a hand. Aftanas, inside, started the motor.

"No you don't!"

Bradford dashed the short remaining distance to the car and yanked open the door before Aftanas could jerk the transmission into gear.

"You boys are asking for trouble that you don't want," threatened Aftanas, jumping out.

"We want to see what's in the trunk," said Bradford.

"Kiss my ass. You ain't gonna see nothing but dirt you keep this up."

"You thinking of taking on all six of us?"

"I can see there ain't but two of you that might give me trouble, and I'll take my chances."

Rudy Wallace stood on the opposite side of the car and was seeming to act boldly, but he had his doubts about what they were doing, here in the beginning hours of the morning. There were no noises issuing from the trunk now and he was questioning if there had been any just a few minutes earlier. Gray's brother had not impressed him. All night he'd been dull and humorless, harboring the characteristics of a social misfit. Even after the graduating teen Cassie had informed them that Asa was intending to lead a group of his friends out to Nesbitt's camp to heist some hidden beer and that she thought there was a good chance that he would vandalize and maybe even set fire to the place, Bradford had argued against going. And it seemed to Wallace that the only reason he was along now was that he didn't want Gray, himself, and a bunch of teachers as a whole to be of the opinion that he couldn't hack a long night. What was he expecting they'd find in the trunk once it was unlatched and open? Paul had suggested a dog, but it was probably only the jack, or some loose wrenches, that had been rumbling around and vibrating through to the exterior panels.

SPINE

Lord had drifted several yards past Wallace toward the rear of the car to intercept Aftanas, should the man be inclined to bolt along that direction. But Lord, too, could not detect any sound resonating from the inside of the trunk and he wondered if his brother wasn't making a mistake that could land them all in hot water. Which was something he certainly didn't need. Sal Rodino would jump at the chance. Serena Cantor herself had warned him to stay clear of further trouble.

For as long as he could remember, his big brother had been a scuffler, a brawler. But unlike Rudy and Paul who—and it wasn't difficult to tell—were regarding Bradford as a bully, a man unwilling to make fair assessment of others, the kind of man who preferred the fist and the gun to reason; and who they regarded also as some kind of Bottles Barton, dreaming up scenarios in order to be heroic; Lord was aware now, as always, that Bradford had never bullied anyone, other than the younger brother himself, which could be expected; and that there had never been a reason to invent scenarios—real ones were unfolding all the time. The truth was, in their fraternal history Brad had often made fair assessment of a situation and then acted upon it when others would have done nothing but pray to God and hope for the cavalry. The scenarios merely required someone's immediate recognition. Paul had thought he was giving the man a shot when he'd mentioned the classroom and asked if Brad had ever desired to teach. Paul hadn't understood. His brother knew too well that his kind could not teach into today's classroom where discipline was negotiated, not demanded. Outside, though, it was a different story. Outside, Paul didn't know that it would be the Brads who would pick up for him. Lord could doubt his brother, but not for long. He didn't believe Brad had enjoyed this evening very much beyond Tilly's, but he himself had, and he was glad that Rita had surprised him.

Aftanas glanced to his left. The second big guy was still by the cars up front, though moving in his direction with two others. The fuckhead before him was foolishly holding out his left hand for the keys.

Bradford hadn't allowed either of his eyes to stray from the tall man. The smirk was too much like the son's, and soon it betrayed Aftanas.

With cat-like swiftness Bradford rammed his right fist into Aftanas' gut. When the tall man grabbed instinctively at the pain, he followed with a knee to the groin. Aftanas collapsed in the gravel filling the berm and Bradford bent to snatch the keys.

257

"Gray, get around here!" he barked. "If he moves, kick him in the nuts again."

"I hope you know what you're doing," Wallace said.

"Then you open it, Rudy." Bradford tossed the keys over the roof of the car. Wallace threw them right back.

"Open it yourself."

Bradford cut short a grin, stepped to the trunk, and unlocked it with Rudy peering from the side. The lid swung upward to release the light. The boy lay drenched in his own blood, one hand gripping a harness of ripped-out electrical wires, his mouth working like a fish out of water, but saying nothing.

"Oh, Jesus," Wallace whispered.

"What is it?" Lord asked.

"I think it might be Rodney Tucker, Gray."

Lord backed several steps away from the Crown Victoria, all the while keeping his eyes open.

It was the first he realized that the car was the same car that the boy had forever doodled.

Chapter 29

The route from the Foss House to the secluded camp required the careful navigation of several outlying roads, mere dirt and gravel swaths whose original use was to haul felled timber out of the forest. Some zigzagged and connected to other, more legitimate roads, those mapped. Some didn't, and the driver who mistakenly chose the latter could remain lost for hours.

Asa Aftanas was aware of the confusion possible of heading out this different way. But traveling back into town to take the familiar route would be a waste of gas.

The others scorned the decrepit condition and musty odor of his car, especially the girls, and would have opted to ride with Little or Dana, but riding alone tonight, this was his choice. He told them he wanted to arrive first, to make certain there were no guests staying at the camp.

"You remember how to get there?" he had asked them.

"We'll find it," Little boasted. "Only don't go sucking down the brewskies 'til we show."

"I told you. We'll have to spend time searching for it, maybe even on our hands and knees. But it's there. I guarantee you it's there."

Part of the plan. He wanted someone else to discover the lid on the hole. And if they couldn't... well, he would. But he wanted the others around. He hoped goddamn Lyle remembered to replace the lid after setting in the cases of beer. Lyle's head was up his ass, as the cops were still searching for him, though in the car he'd wisely gotten rid of, not in the pickup. Another reason to arrive ahead of the rest. To see if Lyle done what he was supposed to. Bring the beer and bring the ice. He was reminded how Lyle had said he would make two trips out to the camp, rather than deliver both the beer and the ice in the darkness. No fucking way was he climbing into a pit with a dead man when the stars were out.

"I'll drive back out around midnight with the ice and wait for you. But I ain't truckin' no beer into that hole without the sun over top me. I don't believe in ghosts, but I ain't crazy either."

Tessie's boy. Asa chuckled to himself, but he was happy to see the green pickup at the bottom of the lane. He parked near the top, so that those behind him wouldn't miss his crate and drive by, especially Little who drove like a goddamn maniac.

With flashlight in hand, he moved down the lane toward the cabin.

"Hey, Lyle," he called softly. "Lyle, where are you?"

He paused at the dented pickup and directed the light inside the cab, guessing that his stepbrother might be stealing a few zzz's while waiting.

"Hey, Lyle," he called again, moving forward, shining the light in various directions.

Suddenly, the answer occurred to him and he mounted the few steps to the porch and cabin. He tried the knob and the door creaked open. The fucker must have taken a bed. Immediately he had another thought to scare the hell out of his stepbrother by putting the big revolver to his sleeping head. Reversing himself, he hurried back to the car to retrieve it.

Nesbitt stood motionless inside the door, a hatchet in hand, choosing the blunt side, knowing that it could kill Asa Aftanas just as easily as the end with the sharpened blade. Through a crack he watched the kid rush back to his wreck of a car, then reach down and withdraw something from under the front seat. Probably a gun, maybe even his own. Lyle wasn't answering and the crazy teen was growing afraid.

Asa Aftanas hustled back to the cabin, now with the flashlight off. He stopped short of stepping inside and directed his vision at the windows to the left and right of him. None was broken, and Lyle wasn't the industrious kind to search for a key hanging off a nail. He retreated off the steps, sensing danger.

He called once more anyway. "Answer up, Lyle baby. You in there somewhere?"

He glanced back at the pickup, unable to figure it. Where the fuck was he? Switching on the light, he directed its rays toward the rise, at the grass on the surface. Staring, he moved in the direction of the pit, slowly, looking left, cautiously, looking right, swinging around at times to check his backside, the gun barrel pointing in the darkness always to where his eyes were probing.

The lid was seated securely and obvious scuff marks in the surrounding sod proved that someone had been in the area. He could see, too, where Lyle had set down the beer cases in order to uncover the pit.

He reached down, removed the lid, and shined the light into the bottom of the concrete hole.

From the outline of the oversized walnut handgrips, Nesbitt soon determined that it was his revolver that Asa Aftanas was wielding. The .44

magnum, a revolver that would put an awfully big hole in anyone on the receiving end. He should have made arrangements to get hold of a gun when he was in New York, that's what he should've done! But he hadn't, and now he better make certain there were no mistakes!

Killing the man named Lyle had been an unavoidable mistake. It was never his intention. But with laws funny and often unpredictable, he could paint a scenario already under construction that might land himself in jail, perhaps even reserve a seat for him on death row.

The two sets of car headlights flashed in a distant curve of the road out front, then fanned skyward to backlight the rich foliage of tall trees, one set close upon the other and both moving fast. Aftanas and Nesbitt became aware of them at the same time. Asa stopped in his tracks and watched as they approached. Nesbitt slipped to the door, unsure of what he would do, now that the kid's playmates would soon be on hand.

The cars careened along the road and their disturbance of the stones and gravel sounded too loud and reckless. They swung into the lane and rushed all the way to its bottom, their occupants jumping out at once and slamming the doors behind them.

"Aftanas! Where are you?" a voice called out immediately. "Show your ass!"

Nesbitt recognized the voice, despite its volume. It wasn't that of any student. The take-charge huskiness belonged to Walt McAllister. Other recognizable voices followed.

Someone reached back inside the first car and flicked on its high beams. The kid could be seen standing at their weakened hem. Everyone saw the gun in hand.

"What are you doing?" said Lord. He moved cautiously toward Aftanas with his eye on the big revolver, his colleagues a step or two behind. When closer and stopped, he repeated the question.

"Protecting myself. What else?"

"Against what?" Wallace asked in a flippant tone of disbelief.

"Check the hole in the ground. Your friend Nesbitt murdered my stepbrother."

"Put the gun away," Lord said, "and get on home. Your father's been arrested, Asa. The police will want to talk with you and your mother."

261

"I ain't fuckin' with you, man! Lyle's dead. He's lying in that open hole up there and your friend Nesbitt's the fucker who killed him."

The exterior yellow light at the cabin came on, capturing everyone's attention. George Nesbitt stepped out onto the porch.

"I knew the cocksucker was in there," Aftanas said.

"Welcome back, George," said Wallace.

Nesbitt greeted them all with a stiff nod.

"The dog, Gray. Was it you?"

"Janey and Rudy, too," Lord said. "We buried him out back." He recalled Clipper's correction that Sy had not been a male and for a moment considered restating himself.

"What made you look?"

"Put the gun down, Aftanas," McAllister said. "Maybe you should get rid of the hatchet, too, George."

"He murdered Lyle."

"What made you drive out and look?" Nesbitt again asked of Lord.

"Some beer cans stuffed inside a desk."

Nesbitt raised the hatchet and pointed it at Aftanas. "He threw the dog in, broke its neck. Then he left me there to die."

"How'd you get out?" Wallace asked while staring at Aftanas.

"Shut up!" the kid shouted.

"Rigor mortis. I stood the poor creature in an upright position once he stiffened and used him to climb on."

"This is crap," the kid said, spitting.

Lord drifted toward the porch and mounted the steps. He held out a hand and Nesbitt clasped it warmly.

"Get rid of the gun, Asa," Lord ordered. "You're making everyone nervous. If what you say is true, then it's a matter for the courts to settle."

Nesbitt took a step back from his friend.

"No, Gray. The kid's right to call it crap. I can't prove any of it. The gun he's holding, it's mine, but I can't prove it by any receipt or document. And who knows what he's done to my car. He's also got my money. This gets to court, I go to prison as I see it, and this bastard of a kid walks away with five-thousand dollars."

Lord believed he could see something of the familiar gloating smirk on the teen's face. He forced his own face toward the cabin.

"Maybe not," he whispered to his friend. Then he turned back toward Aftanas. "I said your old man was arrested, Asa. You don't care to know the reason?"

"Now let me guess. He got soused up again coming out of Domirock's and put that blue piece of shit he calls a pickup in a ditch."

"Wasn't a pickup. What did you say it was, Paul?"

"Crown Victoria," Blake answered.

"You ever hear of that car, Asa?"

"What the fuck do I care what kind of car that crazy old man of mine was driving?"

"There's more. We were driving by that car and my brother there—you remember meeting my brother Brad earlier, don't you? My brother heard something in the trunk of your father's car and he forced him to turn over the keys so we could see what's inside."

The kid spat out a laugh. "Nobody forces my old man to do anything. Where you been?"

"Well, Brad did, whether you like it or not. And venture a guess what we discovered in the trunk."

"I could give a shit, Lord."

"A classmate of yours. Rodney Tucker. He was lucky to be alive. Your old man had tried to split his skull open as though it were a coconut. Anyway, you can figure the rest. It wasn't difficult for me and it wasn't difficult for the police. And now I'm betting it runs in the family."

"You're betting what?"

Lord let the moment play a while. "I'm betting my friend's automobile is still in your possession, Asa. And if that's the case, the question is: Will you give yourself up, or do you intend to kill us all?"

There was an empty, silent stretch of seconds as the kid watched everyone and everyone watched him. What was this teenage bad-ass considering doing now?

The kid carefully, even thoughtfully, released the hammer, as if the game was up; then immediately cocked it again, the solid sound notched in machined metal.

"Then it's only a question to you."

The gun rose to eye level and he trained it haphazardly on each of them, a second for Blake and McAllister and Schenley, longer for the others.

Wallace laughed out loud when his turn came and left Schenley and the others to join Lord and Nesbitt on the lighted porch.

"You got any beer inside, Georgie?... Aftanas, who the hell did you have for math? If it was Stiles, she and I are going to talk. Look at you. You don't have a clue, do you? There's seven of us, boy. That monster revolver in your hand only holds six rounds. What do you think? The seventh man is going to wait for you to reload?"

The kid regarded the gun, but was not put off.

"Well, you can be that seventh man, jackoff. Ain't nobody in the whole school didn't think you were the biggest asshole of them all, anyway. So, yeah, I'll let you watch me reload. Then I'll blow your fucking brains into the bushes. How does that sound?"

In the face of the threat Wallace laughed again. "To hell with him. The idiot won't do anything but pound his pud. Let's have a beer. You did bring beer with you, George, I hope?"

But even as he was saying this, Wallace's body swung away from the cabin. He reached out, ripped the hatchet from Nesbitt's relaxed hand, and sailed it head over handle at the kid. It struck Asa Aftanas in the left shoulder but did not stick. The night air suddenly filled with the roar from the small cannon. The first bullet smashed through the window on the cabin door. A second shot followed, whacked into siding, splintering wood in all directions. Then a third shot.

As the kid dashed toward the men on the porch, Bradford rushed the teen from the rear. He grabbed him about the neck with one hand while the other restrained the wrist wielding the gun.

"Give me trouble and I'll squeeze what little you got for brains right out of your skull."

Wallace, seeing Aftanas subdued by Lord's brother, let out a primal scream and leaped the porch railing. He raced to the now-restrained Asa Aftanas forced to lie facedown in the earth, and with runaway rage he kicked at the head of the youth who had threatened his life, stomped his heel over and over on the temple.

"Jesus Christ!" Bradford swore, and with one hand he tried to shove Wallace away, but the math teacher wouldn't be shoved as he continued to drive his foot down at the Aftanas skull, as if intending to beat it into the grass. "Get him away!" Bradford shouted to the others.

Lord could hardly believe the enraged behavior of his colleague as he watched McAllister and Schenley respond to his brother's order and take hold of Rudy by the arms and drag him off. But even then the math teacher continued to breathe hard and struggle to free himself.

"What are you going to do with him?" he demanded, still in the grip of McAllister and Schenley.

"You know what we're going to do, Rudy."

"I say we kill him!"

"What the fuck's wrong with you, Rudy?"

"I say we kill him! The sonovabitch threatened our lives, Gray! He shot at us. He left George for dead!"

"Let's get him up."

"You sonovabitch! What about you, Brad?"

"This isn't my fight," Bradford said. "But if you want to waste him, I walk before you do."

"Nobody's wasting anyone," Lord said.

"What's the matter with you?" Wallace screamed. "Isn't there even one among you who values his fucking life?"

Car lights lit up the sky.

"That's probably the others. Paul, meet them at the top and take care of things."

"What do you want me to say, Gray?"

"Just tell them the party's over. Tell them to get moving. Don't inform them of anything else."

"You value his life, you won't value your own?" Wallace repeated. "What the fuck do you teach that's worth anything if you don't teach that?"

Lord gazed at his normally comical friend who continued to stare wild-eyed at Aftanas and the rest of them. His brother was restoring the dazed kid to his feet. They all stood at the edge of the light from the cabin, their faces appearing waxed and drained of energy, except for Wallace's. Finally, Lord took the flashlight that his brother had removed from Aftanas, and he and Schenley moved to the pit to look at Lyle Kaster.

"Walt, we need your help," Lord said. "You too, George. Unless that ladder's nearby and has been repaired."

"It hasn't," Nesbitt replied. "But, Gray, I don't want anything more to do with that hole in the earth."

.

265

Lord nodded after a moment, thinking he understood.

"Brad, then you lend us a hand in raising this body out of here. I think the four of us can handle it."

Bradford, who had disarmed Aftanas of the big revolver, waved Nesbitt over and extended him the gun.

"This manstopper is yours anyway, you said. Watch him. Walk him up to the car if you want. We'll put him in Gray's. What about you, Rudy? You have control of yourself yet? If you do, go along with him."

Nesbitt shoved Aftanas in the back, using the round of his palm to jolt the kid's spine, and together they moved uphill toward the cars at the end of the lane. Wallace continued standing motionless where he was, alone and staring at nothing for a time. Slowly, the trance dissolved.

On the rise to his right, Schenley and McAllister, crouching, were pulling up on the stepbrother's corpse. They stretched it on the ground and then reached back into the hole to assist Lord and his brother while they climbed out. Lord made some remark to the others about the incident at the Goldenrod when he was standing upright again.

At the top of the lane Wallace could hear Paul Blake. His voice and the voices of several uncompromising teens blasting from inside the cars were engaged in an altercation. One of them had a light for spotting deer and turned it on. Its illumination sprayed wildly over the forested landscape. And then he listened to a fed-up Blake as his friend threatened the drivers with calling both the police and their parents if they didn't depart at once. Some of the others began cursing with neither restraint nor embarrassment, but Little and Foss, already with too much alcohol on their breaths, took their cue and punched at the gas. The holder of the spotlight kept its bright light deliberately flooding the face of the science teacher who watched as the vehicles diminished to nothing.

Finally, Wallace shifted his vision all the way left in the direction of Nesbitt and Aftanas. The ex-teacher and recent graduate stood between the station wagon and Lord's car, parked at the bottom of the lane. They faced each other, but it was only the face of Nesbitt that he could see, and it was talking. None of the words was audible, but a steady tone, gravely serious, communicated itself to Wallace like white noise. For several seconds, Nesbitt, he observed, let his eyes scan the position of the others. Blake, still up top, staring down the road. Gray, Walt, Jack, and Gray's brother hovering like beetles over the recently deceased stepbrother. And then the eyes came to rest on himself, alone. What are you looking at, Rudy? That's what they seemed to say.

Wallace turned away from his friend and former colleague. He wanted nothing to do with any of them, Nesbitt included.

When he did, the manstopper roared a final time.

Chapter 30

"DeWitt, I do believe the rest of us will have to start addressing you as Dooley if you don't soon learn to be a liar. Put your money away. I'll buy the round, seeing I haven't bought one in quite a while. Which, by the way, Gray, is the reason I think our mutual friend George might have killed the Aftanas boy in cold blood, contrary to what the paper reported he told you and the police."

"Come off it, Warren. You don't really think that, do you?"

"I don't want to. I want to believe the same as you. That the kid attempted to get the gun back and George shot him accidentally in self-defense. Only do you ever remember George buying a round?"

"My god, he treated the bar to plenty of rounds! If you weren't on—"

Warren Hoverton raised a hand and softened his voice. "I'm not saying he wasn't generous. That's not what I'm saying at all. Only I never saw him collect three dooleys even once. Whose deal?"

"So you're saying he's duplicitous?"

Hoverton shook his head. "That's a little different. No, he was always forthright. Look, don't get me wrong. I still like George and I'm not saying I believe what I'm saying. It's interesting, is all."

The farmer Tut grabbed the tall bottle of lager Tilly had placed before him and tipped it to his lips. He never used a glass.

"I don't know, Warren. Aftanas can't hold his liquor and probably his son couldn't either. I saw a lot of vehicles leave that party that night, and if I'm not mistakin' his, he was already gooned up. It's a wonder he found George's camp, being it's way the hell out there."

"Well, I'm just saying—"

"He shot at 'em, too. Three times. Ask Gray."

"I know that, Tut," Hoverton said with annoyance.

"And what about that boy's dog and Nesbitt's story? Face it. The old man is no good and neither was his son. I've two boys of my own, so I don't like to hear about any kid getting shot and ending up dead, but...."

"Give me the deck, Tilly," Boyd Benson said, startling the others and warranting their collective glance. "I'm finding this all very distressing. This sort of thing shouldn't happen in our community."

"We're no different, Boyd," Tut said.

"Well, I like to think we are."

"Where's Mr. Nesbitt now?" DeWitt Wainwright asked. "Is he still around?"

"He left this morning," Lord said. "He was cleared and they returned his car."

"What about the money he said the Aftanas boy stole from him?" Hoverton asked.

"No recovery of it, as far as I know."

Tom Worth spoke out. "Margo wouldn't agree with me and I'm probably the oddball here, but outside Tilly's doors, there's a view of George Nesbitt we've all known about. I have to say that I've never understood how he could just up and leave his son. And now, Gray, you say he's done it again. I don't understand it and I certainly can't respect any man who does it, but especially a man who doesn't even seem to have a reason."

"What makes you believe he hasn't a reason?"

"George has never been hurting for money so that he might feel he was of no benefit to his family. And if there's another woman, when has he found the time?"

DeWitt Wainwright chuckled out loud. "Maybe the boy's not his. Did you ever think of that?"

"What do you mean, 'not his'?" said Worth, constricting his eyes in puzzlement.

"Not his. Maybe it's been sticking in his craw all this time that he's not really the father."

Lord regarded his ex-student and pondered the thought he offered, bringing Stella Nesbitt in at the end. Maybe DeWitt had something there. Maybe it was that, and it was George's part of the compatibility that had made the marriage last for as long as it had. Throw in Janey's theory that he had become numbed by the students he taught and maybe it explained why he fled so effortlessly. When George had spoken of Stella, love had never been mentioned. And he didn't think he had heard it from Stella, either.

"Well, either way then," Worth said. "Walking away from a boy you've been living with and taking care of, how big a jump is it to shoot another man's son and think nothing of it?"

"How could you not see anything?" Boyd Benson said under strain. "There were six of you!"

Lord returned his thoughts to the bar, knowing Benson was directing the question to him.

"We were doing other things," he said.

"Your fellow teacher Rudy Wallace wasn't, according to the rumors."

"You think he witnessed the shooting," Worth said, "and is just choosing to keep quiet?"

"He wanted to kill the child himself!" stressed Benson. "The rest of you testified to that. Or were the papers making all that up?"

"Shuffle and deal," Hoverton said. "I'm sorry I started this. We're not going to solve it here. Go on, Boyd. Deal 'em out. Tilly, I need a refill, too."

Boyd Benson played cards rarely and it showed in his attempts to rearrange the deck. But finally he peeled off five cards in front of DeWitt Wainwright.

"Anything wild?"

"Make it interesting," Hoverton encouraged him.

"Like what?"

"Make it all face cards. What do you think, Tilly?"

Tilly rolled his eyes.

"Multiples of three," Benson said.

"What's that?"

"I think he means threes, sixes, and nines are wild, Tut."

DeWitt Wainwright scooped up the hand and inspected its cards. He folded them and offered them to Tilly who gave them over to Hoverton.

"You staying out on this one, Till?"

"Have to. Kegs to change, cooler to fill."

"So what are you passing me, DeWitt?"

"What are you buying?"

"Doesn't seem like Warren's buying much of anything today," Tut said.

"Look, Gray's already said the boy's the kind who gets up in your face and laughs. I think, maybe when they were standing alone, George asked the whereabouts of the money and the kid did what Gray said he does, never figuring that if George could walk away from his family, he could walk away also from five grand." Hoverton glanced from one man to another, expecting some kind of response to this theory on how Asa Aftanas came to be shot point-blank by George Nesbitt, but there was none. In the end he thought, Just as well.

"All right, DeWitt," he said. "Stir my curiosity. Let's hear it. What are you selling?"

"Five tens, Mr. Hoverton."

"Oh my. How big a fool you think Warren Hoverton is, son?... You're not even going to react to that, are you? Okay, I'll look at 'em."

Tut bobbed with faint amusement, Boyd Benson grinned meekly, and Lord started to think of the upcoming holiday weekend, although Hoverton's theory lingered with him.

"What are you doing for the Fourth, Gray?" Hoverton inquired as he mulled his cards. "I'm having doings out at my place and you're welcome to come on out. I've already invited the rest, but they have plans of their own."

"Well, so do I," Lord said. "But I appreciate the invitation."

"You heading somewhere, are you?"

He was, yes. The day after tomorrow he was taking Janey down home to introduce to his mother and the rest of the family. Brad and Rita were hosting.

"Now that's nice. That's news I like to hear," Boyd Benson said, brightening. "That's news that augurs well for a community."

The five cards had already passed through Tut and were on their way to himself. He read the hand, discarded, and inserted the replacements slid over to him by Benson.

"What's the call, Gray?" Tom Worth asked. "I bought a couple of rounds prior to your arrival and I don't care to buy a third."

"You think I'd lie to you?"

"Funny you ask that. In fact, I don't. Just last night Margo and I were talking about all that's happened and when your name came up, she said what a heckuva year you've hand. She said, with your involvement with everything's that happened, she feared you might become too serious and all."

"Well, she's right, Tom. Margo knows of that she speaks."

"So what are you giving me?"

Lord fanned the hand once more. **K♣ 3♣ 9♣ 8♦ 8♠.**

"Sorry, Tom. There's room, but not much. Read 'em and weep. Five kings."

Printed in the United States
1436900004B/93

9 781588 515711